Another World

Kate Lowe Kerrigan

BALLANTINE BOOKS · NEW YORK

Library of Congress Catalog Card Number: 77-4916

ISBN 0-345-25859-2

Manufactured in the United States of America

First Edition: January 1978

Chapter One

THE dressing room was stifling. Not that it mattered. They hardly gave you time to breathe the air in here, let alone think about it.

"Come on, Davis. Get a move on. You've only got a minute and a half."

"All right, Miss Stanley, all right, all right." With a sigh Rachel pulled the gold lamé evening gown over her head. It was the most gorgeous dress she'd ever laid eyes on, but it weighed a ton.

And nobody to help smooth her hair or freshen her makeup. Nothing turned out the way you were led to believe it would. Being a fashion model at Bryant's Department Store sounded so glamorous. So pampered. So catered-to. Rachel wrinkled her nose at the girl changing next to her. It was like working in a sweatshop.

And on your feet the whole day long—no different from her first job out of high school, when she'd waitressed at that dump of a drive-in on the south side of town. Only there at least they let you alone. Or the boss did anyhow. Here Miss Stanley was on your back over every least thing. Keep moving. Straighten up. Wear the outfit as though it had been designed for you.

Rachel gave a final pat to the shoulder-length dark hair that framed her heart-shaped face and smoothed out the luscious gold lamé as Miss Stanley started yakking at her again. "All right, all right. I'm coming." And a measly twenty percent discount. Who could buy anything worth wanting on that?

She'd thought this job was going to be her first step up, her ticket out of town, the escape she'd been looking for from that hole-in-the-wall apartment on the wrong side of the tracks that she'd shared with her mother for as long as she could remember.

Escape, phooey. This job was a first step to nowhere.

Pushing her way through the jumble of clothes and girls, Rachel stumbled and swayed, and had to grab on to somebody to keep from falling.

Miss Stanley frowned at her. "Are you all right?"

"Yeah, I'm okay." She wasn't, actually. She felt weak and dizzy. But she didn't have time to think about that either.

Outside the dressing room, Fat Millie checked off the gown and accessories on her clipboard. As though they thought she might try to make off with something. Fat Millie. Fat chance. Rachel hurried to the runway. At least doing a show wasn't as boring as wandering around the store and in and out of the restaurant like some showroom dummy. The way those rich women looked you over, that was exactly how they made you feel: like a dummy. A piece of goods they might or might not want to buy. At least, doing a show, the lights were so bright you couldn't see their faces.

And there was always the chance she'd get her picture in the paper, and the Associated Press might pick it up, and some Hollywood producer might happen to see it, and she might be exactly the girl he was looking for to star in his next movie, and he'd pick up the phone, and—

"All right, Davis. Off you go."

Rachel snapped out of her daydream, put on a smile, and started down the runway. Again she stumbled and swayed and started to pitch forward. Somebody screamed, and her last clear thought was to wonder why.

The next thing she knew, she was gasping and choking; somebody hovered over her, holding ammonia to her nose. She pushed the hand away and tried to sit up, but another pair of hands from behind held her down.

"Lie still, miss." A man's voice.

"Where—where am I?"

"In the Emergency Room of the hospital. Memorial Hospital."

Rachel frowned and blinked, and gradually the man's face came into focus and stayed there. She struggled to sit up again. "Well, I've got to get back to work."

The man—a doctor, she supposed; handsome, anyway—shook his head and smiled. He really *was* handsome: tall and slender, with long, thin hands—a doctor's hands—and brown hair that curled a little around the edges, and eyes that were as dark and sparkling as her own. And the sweetest smile she'd ever seen. "Lie still now," he said, still smiling. "You're not going anywhere."

The hands from behind belonged to a nurse, and now she spoke up. "You're not in any shape to go anywhere."

Rachel looked up at her and then down at herself. She was still wearing the evening gown. They must think she was some kind of nut. She rubbed her forehead. "What am I doing here? What happened?"

"You fainted," the doctor said. "And they couldn't bring you around. So you were brought here by ambulance."

"Oh. Well, but I'm all right now, aren't I? I mean, I can't stay here all day. I'm in the middle of a fashion show at Bryant's Department Store, and they'll be screaming their heads off."

Now the nurse smiled. She wasn't bad-looking either. A blonde with blue eyes. The kind of girl who looked as though if you dropped her she'd break. Though she didn't sound that way. She sounded matter-of-fact. "The time it took to send for an ambulance," she said, "and then bring you here, the fashion show must be over by now. So why not relax and take it easy?"

Rachel nodded. "I guess you're right. But couldn't I at least sit up?"

Down came the nurse's hands again, but then a look passed between the doctor and her, and he said, "Let her try, Alice," and she took her hands away.

Rachel struggled up—and would have pitched forward onto the floor if he hadn't caught her. "Now do you believe me?" he asked, holding her a bit longer than he needed to, she thought, his face close to hers, before helping her stretch out again. So long as she had to pass out, she could at least be glad she was wearing the gold lamé. It really did look as though it had been designed for her.

"Now will you lie still and stay that way?"

She sighed. "Okay. Till my head clears, anyhow."

"Good." He picked up a clipboard and smiled at her again. "What's your name?"

"Rachel Davis." She tried a smile on her own. A flippant one. "What's yours?"

"I'm Dr. Matthews. Dr. Russell Matthews. And this is my sister Alice."

"Oh," Rachel said, and then, as what he'd said got through to her, "oh. Matthews?" Her eyes widened. "You mean you're one of the Bay City Matthewses?"

He and the nurse exchanged another look, and it was the nurse who answered. "No. We're two of them."

He nodded. "And there are even more of us at home."

"You're making fun of me," Rachel said.

They laughed, and because it seemed the only thing to do, she laughed with them. But being a Matthews in Bay City wasn't something she'd make a joke about. Not likely. The Matthewses were important people in this town. Their names were always turning up on the society pages. At this ball and that one. Big charity things. And they were rich, too. You had to be rich to live in the part of town they did. Not new rich in a ranch house in the suburbs, either. Longtime, big-old-fashioned-houses rich.

"Now then," Dr. Matthews said, making with the clipboard again. "I need your age and address."

She lied about both. She was only nineteen, but she didn't want him to know it. He must be twenty-five or twenty-six at least. So she said she was twenty-two. And she made up an address in a good part of town. Why not? He wouldn't be checking it out.

"Have you fainted like this before?" he asked.

"No," she said, thinking that would be the end of it. It was only the beginning.

Had she been running a fever? Had she felt dizzy? Weak? Any headaches? Any chills? How often? For how long? Was she on any medication? Had she been sleeping well? What had she eaten for breakfast this morning? Lunch? No lunch?

"I didn't have time for lunch, and if that's all it is . . ."

Once again she struggled to sit up, but this time he didn't let her try. "No you don't. Alice, I'm going to wheel Miss Davis into a cubicle, and then I want you to get her undressed and into a hospital gown while I call Admissions to see about—"

Rachel grabbed his arm. "What? Now wait a minute. You can't do that. There's nothing the matter with me. Now you listen—"

He pushed her hand down as though he were pinning her to a mat, his face close again, his brown eyes intent on her. "No. You listen to me," he said, his voice matching the look in his eyes. A shiver of anticipation ran up her spine. "Something is the matter with you. Maybe something minor, like undernourishment or overexhaustion, but something. And until I find out precisely what it is, you're not going anywhere except to a bed in this hospital. Is that clear?"

Rachel didn't take her eyes from his, but returned look for look, saying—almost without thinking—"Is this how you talk to your wife?"

"I don't have a wife," he said, "but if I did, and if she were in your condition and were behaving the way you are, then yes, I would talk to her like this. Any more questions?"

Rachel smiled. "No, Doctor. No more questions."

Her good mood lasted until she saw her bed—in a six-bed ward, full of a lot of old women coughing and spitting and carrying on, and only a curtain around her own bed to give her any privacy.

"I didn't pick it," he said. "It was the only bed available. Do you want me to put you on the list for a private room?"

"Oh, sure," Rachel said. "Just take the money for it out of your allowance."

He grinned. "Very funny. I'll put you on the list. When a room comes up, you can always say no."

"I don't expect to be here that long."

But she was there that long, and her mother somehow managed to find the money to pay for a private room. How, Rachel didn't know. Nor did she ask. Her mother, Ada Davis, was a beauty operator at Pierre's in downtown Bay City—not all that far from where they had their apartment—and though she didn't make a whole lot of money, she did have some rich clients who had sometimes helped out in the past, so maybe they were helping out this time, too. Her mother was closemouthed about it, the way she was closemouthed about a lot of things. Pride, maybe. Or having to swallow her pride.

Whichever it was, being in the hospital wasn't so bad when you had a private room, except that it was boring having to stay in bed all the time even when she felt okay enough to get up, and having a raft of tests, and doctor after doctor listening to her heart because one of them heard a murmur one time that shouldn't have been there.

And there were a couple of scary times, the first when Russ—she had long since stopped calling him Dr. Matthews—told her she had an inflammation of the heart lining. "What does that mean?" she asked.

"It means you have an infection that has to be cleared up."

"And can it be cleared up?"

"Yes."

"And I'll be all well again?"

"Yes."

She frowned. "You say 'yes,' but you don't sound it."

"It's nothing to worry about, Rachel." He knew how she hated being in the hospital. Or he ought to, anyhow; she had told him often enough. And she was terrified of being sick. He knew that, too. "It's just that you'll have to be careful," he went on, "until we know for sure your heart hasn't sustained any permanent damage. Now you're not to worry," he said again.

"You leave that to me. I'm taking care of you, aren't I?"

"And what happens if you stop taking care of me?"

He eyed her a moment. "I think there's very little chance of that."

The other scary time was when the fever came back and she passed out again and came to to find Russ hovering over her the same as when he had first come into her life. Only this time he looked—well—not quite so cool and professional.

"What happened? What's going on?" she asked him, beginning to get even more scared when he went on listening to her heart long after he should have heard enough.

He shook his head. "I'm not sure."

The fear became dread certainty. "Russ, I'm going to die, aren't I?"

"No," he said firmly. "No, you're not. You've just had a little setback, that's all. Not even enough of a setback to call in Dr. MacCurdy."

Dr. MacCurdy, a full-fledged doctor and an older man, was in charge of her case. Russ himself, as he had told her over and over, was only an intern. But he was Dr. MacCurdy's protégé, and Rachel had learned enough about the hospital by this time to know that meant Russ was going to be just as big a name in medicine someday as Dr. MacCurdy was now. Maybe even more so. And a Matthews to boot. She couldn't believe her luck. Especially if—

"Russ, what are you doing here? I thought you were off tonight."

"I was. The hospital called me."

"But why?"

He smiled. Not the sweet smile. A teasing one. "It seems you were calling my name."

"You mean while I was passed out?"

"That's right."

She smiled right back at him. "Then you can't hold me responsible, because I didn't know what I was doing. And besides, you probably do this kind of thing all the time."

"Come in when I'm off duty? Don't you believe it!"

"You mean you did it just for me?"

He waited a moment before he answered her, and then he said, "Just for a patient—like you—who's very sick. Who needs me."

"But you said I wasn't very sick. Or that it wasn't anything serious, anyhow."

"I didn't know that when they called me."

Russ was sweet. He really was. He didn't have to send his mother to meet her one day for her to know that he was getting serious about her. She already knew that. But still he did it. Maybe to let his mother know.

Regardless, when Mrs. Matthews was at the hospital, visiting somebody else, she stopped by and introduced herself, and they had a real nice visit, although it would have been nicer if Rachel's own mother hadn't happened to be there, too, considering that her mother and Russ's mother couldn't possibly have anything in common.

Russ's older sister, Pat—it was Pat and then Russ and then Alice—came in to visit one day, too. She was as blonde and blue-eyed as Alice, but without the Dresden-doll look. As Russ said, she looked like her name—patrician. She was tall, almost as tall as Russ, and sleek and elegant and wearing elegant clothes. And she was married to John Randolph, one of the biggest and richest lawyers in Bay City—maybe the whole state, maybe the whole Midwest.

Ever since Rachel had been old enough to know she didn't have anywhere near what she wanted in life, Bay City had been mostly a place to get out of, and the sooner the better. But now she began to think it might have some possibilities on its own.

It wasn't a hick town, anyhow, no Podunk, U.S.A., but a city, with maybe fifty thousand people, and that wasn't counting the surrounding area.

The part where she lived was grimy, of course, with factories and diners and old brick buildings with boarded-up windows—and all defaced anyway with graffiti and layer upon layer of moldy old posters. But the right part of town, where the Matthewses and their friends all lived, had beautiful homes with big, beautiful yards, and wide, quiet, tree-shaded streets. And over by the bay it was always pretty, summer or winter.

Sometimes after work when the weather was nice she and one of the other models at Bryant's would take a bus out to the big city park that fronted on the bay, and they'd buy hot dogs and Cokes from a vendor and go watch the people sailing their boats. Or, even better, walk over to the marina, where the motor launches and the yachts were tied up. And they'd imagine what it would be like to own one of those big, gorgeous things, to live that kind of life.

Wouldn't her girl friend have a fit if she knew Rachel was that close to finding out!

Russ had to be coaxed a little, of course. As much as she could tell that he ached to touch her—not as a doctor, as a man—he held back, maybe because of the way he'd been brought up. Probably.

One day he came into her room to make her get back into bed, and since he obviously thought she was weak, she figured she might as well take advantage of it. So she pretended to faint, and he had to catch her, and she managed to get her arms around his neck, and then she just stood there looking at him for all she was worth, until he pulled her close to him and kissed her.

When he finally broke away, he said, "I shouldn't have done that."

She smiled. "I know. But I'm so glad you did."

Then he smiled too, and took her in his arms again. And after that he kissed her every time he got the chance. And held her close, and touched her hair and her face.

But she had to make sure, and though it scared her out of her mind to do it the way she did, it was the only way she knew how.

One evening when he had the night off, and he came in to kiss her good-bye and hold her close, she said, still snuggled up against him, "What are you going to do tonight—go out with some gorgeous blonde?"

"Oh, sure," he said. "Three or four, anyhow. However many are lined up outside the hospital waiting for me."

She sighed. For all she knew, it might not be a joke. "I wish I could go out with you tonight."

He gathered her close. "So do I. But you wait. One day soon you'll be leaving this place."

"I know," she answered. "And then you won't see me any more at all, and you'll forget all about me."

"Don't you believe it."

She rubbed a finger along the sleeve of his white hospital coat. "I've never understood anyhow why you'd look twice at a girl like me."

He frowned. "What do you mean, a girl like you?"

"Oh, you know."

"No, I don't know."

"I don't have any family, Russ."

"You have your mother."

"That's not what I mean. I mean family. Money. Social position." Rachel took a breath. She had gone this far. She might as well go all the way. "I don't have any of those things. Little Miss Nobody, that's me."

He was frowning again. "Rachel, stop talking that way."

"But, Russ, it's the truth. The day I came to the hospital, when you asked me where I lived, I made up an address, because I was ashamed to tell you where I really do live. On State Street. In the four hundred block. One of the grungiest parts of the whole city. In an apartment with one bedroom that I share with Mom. You remember you were saying something the other day about your room at home? Would you believe I've never had a room of my own? Never in my whole life?" She shook her head. "A room? I never even had a father. Not long enough to get to know him, anyhow. But you have a father and a mother and two sisters. And you live in a great big house. And the people in this town know who you are. As for me, well . . ." She shook her head again. "I'm afraid we're not very much alike."

"Is there anything that says we have to be?" His

voice was husky, and he had that intent look back in his eyes.

"No," she said, choosing what she was about to say very carefully. "But then, I'm only a patient of yours. I mean, someday a girl will come along that you'll want to marry, and suppose she's a girl like me. What would your family think of that? Would they approve?"

"They'd better," he said. "If they don't, it's too bad."

She slept very well that night. And without a sleeping tablet.

In fact, except for her mother making waves, it looked to be smooth sailing all the way.

Her mother.

Rachel made a face.

Her mother was getting to be more and more like a broken record every day. Harping and harping on the same old thing.

"The Matthews family is society, Rachel," she was saying now.

"Mmm. And loaded." Rachel applied a last bit of nail polish to her left hand, then looked at the glistening array of color. "How do you like this shade, Mom? I've got the lipstick to match."

"Rachel, will you listen to me?"

"I can listen and do my nails at the same time."

"The Matthewses are going to look right through you, just like there was nobody there."

"That isn't the way Russ's mother acted when she came in to meet me. You saw how she was. She was as nice as pie."

"I didn't say they don't have good manners. They'll say 'Hello, how are you' and 'Nice to see you' and be as democratic as a bartender, but—"

Rachel finished the sentence for her: "But they won't want me to marry their son."

Her mother nodded. "That's it exactly."

"We'll see."

"Honey," her mother said with an anxious look on her face, "don't wait around to see. I don't want you to get hurt."

Rachel blew on a nail to dry it. "What you want is for me to go to Hollywood."

"Well, that's what we always planned, isn't it? After you won that beauty contest when you were only fifteen years old. That's what all those diction lessons I paid for were for, wasn't it? And the dancing lessons and the drama lessons and the charm school. All so you could go to Hollywood and maybe get to be a star."

"Mmm. And suppose I did, Mom. There. How do they look now?" She held both hands out.

"They look fine, Rachel, but will you please stick to the subject?"

Rachel sighed. "Like glue, Mom. Like glue. Okay. Suppose I did go to Hollywood and I did become a star. I'd still have to work, wouldn't I? It says in every movie magazine how hard stars work."

"So they work hard. They get paid a lot better than—"

"You didn't let me finish, Mom," Rachel cut in coolly. "You take a woman whose name is Mrs. Matthews. Married to that good-looking guy with all that beautiful Matthews money. How much work do you think she has to do? No work at all, and the money rolls in just the same. I'd say being Mrs. Matthews is about the best job there is anywhere."

"Rachel, that's a terrible way to talk."

"So? There isn't anybody to hear it except you and me. And neither of us is going to tell anybody."

"You think not?"

Rachel had taken the applicator out of the bottle to touch up a thumbnail. Now she put it back and looked straight at her mother, furious with her. "You wouldn't dare."

Sometimes, when she got angry enough, her mother backed right down. Other times she didn't. This was one of the other times. "Wouldn't I?" she said. "What's to prevent me from taking Dr. Matthews aside and—"

"I'll tell you what's to prevent you," Rachel answered, almost beside herself with rage. "Because the whole thing was your idea to begin with, that's what."

Her mother looked bewildered. "My idea?"

"Yes, yours. Who sat right here in this very room and said her daughter was every bit as good as any of the Matthewses, never mind that Dr. Russell Matthews must have dozens of society girls chasing after him and could probably have any of them he crooked a finger at, nobody—and that included Dr. Russell Matthews—was out of her daughter's league, and if Dr. Russell Matthews didn't look twice at her daughter, then there must be something wrong with his eyesight. Well? Or are you going to pretend you never said that?"

Her mother let out a breath like a deflating balloon. "No. I'm not going to pretend I never said it. I don't pretend things, Rachel. That's your department, not mine."

"So?"

"All right. But I only said it to give you self-respect. I never meant to give you the idea of trying to trick somebody into marrying you."

"Who said anything about tricking? Russ is in love with me."

"Has he told you that?"

"He will."

"And you? Are you in love with him?"

"Well, of course I am." Rachel took the applicator out again and did the touch-up job. "Come on, Mom." Now that she had made her point she could afford to bend a little. "You want me to be happy, don't you?"

Her mother looked a little less pained already. "Well, sure, honey, but . . ."

"And you always said you wanted the best for me."

"I know, but . . ."

"All those things you did for me. All the lessons. They weren't wasted, Mom. They're going to pay off. Not the way you thought, but a better way. They're going to make me a Matthews. You wait. You'll see."

A couple of days later Rachel was standing in front of the mirror of her hospital bureau, trying out some new eye shadow, admiring the color, a cool and silky green, when she happened to look up and saw Russ leaning against the wall behind her, watching her, arms folded, an amused look on his face. She felt the hot blood surge into her face as she spun around to him. "Russ! What are you doing there?"

He grinned. "Admiring the view."

She could have killed him. "How long have you been there?"

"Oh, a couple of days."

"Russ!"

"All right. Not more than half a minute."

She breathed a sigh of relief and put on what she hoped was a demure look. "You must think I spend all my time in front of a mirror."

"I can't say I'd blame you if you did. A girl as pretty as you."

She smiled at him. "Do you really think so?"

"Would I say so if I didn't?"

"You might. To make me feel you cared about me."

"I have other ways of doing that."

"Do you?"

"You know I do," he said, his voice low and husky. He stretched out a hand. "Come here."

She went to him, and he took her in his arms and kissed her.

"Oh, Russ," she said when she could speak.

He held her a little way off from him. "Now do you believe me?"

She pretended to consider. "Mmm. Maybe you could show me again? So I could make sure?"

"Scamp," he said, pulling her to him. He kissed her again, harder than before, and she responded, until finally he broke away from her. "You're going to get us both in trouble."

"*I* am?" She gave him an arch look. "Well, I like that! Who started this, I'd like to know."

He shook his head. "You see? I can't even think straight any more."

"Do you mind?" she said, and would have gone into his arms again, but both of them turned at the sound of footsteps in the hall, and almost before they could move a safe distance apart, his sister Alice came into the room with fresh linen for the bed.

Even so, Alice must have felt the tension in the air, because she said, "Am I interrupting something?"

"No," Russ answered her. "I just came in to tell Rachel the good news that she's getting out of here tomorrow."

"Oh, Russ!" Rachel clapped her hands. "Do you mean it?"

"If that's what you came in to tell her," Alice said, looking from one to the other of them, "what were you holding back for?"

Russ shrugged, a bit of color in his face. "I hadn't gotten to it yet, that's all. I had to check her over first."

Alice gave them that cool Miss Icebox smile of hers. "I see."

"Maybe," Rachel said, nervous—Alice always made her nervous—"maybe Russ was afraid if he just blurted it out I'd think you were all dying to get rid of me."

"I don't know why you'd think that," Alice said— the way she said almost everything, not giving you a clue about which way she meant it or how she felt.

"I guess I think it because I still can't get over how nice you've been to me," Rachel said to her, putting on her nicest smile. "How you've gone out of your way to be nice to me."

"I didn't realize I had," Alice answered in that same matter-of-fact way. But her smile seemed to warm up some. "Well, I'll be back in a few minutes to change your bed. After I distribute the rest of the linens."

When Alice had gone, closing the door behind her, Rachel said, "Do you think she'll ever get to like me, Russ?"

"What do you mean, get to like you? She likes you now."

"Do you really think so?"

"I'm sure of it."

Rachel wasn't sure at all. Alice and Russ were very close, and apparently always had been. It was Russ's becoming a doctor that had given Alice the idea of becoming a nurse. And they always had their heads together over something. And not just patients, either, but some private joke or some little confidence.

And yet Russ couldn't have said much to Alice about what was happening between the two of them, or Alice would have let on more. As it was, the only thing Alice had ever said in any kind of confiding way was to play down how much money her family had and talk about how hard all of them worked and how Russ had to live on what he made as an intern—and who couldn't, considering he lived at home? Maybe that was her and Alice's private joke.

If so, it was their only one. And the way Alice looked at her sometimes, as if she knew exactly what Rachel was thinking. She didn't, of course. She couldn't. But it made Rachel nervous all the same.

Not that it mattered how Alice felt about her, or how any of the Matthews family felt about her. Russ had already made that clear. The only thing that counted was how he felt about her. And she was a hundred percent sure of him. Almost.

The first time he came to see her after she got out of the hospital she was as nervous as a cat—and almost on the verge of tears at what he would think when he saw how shabby her mother's apartment was. Even dusted and straightened up, with all the newspapers and movie magazines and the ironing out of the way, it still looked shabby. You couldn't hide that. The sofa and chairs were scruffy and faded, and the kitchen table had a cheap plastic cloth on it.

But Russ didn't seem to mind. He didn't even seem to notice. All he had eyes for was her.

And that made her surer than ever.

But his family could still put obstacles in her and Russ's way if they wanted to. And apparently they did.

Naturally, Russ didn't see it as that. Not at first, anyhow. One night when she'd managed to get her mother out of the apartment—and Russ onto the subject of marriage—he said, "I haven't talked about it before, Rachel, because I don't feel I have the right to yet. After I finish my internship I still have my residency ahead of me."

She sighed. "You mean you can't get married until after all of that?"

"It isn't that I can't, but I don't think it would be fair to you. I have to be at the hospital so much of the time. Look at the dates I've already had to break with you because some emergency came up."

"Yes, I know, Russ, but the little time you do have free we'd really be together." She snuggled more closely into his arms and rested her face against his chest. She could feel his heart start pounding as he tightened his grip on her and bent to kiss her. Hard. And then harder.

"Oh, Rachel, Rachel."

She pulled away from him a bit. "Do you really love me, Russ?"

"You know I do."

She shook her head. "You can't love me as much as I love you, because I love you too much to wait, Russ, and if you really loved me you couldn't wait either."

"Darling," he said, "I don't want to wait, but it's the sensible thing to do."

"How can you talk about being sensible if you're in love? Don't you know what love means? It means not caring about any of the little things but only about being together. And it's more than that, too. Darling, don't you see? Tonight when Mom gets home you'll take me in your arms—the way we are now—and we'll kiss, and then you'll leave. And that's what I can't stand, Russ—to have you near me, have you hold me and caress me and kiss me and then turn and go away from me, leaving me alone. And crying."

Frowning, he cupped her face in his hand. "Crying?"

She looked away from him. "I shouldn't have said that."

"No, I'm glad you did. I want to know everything about you, Rachel."

She turned to look at him again. "I'm afraid I'm not very good at hiding things from you, Russ."

He was silent a moment. "I only want to be fair to you."

She took a breath. "The only way you can be fair to me, Russ, is to make me your wife. I wish it weren't that way—that I could be sensible, as you call it— that I could sit around and wait for however long it takes. But I can't. I can't go on seeing you like this, being with you like this and not be your wife. I'd have to go away somewhere, leave Bay City."

"No!"

She reached for him, and he swept her into his arms and kissed her harder than before. "Oh, Russ," she said, "if you only knew what you do to me."

His voice was so choked that he could hardly speak. "We'll get married, darling. I promise you."

That was when his family started being heard from. Even her own mother had her two cents' worth to put in, trying to discourage her by lecturing her on what marriage meant, until Rachel cut her off by saying "Considering that my father walked out on you when I was a baby, I don't think you're anybody to be giving advice, Mom, I really don't."

The Matthewses weren't so easy to dispose of. Rachel was sure Russ's family thought she wasn't good enough for him. The women in the family, anyhow. His mother and Alice and Pat. And the one time she'd met his Aunt Liz, the richest and most important one of them all, his aunt had nearly tripped over her feet from looking down her nose at Rachel.

Rachel was careful not to say any of that to Russ. Instead she told him how much she liked his family— and she really did like his father, so that part wasn't hard. As for Russ, he claimed that the only reason his family objected was that he was still an intern.

"As if that made any difference to me," she said.

"They think it should," he answered. "And you can see their point. After all, I'm not able to take care of a wife the way I'd want to."

She didn't say anything for a bit, but took one of his hands in hers, running a finger up and down and around the back of it from wrist to fingertip. "And so you let them talk you out of it."

"No I didn't. I make up my own mind. I said we'd get married, darling, and we will."

Again she was silent. "It does raise a problem, though, if they're thinking that way."

He agreed that it did.

She had the answer for him the very next night—

when she could get her breath back after looking at what he had brought her: the most gorgeous diamond engagement ring she'd ever laid eyes on. And big, too. "Oh, Russ," she said. And said it again. And couldn't find anything else to say except "Oh, Russ," until he started laughing. "Listen," she said, half laughing with him, "listen to me. I figured it out. What we can do, I mean."

He arched his eyebrows. "What?"

He was almost as gorgeous as the ring, with those sparkly brown eyes and that long, lean, handsome face that lighted up so whenever he looked at her. She was giddy with excitement. "On your next day off, why don't we fly to Chicago or somewhere in Illinois and get married there?"

"You mean elope?"

"Why not? What difference does it make as long as we're Dr. and Mrs. Russell Matthews? And it's been done before, you know."

He considered, then nodded. "That's not a bad idea."

And so they did, the only change being that they didn't wait until his next day off.

The Matthews family did indeed live in what Rachel considered the right part of Bay City, though there was nothing particularly grand or pretentious about their home, a two-story white frame house with a wide front porch and a flagstone patio in the back yard. The first floor consisted of a nice, spacious living room furnished with well-cared-for pieces, a bright and cheerful modern kitchen, a dining room that was seldom used—they usually ate in the kitchen—and a den, where Jim Matthews sometimes spent the evening on a client's tax return or auditing a company's books.

Upstairs, the master bedroom was at the back of the house. In front was a large bedroom, with its own small bathroom, that Alice and Pat had shared while they were growing up. Since Pat's marriage to John Randolph, Alice had had the room to herself. Next to it was Russ's smaller bedroom, and down the hall was a full-size bathroom.

Jim and Mary Matthews had bought the house right

after Alice was born, twenty-two years ago. It was sturdy, it was comfortable, it was cool in the summer and warm in the winter, it was attractive, it was familiar, it was home.

The day after Russ became engaged to Rachel, Alice arrived home from the hospital a little after five to find her Aunt Liz in the living room with her mother, the two of them having a cup of tea. "Goodness," Liz said, looking at her watch, "I had no idea it was this late."

Alice's mother was looking behind her. "Isn't Russell with you?"

"No. Did you think he would be?"

"He has tonight off."

Alice sorted through the mail on the hall table, then came in and sat down. "And where does he generally spend his nights off these days?"

"Don't tell me," Liz said, "he's still seeing that dreadful Davis girl."

"Seeing her, Aunt Liz? He's engaged to her."

Liz's mouth dropped open, and she spun around to Mary. "You didn't say a word."

Mary sighed. "It only happened yesterday."

"I'm amazed you allowed it to happen at all. A girl like that. With her kind of background."

"I'm not concerned about her background, Liz."

Liz sniffed. "I think you should be."

"Well, I'm not. I don't have anything against Rachel. What I am concerned about is whether she truly cares for Russ or is dazzled by the fact that he's a doctor and a very attractive young man."

"A good catch is what you mean."

"Yes, that *is* what I mean," Mary said. "That's what I wonder about Rachel. Does she simply consider Russell a good catch?"

"I don't hear you saying anything, Alice," Liz said.

Alice shrugged. "I don't have anything to say. I don't have anything against Rachel either. Or I didn't when I first met her. But I'm not as kindhearted as Mom, and I've seen Rachel go to work on Russ, so I don't have to wonder. I know. She isn't right for him at all. And she isn't just dazzled by his being a doctor and good-looking. She's got this wild idea we're rolling in money."

"Where on earth did that come from?"

Mary shook her head. "Jim says that from Rachel's point of view we probably do seem rich."

"Yeah. By the way, Mom, what is the cook fixing for dinner?"

"I don't know, dear. You'll have to ask the butler."

Alice laughed and turned to her aunt. "Mom said something to Rachel once about having to get home to straighten up the house or something, and Rachel thought she was joking. She thinks we have a houseful of servants. In spite of the fact that she's been here for dinner and seen that we don't. Or maybe she thought it was their day off. Probably."

"Well," Liz said, "why don't you straighten her out? Before it's too late."

"I tried to," Alice said. "It went in one ear and out the other. I don't know. One of these days Russ is going to wake up and wonder what hit him."

"That's what I'm afraid of," Mary said, an anxious look on her usually calm face. "I know this sounds like a trite thing to say, but it happens to be true. When Russell was a child—long before he said he wanted to be a doctor—he was always bringing little hurt things to the house. A dog or a cat or a bird or a frog. Any little animal that needed to be mended and cared for and made well and strong again. And that was exactly what he would do for it. And I can't help thinking . . . Oh, I know Rachel is extremely pretty, and I know Russell is immensely drawn to her, physically drawn to her. But I can't help thinking he also sees her—whether he knows it or not—as a grown-up version of one of those little hurt things."

By the time her mother had finished, Alice had tears in her eyes. "You're right, Mom," she said. "I'd forgotten about Russ and his orphans of the storm. But you're absolutely right. Only this time I'm afraid he'll be the one who ends up being hurt."

"I know," Mary said. "My sentiments exactly. But

at least his father talked him out of getting married right away. Jim made Russell see he has too many obligations at the hospital right now to take on the added responsibility of marriage. To anybody."

"You mean," Liz said, "you hope Jim made him see that."

"Russell gave his word he wouldn't marry until after he finished his internship. And when Russell gives his word, he keeps it."

"In that case," Liz said, getting up, "maybe Russ will come to his senses in time."

After she had gone, Mary went into the kitchen to see about dinner, and Alice went along to help. "It isn't like Russ not to call if something is keeping him at the hospital," Mary said.

"Maybe it's an emergency," Alice said, "and he hasn't been able to get away to call."

Her mother nodded. "Maybe." She brightened. "There's your father's car in the driveway. Maybe Russ is with him."

But he wasn't, and as dinner came and went and the evening turned into night and there was still no word from him, Mary said again, "It isn't like Russ."

Jim put down the book he was reading. "He's not a child any more, darling. There's no need for him to check in and out."

"I know. But he told me this morning he wasn't on duty tonight, and he would be home."

"He probably talked to Rachel," Jim said, "and she changed his mind. After all, they've only been engaged about twenty-four hours, and it's natural they'd want to see each other—even if only for a little while."

"Yes, I suppose so."

Jim looked from Mary to Alice. "Shall I go out to the kitchen to get a knife to cut the gloom with?"

"I'm not gloomy," Mary said. "I'm just concerned."

"I'm gloomy," Alice said; then she grinned. "Just joking, Dad. And anyhow, as Aunt Liz said to me when she went out the door this evening, if Russ does get hurt a little, he's brought it on himself. And furthermore, he's a grown-up man who's perfectly capable of taking care of himself. Without any help from me or anybody else. So I've decided to take Aunt Liz's advice. Whatever happens or doesn't happen, Rachel is Russ's problem. She isn't mine."

Chapter Two

THERE may have been a time when Ada Davis was ambitious for herself, but that time had long since faded away. Or been worn away by too many years of missed opportunities and things gone sour, by too many bills to pay and never enough money to pay them with. And by a husband who had promised her everything and left her with nothing, except a baby daughter, who had come to mean—quite literally—the world to her.

Ada wanted for her daughter what she hadn't been pretty enough or educated enough or quick-witted enough to get for herself. She wanted Rachel to have the best, and for a long time now she had scrimped and scrounged to that end with gritty determination.

To Ada the best meant freedom, independence, being able to stand on your own two feet and thumb your nose at the world. It did not mean marrying into a family who would thumb their noses at you. And Rachel's determination to do exactly that had her mother worried sick.

She sighed as she lit the fire under the coffeepot and reached for the skillet to scramble some eggs for breakfast. Nor did she like the idea of Rachel staying out all night last night—something she'd never done before.

Ada was sitting down to eat when she heard the door to the apartment open and, a moment after that, Rachel's voice.

"Mom, where are you?"

"In the kitchen." Then, as Rachel came into view: "I was asking the same question about you all night long. Where were you?"

Rachel beamed. "Remember what I told you when Russ gave me the diamond engagement ring—that I was going to get the other one to go with it very soon?" She held out her left hand. "One day later. Is that soon enough for you?"

Ada stared from the hand to her daughter's face and back again. "You mean you're married? You and Russ are married?"

"That's right. That's where we were last night. Eloping. The first part of the night, anyhow. And the rest of the night—well . . ." She beamed again. "I guess you could call it making the marriage something more than our names on a piece of paper, in case anybody gets any ideas about wanting to change things back the way they were. Not that anybody will, of course, because they're not going to know. Russ told his parents he wouldn't get married until after he finished his internship, so we're going to keep it a secret."

Ada's head was still reeling. "Won't his parents be the same as me, wondering where he was all night?"

Rachel shrugged. "He'll let them think he was at the hospital, which is where he is half the time anyhow."

"I see. And what made Russ change his mind about getting married?"

"He said he couldn't live without me. What's for breakfast? I'm starved."

"Haven't you had anything to eat this morning?"

"No. We were too busy. Doing other things. You know. Right up until the time we had to check out of the hotel to catch a plane back." She beamed again, more triumphantly than before. "Oh, Mom, I told you I'd bring it off, didn't I? And I did, I did. Mrs. Russell Matthews. Mrs. Dr. Russell Matthews." She laughed and hugged herself.

Ada handed Rachel the toast and scrambled eggs she'd fixed for herself and got up to make some more. She always tried her best to see things from Rachel's point of view, to swallow her own disappointment or put a clamp on her feelings—whatever it took to keep

Rachel happy and satisfied. She tried to feel good now about what she'd just been told, but she couldn't. "You think Russ's family is going to like you any better for having talked him into this hurry-up marriage?"

"Who said anything about talking him into it? It was his idea, not mine. And what do I care whether his family likes me or not? The only Matthews I need is the one I've already got. Make another piece of toast for me, Mom, will you?"

Maybe, Ada thought as she dropped two more slices of bread into the toaster, Rachel was telling the truth about its being Russ's idea to elope, but she was nowhere near the truth about not caring whether his family liked her. It still made Ada wince remembering how Rachel had thrown herself at Mary Matthews that time at the hospital, trying so hard to impress her it was God's wonder Russ's mother hadn't turned on her heel and walked out of the room.

"You should have waited, Rachel. And you could have. Russ will be finished with his internship in another six months. Six months isn't so long to wait."

"Yeah? And what if, while I was waiting, he'd somehow gotten away from me?"

Ada brought her scrambled eggs and the fresh toast to the table. "If he loves you, like you've been saying he does, why would he do that?"

"You were the one who said it to me, Mom—that men like Russ don't marry girls like me. So why take chances?"

So it hadn't been Russ's idea! Ada opened her mouth, then shut it again. What was the use? Rachel wouldn't admit she'd lied. And before long it wouldn't be a lie any more, because Rachel would come to believe that her marriage to Russ had happened exactly the way she was saying it had.

It had always been that way with her. Ada supposed it was her own fault for not putting a stop to it long before now, except how could you put a stop to something you didn't know was even there until it was already too late? Not the dark side of it, anyhow. In the beginning, when Rachel was just a little thing, it hadn't been anything more than fairy tales, harmless little bits of things spun out like cotton candy. Rachel was hardly any different from other kids who, on a rainy afternoon, put on their mother's dresses and shoes and pretended to be grown up.

That was the kind of dreaming and carrying on that all kids did. She'd done it herself a time or two when she was young. The trouble was that Rachel didn't seem to know—or care—where the dreaming ended and the truth began. Or where the truth ended and the lies began.

After Rachel had finished her breakfast and gone off to work—though how she could stay on her feet all day modeling clothes with hardly any sleep, her mother didn't know—Ada sat on at the table. She'd have to get a move on herself pretty soon. But it was only a short walk to the beauty parlor, and her first customer wasn't due until nine forty-five, so she had time for another cup of coffee.

Married. Rachel married. She still couldn't believe it. All her plans, all her hopes and dreams for Rachel gone up in smoke now. Not that Russ wasn't a nice boy. He was one of the nicest, kindest, most decent boys Ada had ever known. And respectful? He treated Ada as though she were royalty. Or the next thing to it.

And he would provide for Rachel. Ada didn't doubt that for a minute. He was a smart young doctor, and a good one, too. Everybody she'd talked to at the hospital when he was helping handle Rachel's case had said that. Dr. MacCurdy and the nurses. People who were in a position to know. Russ would do all right.

It wasn't Russ she was worried about. It was Rachel. The one thing Ada had wanted to give her daughter—a college education—she hadn't been able to. And what good were all the diction lessons and the acting lessons and the charm school going to do Rachel when it came to fitting into the Matthews world?

No good at all.

From the time Rachel had announced her intention of becoming Mrs. Russell Matthews Ada had been scared she would be hurt. Worse than hurt—laughed at; made a fool of.

"Who says so?"

"His mother did. Today. She said that when she and her husband were first married, he was just getting started in business, and they didn't have much money, so she worked as a clerk in a woman's specialty shop."

"So? That was years ago. I didn't say they were born rich. Anyhow, you notice she didn't say they didn't have any money, just not much. So how much is much?"

"Rachel, I've never claimed the Matthewses were as hard up as we are. I don't mean that. But they're not what you think they are, either. It's true Jim Matthews has his own accounting firm—and has had for some time—but Mary Matthews does all her own cooking and cleaning except for a woman who comes in one day a week to help with the heavy work. Is that your idea of rich?"

Rachel shrugged. "It's my idea of people who have money and don't spend it, that's all. Look at Russ's Aunt Liz. You think she does her own housework? I bet."

"How much money Russ's aunt has or doesn't have is beside the point."

But Rachel had already lost interest and was opening the box from Bryant's. She took out a long dress made of some clingy fabric in flaming red and held it up against herself. "How's that for smooth and slinky, Mom? Isn't it gorgeous?"

"It's beautiful, honey." And with Rachel's creamy skin and her thick dark hair, it was. Ada swallowed and tried to sound casual. "Was it on sale?"

"Mom, you're about as subtle as a brick. Will you stop worrying about money all the time? That's all behind me now. Thank heavens."

"Rachel, I'm trying to tell you it isn't behind you. Even if Mary and Jim Matthews were rich—which they aren't—it's not them you're married to. It's their son, Russell. Do you think Russ is the kind of boy who would let his parents support him?"

Rachel was admiring herself and her new dress in the mirror on the back of the bedroom door. "You don't have to support somebody to find ways to give him money. And that's only until Russ finishes his training. When he starts practicing, he'll make plenty of money on his own. Oh, Mom, I'm so excited about tonight. I was thrilled when Russ called to say he'd arranged the double date with Walter and Lenore."

"And whose idea was that?"

"What difference does it make whose idea it was? They're important people, Mom, I told you that. People you want to be seen with. And Lenore and I are going to become good friends. I just know we are. When she gets married to Walter she'll probably ask me to be a bridesmaid. I'm sure she will."

"Rachel, you don't even know the girl."

"I know who she is. And I've seen her at Bryant's plenty of times. Anyhow, I'm not talking about now. I'm talking about later. After tonight and some other times just like it."

Ada shook her head. "I don't see why this Lenore person should mean so much to you."

Rachel smiled. A dreamy smile. "Because one of these days I'm going to be just like her. You should see her, Mom. She's every bit as elegant as Russ's sister Pat. Maybe even more so. And she knows how to act without even thinking about it. She's all smooth and easy, like velvet. That's what money does for you." The smile vanished, and a hard look came into her daughter's eyes. "And that's what money is going to do for me, Mom. You think I can't make it with the Matthewses, but I will. And I'll be every bit as smooth as Lenore is, too."

Ada made one last try. "If you're so interested in making it with the Matthewses, you might try living the way they do. They don't go out dining and dancing night after night. And I don't know how you expect Russ to keep up this pace when he has to work all day every day at the hospital, and all night, too, every other night."

"Oh, Mom, he's young. And he likes going out as much as I do. And, Mom, before I forget, could you arrange to spend tonight at your friend's house, like you did on Tuesday? I mean, Russ and I hardly ever get to be together, and . . . well, you know."

"All right, Rachel. Yes, I suppose I can. But I'm getting tired of being thrown out of my own apartment all the time. Why don't the two of you get a place of your own?"

"How can we do that and keep our marriage a secret?"

Ada didn't answer, because there wasn't any answer to that. Except, as it turned out, there was.

After Rachel complained of a headache and feeling dizzy for a few days in a row, Russ tried to talk her into going to see Dr. MacCurdy, but she talked him into going dancing instead at the Top of the Tower, where she passed out cold in Walter Curtin's arms.

After that Russ put his foot down—something he didn't do often enough, Ada felt, though she was hardly one to talk, considering all the times in Rachel's childhood that she hadn't put hers down either. Russ put Rachel in the hospital to find out what was wrong with her. And, as scared as Rachel was that it might be her heart infection coming back, the way she acted when she found out what it really was made her mother think she would have preferred the business with her heart.

Rachel stared at Russ. "I'm what?"

He was grinning like a fool. "What I said. You're pregnant."

"But, Russ, I can't be! There's got to be some mistake."

"You want to hear it from Dr. MacCurdy?"

"No. But, Russ, what are we going to do?"

"We're going to have a baby," he said, still with that same fool grin on his face. "That's what we're going to do."

She moved her hand impatiently. "You don't understand. I'm not talking about that."

But he was already nodding. "You mean about making our marriage public. We'll just have to announce it, that's all. I think maybe the two of us should go to my parents first—either together, or I can go alone if you want me to."

"No, I— Oh, Russ," she wailed, "this wasn't what I had planned on at all."

"I know," he said, grinning again. "It wasn't what I planned on either, and I'll admit it makes some complications. But that's all they are. It's nothing that's going to be impossible to overcome. Darling, don't look so panicky. It's going to be all right. Mother and Dad will accept this thing just fine, and you're going to have fun getting ready for the baby. Mom and Alice and Pat and everybody in the family will be there to help you, and then we'll have a wonderful, beautiful baby—just like its wonderful, beautiful mother."

"Oh, Russ, I"—she took a deep breath—"Russ, do we have to have the baby?"

He stared at her. "What?"

"Russ, I'm scared." And she was—scared out of her wits. "I mean, I know you probably think it's silly."

He'd gotten over his look of shock. "No," he said, "I don't think it's silly. I understand. It's a perfectly natural feeling. A lot of women are afraid. That's their first reaction when they find out they're pregnant— just as yours was."

Scared or not, she had made a bad move, and she knew it. She hurried to repair the damage. "No, Russ. That wasn't my first reaction. My first reaction was like yours—pure joy. It was so wonderful, and I was so happy that you and I . . . but then I got scared. I got such a feeling, thinking about it, that—"

But a phone call summoning Russ to a patient in another room cut off her pleading, and he hurried away, saying they'd talk about it later. For all the good it was likely to do her, Rachel thought.

The food cart holding the lunch she'd eaten stood by her bed. She gave it such a violent shove that it slammed across the room and crashed into the wall in an avalanche of broken glass and china that was sure to bring somebody on the run. Furious, frustrated, Rachel buried her face in her hands and burst into tears.

And her mother wasn't any more understanding that evening than Russ had been.

"I like the idea of having a grandchild," she said.

"Sure you do," Rachel answered, making a face. "You don't have to get fat and go all out of shape and wait around all those months for something you never wanted in the first place. Oh, Mom, I'm scared. It's all I can think about."

"You'll get over that," her mother said. "Has Russ broken the news to his parents yet?"

That was the only good thing about this whole business, having to tell his parents. Because she wanted them to know. And had all along. "He's doing it now. Tonight. He wanted to tell them together. And I don't care what you're thinking, Mom. Or what they are, either. They'll have to accept me, whether they like it or not. Russ and I wanted to get married, and we did get married, and that's that."

The words were hardly out of her mouth when Russ came in with a big smile on his face. "I have a surprise for you, sweetheart," he said, bending to kiss her. "Hello, Mrs. Davis."

"Hello, Russ."

"What's the surprise?" Rachel wanted to know.

He cocked his head at her, a teasing look on his face. "Well, don't you want me to lead up to it? You don't just want me to come right out with it, do you?"

In spite of her misery Rachel began to feel excited. "Oh, Russ. Yes, I want you to come right out with it. What is it?"

"Look," her mother said, "I'll go on home and let you two be together."

"Mom, don't you want to know what it is?"

"You can call me later." She looked from Russ to her. "Good news always keeps. Good night, honey. Good night, Russ."

When her mother had gone, Russ took her in his arms and kissed her again, passionately this time. "This is more like it," he said.

She responded for a bit, then pushed him away. "I want to hear the surprise. Is it good news?"

"I'd say so, yes."

Anxiety came flooding back. "What you think and I think aren't always the same. It's about your parents, isn't it?"

"That's right."

He tried to kiss her again, but she turned her face away. "They wish you'd married somebody else."

"No," he said. "Absolutely wide of the mark."

"Well, then, they wish you hadn't gotten married at all."

He half agreed. "Let's say they wish I'd waited— as I told them I would. But since I didn't, and since they know I love you, they're delighted to have you as part of the family."

"Oh, Russ. Honest?"

"Honest and truly."

Now she let him take her in his arms again, and this time she responded so fiercely to his kiss that he started trembling.

"Oh, what marvelous news," she said, when she could manage to say anything.

As much as she could tell he didn't want to—that if this weren't the hospital and he weren't Dr. Russell Matthews, he'd jump into bed with her right then and there and take her so fast he would leave her dizzy— he pulled back from her. He shook his head. "That isn't the news."

"You mean there's more?" she said.

"Much more."

"More good news?"

He nodded.

"Oh, Russ. What? Tell me. Please."

He took one of her hands in his, caressing it—he hardly ever was able to leave her alone. "I told the folks you'd be coming home from the hospital in a couple of days, and that you and I would like to live together instead of the way we have been, but I didn't want you taking care of a house during your pregnancy. Doing the dishes and scrubbing the floors and all the things you have to do to take care of a house."

Rachel nodded, eager to hear the rest. She didn't want to do any of those things either. Maybe being pregnant had some advantages. Except . . . Anxiety stirred again. "You mean Dr. MacCurdy thinks my heart's going to give me trouble again?"

Russ stopped caressing her hand long enough to pat

it. "No, he doesn't think any such thing. But you do have a history, so he wants to take precautions, that's all. The same as I do."

"Oh."

"So guess what?"

"What?"

"You're coming home to our house to live. Until the baby is born."

"Your house?" Her eyes went wide. "That great big house of your parents'? Oh, Russ."

He smiled. "Is that okay? I mean, I know it isn't like being alone, but——"

She cut him off. "Okay? It's the most thrilling thing I ever heard. Oh, Russ!" She pulled him to her and hugged him tight. "You wait. The first night we're together you'll see how thrilled and excited I am. Oh, Russ!"

He kissed her, and she kissed him back, until both of them were trembling with desire.

Alice woke up aware that something was the matter, wondering what it was. She propped herself up on one elbow and looked around. Bright spring sunlight streamed through the windows. She blinked and looked at the clock. It was after nine, but she was on the three-to-eleven shift this week, and she didn't have a class this morning until eleven thirty.

There was something going on out in the hall. Maybe that was what had wakened her.

Her mother's voice, muted: "It will fit, Jim. I know it will. I measured it. Try angling it a little. There."

Alice sighed and lay back down. She knew now what the something was. Today Rachel was coming here to live.

After a bit, she got out of bed, put on her robe, and went out into the hall. Her parents had moved an old double bed into Russ's bedroom; the bunk beds that had been there were stacked in the hall.

"Do you need any help?" she called to them.

Her father stuck his head out the door. "No, darling. We're almost finished."

"You should have called me."

Her mother's face joined her father's. "We didn't have all that much to do. But now that you're up, come take a look."

Her mother was obviously pleased with her efforts, and Alice thought she had a right to be. The bed had a smart new spread in shades of blue and green, and matching curtains hung at the double window. Next to Russ's bureau was a dressing table for Rachel.

"Do you think it looks too cramped?" her mother asked. "With Russ's desk and all?"

Alice considered, then shook her head. "No. I think it looks nice and bright. And very cozy. And I'm sure to Rachel it will look like a palace."

Her mother smiled. "Well, hardly that."

· Over breakfast her father said, "Are you feeling better about Rachel's coming here to live?"

Alice looked at him a moment. "If you want an honest answer, no, I'm not." Hardly designed to please her father, but then, a far sight milder than her first reaction: "Have you two taken leave of your senses? Do you realize what you're doing, asking her here?" And to their protests that Russ had good reason to be concerned about Rachel's health: "Nonsense. He's letting his emotions get in the way of his judgment. Sure, Rachel has a history of endocarditis. But it's all cleared up, and there are no signs of it now, and furthermore they'll be checking her throughout her pregnancy. There's nothing at all to prevent Russ and Rachel from getting a little efficiency apartment that's easy to take care of." And when they still wouldn't listen: "Mom, can't you at least see it won't work out? You know as well as I do that Rachel is a completely selfish person." She had shaken her head. "It will be a disaster."

And for all she'd accomplished, she might as well have saved her breath.

Alice was in her room, finishing dressing, when Russ brought Rachel home. She heard the flurry of voices at the front door, and, bearing in mind her parents' admonition to join them in making Rachel feel welcome, she pulled on a turtleneck and went downstairs.

"How are you feeling, Rachel?" her mother was asking. Her father had already left for work.

Rachel smiled brightly. "Oh, just fine, thank—" The smile faded as abruptly as her voice, and she seemed to wilt visibly. "Oh. Well, not fine, really. I mean, you know how you say that automatically when somebody asks you, because you're so used to saying it." She shrank back into Russ's protective embrace. "Actually, I get tired very easily and need to rest."

Shutting what she was thinking out of her mind, Alice stepped forward, smiling as warmly as she knew how. "Welcome to the house, Rachel. Or maybe I should say 'Welcome home.' "

Rachel turned to her with a look at once so pathetic and so eager, so like a puppy that had unexpectedly been hugged and was squirming for more, that Alice's heart went out to her. And then, as soon as Rachel opened her mouth, she spoiled it: "Oh, Alice, I'm so glad you've come around."

Alice frowned at her. "I don't know what you mean. Come around about what?"

"About our getting married, Russ and me. I mean, I don't think you were very happy when you heard about it. I mean, not that you ever said anything, of course, or ever would. You're much too well brought up for that."

Embarrassment settled in the living room like a haze, but Rachel plunged ahead, a too-bright smile fixed on her face. "But anyway, all I wanted to say was you're going to be glad of our marriage, Alice." She waved an all-encompassing hand. "You all are. Wait and see."

Alice's mother saved the day. Or tried to. "But Rachel, dear, we already are glad. That's what I've been trying to tell you. It's true we wanted you and Russell to wait. But that had nothing to do with you. And we can understand why you didn't want to wait. And so we're happy to welcome you into the family."

"Oh, thank you," Rachel said. "It's just that—"

Russ cut in on her, his voice a bit too loud. "Look, darling, I'm going to take these suitcases upstairs to the room. Do you want to come with me?"

"Oh. Well." Rachel looked from the stairs to the couch to her mother-in-law, and Alice could almost see the forces warring in her mind. Eagerness to see the new room against the need to impress on all of them—and particularly the lady of the house—that she was a semi-invalid who needed tender, loving care. Not surprisingly, the need won out. "Oh, Russ, I don't think so. Not right now. Your mother said something when we first got here about a cup of coffee, and I really would like to rest down here for a bit."

Instantly Russ was all solicitude, settling her on the couch before taking her luggage upstairs.

"Here, Russ, let me help you," Alice said, picking up one of the suitcases. She took it upstairs for him, set it inside the door of his room, and started back down. Halfway downstairs, she stopped and stared. When she and Russ had gone upstairs and their mother had gone into the kitchen to put the coffee on, Rachel had been stretched out like Camille. Now she was walking around the room looking like anything but an invalid, semi- or otherwise. She ran a hand along the coffee table, gave a proprietary pat to the tallboy, then turned to the antique silk draperies at one of the windows, handling the fabric as if she were caressing it. But it was what she said, her voice low and intense, that startled Alice the most. "Mine," she said. "My home now."

After she got over her astonishment, Alice's first reaction was—as it had been earlier—a rush of pity. It had never occurred to her that Rachel would feel so strongly about what was, to Alice, just a house. And a fairly ordinary house at that.

Nor did it occur to her the following day, when Rachel spoke so admiringly about her big, sunny bedroom, that there was anything more in Rachel's mind than that same childlike wonder.

She should have known, of course. And would have, had she been privy to the conversation that took place the following morning when Rachel came downstairs late after a bout with morning sickness—or so she claimed—and joined Mary in the kitchen.

To her mother-in-law's query as to how she felt, Rachel said, "Well, Mrs. Matthews, not so hot, if you want to know, but I felt worse staying in my room. I felt so cooped up in there. I mean, the room is kind of small, and for two people . . . I mean, don't get me wrong, Mrs. Matthews. It's a nice little room, and you've fixed it up just beautifully, but . . . well, I was sick this morning, and the four walls made me feel . . . well, nervous, as if they were closing in on me." She laughed a little. "I thought maybe I'd go see Alice for a while—to take my mind off things and get a change of scenery and . . . well, sort of stretch out. I mean, her room's so huge and all, it gives you that feeling—that you can just stretch out and let the world go by." She shook her head. "But Alice wasn't there."

"No," Mary said. "She left for the hospital when her father went to the office."

"But I thought she was on the swing shift this week."

"Yes, but you forget, dear. Alice is still a student nurse, and she has classes this morning."

"Oh," Rachel said. "That seems a pity."

"A pity? I'm afraid I don't know what you mean."

The deprecatory little laugh again. "Well, I just meant—to have that great big marvelous room, and then to spend so much time at the hospital she's hardly ever in it."

When her own mother came to visit her, remarking on what a beautiful house the Matthewses had, Rachel didn't waste her breath on the amenities but said contemptuously, "You want to know what's really beautiful? Russ and I have to share one tiny room, and Alice has a huge one all to herself. With a private bath. Do you call that fair?"

But it was for Russ, of course, that she saved—and used—her most powerful ammunition. One evening when he came home and went upstairs to their room to find her stretched out on the bed, she sat up and said, "Oh, Russ, I didn't expect you home this soon."

He came over to kiss her, sitting down on the bed beside her, taking her in his arms and holding her. "This is what I've been waiting for all day."

"Mmm," she said, "me too."

Her first thought was to break away before he became so interested in having her that he wouldn't pay any attention to what she had to say to him, but on second thought, if she gave in to him, it would put him in a perfect mood. And so, as he pulled away from her, she drew his face back to hers, and this time she kissed him—with such intensity that he said, his voice gone husky, "Well. What have we here?"

She smiled her most seductive smile. "Us. And time. At least time enough, don't you think?"

He smiled. "I guess so."

She undid a button on his shirt and laid a hand against his bare chest. "And isn't that really what you've been waiting for all day?"

He pressed her to him. "Oh, Rachel."

And then there was no stopping him.

Afterward, while they were getting dressed again, she said, "I meant it when I said I didn't expect you home this soon. I mean, I needed to rest, and so that's what I was doing, but in a few minutes I was going to try to do something about this room."

The room could hardly be described as neat. Several of Rachel's dresses were hanging over whatever chair back or open drawer or bed rail was available. Some dirty plates and cups and saucers were stacked on the bureau. The top of the dressing table was a jumble of cosmetics and movie magazines and even orange peel. But Russ apparently hadn't noticed.

"Something about the room?" he said blankly, buttoning his shirt.

Rachel waved a hand. "Look at it. Those dresses of mine should be hanging in the closet, but there isn't any room for them. That little dinky closet is about big enough for your clothes, and that's it."

"Well, take mine out. Your clothes are more important than mine."

"That's not the point. Oh, Russ," she said, giving him a reminding hug of what had been and what could be again—maybe later that same evening. "I want the place we live in to be nice. Nice for you. I want you to come home to a room that's all picked up and neat —but what can I do here?"

"Honey," he said, touching her face, "don't get upset about it."

She looked up at him. "Do you think I want my husband to stop loving me because I don't know enough to hang up my clothes?"

"Stop loving you?" He grinned. "Don't you count on any such thing." And, as if to prove it, he took her in his arms again.

But Rachel was too interested now in getting to her point, so she freed herself from him as gently as possible and picked up the nearest dress, as if that had been her point in walking away from him. "But, Russ, I really care about how things look when you come home. If I only had another closet or . . . what I really need to make things really nice for you is a bigger room. You know. Like Alice's. I mean, it was designed for two people. Alice told me that herself. That she used to share it with Pat, I mean. Before Pat married John Randolph. And . . . well, there it sits empty all day long, with Alice hardly ever in it, while I'd get so much more— Oh, darling," she hastened to add, fearful she had gone too far too fast, "I don't want you to think I'm ungrateful, because I'm not."

But he was still basking in the afterglow of lovemaking. He grinned at her. "Have I accused you of being ungrateful?"

"No, darling," she went on, fearful now that he'd heard nothing of what she'd said to him, "I mean it. Your folks have been just wonderful to me, the way they've taken me in and made me feel at home, and the way your mother fixed up this room as best she could, but I'm sure she knows herself it's too small for two people."

"And you think we should swap rooms with Alice."

So he had been listening after all. "Well," Rachel said, trying to sound as if the idea were new to her, and one she was reluctant to consider, "only if Alice doesn't mind, of course. Of course, she might not mind. She probably wouldn't mind, considering how fond she is of you. And anyhow, it would only be for a few short months. Yes, darling, you're probably right. That probably is the answer, swapping rooms with Alice."

All that remained now was the problem of how to go about it.

Alice should have been able to figure that one out, too, but she was still doing her level best to give Rachel the benefit of the doubt. Every doubt. Especially after what her father had said to her one morning as she rode to the hospital with him on his way to the office.

"Darling," he said, "I know you don't like Rachel, and I know you don't like the idea of her living in the house with us, but try not to pick on her for every little thing."

"What do you mean, every little thing?" Alice said, immediately on the defensive—as she seemed to be more than half the time now where her father was concerned. Something else she could thank Rachel for.

She tried to put the thought out of her mind, and said as reasonably as she could, "Dad, you know what hideous hours Russ has to put in at the hospital. I've seen interns fall asleep standing up, and I mean it. So there he is in the kitchen, fixing her a breakfast tray because she has a little morning sickness. That's the most ridiculous thing I've ever heard of. She's just plain lazy, and you know it."

"Alice," her father said, "if Russ didn't want to do it for her, he wouldn't do it."

Alice sighed. "No. I suppose not."

"So why not leave what are their affairs to them?"

"All right. I guess you're right."

They rode in silence for awhile. Then Alice said, "Dad, do you like Rachel?"

"Yes," he said. "I do. She's got a few things to learn in certain areas, but . . . well, I think you miss the fact—and it is a fact—that she's rather pathetic."

"No, I haven't missed it. I know what you mean. Or at least I think I do. But it seems to me you're missing something. I mean, last night at dinner she literally turned on the charm for you, and you sat there and lapped it up."

He nodded. "I know I did. But don't think I didn't know very well that she was, as you put it, turning on the charm. That's part of what I mean about her being pathetic."

Alice turned to stare at him. *"That* is? Well, then

I don't know what you mean after all. What's pathetic about that?"

"What's pathetic," her father answered, "is that she feels she has to play up to me. Alice, you have to remember that Rachel never had a father. He walked out on her, abandoned her. And you know as well as I do that that's about the worst thing that can happen to a child—that abandonment is every child's greatest fear."

"Yes, I know."

"And I'm sure it's made a big difference in Rachel's life—a bigger difference than you and I can imagine."

"Yes, I suppose you're right, Dad."

What her father didn't say—didn't have to say—was how lucky she had been compared to Rachel. Lucky to have the family she did, to have good friends, to be well provided for, to have a college education and training for a job that she not only enjoyed but that gave her satisfaction. More than satisfaction: fulfillment. A feeling she was doing something that mattered, that needed to be done.

When you put all that up against what Rachel had had—or hadn't had—you couldn't help feeling sorry for her.

So Alice tried harder to like Rachel, to understand her, to accept her at face value even when, as now, she suspected that Rachel was leading up to something, though exactly what she couldn't imagine.

"I don't see much of you, Alice," Rachel was saying.

Alice smiled. "I'm here every day."

"You mean every night."

"Well, all right, every night."

"But that's the point. I mean, I'm around here all day long, you know, and it would be nice if you could be, too. I'd like that. Wouldn't you?"

Trying not to sound as puzzled as she felt, not knowing quite what to say, Alice said, "Well, I kind of like the work I'm doing, you know."

"Oh, sure," Rachel said vaguely; then: "I spend most of my time up in that room of Russ's, of course."

"I don't see why, Rachel," Alice said. And she didn't. "The whole house is at your disposal. You're one of the family, don't forget."

Again Rachel seemed a little vague. "Oh," she said, "you're nice to say that. But there's so much to do in that room—so much work."

Alice felt her eyes go wide. "In one room?"

Rachel nodded. "Well, sure. Not because it's one room, but because . . . well, it isn't big enough for two people, and the picking up I have to do . . . I mean, the thing is, it never really gets picked up." She laughed that little self-deprecating laugh of hers. "So finally Russ had this idea."

Alice waited, but Rachel didn't go on, so she said, "What idea?"

"He . . . well . . . he thinks it would be nice if we had a bigger room. Of course, I told him I certainly wouldn't want to do it unless it was okay with you."

And there it was. Or very nearly. "You wouldn't want to do what unless it was okay with me?"

"Oh," Rachel said, not batting an eyelash. "I mean swapping rooms."

Alice stared at her. Even with the last-minute fore-warning it was still unbelievable. Nor could she think of anything to say. And apparently she didn't need to —Rachel was going right on.

"I mean, Russ said here we've got a single room and two people, and you've got a double room and one person. And besides that, you're away all day, and it would be only temporary anyhow."

Alice was still staring at her, but she had found her voice. "Russ said all that?"

"Yes," Rachel answered, all wide-eyed innocence, but Alice didn't believe for a minute that he had. Or that he knew anything about what Rachel had done, for that matter.

Not that that seemed to matter either. When it came out the next morning in Russ's presence that Rachel had asked Alice to swap rooms, Rachel burst into tears and claimed she hadn't asked her, she'd only mentioned it in passing and in fact had gone out of her way to assure Alice she wouldn't think of changing rooms with her. This whole thing was all a misunderstanding.

When her mother reported that to her, Alice didn't know whether to laugh or cry. And when, a few days later, Rachel gave her a smart little canvas tote bag to "make up for the misunderstanding" about her room, Alice did the only thing she could do under the circumstances. She gave her room to Russ and Rachel.

As her father had pointed out to her, there was some merit in the idea, whoever had come up with it. Russ and Rachel did need a larger room, Alice wasn't in it much, and she would be inconvenienced only until the baby was born.

In any event, she didn't want to seem selfish or thoughtless or mean.

But when her father commended her for her generosity, she shook her head, saying, "No. If I were truly generous, I would have come up with the idea myself." She smiled. "So no honor to whom no honor is due."

Her father smiled back at her. "Nevertheless, I think you're quite a girl."

"And no need to turn on the charm?"

"No need at all." He squeezed her shoulder. "Maybe things will be easier here now."

She nodded. "Maybe."

He eyed her a moment. "But you're not convinced."

Alice shook her head again. "No, I'm not. The main thing I've learned from this, Dad, is that Rachel is covetous. She wants anything nice that anybody else has, and never mind who gets hurt in the process."

"Oh now, darling," her father said, skeptical, "don't you think you're overreacting a little?"

Alice shrugged. "Maybe. But I can't help wondering what Rachel will want next that's mine."

Chapter Three

THE heady satisfaction of being Mrs. Dr. Russell Matthews began to dissipate—just as her mother had feared it would—as soon as Rachel began to understand that in marrying Russ she had indeed tricked herself as well as him.

There was, for one thing, the question of how he spent his time, which was too much at the hospital and too little taking her out—or even being at home with her.

In the beginning Russ interpreted this as devotion, saying to his mother after Rachel made him promise to come home for dinner that first evening at the Matthews house and not just try to, "See, Mother? This girl really loves me."

Mary Matthews didn't see it that way at all. After Russ had left for he hospital she said, "I'm afraid you're going to have to get used to an intern's hours, Rachel. We've had to."

"Well, I suppose so," Rachel answered, "but a girl does want her husband around. And there are lots of ways to get out of work for a while. He just has to get somebody to cover for him, that's all."

While Mary was digesting that, Rachel went on to say, with an elaborate sigh, "I'll be so glad when Russ finishes his internship and all this will be over."

"But it won't be over, Rachel. He'll have his residency to go through."

"If he decides he needs it."

Mary frowned. "He not only needs it, he wants it. And with reason. It means he'll be much more thoroughly prepared when he does go into practice."

"Oh," Rachel said, "I know he's a dedicated young

doctor and all that, and I suppose I'm glad of it, but he's still a normal human being, isn't he? I mean, he has a right to enjoy life, doesn't he? And anyway, after a young doctor has hung out his shingle, who knows the difference?"

With an effort Mary restrained herself from saying anything. How Russell pursued his career was, after all, his business. She hoped she could rely on his intelligence and judgment to do what he knew was best for him, that he wasn't so bewitched by Rachel that he had taken complete leave of his senses. Or —a more forlorn hope—that Rachel would begin to develop some understanding of Russell's needs, to show some concern for him as well as for herself.

It was not only a forlorn hope, it was a futile one.

"I don't see why," Rachel said to Russ one night when they were getting ready for bed, "you have to go through a residency. Other doctors don't."

"The good ones do."

She came over to him and asked him to unzip her dress, then turned around to him, half holding the dress against her in a way that she knew excited him. "I don't see why. I mean, why couldn't you go in with some established doctor and go into practice right away?"

He put his hands on her bare shoulders. "Darling, I've tried to tell you. There are many, many things I need to learn yet before I go into practice."

"Well, you could learn them from him."

He shook his head. "This isn't the middle of the nineteenth century. The kind of experience I need I have to get in a hospital environment. And suppose I decide I want to specialize in cardiology. I can't do that without a residency."

Rachel stepped out of the dress and threw it aside. Then she put her arms around him, pressing her body against his. "But, Russ, it takes so long."

"Not when you think of what you're getting. And it's only two or three years."

He bent to kiss her, but she reared back. "Two or three years? Russ, that's forever!"

She would have turned away from him altogether,

but he didn't release his hold on her. "It's not forever, darling," he said, pulling her to him again. "And when it's past you'll see it was all worth waiting for." He smiled at her. "The same as this."

Which she was no longer in the mood for.

The thought of two or three more years of living the way they were living now—and in a few more months with a screaming baby on her hands as well—was enough to drive Rachel up the wall. On a visit to her mother's apartment she astonished Ada by saying "It's good to get out of that place for a while."

Her mother's eyebrows shot up. "You mean the Matthews house? That beautiful place?"

Rachel's lips curled. "Sure, it's beautiful, but I'm practically a prisoner there. Russ has to work all night every other night. Or be at the hospital on call, so he can't come home."

"Well, he's an intern, and—"

Rachel cut her off. "Don't you remind me of that. Everybody else does. I stay cooped up there, we don't go out, we haven't been dancing, we haven't had any fun at all."

"Rachel," her mother said, "you're talking like a schoolgirl. You're a married woman, and you're pregnant. That's your lot in life right now."

"My lot in life," Rachel said contemptuously.

"Yes. And one you asked for."

"I didn't ask to be pregnant."

Ada sighed. "Honey, can't you ever learn to be satisfied with what you've got?"

"Not when it's not what I want."

But how Russ spent his time wasn't the only irritant. There was also the matter of money.

When Rachel's mother criticized her for spending so much money on maternity clothes, Rachel brushed the criticism aside, saying she had to have them, as Russ's wife she was expected to be well dressed, and she was getting so big and fat she couldn't get into any of her old clothes. And anyhow, she hadn't paid cash for them, she'd charged them, so what difference did it make?

When her mother tried to make her see the difference, she brushed that aside too, saying impatiently, "Mom, it has to cost something for a man to support a wife. Don't I deserve anything?"

Apparently she didn't.

When Lenore announced her engagement to Walter Curtin, and Rachel announced to Russ that she had invited Walter and Lenore to celebrate the great event as their guests for dining and dancing at the Top of the Tower, Russ said that interns usually celebrated some place where there were checkered tablecloths and steins of beer.

"Do you have any idea how much this is going to cost?" he asked.

"I don't see why that should matter," she answered. "We haven't spent any money in ages. We haven't been anywhere to spend it."

"Maybe we haven't," he said, waving a hand toward her closet. "But you have. You bought enough new clothes for three babies."

"Oh, Russ, I didn't either. And what am I supposed to do—wear the same old thing day after day? You'd get sick of seeing me in it."

"Darling, it's you I care about, not what you're wearing."

"Well, I care about what I'm wearing. And I care about what people say, too."

He gave her a puzzled look. "What does that have to do with anything?"

"It's why I invited Walter and Lenore to go out with us. Because it seemed the right thing to do. After all, they're practically our best friends."

"This is the first I've heard of it."

And the evening was a bust at that.

Never mind that she'd ordered French champagne, and the orchestra played the most divine music. Russ gave her such a look when the waiter brought the bottle to the table that she couldn't enjoy it, and he absolutely refused to let her dance at all except for one poky number at the very end.

All they did the whole time was sit and talk about Alice and what a wonderful person she was, making Rachel feel left out of things, and then when she finally tried to join in the conversation by saying what good friends she and Alice were, and not just because she was Russ's wife, either, the others acted as though they were so embarrassed they could hardly stand it, though why they should be, she certainly didn't know.

Unless it had to do with swapping the bedrooms, and how could it be that when that had been Russ's idea, and Alice had been the one who insisted on doing it?

It was all too tiresome for words.

And to top everything off, Lenore said she was going to have only one attendant at her wedding, and that would be Alice, naturally.

Naturally.

Rachel wrinkled her nose just thinking about it. Of course it would be Alice. Alice always got everything she wanted. Rachel never did.

So now she would miss out on all the fun of the preparations and the rehearsals. And probably the reason Lenore hadn't included her was not because she didn't want her. Of course Lenore wanted her. Why wouldn't she when they were practically best friends?

That must be why Lenore was having only Alice, pretending she wanted a small wedding, so she wouldn't hurt Rachel's feelings by telling her the real reason she couldn't have her. Because she was six months pregnant, that was why. And sticking out so much nobody could miss it. And what bride wanted some fat frump in her wedding procession? Darn Russ anyhow for getting her that way when he could have been more careful.

So she pretended one day she was going to be in the wedding, coming downstairs at the Matthews house as a bridesmaid would, imagining herself sleek and slender again, thinking how really smashing she looked in a pale blue—no, a pale yellow gown of misty chiffon, her dark hair curling out from under a picture hat, the ribbon tied under her chin.

She was carrying a bouquet of yellow daisies—and white ones, too, to match the bride's bouquet—and everybody drew in their breath when she came into view, because she was so very pretty. If the truth be told, far prettier than the bride herself.

And because she and her husband, Dr. Russell Matthews, were such close friends of the bride and groom's, they hosted the wedding reception in their Magnolia Street manor, that famous old house that dated back to the nineteenth century, the kind of house that wasn't built any more, a landmark house people would give their eyeteeth to be invited to.

"Naturally," Rachel said to one of the eyeteeth people, "my husband and I bought this house as soon as we heard it was up for sale. Yes, of course it's very expensive to maintain, these big old houses take a lot of care, that's why we have so many servants, but then"—she laughed her little polite-hostess laugh— "what's the good of being a doctor if you can't live like one?"

She was turning to greet her next guest when Russ's mother came in from the kitchen—where she spent about half her life—saying, "Is that you, Rachel? Is somebody with you?"

Rachel sighed. "No. I was on the phone."

"Oh. Well, I didn't mean to interrupt you."

"You weren't interrupting anything."

She winced, and her mother-in-law looked anxious. "Is something the matter, dear?"

"Not really. It's just a twinge. Or maybe the baby kicked me, I don't know."

She was only saying it to be polite, not even to ask for sympathy, but she wished she hadn't said anything at all, because getting her mother-in-law started on the baby and how they were all looking forward to it was like turning on a faucet and then breaking the handle.

And Russ's sister Pat didn't exactly add to her joy either. The whole family assembled for Alice's graduation from nurses' training, and when Rachel complained to Pat that she never saw anything of Russ, Alice saw more of him than she did, and now that Alice was a registered nurse she'd probably see even more of him around the hospital, and Rachel couldn't wait for Russ's training to end so they could really start living, Pat said, "You may be in for a surprise,

Rachel. You know, professional men don't have sched-
ules, and they put in pretty long hours."

Since John Randolph was such a big-time lawyer,
Rachel figured sourly that Pat must know what she
was talking about.

But the surprise Rachel really was in for didn't take
two or three years to happen. Though she was neither
prepared for it nor aware of it at the time, it happened
the very next evening, at the wedding reception for
Walter and Lenore Curtin—just when some of the
magic of being a Matthews in a Matthews world was
coming back to her.

From the beginning of his involvement with Rachel,
Russ's friends and family had puzzled over what he
saw in her. Oh, everybody understood the physical
attraction. Rachel was extremely pretty, and she had a
small and lovely figure—and a saucy way about her
that heightened her attraction.

And Russ, like any other healthy male in his mid-
twenties, had powerful drives that were largely frustrated.

So, all right, yes. Me Tarzan, you Jane.

But beyond that, what?

Contrary to Rachel's conviction—and her mother's,
too—none of Russ's friends or family held Rachel's
background, or lack of it, against her. There was, to be
sure, Russ's widowed Aunt Liz—Mrs. William Matthews. But then, Liz Matthews, as Mary herself
pointed out to Ada at their get-acquainted luncheon,
had a tendency to put on airs, wanting to give people
the impression that she was quite the great lady, a little
grander than she really was.

To that end—and because she had very little else
to do—Liz devoted herself to a great many charitable
endeavors. Indeed, it was her name that turned up so
often on the society pages, leading Rachel to the erroneous conclusion that Russ's parents were very rich
and high-society, when in fact they were in comfortable circumstances and were highly regarded in the
community, where the Matthews name had been
known for three or four generations.

One friend of Russ's who saw through Rachel from the moment he met her was the district attorney, Walter Curtin. A man in his early forties who had the ability to be objective about everything but himself. Even he could not foresee—as who could—the tragedy Rachel was going to set in motion for Alice and Russ and all of the Matthews family.

His new wife, Lenore, who had grown up with Alice and Russ, and who was far too kind and generous a person to see through anybody, simply couldn't understand how Russ could be interested in somebody so different from himself. He was such a solid, settled, down-to-earth person, while Rachel wasn't serious about anything, a good time being about the only thing she ever had on her mind.

Without realizing it, Lenore had put her finger on the mark. Apart from the physical attraction, it was precisely that difference between them that drew Russ to Rachel. Until he met Rachel Russ didn't really know how to have a good time. Absorbed first by his studies and then by his medical training, a little on the shy side, and failing, until Rachel came along, to meet any girl who aroused any special interest on his part, he hadn't dated much and had partied not at all.

Rachel opened a new world to him—a world he found delightful.

Love, of course, is blind. And Russ was very much in love. If Rachel was dazzled by his being a Matthews, he was infinitely more dazzled by Rachel herself.

As to why he continued blind to her trickery and her shallowness long after he should have begun to see her for what she was, there were several reasons. For one thing, nobody likes having to face up to the fact that he's been taken, made a fool of—particularly by somebody he's given his heart to so completely—and Russ was no exception. For another, Rachel was careful for quite some time to show a different face to Russ than to other people, to hide her scheming and her shallowness in the guise of ignorance or fear.

And part of Rachel's fear and ignorance was genuine. As her mother had figured, Rachel did make a fool of herself—and on more than one occasion. She didn't know how to dress properly, her sense of values was wildly inappropriate, she prattled away about how marvelous it was to be rich and how thrilling it was to be a Matthews and how they wouldn't regret she'd married their son and brother.

The Matthewses didn't laugh at her. They were embarrassed for her, and Russ more so than the others, because he understood better than they did how painful it was to Rachel to have to live among strangers and, much of the time, to have to do it without him there to smooth her way.

But Russ, making one of the most common errors known to man, was confident that with his love and understanding Rachel would learn, would grow up, would overcome the very real disadvantages she had suffered as a deprived child and adolescent.

Although Russ teased Rachel for being a doctor's wife who was afraid of doctors, he also understood her fear of illness and her fear of being pregnant and thought—again—that he could help her overcome this.

That Rachel was not so ardent in her lovemaking as when they were first married could be put to her advancing pregnancy, with its attendant aches and pains and queasiness. For that matter, Russ wasn't always so ardent himself. His schedule at the hospital was brutal, and when he did come home he was often desperately tired and aching for sleep. Which didn't add to his perceptiveness, either.

And, finally, Rachel's childlike quality, far from putting Russ off, was one of the very things that drew him to her. As his mother had guessed, he did indeed see her as a little hurt thing that he would care for, mend, make well.

The childlike quality had its endearing and amusing side as well—at least in the beginning—and this was never more evident than at the reception for Walter and Lenore, which was held at the Bayside Country Club in the massive wood-paneled reception hall with its crystal chandeliers, the impressive gold draperies at the old-fashioned floor-to-ceiling windows, the great fireplace, and the general air of solid luxury.

"Oh, Russ!" Rachel exclaimed as they came into the room and she looked about her, wide-eyed. "Oh, Russ!" she said again. "Isn't this fabulous!"

He nodded. "It's very nice."

"Nice! It's a lot more than that. I think it's scrumptious." She pulled him to her and whispered, "Do you know how much it costs to belong to a country club like this?"

"Plenty."

"Could we afford it?"

He shook his head. "Not at the moment, I'm afraid."

"But someday? Oh, Russ, I bet all the best doctors in town belong here."

"Best in what way?" he asked, though he knew full well.

"Oh, you know what I mean." She looked around her again. The wedding guests were arriving in droves now, bunched up at the door, waiting to go down the receiving line. "Just look at everybody," she said as he guided her from the line to where the champagne was being served. "All those gorgeous clothes, all the people. Oh, it's exciting!"

He handed her a glass of champagne, grinning at her. "You excite very easily."

"Russ, don't make fun of me."

"I'm not, darling. I'm just teasing you a little."

"Well, I don't care. It *is* exciting. We don't do this every day in the week."

"Thank heaven for that."

She made a face. "Oh, Russ. Now I don't want to hear how tired you are or how you were up all night last night without any sleep."

"Which I very nearly was."

"I don't care. I don't want to hear about it. We came here to have a good time, and that's what we're going to have."

He gave her a mock salute with his champagne glass. "Yes, ma'am." Then he frowned. "Rachel, what's the matter?"

"Nothing."

"Are you sure? You looked as if you were in pain."

"It was nothing, Russ. Honest. Just a little passing twinge."

"I don't want you to overdo."

"Oh, Russ. Now, I came here to dance, and I'm going to dance, and don't you be a spoilsport."

"All right," he said, but he did not intend to let her overdo. She was, after all, six and a half months pregnant.

The reception had been going on for about an hour when Rachel turned to him and said, "Who's that over there with Alice? That good-looking guy with the dark eyes and the intent look on his face."

Russ turned in the direction she was pointing. "I don't know."

"You can almost read his lips," Rachel said, "he compels you so to look at him."

Russ shook his head at her. "So what's he saying?"

"Oh, Russ. I only said 'almost.' "

What the dark-eyed man with the intent look on his face was saying to Alice was "I've been waiting for Walter or Lenore to introduce us, but somehow I don't think they're going to get the time. So hello."

She smiled. "Hello to you."

"I should have met you on the reception line, but I'm afraid I missed it. I had some business to take care of between the church and here."

"Yes, I've been told you manage to keep busy."

"Most of the time I do. But not tonight. Tonight . . . well, may I have this dance?"

"Yes, thank you. I'd like that."

Russ had long since lost interest, but Rachel watched Alice and her partner join the other dancers. In spite of her announced intention, Russ was making her sit out most of the dances. So her first reaction regarding the man Alice was dancing with was envy.

She was also curious to know who he was.

Her curiosity was at least partly satisfied at the end of that set, when Alice brought the man over to introduce him: "This is Steven Frame."

Chapter Four

"TELL me something," Steven Frame said as he and Alice left the wedding reception and headed for the country club's parking lot. "This business of being a nurse. Do you like it?"

Alice smiled. "I never heard it put quite that way before, but, yes, I do." Her smile widened. "And what about you? This business—well, let's see now—of being in the construction business, and the football-team business, and heaven only knows what other business, do you like doing that?"

He laughed. "Yes, especially the heaven-only-knows one. That's one of my particular favorites."

Alice laughed too. "All right. Touché. As the French put it. I want you to know this nurse has class."

Steve touched her elbow to guide her toward the car. "This way. And I didn't need the French to know the nurse has class. I knew that the moment I set eyes on you."

"Now you make me feel terrible," she said. "I wasn't fishing for a compliment. Or at least I don't think I was."

"I'll give you the benefit of the doubt. Here. It's the red Porsche."

"How elegant," she said as he bent to unlock the door on the passenger side.

"Some people think it's ugly."

She stepped back to inspect the car. "Well, in a way it is. But not ugly ugly like some cars. I'd say handsome ugly."

He laughed again and held the door for her. "Watch your head getting in."

As they turned into the driveway Alice said, "If you want directions . . ."

He shook his head. "I don't need them, thanks. I know where you live. I looked it up in the phone book."

"Oh."

He turned to glance at her. "Now why should that fluster you?"

"Did I say I was flustered?"

"No," he admitted. But it was obvious that she was. She was looking straight ahead through the windshield, her fair skin suffused with pink, the upswept blond curls only emphasizing the vulnerability of her round and pretty face. No. More than pretty. Lovely. Enchanting. A creature out of Hans Christian Andersen.

From the buildup his friend Walter Curtin had been giving him about Alice Matthews for the last few weeks, Steve had hoped for something special. He hadn't expected she would take his breath away. Suddenly he wanted to whoop for joy.

Instead he told himself to go slow, take it easy. She also struck him as someone who could frighten very easily. Under that cool demeanor, the charm, the ready wit, he sensed a shyness, a reticence, the wariness of someone who wounds easily. And, once wounded, twice shy.

Look at what he had done to her just now. "But you're right," she was saying. "I am flustered. And, to answer your question, I don't know why. Change of subject, please?"

"Sure. Fine."

She frowned in concentration. "If only I can think of one. Why is it, at a time like this . . . All right. Back to your favorite business—the heaven-only-knows one. Why do you like it?"

"For the same reason I like them all. But it may not be the reason you think."

"Oh," she said, turning to him, "I know so little about business that I have very few preconceived notions about it. My father has an accounting firm. He likes it because he likes working with numbers. And you?"

He could go slow and easy, but he couldn't—and wouldn't—play games. He believed in laying things on the line. And that included himself. "I like figuring out how to outfox the competition."

"Oh."

After a silence he said, "Not that I do anything illegal."

"I wasn't thinking that."

"But it shocks you."

Alice shook her head. "No, it doesn't shock me. I guess that's part of business, isn't it—beating the competition?"

He nodded. "It is indeed. A basic part. Let's see. I should have turned back there, shouldn't I?"

They were approaching the outskirts of Bay City on the Saginaw River Road. "I'm sorry," Alice said. "I wasn't paying any attention. When you said you knew where I lived I assumed you knew how to get there." She peered out at the next sign looming up ahead. "No, you're all right, Steven. Ravenswood's the next turnoff. That's the one to take."

"Thanks," he said. "I know my way around the city fairly well by now, but these freeway approaches still throw me from time to time."

"How long have you lived here?" she asked.

"About a year. Next question—why did I move here?"

Alice smiled. "How did you know I was going to ask that?"

"Because everybody does. And the way people ask it, you'd think I was missing some brain cells." He shook his head. "I like Bay City. I like its location, I like its size, I like the people, and the scenery is fantastic. The first couple of times I came here on business I found myself wishing I lived here. So I said to myself, why not? One advantage of having money is you can afford to indulge a whim now and then. Will you have dinner with me tomorrow night?"

She looked at him in astonishment. "Where did that come from?"

He grinned. "I thought if I slipped it in when you weren't expecting it I could surprise you into saying yes."

"Meaning otherwise you wouldn't stand a chance?

You're not living up to your advance billing. Walter Curtin told me you were very self-assured."

"Walter Curtin only knows me as a businessman. As a person I'm so much quivering jelly."

She gave him a sideways glance. "Or so you would like me to think." They had turned onto her street. "It's the white house—there—in the middle of the block."

He pulled up in front of the house, cut the engine, and turned to her. "Will you have dinner with me tomorrow night?"

"You make me feel it's a boardroom decision of far-reaching consequences." When he didn't respond, but only went on looking at her, she said, a little breathlessly, "All right, fine. Tomorrow night."

"Good," he said. "I'l pick you up at seven."

As he was walking her to the front door she glanced up at the windows of her old room. "That's funny," she said. "Russ and Rachel left the reception well before we did, but the lights are still on."

"So what's funny about it?"

"If you were an intern you wouldn't have to ask. I would have expected Russ to be in bed and asleep an hour ago."

"Do you think something's wrong?"

"I don't know. Maybe Rachel isn't feeling well, though she certainly didn't act like anything was wrong with her at the reception. Did you think?"

"You're asking the wrong fellow," Steven said. "I've only just met her. And had one dance with her. The one thing that did strike me about her is she seems a bit impressionable."

"A bit?" Alice burst out laughing. "When Russ was talking to you about your football team, I thought Rachel was going to ask you your net worth." She laughed again, and he laughed with her.

At the front door she said, "Thank you for a lovely time, Steven."

"Thank you," he said. "Tomorrow at seven?"

"Yes. Fine."

He took her hand in his and held it a moment, then released it. "Good night, Alice."

"Good night."

Driving home, he couldn't take his mind off her. She was everything he'd always wanted. Or she seemed to be, anyhow. He reminded himself that he hardly knew her. One evening—even an evening as spectacular as this one—didn't add up to a lifetime. And yet he had a genius for sizing up things and people very quickly. That was part of his success in business—a good part of it. That and knowing exactly how to go about getting what he aimed to have.

This time he not only wanted to whoop for joy—he did.

After saying good night to Steven at the door, Alice went inside. Her father was in the living room, turning out the lights. "Is something the matter with your hand?" he said.

Alice gave him a blank look. "My hand?"

"You're rubbing it."

"Oh," she said, staring at it. "No. Nothing's wrong."

He turned out the lamp by the sofa. "Your mother and I thought Walter and Lenore's reception was a pretty splendid affair."

"Yes, it was, wasn't it?"

"I was going to ask you for a dance, but all of them seemed to be taken. He's a very intense-looking young man, Mr. Frame."

"Oh. Mr. Frame. Yes. He's interesting, isn't he?"

Her father eyed her a moment. "The word I would have used is 'attentive.' Not to say 'remarkable.' "

"Why 'remarkable,' Dad?"

Again her father eyed her. "How many other twenty-eight-year-old self-made millionaires do you know?"

"Oh. That. Yes, I guess he is remarkable."

Her father smiled. "And nice, wouldn't you say?"

Alice smiled back at him, fully out of her spell now. "I wouldn't dare say that, Dad, for fear of what you'd make of it. Where's Mom?"

"Gone up to bed. Which is what I'm about to do."

"Yes, so I see. Did you know Russ and Rachel are still up?"

Her father gave her a surprised look. "Still up? They went upstairs an hour ago."

"The lights are still on in their room. I was wondering—" Alice broke off as a door opened and Russ came pounding down the stairs. "Russ, what is it?"

"It's Rachel. She's in labor." He ran to the phone.

"In labor?" Alice said, her father echoing her. "But she's only— Russ, are you sure?"

He was dialing. "Yes, I'm sure. Hello. Yes. Ask him to call Dr. Matthews—Russell Matthews. And, operator, it's an emergency." He cradled the phone. "I think she ought to go to the hospital, but I thought I'd check it out with Dr. Clater, since he's her doctor."

"What brought it on?" her father asked.

"Who knows, Dad?" Russ answered. "It could have been overdoing, but then, it could just as easily have been any number of other things. What concerns me now is trying to save the baby. At barely six and a half months, it's not going to have much of a chance."

"Russ," Alice said, "maybe it's false labor."

"Maybe," he conceded, but he didn't look convinced.

Some sort of sound came from upstairs, maybe only a night creak of the house, but Russ cast an agonized glance up the stairs, and would have gone pounding back up had Alice not put a hand out.

"No. You stay here and wait for Dr. Clater's call. I'll go to Rachel. Dad, maybe you'd better get Mom up. She'd want to be up, I'm sure."

"Yes, I'm sure of it too," he said, and together they hurried upstairs.

In her old room Alice found Rachel huddled on the bed, looking terrified. "Oh, Alice," she said, "it isn't true, is it? I'm not going to have the baby now, am I?"

"I don't know, Rachel." Alice tried to sound as soothing as she could. "It may be false labor. Russ is waiting for Dr. Clater to get back to him."

"I don't want Dr. Clater. I want Russ."

"Russ can't take care of you, Rachel. I mean, he can't be your doctor."

"Why not? He was the last time."

"You weren't married to him the last time."

Rachel winced as another contraction started, and Alice tried to get her to stretch out, relax, ride with it instead of fighting it—but not with much success.

"Try not to be frightened, Rachel. Russ will be with you all the time. He'll see you're taken care of. You know he will."

"I want him now."

As if on command, he appeared in the doorway. "Dr. Clater wants us to go to the hospital."

Alice breathed a sigh of relief, but Rachel cried out, "No! I don't want to go to the hospital! Russ, I can't have the baby now!"

"Honey," Russ said, cradling her in his arms, "we've been all through this. I don't want you to have the baby now either, but it can't be helped."

Rachel clung to him, white-faced and trembling. "Then why can't I have it here? Why can't you be my doctor? Oh, Russ, don't let me die. Please. Please don't let me die."

There was a gasp from the doorway, and Alice turned to see her mother standing there, alarm on her face. Alice gave a warning shake of her head, then took her mother a few steps down the hall, explaining what had happened.

"Do you want me to get dressed and go to the hospital too?"

"No, Mom, I don't think so. The more people who go along, the more panicked she's going to be, and she's panicked enough already. I'm going, and Russ, and I expect he'll call her mother."

"Is there any danger, Alice?"

Alice shook her head. "Well, she's two and a half months early, and I don't like that."

"And the baby?"

"I don't know."

Her mother looked at her in silence, then said, "You're thinking what I'm thinking—the baby doesn't have a chance."

Alice nodded and squeezed her mother's arm.

Although Rachel was convinced she was going to die—so convinced she didn't care what happened to the baby—it was the other way around. Throughout her somewhat protracted labor, Rachel was never in any particular danger, but the baby was stillborn.

When Russ told Alice, her eyes filled with tears. Exactly what she was crying about—or to whom— she didn't know, but the person she couldn't get off her mind was Rachel's mother.

Ada had stayed at the hospital the same thirty-six straight hours Alice had. One time Alice came back from the cafeteria to find Ada standing in the corridor outside Rachel's room, staring out the window, with a look of such infinite sadness on her worn, lined face that Alice caught her breath, fearful that something had happened while she was gone.

Ada shook her head. Nothing had happened. She had just been talking to Rachel, that was all. "You know," she said, "I always thought that since Rachel didn't know her father, she wouldn't really miss him. I know now that isn't true. She was talking about him just now, wondering where he is and whether he thinks of her. After all these years. It makes me feel like I've failed her. Like it's my fault. I always thought I could make it up to her in other ways—by giving her things she wanted. I gave her everything I could, but it wasn't enough."

Alice put a comforting hand on Ada's arm. "Who says it wasn't?"

Ada shook her head again. "Rachel. She says it in practically everything she does. You must have noticed it, Alice, the way she has to have things."

"Well . . . yes."

"And you should have heard what else she said in there just now. She's so scared she's not going to"— Ada blinked and swallowed—"well, you know. And so she went on and on about how sorry she is for all the bad things she's said and done. To me. And to Russ. And how she's going to make it up." Ada swallowed again. "It's all so sad, because I've heard it all before, and then she's gone right on being herself somehow. And try as I have, over and over and over again, I can't seem to help her either. Maybe if the baby lives."

But the baby didn't.

And a slight recurrence of the endocarditis kept Rachel in the hospital a few weeks longer, at first feeding her fears, and then depressing her. Russ thought she was depressed about losing the baby. Although Alice knew better—and knew it straight from Rachel—she let Russ go on thinking what he did. She was determined to stay out of their affairs.

Alice had canceled her dinner date with Steve Frame—or postponed it, rather, until the end of the week following the stillbirth. When he came to pick her up on Friday evening, she was still in her room, dressing, but it was warm out, and her window was open, and as he joined her parents on the front porch beneath her, all three voices floated up to her.

"Would you like some lemonade?" her mother asked.

"Yes, thank you, Mrs. Matthews."

Alice heard the clinking of ice cubes and the pouring of liquid and then Steve's laugh. Steven Frame was not a man she would describe as merry. He was a brooding, intense sort of person, a man of considerable inner tension. Or so he had seemed to her in their one evening together. But, in striking contrast to those qualities, he had a merry laugh, and, hearing it now, Alice smiled.

Her mother apparently was puzzled. "Is something wrong?" she asked.

"No," he answered. "I was just thinking of something. My first business venture was lemonade. When I was eight, I had a stand outside my house."

"And was it successful?" her father asked.

"Not at first," Steve said. "You see, I'd got the idea from some bigger kids in the next block. When they realized they had some competition they came over and tried to put me out of business."

"And what happened?" her mother said.

"Well, it's a long story, Mrs. Matthews, but what happened is we made a deal. By the end of the summer I had five lemonade stands."

Sitting down at her dressing table to brush her hair, Alice smiled again.

And caught her breath at how excited she was to be

going out with him. He was so handsome. Well, maybe "handsome" wasn't the word for it. But distinguished-looking, certainly, with those dark, brooding eyes and that craggy-jawed face and the dark brown hair with the long sideburns.

And an absolutely captivating smile. A little-boy smile. The little boy of the lemonade stands twenty years ago.

"I gather," her father was saying, "you learned some valuable lessons from that."

"I learned my biggest lesson the next summer," he said. "I was ambitious. I was going to have stands all over town." Again that merry laugh. "It rained about every other day. By the end of the first week I was wiped out."

"And what was the lesson you learned from that?" her mother asked.

"Diversification. Don't put all your eggs in one basket."

"Well," her father said, "I'd say you learned the lesson pretty well. From what I've read, your holdings are very diversified. And I understand you've bought the Bay City Bengals."

"That's right."

"I was rather interested in that transaction," her father went on to say. "You see, I'm an accountant, and the people who were bidding against you are clients of mine."

"Yes, I know that," Steve said.

"You do?" Her father sounded surprised.

"Well, business is a lot like war, don't you think?" Steve answered. "In a war the side with the best intelligence network usually wins. So I try to find out everything I can about my opponents."

"I see." Her father sounded taken aback, and Alice, putting on lipstick, stopped to smile again. She knew exactly how he felt. Get Steve Frame talking about business and he was like a whirlwind. Or a dynamo. Or a torpedo. Something that took your breath away, anyhow.

As she went back to applying her lipstick, Steve said, "If it will make your clients feel any better, you can tell them it's probably the worst investment I've ever made."

"Then why did you make it?"

"I guess you could call it a whim. When I was growing up I didn't have much time for games. Maybe I'm compensating for it now by buying myself an expensive toy."

The football team and why he bought it came up again at dinner. It began when he said he wanted to talk.

"Fine," Alice said. "What about?"

He was looking directly at her. But then, he always looked directly at her when he spoke to her, as if nothing else in the world were of any consequence. As if there were nothing else in the world, period. It had disconcerted her at Walter and Lenore's reception, and it still did.

"About you," he said. "And about me. To find something out about each other. And to find out whether we want to find out more."

"My goodness," she said, feeling breathless again. "You don't pretend much, do you."

"People who pretend are scared."

If she was going to be spending time with Steve Frame—and she had the feeling she was—she might as well lay a few cards of her own out on the table. "Sometimes people who push too hard are scared, too."

He got the point. She had expected he would. He had said earlier that she was smart. She was willing to acknowledge that, but he was smarter. And not by just a little bit, either. "All right," he said, taking a sip of wine. "Let's see if I'm scared of anything. Maybe I am. Maybe I'm scared of living my boyhood over again. Scared of never getting what I wanted."

She started to say that he was just like Rachel, but she didn't. For one thing, he wasn't anything like Rachel, and for another, Rachel had just pulled another trick on Russ—a really nasty one this time—and Alice didn't want to spoil what was otherwise a pleasant evening by bringing Rachel into it. She said instead, "And owning a football team was one of the things you wanted?"

"I was telling your folks this evening—"

"I know. I heard all of you through the bedroom window. You said it was an expensive toy."

"And a bad investment. Because I need a bad investment. Do you understand taxes?"

"The only thing I understand about them is I have to pay them."

He smiled. "Okay. I bought the ball club to take a loss so I could make a bigger profit because the taxes wouldn't be so heavy. Of course, that's a simplification."

She grinned. "If that's a simplification, please don't say anything complex." He laughed, and she laughed with him. She was having an even better time than she had expected. "So it was just on account of taxes?" she asked.

"No. I had another reason. So I could say to myself Steve Frame owns a football team."

"Status, in other words."

He shrugged. "Why not? In other people's eyes, and in my own, too. So I could say to myself I did it." The brooding look was back in his eyes, and they were riveted on her face. "Me. Myself. With nobody's help. Can you understand that?"

"I guess so," she said, trying to sound more casual than she felt. She suddenly did not understand this man at all. One moment she was reveling in the pleasure of his company, and the next she was so taken aback by him that she was almost frightened. And didn't know what she was frightened about. "But, Steven," she said, "this I-made-it-myself syndrome of yours, is that really the way you feel about things?"

"I don't depend on other people, if that's what you mean. And you shouldn't either. Be what you want to be, and never mind if somebody else . . . well, disillusions you. Don't have illusions in the first place."

"That sounds so hard."

He shrugged. "I only meant if you don't want to get hurt, don't count too much on others. That's all. And don't worry about them, either. Either they'll help themselves or they'll dig their own graves. Without your help or your tears or your worry."

She was astonished, and she knew it showed. "You're telling me not to care about people."

"I'm telling you it does no good."

"Meaning I should be selfish instead?"

" 'Realistic' is the word."

She was back to not understanding him. He wasn't like anybody she'd ever known. She wasn't even sure she wanted to see him again. Maybe it would be better if she didn't.

But then when he was driving her home he said, "Would you like to go sailing this Sunday?"

"Oh," she said, turning to him in delight. Sailing was one of her favorite pastimes. She had no idea it was his as well. "Have you got a boat?"

He smiled. "I'll have one by Sunday. How about it?"

She burst out laughing. What could you do with a man like that? Lenore must have told him how much she liked to sail. "Steven, all right, yes, I'll go sailing with you Sunday. But not if you buy a boat for the occasion. At least find out first if it's something you enjoy. You can rent a boat, you know."

He showed still another side when he said good night to her at the door. "Something was bothering you tonight, wasn't it? I mean something not having anything to do with me."

"Am I that transparent? But yes, you're right. I'm sorry."

"Why be sorry?"

"Because I shouldn't have burdened you with something that doesn't concern you."

He smiled. "How have you burdened me with it, Alice?"

"By letting you know it was bothering me."

"It was a very gentle burden then. No heavier than a breeze." He took her hand in his and brushed his lips across it. "About like that." He squeezed her hand and released it. "Whatever it is, I hope it works out all right for you."

"I don't see how it can, but then, it isn't me it will work or not work out for. It doesn't really concern

me any more than it does you. It has to do with my
brother and his wife. Good night, Steven."

"Good night, Alice."

She thought for a moment he was going to kiss her,
but he only looked at her, touched her hand again, then
turned and left.

She lay awake for some time, thinking about him.
And about the near fight she had had with Russ over
his latest capitulation to Rachel.

Since his earliest days in medical school Russ had
wanted a residency at Massachusetts General Hospital
in Boston. A few months ago he had applied for it,
and a few days ago, to his great excitement, a letter
had arrived saying he had been accepted. And then
he had stunned everybody by turning the residency
down.

When he told Alice his decision, she asked him
straight out if it was Rachel. And of course it was.

"Rachel isn't well enough to travel yet," he said.
"Not for a month at least. And maybe longer."

For some time Alice had observed that where
Rachel was concerned, Russ's medical judgment went
out the window, but all she said was "Then I'll stay
with her and take care of her until she is well enough
to travel. And when that time comes I'll fly out to
Boston with her—to bring her to you."

He started to object, but she went right on. "Russ,
you're not to throw away an offer that you've killed
yourself to get. You are not to sacrifice a goal that
you've stayed up nights to realize."

But it wasn't any use. "Alice," he said, "please try
to understand. It isn't as though I'm throwing away
a career. Dr. MacCurdy wants me here at Memorial,
so that's what I'm going to do."

"That isn't the same."

"My life isn't the same. It isn't just my life any
more. It's Rachel's, too. And I have to take her problems into consideration as well as my own. It isn't
only the physical move that she objects to. It's
the new surroundings—a new place, new people. She
isn't really up to it."

"But, Russ, there's no reason for her to feel that way. She'll be better soon, and stronger."

"Alice, you don't understand. Rachel doesn't adjust to things the way other people do. She's had a lifetime of uncertainty. And she's going through a bad time right now. I can't take her with me, and I can't go off and leave her here alone. So we're staying here. Both of us."

Some of what Alice was feeling must have shown on her face, because he went on to say "You think Rachel demands too much."

"I didn't say that."

He nodded. "I know you didn't, but it's true. She does demand too much. And I know she does. I'm not a fool, Alice. I know Rachel has angered and upset a lot of people because she seems willful and spoiled."

"We only want to help you, Russ. Why can't I help you now the way I just suggested?"

"Because Rachel is my responsibility, that's why. Alice, I know Rachel isn't like some other girls, but I happen to love her the way she is. And first things have to be first. Right now she's ill. She needs me, and she needs Bay City. This is her home. She can't be uprooted feeling the way she does."

"Then that's it? All the plans over all these years —all of it thrown away?"

"No. I've passed my boards, and I'm going to be a resident. I'm going to be a doctor, just as we planned. But I'm also going to be a husband, and I'm going to take care of my wife."

"And you can't take care of her in Boston?"

It came out more harshly than she had intended, and he frowned at her. "Alice, I've made my decision, and that's that. And don't get any ideas about talking to Rachel about this. I don't want anybody meddling in our affairs."

"I had no intention of speaking to her," she said stiffly. "I'm not about to speak to Rachel about anything. I'm not looking to get my head chopped off." And before he could say another word she had walked away from him.

Alice punched up her pillow and concentrated on falling asleep, and eventually she did—and she dreamed of falling overboard.

But in fact it was Steve who fell overboard on Sunday afternoon, while he was trying to jump out of the way of the boom in a sudden shift of wind. And when he came bobbing up again and grabbed hold of the boat, she was peering so anxiously over the side that she lost her balance and tumbled in after him, and they both shrieked with laughter until they nearly drowned.

She had made up her mind not to let her concern for Russ burden her date this time even so much as a breeze, and she didn't, but a few nights later, when she and Steven were with Walter and Lenore, she was so depressed that they all commented on it, so she told them what had happened.

The four of them were walking along Bayside Boulevard, on their way to a new French restaurant Lenore had heard about, Alice and Lenore a few steps behind the two men, Walter towering over Steve as he towered over most of the men Alice knew, though he was such a sensitive—and sensitive-looking —man, with finely chiseled features and brown eyes like liquid velvet, that she never thought of him as towering.

He and Lenore were a handsome, well-matched couple, despite his being about fifteen years older than she. Lenore was tall and regal-looking, with tawny hair, long and thick, and the bearing of an aristocrat. Alice could easily understand why it was Lenore Rachel wanted to be like. Lenore was elegant, cool, in command. Without ever apparently giving it a thought.

As if they had read her thoughts, Steve and Walter began talking about Rachel, and Alice and Lenore fell silent, listening.

"Believe me," Walter said, "this won't be the last time Russ will make a large-size sacrifice for Rachel. That's the kind of girl she is."

"Meaning . . . ?" Steve asked politely.

"Oh," Walter said, "she's a very mixed-up kid. She

likes material things. She feels she's got to latch on to every piece of evidence that she's 'in,' that she's important, that she's . . . well, I'll say it—that she's well off."

Steve laughed. "She sounds like me."

"No. I can't buy that one."

"Why not?"

"Because, my friend, you may be as ambitious as anybody else around—in fact, I'm sure you are. But you know how to go about getting what you want. Rachel doesn't. She always picks the wrong way. I like her, I get annoyed with her, and I feel sorry for her all at the same time."

"It's interesting, isn't it," Lenore said to Alice in a low voice, "how the men all find excuses for her. I wonder why."

"I don't know," Alice said. And she didn't, but she had to admit that it was true.

Even her own father, as upset as the rest of them that Russ was throwing away such a great opportunity, managed to find excuses for Rachel, saying she couldn't be blamed for being frightened of a move at this time. "And don't forget, she doesn't understand the importance of where a residency is taken. I imagine one hospital or another—they're all the same to her."

"Oh, sure," Alice said. "Of course. And since Rachel knows Dr. MacCurdy has offered a residency to Russ, staying in Bay City makes sense to her. I never said Rachel didn't have her reasons. I'm only saying Russ is irresponsible for giving in to them. And to her."

One afternoon a week or so before Rachel was to be discharged from the hospital, Alice came into her room with some medication, and Rachel tried to draw Alice back into the controversy, saying "People know Russ did this for me, don't they?"

Trying just as hard to keep out of it, Alice said, "That's what Russ tells us."

"Well, do they think I made him do it?"

Alice shrugged. "I suppose most people figure Russ talked it over with you."

"And they think it's wrong, don't they?"

Alice handed Rachel the tiny paper cup with the pill in it, then filled a glass of water from the pitcher on the bedside table and handed her that as well. "Mom and Dad are a little disappointed."

"And you, Alice?"

"I don't have any opinion about it."

Rachel made a face. "Not much. You think I'm not a good wife to Russ."

"Rachel, I never said that. Now take your medicine, please."

"All right." She took the pill and drank the water. "And of course you didn't say it. You've been brought up to be polite. But I can tell. Everybody thinks I did something terrible to Russ. But I didn't. Alice, it was Russ's own decision."

"Well, fine, then. Look, I'll see you later."

She started out of the room, but Rachel called her back, saying she didn't want people to think she wasn't a good wife to Russ. Alice wondered who had been talking to her, and in the next breath Rachel told her —reversing things, of course.

"I was saying to Mom last night when she came to see me that a wife should do whatever the husband thinks is the best thing for his profession. Isn't that right?"

"I suppose so, yes."

"If it's not too late."

"Too late for what, Rachel?"

"For Russ to take that residency. I mean, that would be being a good wife, wouldn't it? Encouraging him to take the residency."

Alice stared at her. "Are you saying you want Russ to take the Massachusetts General residency now?"

Rachel smiled demurely. "I want whatever is best for Russ's career. That's what a good wife should want, isn't it?"

Alice was thinking that Rachel's mother must have really lit into her. It wasn't surprising. Ada was as distressed as all the Matthewses were over this latest turn of events. "I'm sorry," she said, aware that Rachel had gone on talking. "What did you say?"

"I said I want to talk to Russ about it. So if you run

into him in the corridor or wherever, tell him I want to see him, okay?"

But Rachel's supposed change of heart was only another ploy in her arsenal of tricks. While seeming to urge Russ to take the residency in Boston, she managed to come up with yet another reason for their staying in Bay City: Her mother was upset and needed Rachel's support. Of course, Rachel said, after she was well enough to join Russ in Boston, she could fly back to Bay City for a couple of days each week to give her mother that support. That way she could take care of both Russ and her mother.

But—as Rachel must have known—Russ wouldn't hear of that.

And when she pressed him, asking if this was his decision or was he doing it because it would be the best thing for her—did he really and truly want to stay in Bay City—what else could Russ say but that he really and truly did?

Or, as Rachel said to Alice in front of Russ, "I've been trying and trying and trying to convince Russ that he ought to take that residency in Boston, but he insists on staying here. This is really where he wants to be."

When her brother offered no protest, then or later, Alice figured the matter was settled, once and for all. And in a way she was relieved. She was sick to death of hearing about it.

But the matter was far from being settled. It was, in fact, the first flick of the tiger's tail.

Chapter Five

STEVE Frame's initial exposure to Rachel's talent for manipulation occurred shortly before she was discharged from the hospital at the end of August. Stopping by to see one of his football players who had been injured in practice that morning, he ran into Russ and Rachel walking down the corridor.

"Well," Russ said, "look who's here. What's the occasion, Steve?"

Steve grinned. "I'm pretending to visit one of my football players who got hurt, but actually I came here to ask your sister to have dinner with me tonight. And what's more, she said she would."

Rachel beamed. "Oh, I think that's marvelous."

"So do I," Steve said. "And it's nice to see you up and around, Mrs. Matthews. Are they letting you go home soon?"

"Very soon now," Russ said. "Maybe in a day or two."

"And believe me," Rachel added, "it can't be soon enough."

"You've missed a lot of nice weather," Steve observed.

"Oh, I've missed a lot more than that. When I get out I'm going to make up for lost time, and one of the things I'm going to do is make Russ take me to a football game as soon as the season starts. One of your football games, Mr. Frame."

He smiled politely. "We're always glad to have another fan."

Rachel smiled back at him. "I read in the paper yesterday that everyone's trying to get season tickets."

76

She turned to Russ. "Wouldn't it be nice to have season tickets, Russ?"

"Honey," he said, but got no further.

Rachel had turned back to Steve and was saying, "But they're impossible to get, aren't they?"

"Not if you know the owner of the team."

Rachel's eyes widened. "You mean you could get them for us? Oh, that would be marvelous!"

Russ started to protest, but Steve cut him off. "They'll be in the mail tomorrow, and you can consider them a gift."

Now Russ did protest. "I can't do that."

"Of course you can," Steve said. "Think of it as a get-well present for your wife. Besides," he added with a grin, "if the seats just happen to be in my box, it gives me a good excuse to ask your sister to come along." Turning to Rachel, he said, "You get well now, Mrs. Matthews, and I'll see you both soon."

As soon as he had gone, Russ said, "Honey, that was awful. You practically asked him to give us those season tickets."

"I did no such thing," Rachel said vehemently. "I didn't ask him to *give* them to us."

"Well, how else could we have gotten them? Season tickets cost sixty or seventy dollars."

Before Rachel could answer, Alice came along to tell Russ he was wanted in pediatrics and she would see that Rachel got back to her room all right. As they started toward it, Rachel said, "Russ and I just had a nice chat with your Steven Frame."

"He's not my Steven Frame, Rachel."

"Alice, how can you be so blasé? If I had someone like him hooked the way you do—"

"Rachel," Alice cut in, "I don't have him hooked."

Rachel arched her eyebrows. "No? You should have heard him just now. He was doing everything to get your name into the conversation. Alice, he's yours for the asking. I can tell."

Alice smiled. "But suppose I don't want to ask?"

"Well, then, you'd be a fool. Believe me, when you've got somebody like that on the end of your line, you reel them in just as fast as you can."

That night at dinner Steve startled Alice out of a reverie by handing her a dollar bill. "That's in keeping with my reputation as a big spender. A dollar for your thoughts." When all he drew from her was a faint smile, he said, "Sorry. It wasn't a very good joke, was it. You're not impressed with my money."

She shook her head. "Not as much as some people are."

"Like your sister-in-law, for instance? Did she tell you about the tickets I gave them?"

"Yes, she did. It was very nice of you, Steven."

He eyed her a moment. "But you don't think I should have done it."

Alice shrugged. "I suspect she hinted for them, and that embarrasses me."

"Don't let it," he said, refilling their wineglasses.

"I guess you're right. I mean, if you wanted to give them to her . . ."

"Not particularly."

"Then why did you do it?" she asked, surprised.

"Let's just say I can understand a schemer."

Alice took a roll, broke off a piece, and buttered it. "From what little you've seen of her, you think Rachel's a schemer?"

"I don't have to have seen much of her. Your brother isn't taking that residency in Boston, is he?"

"No, but—"

"You said yourself—that night we were with Walter and Lenore—that Rachel talked him out of it."

"Then I probably shouldn't have said it, because I don't know it for a fact. And it's true she has been sick."

Steve nodded. "And you're bending over backward to be nice. Haven't you ever seen anybody use sickness like a club? I don't know whether Rachel wheedled and begged and cried a little, but I know she ended up with what she wanted. Her kind usually do."

"Especially if people keep giving her what she wants."

"You mean about the tickets? Look, Alice, what did I lose? If I hadn't given them to her, they'd have gone to somebody else—some builder I needed a favor

from, some politician, some other conniver." He
raised a hand to keep her from interrupting. "Now I
know that isn't a nice thing to say about your sister-
in-law, but . . . well, look at it this way. One of the
tickets went to your brother, and I happen to think
he's a very nice guy."

Alice smiled. "So do I."

For the next few minutes they devoted their attention to eating the bay scallops Steve had ordered for
both of them. Then he said, "You're worried about
him, aren't you? Russ, I mean."

She nodded. "Yes, but I don't know if you can
understand that."

"Why not? Some more wine?"

"No, thank you. Because of things you've said to
me before."

"You mean about looking out for yourself and forgetting other people."

Alice nodded. "I can't do that, Steven. People are
too important to me."

"And the word 'people' covers too much ground for
me to appreciate. Individuals, one person at a time—
that's something I can understand. Alice Matthews,
Steven Frame. Those are people I care about right
now."

"That sounds like Rachel's philosophy."

Again he eyed her a moment. "Maybe it is, but
there's really a great deal of difference between Rachel
and me. You see, Rachel says one thing but means
and feels another. I don't do that. For better or for
worse, I say what I think and mean it. Now, I probably
could do a lot better with you if I didn't operate that
way. I know a lot of things I say annoy you, but at
least they're me. There's no pretense at anything else.
Alice, when I started out I didn't have anything except
my honesty, and even if I lost all the money tomorrow,
that's the one thing I'd want to hang on to. I call things
as I see them, because I couldn't live any other way.
Rachel and I may sometimes seem a lot alike, but
believe me, we're two different breeds of cat."

Later that same evening, after Steve had taken Alice
home, and she and her father were foraging in the re-

frigerator for a late-night snack, he said, "I stopped off at the hospital this evening to see Rachel. She's very impressed that you're going out with such a big tycoon as Steven Frame." Her father's eyes twinkled. "Her very word. 'Tycoon.'"

Alice poured herself a glass of milk. "I know. And Russ thinks it's a big joke. That she's so impressed by him. And do you know her reason? Well, of course you do. You just said it. 'Tycoon.'"

Her father unwrapped a slab of cheese and cut a slice. "You want some of this?"

"No. I settled for a brownie that Russ somehow or other seems to have overlooked."

The cheese went back into the refrigerator. "Of course, you have to admit," her father said, "that Steven Frame is a rather impressive young man."

"He's a date," Alice said. "And kind of a nice one. But I don't sit at a table opposite him in a restaurant and say 'Look, across the table from me is a real live tycoon.'"

Her father nodded. "No, I know you don't. You don't think the way Rachel does."

"But that's just my point, Dad. Does Rachel have to have the particular set of values that she does?"

"At the moment, yes, I think she does have to have them. I think those values give her some kind of security."

Alice shook her head. "Everything measured by money?"

"And position. And—oh, the thing they call glamor these days."

"But there's no security in that."

"I don't think so either, Alice. But Rachel's needs are not yours or mine, and they're not necessarily permanent. I think Russ will give Rachel security as time goes on. And I don't mean money or material things. I mean simply by being Russ. He's a fine young man, Russ is, and we can only hope Rachel will gradually realize that what he has to offer is more precious than his picture on the cover of *Time* magazine or a mink coat."

Alice drained the glass of milk. "And if she doesn't realize that, Dad?"

"We have to hope she will, and I have some faith she will."

Alice put the empty glass in the sink and ran cold water into it. "You have more faith than I do, I'm afraid."

The evening of the day Rachel came home from the hospital, Steve came to take Alice to a dinner party that Walter and Lenore Curtin were giving. Upset that she and Russ hadn't been invited, unhappy that Russ was on duty that night, feeling let down and left out, Rachel nevertheless made a point of being on hand when Steve arrived, and she listened bug-eyed as he talked to Jim about the football team and how he would like to transform it from a tax loss into a capital gain, as he had done the previous year with some real-estate holdings.

"Real estate!" she exclaimed. "I mean, football teams and construction work and real estate, too?"

"It's just a diversification of holdings," Steve said.

"Oh," Rachel said, trying to look as if she knew what he was talking about. "I was wondering," she began, but she no longer had his attention. Alice was coming down the stairs.

"Don't you look lovely," he said, standing up, and Rachel had to admit that Alice did. She was wearing a long pale blue silk jersey skirt with a blue-and-white figured blouse that made her eyes bluer than ever, and she had her hair done up on top of her head in a fancy braided coil.

"That's a very pretty dress, darling," Alice's father said.

"And a very pretty girl inside it," her mother added.

Alice beamed at them, then turned to Steve. "It's getting much too sticky around here, Steven. Have you got your pumpkin and all six mice out there?"

He nodded, smiling. He hadn't taken his eyes off her since she came down the stairs. "Yes. They're out there. Shall we go?"

"Let's," Alice said. She kissed her parents. "I'll be home early, no, I won't forget my manners, and I won't ask for second helpings, and I'll thank the hostess for a lovely time. Good-bye."

Everybody laughed—except Rachel, who felt so envious of Alice that she could hardly bear it, and spent the evening brooding about how Alice always got everything she wanted and Rachel never did.

When the Matthewses went to bed, Rachel said she wanted to stay downstairs awhile and read, and for a while she did, leafing through one magazine after another, but when she heard a car pull up out front, she turned out the lamp and went to stand by the open doorway.

As Alice and Steve came up the walk Rachel heard Steve say, "And you were the smallest girl in your third-grade class."

Alice laughed. "So far, so good."

"And I bet your dresses were starched."

"That's sizing my mother up correctly, not me."

They came up the front steps and sat down on the porch glider. "Pigtails?" he asked.

Alice laughed again. "I'd like to say crew cut just to confound you, but pigtails, yes."

"You see, shortly after I was introduced to you I realized I'd known you for a long time. I've just proved it, haven't I? How can you be so bright and so—I don't know—innocent, fresh—"

"Oh, Steven, please," Alice said. "If I took you seriously . . ."

"Why shouldn't you?" he said, his voice so low that Rachel had to strain to hear him. "Do you find me too brash and outspoken?"

"I don't find you too anything, Steven," she answered, and now her voice was as low and as intimate-sounding as his. Rachel began to wish that she had let Russ make love to her today before he went back to the hospital, but Russ wanted her to have another baby and to start it any old time now, for crying out loud, when having another baby was the last thing in the world she wanted, now or any other time. It was all very well for him; he didn't have to lie around feeling sick and miserable and getting big and fat. Well, she wasn't going to do it, and that was that. She was going to have some fun for a change.

"But you're certainly frank, Steven," Alice was saying. "I don't mean when you're saying flattering things. I mean ordinarily. And you're kind of fresh in a way you don't mean, and I . . . well, I'm remembering what you said about not bothering your head with other people and advising me not to. You're rather cynical."

"I guess you're right," he said; then there was such a long silence that Rachel leaned as close against the screen door as she dared, to see if they were kissing, but they weren't.

"Alice," he said, "I don't want to sit here talking about me. I want to sit here talking about you, but I know that unless you can approve of me I'll never be sitting here again talking about anything, so do you mind if I talk about me?"

Alice laughed. "Do you realize what a complex sentence you just uttered?"

Rachel wondered why in the world Alice didn't put a stop to the talking. If she were the one sitting out there with him all cozy and nice on this warm summer night, she wouldn't be wasting time talking. She'd be in his arms. Maybe if she called the hospital Russ could get somebody to cover for him at least long enough to—

"What I want to let you know right now, Alice," he was saying, still in that same low, intense voice, "is that you and I were brought up differently. We had —oh, did we ever have—different backgrounds, and yours has made you into everything you are, and it's nice. And on the other hand mine has made me into whatever un-nice kind of a guy I am. But that's me, all right?"

"Of course it's all right."

"I've knocked around a lot, Alice, and if I'm fresh or cynical, well, those are the scars, I guess."

"Steven, I didn't mean it as a criticism. It was just an observation."

"You're nice to say that. I hope I'm not too annoying to you."

Rachel couldn't believe her ears. How could a man

as rich as Steven Frame possibly be annoying to anybody?

"You get less annoying every minute." Alice
laughed again. "Saying which, the girl glanced at the
village clock and said, 'My, it's late.' "

He laughed, too. "On which cue, the man rose."
Rachel saw him get up. "How's that?"

Was it possible that Alice was going to let him
leave without doing anything to guarantee he'd come
back?

"I've had a good time, Alice."

"I have too, Steven."

Again there was a silence, and again Rachel strained
against the screen door. Steve had his hand on Alice's
arm. And then finally he leaned over and kissed her.
It was not much of a kiss, in Rachel's opinion, but it
seemed to satisfy him. Or maybe "satisfy" wasn't the
word, because when he said good night there was a
huskiness in his voice.

Alice stayed out on the porch, watching him go, and
after a minute or so Rachel opened the door and went
out to join her.

"Rachel!" Alice exclaimed, spinning around. "How
long have you been standing there?"

"I haven't been standing there at all. I just this minute came downstairs, and I heard a car pull away, and
I came out to see if you might be here. I just wanted
to talk to you, Alice, that's all."

"Oh? What about?"

"About anything. You don't have any idea what
it's like being all cooped up here without anybody to
talk to."

"Oh, now, Rachel, you make it sound as if you're
living in a hermitage. You have plenty of people to
talk to."

"You mean like Russ, who's never home?"

"For a resident, it seems to me, he's home a lot."

"Yes, but when he isn't . . . Honestly, Alice, I know
it's silly, but when he isn't, I get so scared."

Alice stared at her. "Scared of what, Rachel?"

"Of everything. I can't really put it into words. Oh,

Alice, I know you can't understand that. You're so sure of yourself—about everything."

Alice shook her head. "I wouldn't say that." But she looked as if she cared about what Rachel was saying, and she sounded as nice and as sympathetic as Rachel had ever heard her.

"But you are," Rachel said. "And that's why I want us to be friends, Alice. You're really the only other person here I can talk to. With your mother and dad I'm always making mistakes. And even with you. I know you get mad at me for some of the things I say."

Alice was looking more concerned than ever. "Well, look, Rachel," she said, but Rachel went right on.

"And when your mother said something to me the other day that you were thinking of moving out and getting your own place, I knew it was probably because of me. But please, Alice, don't move out. If you did, and with Russ gone so much of the time, I'd really be all alone, and I don't think I could stand that. I've got to have a friend—somebody I can talk to—or I don't know what I'll do."

Alice patted her hand. "I'm not going to move out, Rachel. At least not now. So don't worry about it. Okay?"

Rachel smiled. "Oh, I'm so glad to hear that, Alice. I know you probably think I complain a lot, and I guess I do, but I get so lonesome for Russ, and then of course when he does come home, all he wants to do is sleep."

Alice started to say something, but Rachel shook her head. "No, I know he needs the rest. I understand that. But there are things I need, too. And one of them is to have some fun once in a while. I know I probably shouldn't say that either. I mean, I realize I'm a married woman and all that, but I'm even younger than you are, Alice, and you have fun."

"I also work, Rachel."

"Sure, but you go out with Steven Frame, too, like tonight. That's what I'm talking about. I mean, all I ever see of you and Steve is when he comes to pick you up, and he says how-do-you-do to me, and I say how-do-you-do to him, and . . . well, what I'm trying to say, Alice, is couldn't you and Steve and Russ and I go out together sometime?"

"Oh. Well, sure, Rachel. Why not?" Alice smiled. "On one condition."

"What?"

"That you don't talk about his money."

Rachel smiled too. "I won't. I promise."

The next morning Russ and Alice were up before the others and had breakfast together. Alice told Russ about her talk with Rachel the night before, saying, "I think I got to understand her a little better than I ever have."

"In what way, Alice?" Russ asked.

"Well, Rachel's . . . she's a kid, sort of. She just wants to be reassured. And I remember times in my life when I've wanted that. Everybody does. I just think maybe in Rachel's life there are a few things that make it more necessary to her than to some of the rest of us."

Russ's face had lighted up. "I know what you mean, Alice, and I'm glad you see it too. That she's kind of afraid underneath."

Alice nodded. "Yes. And, oh, Russ, I felt good about our conversation last night. And the reason is I think Rachel felt good about it. You know, she's lonely when you're not here."

"I know that."

"And, as she pointed out, she's even younger than I am, and maybe another girl wouldn't mind being here and seeing Steven and me go out for a date, but I do understand how it makes Rachel feel, and so we sort of tentatively fixed up the idea of a double date —Steven and I and you and Rachel."

Russ brightened some more. "Hey, that's fine! I'd like that. And Rachel certainly would, too. So by all means, fix it up."

A few days later, riding home with her father after work, Alice mentioned the prospective double date to him, and he said, "You've been seeing quite a lot of Steven Frame, haven't you?"

She smiled at him. "Do I feel a father-daughter talk coming on?"

"Well, honey," he said reasonably, "am I wrong to think we should talk about it?"

"No, of course you're not, but I think it's too early for that. Oh, I know he's different from any of the boys I've ever gone out with."

Her father maneuvered into the left-turn lane and waited for the green arrow to come on. "Different how?"

"Well, I guess it's just that. The others were boys. You see, Steven doesn't have to talk about what he's going to be when he grows up. He's been grown up for a long time now. And it's nice to go out with someone like that. It makes you realize you're grown up, too."

"Which may be exactly what I'm worrying about," her father said as the arrow came on and he turned left onto the outer drive that would take them non-stop to the section of Bay City that they lived in.

"Well, don't worry about it, Dad," Alice said. "The situation hasn't gotten serious yet."

"Not for you maybe, but how about Steve?"

"Oh. Well, no, Dad, I don't think so." They rode in silence for a bit, following the curving shoreline of the bay. Then Alice said, "What do you think of Steven, Dad?"

"That's hard to say, honey. I've talked with him a few times when he's come to pick you up—briefly— and I've read and heard a little about him."

"But that little is pretty impressive, isn't it?"

"You said not two minutes ago the situation hasn't gotten serious yet. Now you sound as if he's sweeping you off your feet."

There was another little silence. "Maybe the key word is 'yet,' Dad. I have the feeling sometimes that if I'm not careful that's exactly what could happen. Something else I said a couple of minutes ago—about how nice it was to go out with a man instead of a boy. And yet that's part of the problem, too. I mean, Dad, do you have any idea what it's like? I mean, with the boys I've been used to going out with, I've always had to be so careful what I ordered, so I wouldn't strain their budgets. With Steven, why, half the places he takes me to don't even have the prices on the menu."

"Do you think he's trying to impress you?"

"No. Not with his money, anyhow. I'm far more concerned with that than he is."

Her father glanced at her. "That doesn't sound like you."

"I don't mean concerned with it the way Rachel is. I mean the opposite. Being a reverse snob about it. Until the other night, anyhow. I've always kept waiting for him to prove he has something else to offer."

"What do you mean, until the other night?"

"Well, the more we go out, the more we talk. It's been slow, but he keeps giving me little glimpses into what he's like. And he's really quite a guy, Dad. I still don't always agree with him, especially the way he feels about people, but . . . well, he is honest, maybe more honest than anyone I've ever met before. And that's a lot more impressive than all the other things put together."

Again they rode in silence until her father spoke. "But is that enough, Alice—just honesty?"

"Enough for what? Oh. Look, Dad, this father-daughter chat has taken a far more serious course than I intended. Or than is warranted. I know that in the last few minutes I've been talking as if Steven is going to pop the question any second now, and that simply isn't true." She laughed self-consciously. "At least, I don't think it's true."

Again her father glanced at her. "But you know he likes you."

"Well, yes. Yes, I'm sure he does."

"And you like him."

"Yes, I do, and maybe that's the strangest thing of all. He has this habit of coming on strong." She shook her head. "Well, in the beginning I was totally prepared for it. I kept telling myself, fine, you just play your little game and I'll play mine, but . . ."

When she didn't continue, her father said, "But suddenly it isn't a game any more?"

"Well, that's just it, Dad. I don't know."

That it wasn't a game any more was made clearer to Alice that night, when Steve brought her home from a dinner date with Walter and Lenore. "I don't think I would make the same mistake that Walter did," he said.

Alice was puzzled. "What mistake?"

"Of waiting so long to get married. He's around forty, you know."

"Yes, I know."

"There comes a day—and long before you're forty, too—when you suddenly stop and take a look in the mirror and ask yourself what it all means. You look around at people who are married, and you say, hey, maybe it's time I thought about that for me." He gave her a shy smile. "I hope I'm not scaring you off, talking like this."

"I don't scare that easily," Alice replied, "but you do make it sound as if you're cooking up some big business deal."

He nodded. "Maybe I do at that. But then maybe you can teach me not to approach it that way." Again the shy smile. "What do you think?"

What she found herself thinking, though she wouldn't have told him for the world, was that she wanted him to take her in his arms and hold her so tightly she might break.

Something of what she thought got through to him. He looked at her, touched her face, then took her gently into his arms—as if he were indeed afraid of breaking her—and kissed her.

Then he pulled away and looked at her again. "Good night, Alice."

"Good night, Steven."

She watched him leave, then went on standing where she was, looking at where he had been.

True to her promise to Rachel, Alice had mentioned the double date to Steve, and he was agreeable to it, and so it was arranged for the following Saturday night. But at five o'clock that Saturday Russ was called to the hospital on an emergency—his cousin Bill had been badly injured in an automobile accident. Rachel was furious—until Alice called from the hospital a couple of hours later to say she had been kept there by the same emergency, she had tried to call Steven to say she couldn't keep her date with him, but by the time she was able to get to the phone it was too late, he must already be on the way. Would Rachel please explain to him?

Rachel was only sorry that she didn't have time to change into something more glamorous before he got there.

Chapter Six

WHEN Steve arrived and heard what had happened, he wanted to go immediately to the hospital, but Rachel told him that Alice had specifically asked him not to, that there were too many friends and family already there, and she would call as soon as there was any news.

Rachel smiled. "As long as you're here, wouldn't you like a drink or something?"

He shrugged. He didn't want to stay, but he didn't want to be rude. "I was really thinking of going back to the office."

"After you'd already planned an evening out? Why, that's terrible. I mean, I know how disappointed you must be. I'm disappointed too. Russ and I were both looking forward so to this evening with you and Alice, but of course as soon as we heard his cousin had been hurt I told him to stay at the hospital as long as necessary. Even if it takes all night. I mean, Russ is such a marvelous doctor, and it wouldn't be fair for his cousin not to have the best."

Steve nodded. "Well, I imagine your husband felt the same way about it, didn't he? I mean, I doubt if he'd want to be any place but there."

"Oh, yes, of course. But now come on. Please let me get you a drink. Alice might call any second, and I'm sure you'd like to hear the news."

He hesitated, then shrugged again. "Well, all right. One drink."

Rachel beamed. "Marvelous. I have to warn you that the Matthewses don't have a very elegant bar. They keep the stuff hidden in the kitchen, but I think there's some bourbon and—"

"Bourbon's fine," he cut in. "On the rocks. With a touch of water."

"Fine," she said, beaming again. "I'll be right back. Don't go away."

He gave her an amused look as she flounced out of the room, then looked around him. Spotting a picture of Alice on the mantelpiece over the fireplace, he went over to it for a closer look. It was a picture of her in her nurse's uniform—her graduation picture, he supposed. Not smiling, but looking very serious. And very vulnerable. And breathtakingly lovely.

He still had the picture in his hands when Rachel came back with a drink for each of them. "Now, that didn't take long, did it? Oh. You're looking at that picture of Alice. Honestly, that's so beautiful of her I could just die with jealousy."

He put the picture back on the mantelpiece. "It's no more beautiful than she really is."

"No. You're right. You know, we're very close, Alice and I, and . . . well, she's just a dream. She's so unspoiled and all."

Steve smiled as he took the drink she handed him. "In another minute I think you're going to tell me I'm a lucky guy."

She laughed and held her glass out to him as if toasting him. "Well, you are. Of course, I think Alice is lucky too."

"Do you really?"

"Well, yes. I mean, you're so successful so young, and you have all those marvelous things written about you in all the magazines and the newspapers and—oh well, you know."

He took a sip of his drink and sat down in an armchair while Rachel perched on the sofa. "Well, I wouldn't say they've been so marvelous, but thank you."

"You're welcome. Well, I think we should drink to something, don't you?" Again she raised her glass. "We've been sort of deserted tonight, so how about to the both of us?"

"Whatever you say." They drank.

"Maybe we can have our double date next weekend," Rachel said.

"No, I'm afraid not," he answered. "Not next weekend. I have to fly to Washington."

Her eyes widened. "Washington? I bet you're going to talk to some senators and congressmen and people like that."

He agreed he was.

"Oh, that's too much," she said, still wide-eyed.

Enjoying her impressionableness, he added, "I've got to touch down at Cleveland and Detroit, too, before I come back."

"All in one weekend? My, how exciting!"

"Do you like traveling?" he asked.

She nodded eagerly. "Oh, yes, I adore it."

"You do? I'm surprised. If you honestly like to travel, I'd think you would have jumped at the chance to go to Boston."

She was looking at him blankly. "Boston?"

"Yes. When your husband was offered the residency there."

"Oh, that. Oh, yes. Well . . . Of course I wanted Russ to take it. Boston's always been one of my favorite cities. I mean, to be there and do all of those things. But you see, I wasn't well at the time, and Russ just absolutely refused to leave my side."

"That's too bad," he said, more amused than ever. She was really something, this kid. "You know, there are only a few opportunities a man gets in a lifetime, and when one comes along you'd better swing with it while you can."

"Oh, well, I believe that too. Absolutely. And I wanted Russ to take that residency, and I probably

manipulator, but she was also intensely insecure, with no self-confidence. And although she wasn't stupid, she wasn't brilliant, either.

What she had her mind on, what she was working toward, was making it possible to set her cap for him.

It was to this end that she schemed and lied and manipulated—or, as she saw it, shaped the truth to her advantage and her opponents' disadvantage.

Her primary opponent, of course, was Alice.

Where she had initially taken the attitude that it was a pity Alice and Steven had had a falling out and she hoped they could get back together again—indeed, urged Alice to make it up with Steve—she now saw Alice as not being really suitable for Steve. As she remarked to Lenore, "Steve is a very strong man, you know. That's why he's so successful—because he's strong. When Steve Frame wants something, he just goes after it. That's the way he thinks a man should be. And with that kind of personality—well, a girl can't be stubborn the way Alice is being. I mean, you just can't treat a man like Steve Frame that way."

To Liz Matthews, taken aback by the contributions Rachel turned over to her from three wealthy businessmen—until Rachel admitted she had been directed to those men by Steven Frame—Rachel put it that "Alice is used to . . . well, you know, schoolkids. A guy like Steve . . . well, he's a real man."

She even played Alice down to Steve himself. She went back to his office for the names of still more potential contributors, and while he was in the middle of giving them to her she said, "It's a shame about you and Alice."

"You think so?" he replied. "Now where were we? Oh, yes. After McLaughlin try Larry Townsend. I buy equipment from him. And then after you see Larry, go see Chuck Barrett."

Adding the new entries to her list, Rachel said, "Steve, you know what I think? Alice doesn't appreciate you."

"Oh, is that what you think?"

"Well," she said, "what else can I think? I mean, it's very sad and all, but on the other hand, it's only natural that you and Alice would stop seeing each other eventually, because . . . well, as I said, she just doesn't appreciate you."

He eyed her skeptically. "The way you do. Is that what you mean, Rachel?"

Steve was fond of saying that Rachel couldn't trick him, and for the most part she couldn't. But because of his differences with Alice, he accepted with hardly any question Rachel's outrageous lies about how the Matthews family treated her.

"Steve," she said on one of her visits to this office—all of them unannounced—"you've got no idea of what it's like living there. They treat me like I don't even belong, like they'd done me some big favor by letting me marry their precious son."

"And what have you done to convince them they're wrong?" he asked.

"Well," she said, "I try to help. I really do. But they just smile at me like I was too stupid to even know how to boil water or anything."

"And do you know how?"

"Of course I do. I can do a lot of things, but I'm not going to do them for people who don't even care about me, for people who don't even bother to talk to me any more."

The skeptical look again. "Now surely, Rachel, your husband talks to you."

"Oh, well, sure. Russ tries, but he isn't home a lot of the time, and even when he is, he always agrees with them. As far as he's concerned, they can't do any wrong. You ought to know what I mean. You had the same trouble with Alice."

"Not exactly."

Rachel persisted. "But your trouble with her was over family. That stupid idea of loyalty they all have. Everybody bands together, and an outsider doesn't stand a chance."

"Well, maybe," he admitted. "But is that what you consider yourself—an outsider?"

She nodded vigorously. "I don't just consider myself one. I am one. I mean, who pays any attention to me? I— Oh, look. You don't need to hear my problems.

I'm sure you have plenty of your own. What time is it, anyhow?"

Steve glanced at his watch. "It's ten minutes to twelve."

Her eyes went wide. "Is it really? Oh, listen, I had no idea. I'm probably keeping you from an important lunch date or something."

He smiled. "No. As a matter of fact, I don't have any plans for lunch today."

"Oh, really? Oh, but listen, I'd better leave anyway. I've taken up too much of your time as it is."

"I haven't minded," he said. "And as long as I don't have any plans, why don't you have lunch with me?"

"Oh. Oh, well, no, I couldn't," she answered, but then, on thinking it over, she decided she could after all.

He laughed. "Which is why you came here in the first place, isn't it?"

She started to protest, then laughed with him. "You know, you're right. I can't fool you. Okay, I admit it. I did want to have lunch with you. I sometimes need somebody to talk to."

If Rachel didn't fool Steve—except in how the Matthews family treated and regarded her—she also no longer fooled Russ. All of the Matthewses felt that Rachel had a lot of growing up to do, and Jim and Mary suggested to Russ that he and Rachel get their own apartment as a step in that direction. In any event, since Rachel was no longer pregnant and in need of special looking after, there was no valid reason for them to continue living in the Matthews house, depriving Alice of her room.

Russ was enthusiastic, but Rachel resisted the move mightily. She claimed that she wasn't up to keeping house, that she was only just out of the hospital, that his family didn't want her in their home, that his mother probably thought Rachel didn't help her enough, and why couldn't things just go on the way they had been?

One afternoon after Russ and Rachel had been out looking for an apartment, she came home claiming to be exhausted.

Russ grunted. "If we were going to Walter and Lenore's or the Top of the Tower you wouldn't be exhausted. You've been running all over town canvassing for Aunt Liz. That must have kept you on your feet, but that didn't bother you at all. It's only when you look for an apartment, where you and I can be alone, that you get tired."

Rachel flopped down on the bed, not bothering to answer him.

"How did you like the place on Pleasant Street?" he asked, loosening his tie.

She made a face. "It's dingy, and it's too small."

"Rachel, it's not dingy, and I thought we agreed we wanted a small apartment. You didn't want to take care of a big one, for one thing."

"I don't want to take care of a big one, or a small one either. What I want—"

"What you want," he said, cutting in on her, "is a stack of servants."

"Well, I don't want that apartment on Pleasant Street."

"It had beautiful closets," he said.

She made another face. "Oh, closets."

"Rachel, at the rate at which you buy new dresses, closets are quite a consideration."

"Whatever I say, you're going to turn it against me."

He came over and sat on the foot of the bed. "If I do, it's not because I want to. I have some time off tomorrow. Shall we go look at some other apartments?"

She shook her head. "I don't want to."

He eyed her a moment. "Rachel, why are you resisting the idea of our getting an apartment so hard?" He put up a hand. "And don't say you're too ill. You're not ill at all. I'm a doctor, so stop pulling that on me. Why don't you want to live alone in an apartment with your husband?"

"Russ, it isn't a question of that. We're just not ready to move into an apartment yet, that's all."

"And why aren't we?"

"Because we haven't arrived."

He frowned at her. "Arrived where?"

"Socially. We haven't arrived. And besides, you can't afford the kind of place that—well . . ."

He finished it for her. "That we should rent if we do arrive? Is that it?"

"Yes."

He frowned again. "Rachel, what difference does any of that make? I'm a doctor—a young one, not out in practice on my own yet, and frankly, when I am, I hope I'm not going to live a life that's all parties and entertaining and Charity Balls, because that's not all that important to me."

"Well, it is to me. You want to hold me down. You want to put me in a little bit of a dinky apartment and make me have babies, and I just don't want that, Russ. I want to be somebody. I want to be important in this town. And you haven't been any help there either, but I've been getting to be more important even without it. I'm getting to the point where the best people are ready to accept me. And I'm not going to have you spoil it by putting me in the kind of place that—that—"

Once again he finished it for her. "That a husband and wife could be happy in, is that it? You want some kind of showplace—and a husband who'll provide all the money that's needed to keep it up? Is that it, Rachel?"

"I don't want to be a nobody. I want to be somebody. Everybody thinks I don't know anything."

He shook his head. "Nobody thinks that."

"You do."

"No, I don't, Rachel." He moved to sit beside her on the bed, held out his arms to her, and—somewhat surprisingly, because there had been very little physical contact between them since she'd come home from the hospital—she let him take her in his arms. "I just think you haven't decided yet which things are important and which things aren't, that's all."

"I know what's important," she said, but she stayed in his embrace.

"The most important thing is for us to get a place of our own to live in."

Now she started to pull away. "Russ, don't start—"

Again he cut her off—and pulled her back to him.

"I know it's fun for you to go out with Walter and Lenore, and I like to do that too. And I know you think Steve Frame is very impressive. I'm impressed too." He smiled down at her. "Only I'm not very impressed. Just a little bit impressed."

His smile was as sweet as ever. That, and the soft smoothness of his voice, and the male closeness of him —it was all very tempting. And it had been so long since . . .

"And I know," he was saying, "you like canvassing for money for the Charity Ball. Okay. All these things are perfectly all right. But they're not the most important things in life."

"I never said they were." Maybe she would let him make love to her. After all, he was her husband. Maybe she even had to let him.

"You act as though they were, and that has got to stop." His voice was more firm than smooth now.

She frowned. "What do you mean?"

"I mean that you and I have got to settle down and lead our own lives. The two of us. Husband and wife. Walter and Lenore and Steve Frame and even your mother and my mother and my father and Alice— those are all people we like or love or are fond of, and we're interested in what they do and what happens to them, and we hope they're interested in us and are fond of us. But they're out there somewhere." He drew her more closely to him, making a circle of his arms. "Here there's only you and me. Understand?"

She nodded. "I guess so." She could feel his heart starting to beat harder. Maybe . . .

"This is the center. This is the core. This is the root of everything. From this everything grows. Do you know what I'm talking about?"

She nodded again. "I think so." Maybe she should settle for . . .

"Please understand, Rachel. It's so important."

He bent to kiss her, but she pulled away. No. She wouldn't settle for this. Not any more. Not when she could have so much more than he was willing to give her. "I understand only—"

He pulled her back to him, looking upset. "Don't you even want me to kiss you?"

"Russ, of course I do," she protested.

"Do you know how long it's been since we really kissed each other?"

She supposed now he would insist upon it. He probably thought he had the right to force her into it. "Well," she said, stalling for time. "We're always arguing lately, it seems like."

"Then let's not argue any more," he said.

"All right," she agreed. "I don't want to argue." He had loosened his grip on her, and she pulled back a little from him.

"That's more like it." Once more he bent to kiss her, but this time she slipped out of his grasp and stood up. He didn't reach for her but simply sat where he was on the bed, looking up at her, a frustrated expression on his face. "Rachel," he said, "I think I'm a patient man. I'm trying to be. But there are limits to any husband's patience. You know that, don't you? You understand what I'm saying?"

She understood very well. In fact, Rachel understood her situation—where she was, where she was headed, what she might win, and what she might lose —far better at that particular time than Alice understood her own situation.

The day Steve stalked out of the hospital cafeteria saying if she changed her mind about seeing him to give him a call, Alice thought it was just a remark made in anger, not something to be taken seriously. But as the days and then the weeks went by and she heard nothing from him, she began to realize he had meant what he said.

Several of her friends suggested she call him. Her own brother suggested she call him, but she said too much time had gone by for them to get back together now, and anyhow she wasn't sure she wanted to.

She said to Lenore, "You know he interfered in a private matter between Russ and Rachel, and I think that's unconscionable. But it isn't only that. It's his whole attitude. He's got a thing about being a strong man. I'm not sure I like it."

"Well, but surely," Lenore protested, "you wouldn't want him to be a weak man."

"No," Alice agreed, "but there must be something in between, mustn't there? A man shouldn't be tough all the time. He's got to be tender, too."

"All right," Lenore said, "but don't you think part of the problem is you—that you're too proud to take the first step on your own and call him as he asked you to?"

"Maybe. And maybe not. Look, Lenore, I don't have any hold on Steven, and he doesn't have any hold on me. We went out together, we had some good times together, we liked each other, and now it's finished. Over. The end. Fade-out."

"I see," Lenore said after a bit. "But you don't sound very happy about it."

Alice shrugged. "I'm just telling you how it is."

But Lenore would not be put off. "You're not happy about it, are you?"

Alice looked at her, then said, "Lenore, if you weren't one of my best friends I wouldn't say this. But no, I'm not happy about it. Not at all."

To her sister, Pat, Alice confided that not only did she like Steve a lot, maybe she liked him too much for her own good. And maybe it was better that she not see any more of him.

"Darling," her sister said, "don't you realize that when there is this feeling between a man and a girl it's too precious, too rare to be treated lightly?"

"I'm not treating it lightly."

"But not seeing him, not going near him or anything —you could lose him, Alice, and it just might turn out that you'd lost the most important thing in life. A man who loves you."

"Maybe," Alice said. "But the thing is, I'm not sure Steven is the man who can make me happy."

"But what if he is," Pat said, "and you lose him. Then what? Don't you think you'll spend the rest of your life wondering if maybe everything could have been different if you just hadn't been so stubborn?"

Alice gave her sister a troubled look. "Maybe. And maybe I'm being stubborn because I'm afraid to find out that Steven is the man I want—the man who could make me happy. Because once I find that out, then I couldn't back down or run away, now could I?"

Having taken Alice to task about pride, Lenore now did the same to Steve.

"Are you trying to tell me," he said, "that my pride is keeping me from asking Alice to take me back?"

"Well," Lenore answered, "I don't know exactly how things stood between you and Alice, and it's certainly none of my business, but . . ." Her voice trailed off.

"Then I'll tell you, Lenore. I don't know how Alice felt, but I was thinking very seriously of asking her to marry me. Until she tried to change me. I'm not a man who can be changed."

Lenore's eyebrows shot up. "Are you really so inflexible?"

Steve nodded. "I guess I am. Oh, I know Alice would be a wonderful wife, and I've thought for quite some time now I ought to get married. I'm no kid any more. And that's why I was taking Alice out a lot. However, maybe it's just as well I never got around to proposing, because—"

Lenore interrupted him. "Steve, forgive me, but you talk about marriage the way you would about a business deal."

It wasn't the first time Steve had heard that criticism, but still he challenged it. "Do I?"

"I think so. This deal happened to fall through, but maybe it's just as well. Maybe it wasn't such a good deal after all. That's the way you sound."

He shrugged. "Not very romantic, huh? All right. But that's how I am."

In a way, Russ and Alice propelled Rachel and Steve toward each other, though unwittingly. By refusing to make the first move toward a reconciliation with Steve, Alice was—in Steve's opinion—demonstrating that she was in fact what he had always believed her to be, what had attracted him to her in the first place: unattainable. A man who was always reaching up, who had become accustomed to getting what he went after, he was frustrated and angered that Alice was eluding him, yet he was damned if he would crawl to her.

As for Russ, in trying to make Rachel see what mattered and what didn't matter, in trying to help her mature, in trying to preserve their marriage by being as patient and understanding as he could be, he only succeeded in convincing her of what she wanted to be convinced of: that she was misunderstood, mistreated, and despised.

When Russ learned from his Aunt Liz that Rachel had had lunch with Steve at the Top of the Tower, he was hurt that Rachel had kept it from him, saying that everybody in and out of the family had known about it except her husband. "I know how much Aunt Liz and the Charity Ball and Steve Frame and the Top of the Tower and collecting money from all those rich people—I know how much all that stuff means to you, Rachel."

"What's wrong with all that stuff?" she flared back at him.

"Nothing," he replied, sounding as reasonable as he could, "only you go at it as though you want to make it your whole life. You get all thrilled by it. I know you do. I've seen you. I've seen what you're like. And I think you mentioned having lunch with Steve Frame because you thought it would impress Aunt Liz."

She was staring at him, wide-eyed. "Oh, that's the most terrible thing you've ever said to me. Ever."

He spread his hands. "Honey, it's not so terrible. Really it isn't. If you'll only stop to think about it."

"I don't have to stop and think about it," she snapped, "thank you very much. It is definitely the worst thing you've ever said to me. How can you even think such a thing?" She shook her head. "Don't bother to answer, because I know it's Alice."

He looked at her, bewildered. "What's Alice? What are you talking about?"

"Never mind. I know what Alice thinks of me, and don't think I don't. Besides, she's jealous."

He looked more bewildered than before. "Rachel, Alice hasn't got a jealous bone in her body."

She sighed—a long, drawn-out, exasperated sigh. "Oh, there you go again. Alice can do no wrong. Your whole family can do no wrong. Only me. And every single little tiny thing I do is wrong."

Unable to follow her from one accusation to the next, Russ started out of their room, but she grabbed his arm. "Don't you walk away from me. You wanted to talk. All right. We'll talk. I have some things to say too. I'm not just going to sit here and take a lot of abuse from you. Alice is jealous because Steve doesn't call her up any more. She's jealous, and your family is upset because she lost him."

Russ was staring at her. "Have you ever once heard any member of this family say anything about Alice seeing Steve or not seeing him, either for or against? Have you?"

"I don't have to hear them," Rachel answered. "I can tell they're very upset about it. For a while there your mother was rushing to the phone, breaking her neck every time it rang, hoping it was Steve calling Alice."

"All right. If she did it was because she thought Alice might be unhappy that Steve didn't call her, and that is all. All she was concerned about was Alice's happiness."

Rachel sniffed. "Plus a few other things."

"Like what?"

"Oh, just things."

"You're going to have to do better than that, Rachel. What things?"

"All right. Like losing Steve Frame for a son-in-law."

He was staring at her again. "Do you really think my father and mother care about that?"

"Why wouldn't they? A man like Steve."

Russ shook his head. "You're the one who cared about that, Rachel. Nobody but you."

Rachel sniffed again. "Your Aunt Liz did, too. She thought Alice was all kinds of a fool to let Steve get away from her."

"Don't tell me what Aunt Liz thought."

"Why not? She's part of your family—the great Matthews family."

"She married my father's brother. That doesn't make her part of my family."

"I see," Rachel said. "And what about me? Am I part of your family?"

Russ frowned. "What are you talking about?"

"I thought maybe I was an outsider too. Goodness knows, that's the way I feel most of the time."

Russ was back to looking bewildered. "You don't mean that. You can't."

"I do mean it," she said. "I'm all alone here. The rest of you ignore me. You make fun of everything I say. You don't like anything I do. You all hate me."

He stared at her for a long time without saying anything. Finally he sighed. "I just don't know what to say to you, Rachel. It's all so wrong, so ridiculous."

She even managed to twist that around. "See?" she said. "That's what I mean. Everything I say is ridiculous. Well, let me tell you something, Russ Matthews. Everybody doesn't think I'm stupid and wrong and unattractive. There are a few people who think I'm very smart and attractive and who like to spend time with me."

He frowned again. "What are you talking about now?"

"I'm talking about plenty of people."

"Who? Steve Frame maybe?"

She tossed her dark head. "Well, all right, yes. He's my friend. He helps me. He doesn't put me down all the time. He helped me with the canvassing, and he's helped me in lots of ways, because he likes me, he's my friend."

"Yes, so you keep saying."

Unable to reason with Rachel about what was important and what was not, Russ took a firmer stand. The following day he informed her that from now on he was going to make the decisions. She was to cut out all her canvassing for the Charity Ball or anything else for the time being. She could go back to it later if she wanted to, after they had set their own house in order. In any event, she wouldn't have the time to give it, because they would be moving very soon now into their own apartment, and she would have to get used to taking care of it: cooking meals, making beds, sorting laundry, cleaning house, keeping a budget—all of the things wives customarily did.

"We got off on the wrong foot right from the start," he said. "I think it was my fault, because I loved you so much I didn't realize. But—well, anyway, that's the way it's going to be."

Appalled by this turn of events, Rachel accused Russ of being mean, of not caring a scrap for her, of being careless of her health and well-being. "Why did I ever get into this?" she stormed at him. "Why did I ever marry you? Why was I such a fool?"

To all of which he merely replied that one of the doctors at the hospital was moving to a new apartment because his wife was pregnant, and he and Rachel were going to go look at their present apartment the following afternoon.

Russ's unexpected firmness did more than drive Rachel up the wall. It drove her straight into Steve's arms. Or almost.

That same night Liz hosted a party, to which Alice and Steve and Russ and Rachel were invited. Steve went, hoping to reconcile with Alice, but she didn't come. Russ put in an appearance and then returned to the hospital, where he was on duty all night. Rachel persuaded Steve to dance with her and then insisted she had to see him privately; she couldn't have lunch with him because of what people would say, but later that night, when the rest of the Matthews family was in bed, she would take a cab to his apartment.

Steve's apartment occupied the penthouse floor of his office building and was reached by a private elevator that opened directly into the living quarters. Furnished by a decorator to cater to Steve's taste, the living room was very masculine and very modern in tone, with a steel-and-leather sofa and chairs and with glass coffee table and end tables. The lighting was indirect and controlled by dimmers. One entire wall was given over to stereo equipment, with a master console and various components. In addition to being masculine and modern, the living room said money, and that was the first message Rachel got from it—when she got over the private elevator opening right into the foyer of the apartment.

"But," she said, "anyone can come up and come right in."

"Not unless they have a key," he said. "Or get clearance from me via the intercom to the doorman."

"Oh." She looked around her. "What a fantastic place you have." She took a few more steps into it, then turned to him. "I bet you thought I wasn't going to show up, didn't you?"

He shrugged. He had changed from his party clothes to jeans and a turtleneck white wool fisherman's sweater. "The thought crossed my mind, but I should have realized you'd come." He held out his hands for her coat, and Rachel took it off and gave it to him. She was still wearing what she had worn to the party —a sleek black cocktail dress that hugged her figure and was cut very low in front. "You're a lot like me, Rachel," Steve went on as he hung her coat in the foyer closet. "You don't let anything stand in the way of what you want, do you?"

She didn't answer him but moved on into the living room, where she did some more admiring. "I can't believe it," she exclaimed. "It's absolutely gorgeous!"

He cocked his head at her. "You really think so? That's surprising. Most women don't like it at all."

Rachel turned to him, aghast. "Why?"

"They usually say it's too cold." He went to the glass-and-mirror bar adjoining the stereo wall to fix drinks for them.

Rachel joined him there, standing quite close to him as he poured the Scotch. "And is that why you like it?" she said in a teasing tone of voice. "Because it fits your image as a cold, ruthless businessman?"

He didn't move away from her, and when he handed her her drink and she managed to clasp his hand in hers while taking it, he let her do that, too. "I'm not always ruthless, Rachel." He took his hand away. "Or cold, either."

She raised her glass to him. "No, I bet you're not."

He responded to the salute, locked eyes with her for a few more moments, then moved away to break the mood. "Sit down," he said, indicating a chair. He sat on the sofa. "So now what did you want to see me about anyway? What was worth sneaking out this late at night for? You risk getting caught, you know."

She nodded. "Well, I told you I wanted to talk."

He waited. When she didn't go on, he said, "Yes. What about?"

"Well, about the things you've told me before— about how people ought to live their own lives."

"Yes, I know I told you that. So what's the problem?"

She made a face. "Russ is the problem. He wants us to move to our own apartment."

"Fine. What's wrong with that?"

Rachel made another face. "It's not fine, and everything's wrong with it. I can't take care of an apartment. I'd have to dust and mop floors and do dishes. I've been very sick. I was in the hospital—"

He cut her off with a laugh. "Oh, come on, Rachel. You sound like a schoolgirl trying to con the school nurse into sending you home so you can miss the exam. You're perfectly healthy."

"I'm not, Steve. Not really." She considered a moment, then changed her tack. "But all right. I'm not going to move into some dinky little apartment for Russ or anyone else. Oh, I want to move someday," she added hastily. "Nothing would give me greater pleasure than to kiss the rest of the Matthewses goodbye, but when I do I want a place like—well, like that fine house of Lenore's, with servants and the works."

Steve smiled. "Just like that, huh?"

"No, not just like that. I know it's going to take time."

"Not to mention money. Especially for the things you're talking about."

"Well," she said, "the money could start taking care of itself if only Russ wouldn't be so stupid. He doesn't have to be a resident. He could open an office to-morrow."

"As a general practitioner."

"Well, so what?" Rachel flared at him. "With the rich people I'm meeting now, thanks to you, I could bring him all kinds of patients."

Steve laughed again. "Rachel, rich people don't have just ordinary illnesses. They have the best money can buy. And they want specialists. And besides that, you really don't know any of these rich people you're talking about. You've just collected some money from them, that's all."

She was frowning at him. "Well, but that's important, isn't it?"

"Oh, sure. Every organization needs people to do the little odd jobs." There was a hardness in his voice now. "Look. You collected some money, but so what? Have you thought about what it's like up there in the big leagues? When you go to a luncheon and all the ladies start raising their hands and making pledges? Rachel, you've made a start. You've got your foot in the door. But you're still only on the outside looking in."

Rachel got up and came to sit beside him on the sofa. "Oh, but, Steve, Russ wants me to stay there. He wants to take away even my start. He says I have to give it all up, that I can't do any more canvassing, that I have to move into some awful little apartment." She moved a bit closer and turned to him, her eyes wide and anxious-looking. "Steve, that's why I came to see you. Because I value your advice." Tears shimmered on her lashes. "Because I need it."

He moved away from her. "Oh, come off it, Rachel. You need my advice about as much as you need a handkerchief for those fake tears of yours. Look. People like us don't waste time worrying about what other people think we should do. We know what we want and go after it, because we know that life's too short to worry about anyone else's sensibilities. When we see that golden ring we make sure we come up with it, because we know you just don't get that many chances."

"Oh, Steve," she said, wiping her eyes with the back of her hand, "that's so true, but—"

"And I'll tell you something else, Rachel. You came here tonight for the same reason you wanted me to take you to lunch that second time—because you wanted to defy everybody and show them all that you do what you want when you want, and you don't care what they think. I wouldn't be a bit surprised if deep down inside you were really hoping to get caught." He got to his feet and pulled her to hers. "Now go home before it's too late and you do get caught. For the things you want, it's better to deal from an offensive position rather than a defensive one."

She moved toward him, putting her hands on his arms. "But, Steve—"

He gently removed her hands and took her by the elbow. "I mean it, Rachel. You made a mistake now, and the game's all over." He started steering her to the elevator.

"All right, Steve. I guess you're right."

He went to the closet for her coat, then held it for her while she slipped into it.

Buttoning it, she turned to him, again standing close to him. "But I do want to thank you."

"For what?"

"For everything. For being the one person I can really talk to." She smiled. "We *are* a lot alike, aren't we?"

He raised an eyebrow. "Are we? How do you know I wasn't just saying all that because I knew it was what you wanted to hear?"

She shook her head. "Because you weren't. Because I know better. Because we *are* a lot alike."

For a moment he thought she was going to come into his arms whether they were open to her or not, but she turned and stepped into the elevator. "Good night, Steve," she said.

Almost in spite of himself he kissed his fingers and placed them on her cheek. "Good night, Rachel." Then he pressed the lobby button and closed the elevator door, already shaking his head at himself.

Chapter Ten

SHOPPING together one afternoon a few days later, Alice and Lenore stopped in a luncheonette for a cup of coffee, and the talk turned to the party at Liz's house, which Alice had not shown up for. Asked if she was happy at not giving Steve the satisfaction of seeing her there, Alice said, "Do I look happy?"

"No," Lenore said. "You don't."

Alice stirred sugar into her coffee. "Well, if my face gives me away so easily it's probably just as well I didn't show up."

She offered the sugar to Lenore, but Lenore declined it. "Alice, I can't pretend to always understand Steve. In many ways he's the most complex man I've ever met. But I do know he cares for you, and . . . well, the real trouble may be he just doesn't know what love is."

Alice took a swallow of coffee. "Then should I bother with him?"

Lenore sighed. "I may be wrong, you know. I probably am. But I do know you, and I know you do care. If that's so, then you mustn't let him walk out of your life without doing something about it—without at least sitting down and talking about it."

"In other words, you think I should call him."

Lenore took a sip of coffee. "Well, have you thought about it?"

"Only about once every two minutes. The rest of the time I'm wondering why he doesn't call me."

Lenore smiled. "Well, there's that pride of his."

Alice arched her eyebrows. "But I'm not supposed to have any."

"Oh, Alice," Lenore said, "I really wish I could tell

you what to do, but you know as well as I do you're the only one who can decide that."

"Yes, I know," Alice agreed. "And it's funny we should be talking about it like this now. You don't know how many times I looked at the phone in the kitchen this morning and almost picked it up to call him."

Lenore took another sip of coffee. "And why didn't you?"

Alice shook her head. "I don't know. Maybe because I still think it should be up to the man. And then again, maybe what I'm really afraid of is that the man just plain doesn't care."

She was handed the opportunity of finding out a few hours later, when she went home with Lenore and found Steve there having a drink with Walter.

In spite of his being on her mind so much of the time, she hadn't given much thought as to how she would feel if—when—if—she did see him again. Seeing him now, smiling, saying polite hellos to him and Walter, she felt she was holding her breath. Or that she was standing outside of herself, watching some other Alice go through the motions.

She heard herself agree to stay for a drink, and the next thing she knew, Lenore had somehow maneuvered Walter out of the room and she was alone with Steve.

"Well," he said, giving her a sideways glance, looking as if he might be holding his breath too, "I guess I could say long time no see."

She had forgotten the funny side of him. She smiled. "Yes, I guess you could say that. It's a really nifty line."

He colored a little. "Look, Alice, I didn't know you were coming by."

She wished she didn't feel so brittle—like a piece of glass that might shatter at any moment. "And I didn't know you were going to be here when I did."

They seemed to have run out of things to say.

"Alice," he said after a bit, "we don't have to go around making a point of avoiding each other, do we?"

"Not as far as I'm concerned. No."

"Then, fine," he said. "Here we are."

She nodded. "Yes. Here, as you say, we are."

Once again they stood silent. And once again he finally came up with something. "Alice, I'm not about to back down on any of my principles, but . . . well, don't you think this is all just a little silly? I mean, to let things get out of hand the way they did. I don't see any reason why we can't sit down and try to talk things out. Do you?"

Alice shook her head. "No, Steven, but you'd have to understand I'm not about to back down on my principles either."

He laughed, and suddenly everything began to seem all right again. "I never thought for a minute you would, but at least we can sit down and talk like adults."

She smiled. "And then the next time we quarrel we'll be able to do it with dignity."

He laughed again. "How about dinner tonight?"

"I'm sorry, I can't. I'm on duty at the hospital."

So that, for the time being, was that. But at least, as Alice put it to Pat a few days later, she and Steve were talking and being pleasant again, the matter of his having interfered in Russ and Rachel's private affairs forgiven and forgotten—though, as she also put it, the real problem between herself and Steve had been and still was that Steve didn't want her to have a point of view that might possibly differ from his.

On Alice's first day back on the day shift Steve appeared at the nurses' station on the dot of twelve to take her to lunch, saying he could have waited forever before she would have called him to let him know her nights were now free. He had had to ferret out the information from somebody else.

"The man is supposed to call the girl," she said as they stepped into the elevator and started down to the basement, where the hospital cafeteria was located.

"Oh, come on," Steve said. "That idea is old-fashioned."

"It may be," Alice said, "but that's the way I was brought up."

He shook his head. "I don't believe it. It doesn't go with the rest of you. You're so honest, so forthright, so independent. You earn your own living, you form your own opinions—and defend them like a tigress, I might add. You ask nothing from anybody. Then all of a sudden it's 'the man is supposed to call the girl.' It's incongruous."

The elevator arrived at the basement, and they stepped out and headed for the cafeteria. "But anyhow," he added, "I'm glad we ran into each other at Walter and Lenore's. If only because it broke the ice."

There was a line ahead of them in the cafeteria. They picked up trays and joined it. "We've both been silly," he went on to say. And, when she said nothing in reply: "Come on, Alice, give a little. Don't make me take all the blame."

She smiled at him. "What if I say you're nice and I'm glad you showed up today?"

He beamed. "Beautiful." And added, "So am I."

While Alice and Steve were getting back on a better footing, relations between Russ and Rachel were rapidly deteriorating. When she refused to go look at the apartment he had heard about at the hospital, he went to see it and rented it. When she refused to look at furniture, he asked Pat and Alice to look at some for them. And when she further refused to go with him to see what his sisters had picked out for them, he did a little storming of his own.

"I'm fed up," he said. "Fed up with your brushing off the whole business of taking an apartment and furnishing it and moving into it. I found the apartment. I've paid two months' rent on it. I've had to get Alice and Pat to help shop for furniture, because you wouldn't. But now get it straight, Rachel. We are going to buy furniture. We are going to have it sent to that apartment. And next week we're going to move in, because that's when the lease starts. And don't tell me you can't. You can and you will."

Because she had no choice, Rachel went with Russ to look at the furniture, but the moment he left her to go back to the hospital, she hotfooted it over to Steve's office, where another kind of storm had just erupted.

Steve had asked Alice to a party, and she had

accepted. But then the party was switched to another night—a night on which Alice was scheduled to go to dinner and the ballet with a resident at the hospital. Upset at having to break her date with Steve, but feeling that was her only choice, Alice called him at his office to explain. Not only did he not take kindly to her explanation, he was—it seemed to her—totally unreasonable about it.

When told of her date for the ballet, he said, "Break it."

"I can't," Alice said.

"Of course you can," Steve countered. "But you don't want to, is that it?"

"No, that's not it. Steven, I'm terribly sorry, but—"

He cut in on her. "I don't want to hear how sorry you are. I want you to break whatever date you have and go to that party with me the way you said you would."

"I can't," she said again. "Steven, listen—"

"No. You listen," he said, starting to get angry. "What happened to all those things we were saying to each other the other day at lunch—about starting to see each other again, finding out about each other, discovering where we're alike and where we're different. What happened to all that?"

She started to say something, but he didn't wait.

"I think we've made a little progress. I think we've found out one big important way we're different. We made a date. I can't think of anything on this earth that would have prevented me from keeping that date with you—not a thing. But with you, an invitation to go to the ballet is apparently enough. Well, thanks a lot. Now I know exactly where I stand." And he slammed down the phone.

A knock on the door, and in came Rachel.

Still angry and upset about Alice, he hardly saw or heard her, but finally he took the coat she held out to him and sat her down in one of his big leather armchairs, where she immediately started in on how everybody was giving her a hard time again.

"Steve," she said, "I can't tell you how awful it is. If I couldn't talk to you, I think I'd die."

"All right," he said, with a sigh. He sat down behind his desk. "Tell your Uncle Steve all about it. Now what is it?"

"It's the whole Matthews family," she said, reiterating her accusation that they were plotting to get her out of their house. "They walk all over me. Honestly they do. They decide what's best. They decide what's going to happen. Then they go ahead and do it, just like that. And I'm supposed to smile and say, thank you, aren't you sweet to me, and all the time burning up, because I'm not grateful, I don't think they're sweet, and it's not what I want."

Rachel got up from the chair and paced back and forth in front of his massive desk. "Steve, you've said it so often. The thing is to know what you want and go after it, right? It's true, isn't it? It's not right to let people push you around, is it? And that's what the whole Matthews family is doing to me. All of them. They're all alike. Always talking about their values, their principles, their whatever, as though I didn't have any values or principles at all."

She stopped her pacing and came to the side of his desk and put her hands on it, leaning toward him. "Do you think I'm wrong, Steve?"

He didn't answer her at once, but sat looking at her, his dark, brooding eyes on her face, his right hand inches from one of her own. "No," he said at last, "I don't think you're wrong."

Rachel smiled. "Thank goodness, because you're about the only friend I have in the world." She touched his hand, then picked it up and squeezed it. "You think I'm exaggerating, but I'm not. It really is as bad as that."

Steve stood up, and Rachel made a half-mock gesture of tugging him toward her. Then she released his hand. He stroked her hair. "Poor little Rachel," he said, maybe kidding and maybe not. "Poor little kid."

She bridled a bit. "You don't have to feel sorry for me. I'll show them. I'll get even with them."

He was still looking at her in that intense, brooding way of his, and excitement skittered through her. "Is that what you want?" he asked.

She lifted her chin. "It's part of it."

"What else?"

The excitement in her intensified. "Other things." She smiled her most seductive smile. "Wonderful things. Marvelous things. Exciting, wonderful things. I'm going to get them, too."

He hadn't moved. "You sure?"

She took a step toward him, until her body was almost touching his. Lifting her face to him, she said, "I'm going to try."

He put his hands behind her neck, brought her face to his, and kissed her, slowly, deliberately, hard.

Abruptly he let her go and moved away, a look of dismay on his face.

"Are you sorry you did that?" Rachel said, the excitement churning in her.

"I don't know," he said. "I know I ought to be. And you ought to be too, Rachel. And I think you should go away and think that over."

But Russ seemed to be the only one in that duo who was doing any thinking. Seeking advice from John Randolph on how to cope with Rachel's resistance to moving into a home of their own, he said, "She acts like a little girl. She thinks like a little girl. She feels like a little girl. She just wants to get her own way in everything. She doesn't listen to a word I say. The only voice Rachel hears is her own."

The day the furniture was delivered to the new apartment Rachel condescended to be there to let the deliverymen in, but that was about the extent of her endeavor, and when Russ came home in the middle of the afternoon to help her unpack, she told him he was the one who had wanted the apartment; well he could have it, she was going out.

Where she went, of course, was back to Steve's office. He wasn't very pleased to see her, saying there was nothing he could do for her and stop whining.

She burst into tears. "I was a fool to come here.

You're like everybody else. No one cares. My feelings don't count at all. Everybody pushes me around."

He reached in his pocket for a handkerchief and handed it to her. "That's not true, Rachel. People do care. But you keep making problems for yourself."

She wiped her eyes and sniffed, then shook out the folded handkerchief and blew her nose. "Why do I always have to be the one to give in? Russ takes advantage of me. And after all, you're the one who's always saying—"

"What I've said, Rachel, about going after what you want is good for me but not necessarily for you. You and I are different. There are a couple of important differences. I've never once lied or cheated to get what I wanted. I drive a hard bargain, and I don't offer many concessions, but if I don't get what I want, I don't stand around crying about it. I just go out and start all over again somewhere else."

She handed the handkerchief back to him, and he stuffed in in his pocket. "The difference," he went on, "is you're a schemer. And while I'll walk away from something that doesn't pan out, you'll hang on just as long as you can, trying to have your cake and eat it too."

She started to protest, but he shook his head. "It's true, and I can prove it. You say you don't want to move, and the answer is simple. Don't."

"But I can't," she said. "It's what Russ wants."

Steve raised an eyebrow. "And if you don't move, you're liable to lose him, right?"

She nodded. "Yes."

"And you're not ready for that, are you? At least, not yet."

"I don't know what you mean," she said, frowning. "You make it sound as though I don't love Russ. And of course I do."

He gave her a skeptical look. "How much and for how long? For richer, for poorer, till death do you part, or just until someone better comes along?"

"Oh, Steve," she said, "you make me out to be a terrible person. Someone who lies and cheats. Someone who's selfish. But it's Russ who's selfish. He's trying to change my entire life. No time for working on committees. No time for friends. He wants to coop me up in some tiny apartment. He didn't even like it that I had a couple of perfectly innocent lunches with you at the Top of the Tower."

Steve shrugged. "I'm afraid there's not much I can do about it."

"Oh, but there is." She came up to him and clasped his arms, her face close and pleading. "Please don't leave me, Steve. I'm so alone and so helpless."

He drew her to him and held her close. "I know," he murmured, "I know."

"Help me. Please help me," she said against his chest. Then she lifted her face to his.

For a few minutes they simply stayed that way, looking at each other. Then he kissed her as he had before: slowly, deliberately, hard.

"Oh, Steve," she said, clinging tightly to him. "Oh, please, oh, please."

But he pulled away from her, and before she had a chance to do anything the phone rang.

He answered it, said, "Put him on," and began talking about some business deal. Rachel tried to interrupt him, gesturing to him to call the man back. He said, "Excuse me a sec," and covered the mouthpiece with one hand. "Rachel," he said, his voice now as hard as his kiss had been, "the first kiss meant nothing, and this one doesn't either. You're a married woman. You've got a husband. Go home to him. I'm sorry, Rachel, but that's the way it is."

He went back to his phone call, and after another moment she left the office.

Because she had nowhere else to go, Rachel went back to the hated new apartment, where she promptly got into a fight with Russ, who had made the mistake of trying to make love to her.

"Just because you finally trapped me into living here," she said, "I'm not going to be some tired old thing slopping around in some housecoat, trailed by a bunch of dirty kids." And when he moved toward her she screamed, "Don't touch me! Don't touch me! I mean it! Leave me alone!"

If there was any surprise in it for Russ, it could only have been her vehemence. Using one excuse or another, she hadn't allowed him to make love to her for some weeks now.

When he came home from the hospital the next evening she was gone. She had left a note: "Russ, I'm going away. I don't know when I'll be back. There's something I've got to do. I can't tell you what it is, because you wouldn't understand. Just the way you've never understood how I feel. Rachel."

She was gone for several days, and though Russ had no idea where she had gone or what she had gone for, he covered for her to family and friends, saying she was shopping or she was at the movies or wherever, confiding only in her mother.

Ada had no more idea where Rachel was than Russ did. Maybe she should have. The day before Rachel left she had pestered Ada for some word of her father's whereabouts, accusing Ada of having driven him out of the house. Ada said she hadn't driven him out, he had left of his own accord, and since he hadn't bothered to get in touch with either one of them for over twenty years, Rachel should forget him. But Rachel claimed she couldn't.

But then, Rachel had had these conversations with her mother before, wondering where her father was. So it didn't occur to Ada that Rachel was at long last doing something about trying to find him.

When she returned, she told her mother she had gone to Evansville, a town some five hundred miles south of Bay City. In the courthouse there she had found a record of her father's birth on April 20, 1924. She hadn't known before when his birthday was—or that her father had been born in Evansville. The hunch that had sent her there came from the name and address of the photographic studio stamped on the back of the picture of her father that Ada had come across that day.

"What else did you find out?" Ada asked.

Rachel started crying. "Nothing. That's all. Just his birthday. I walked all over Evansville trying to find somebody maybe who'd known him, but nobody'd ever heard of him."

"And what about the studio? The photographer?"

"It isn't there any more. Nobody knew anything about that either."

Ada put an arm around Rachel. "Honey, I'm sorry."

Rachel nodded and wiped her eyes with the back of her hand. "Next I went to the Army camp in Fairchester, a few miles away from Evansville. I thought maybe they'd have records or something. But they didn't have anything." She shook her head. "It was a dumb thing to do. For all I know, he wasn't ever in the Army. Oh, Mom, I don't know anything about him—except his name. Gerald Davis. And now his birthday and his birthplace. For all the good that did me. That's why I came back. I didn't have any more money, and I couldn't think of anyplace else to look."

To Russ she wouldn't say anything about where she had been, but claimed he was probably glad she went, good riddance, he probably hoped she'd never come back at all. To demonstrate that he didn't feel that way, he told her how he had covered for her to save her embarrassment, but she turned that back on him, too, saying he was only trying to protect himself. And when Russ persisted in trying to find out where she had been, Rachel finally said, "All right. I'll tell you. I went chasing after another man, that's where I went. You wanted to know, so now you know. I went looking for another man. But don't you fret, dear husband, because I didn't find him. He wasn't there. How do you like that for luck? I looked all over, and he wasn't there."

It didn't add to Rachel's joy that several telephone calls to Steve did her no good either. He was in conference and couldn't be disturbed. When she left word for him to call her back, he didn't. But Rachel was not easily deflected. One evening a few days later she left another note for Russ: "Don't blow your top. I'll be back. Probably tonight." And off she went, chasing after the man she really hoped to catch.

Steve was home in his apartment, exhausted after a few days of nonstop grueling work. Stretched out on the steel-and-leather sofa, dressed in jeans and sweater, working on his third martini, he wasn't particularly pleased when the doorman buzzed him to say that Mrs. Matthews was there to see him, but he told the doorman to send her up.

Rachel complained about his not returning her calls and then made up an outrageously transparent story about Russ running out on her in the midst of a discussion.

"So after Russ ran out," he said dryly, "you ran out, is that it?"

"Well, I came here, yes." She was wearing a black sweater and pants that fit her like skin. And she had headed straight for the couch when she came in, curling up on it, taking his place, leaving him no choice but to drop into one of the leather chairs and stretch out in that. Lord, he was tired. "I started to call you," she went on, "but I was afraid you wouldn't talk to me."

He shook his head. "Have I ever refused to talk to you?"

She had the grace to look ashamed. Then she leaned forward and reached across to the chair to put her hands on his. "I couldn't stand it if you ever did. Honest, Steve, I couldn't."

He pulled his hand away and took a sip of his martini. Liquid fire was more like it. "It's been my experience," he said, "that we can stand a lot more than we think we can. Rachel, do you really think you should be here?"

For answer she lay back against the sofa pillows, curling up again like a lithe and graceful cat.

"I'm exhausted," he said.

She looked distressed. "I wish I could do something to help you."

Yes, I'm sure, he thought. And I know how.

"I'll make you another drink," she offered.

"I don't need another drink. I've had more than enough already."

"Have you had any dinner?"

He put up a hand. "Rachel, don't start bustling around making scrambled eggs. When I feel like eating, I'll eat."

She smiled her Cleopatra smile. "Whatever you say."

In spite of himself, he was drawn to her. Aroused by her. He shouldn't have let her come up here.

"It sounds to me," he said, "as though your marriage to Russ is on the rocks. What are you going to do about it?"

"I don't know. What do you think I should do? If you'd tell me what to do, I'd do it." The smile again. "I mean it."

He looked at her for some time without saying anything. He was tired, he'd had three drinks, she was lovely. She was also available—she'd made that clear enough. He held out his hand to her, and she took it. Pulling her down onto his lap, he kissed her. She clung to him, pushing her body against his, returning his kiss with such passion that it was almost overwhelming.

Maybe for her, too, because this time it was she who broke away, looking at him like a startled fawn. "Oh, Steve," she said in a breathless little voice. "Oh, Steve. What have we done?"

He might have known. If he wasn't careful she was going to get him in trouble one of these days. "We haven't done anything," he said, unwrapping her arms from around his neck, pushing her to her feet, sitting her down on the couch, sitting up straight in his own chair.

"Oh, Steve," she said again. "I don't know."

He must look bleary-eyed. He felt it. And bleary-brained as well. "Don't know what?"

She smiled the Cleopatra smile. "I don't know what to think of us. I mean, you just kissed me, and . . . well, I mean, what are we doing? What are we getting into?"

"Rachel," he said, "we did not go off to Atlantic City for the weekend. All I did was kiss you."

"And if I'd stayed there on your lap you would have kissed me again. What are we getting into?"

"The answer is nothing."

She was back to looking distressed. "How can you say nothing? You were just saying my marriage is on the rocks. You said that, and then you kissed me."

He made a face. "I get it. Okay. And I'll kiss you again, Rachel, and it will mean nothing. Understand?"

She did not answer him, but merely said, "I'm going home."

He finished his drink. "If you're looking for this to mean more than it does, Rachel, then I guess you'd better."

When Rachel got home Russ was asleep. The next morning at breakfast he asked her where she had been. She smiled and said she had gone to the same place she went the last time she went looking for a man, but this time her ploy didn't work.

"I know you've been using this business of looking for a man," he said, "just to get a rise out of me. But I know who you were looking for. Your father."

"That's not true."

"Rachel, your mother told me."

"Well, she shouldn't have. It's none of your business."

"But it is, Rachel. Don't you see? If I'd only known—"

"What would you have done?" she said. "Gone with me?"

He shook his head. "No. I would have shown you I understand. I wouldn't have gone with you, because I don't think running off was the proper way to start looking for your father."

She sniffed. "Then what is, Mr. Know-it-all?"

About to take a swallow of coffee, Russ put the cup down. "Rachel, why are you acting this way when I'm only trying to help?"

"I don't want your help. I didn't even want you to know about it."

Russ frowned. "Why? So you could keep on telling me a story about looking for a man? So you could use it just to make me jealous? Rachel, I don't want to believe that."

But she wouldn't relent. "Nobody's asking you to," she said. "Nobody's asking you for anything."

He eyed her a moment. "I understand about your father. I know it's important to you to find him. I want to help. Believe me, I do."

She looked at him coldly across the table. "How could you help?"

"I don't know, but—"

"There," she cut in on him. "You see? Big help."

"Honey," he said, "please let me finish. Look, I'm no expert in these things, but I do know there has to be a better way than just running off aimlessly."

She made a face. "Oh, sure. Because that's dumb, right?"

"Rachel," he said, ignoring her response, "there are people who specialize in finding missing people."

Her eyes widened. "And you'd hire someone like that for me?"

"I don't know how much it might cost—"

"Then why even bother," she said contemptuously, cutting in on him again. "All you have to do is look around, and you can see how little we can afford."

"Rachel, that's not the point. We can at least look into it and see how much it would cost. The only thing is, I think you have to consider that finding your father may not mean all the things you want it to."

She sniffed again. "How do you know what I think?"

"I don't want you to be disappointed, that's all. It's been years since he left your mother. He never tried to get in touch with her or you. I'm trying to be understanding."

"Don't bother," she said, stung. "I told you I don't need your help or your understanding or anything. Just forget you ever heard about my father. All right?"

Russ finished his coffee and got up from the table, saying he had to go to work. At the door he turned back to her. "It doesn't make any sense to talk to you about this. It's apparent that all you want to do is fight, and I'm sorry, but I'm not in the mood for that." And he walked out of the kitchen.

"Russ Matthews," she yelled after him, "don't you

tell me what I want to do, and don't you walk out on me when I'm—"

The door to their apartment slammed shut.

As might be expected, Rachel went straight to Steve.

A few days earlier Steve had called Jim to say he was merging with an international firm whose headquarters were in Los Angeles, and he would like to engage Jim to do a complete audit of the firm's books. It would mean trips to the West Coast, to South America, Japan, and Western Europe. Delighted at the opportunity the job offered, Jim accepted, and he was at this moment closeted with Steve in his private office.

Waiting for Steve in his outer office, Rachel beamed with pleasure when Steven emerged to tell a salesman who was waiting for him that he wouldn't be able to see him that day.

When the salesman had gone Rachel said, "Steve, I'm sorry. Please don't be angry, but I had to see you."

"All right," he said brusquely, "you've seen me. Look. Do you have any idea who's in that office right now?" He jerked his head toward the inner office. "Your father-in-law. Any second now he might think of some question he wants to ask me and open that door and stick his head out. Is that what you want?"

Rachel's smile had vanished. "No, of course not. But, Steve—" She caught at his arm. "You can't be cruel to me. Not after last night. You know what I mean." She smiled again. "We were closer than we've ever been."

He grunted. "Not that close."

"We almost were," she insisted. "Almost. Steve, last night you told me my marriage was falling apart. You as much as suggested that I should end it."

"Rachel," he said, removing her hand from his arm, "if you want to end it, all you have to do is go over there and open that door. You know what will happen if your husband hears you were stopping by and asking for my advice again? Is that what you want?"

Up went Rachel's chin in that defiant mannerism she had. "Yes, maybe it is." She walked over to the door and put her hand on the knob, giving him a taunting look. "Shall I do it?"

If she had hoped to make him nervous, she failed. All he said was, "It's up to you, baby. You're the one who's risking everything, not me."

She looked at him a moment, then took her hand off the knob.

He strode over to her, moved her aside, then said, "Okay, now that that's settled, let's get something else straight. If you've got to prove something, prove it some other time." Then he opened the door, went into his inner office, and closed the door behind him.

Steve had been brusque with Rachel partly because he didn't like the idea of her continually turning up un-announced—and unexpected—at his office, partly because he did have more important things to do than act as her marriage counselor or wailing wall, and partly because there were other dangers in having her around than that her father-in-law might find her there.

But there was still another factor. If Steve had been unreasonable about the broken date with Alice, it was now Alice's turn to be unreasonable.

Chapter Eleven

WITHIN a day or two of getting Jim's acceptance of his job offer, Steve called back to say things were breaking even faster than he had expected and Jim would have to be ready to leave for the West Coast in twenty-four hours, from there to go on to Japan, Western Europe, and South America.

The call had come to the Matthews house early in the morning, while the family was at breakfast. After telling Mary and Alice what the call was all about, Jim said, "The type of operation Steve is involved in,

I guess it's not uncommon that decisions have to be made in a hurry."

"Yes, I know," Alice said, a set look on her face. "It's the same way he runs his personal life."

"Darling," her mother said, concerned, "your father wants this job. It's a big opportunity for him."

"That's right," Jim agreed.

"Oh, don't mind me," Alice said, getting up from the table.

"Alice," her mother protested, "aren't you going to finish your—"

But Alice was already storming up the stairs.

Mary looked from Alice's breakfast plate to Jim. "I've never seen her act that way before."

"No," Jim said, "but then, you've never had Steven Frame call here before and never even ask for her, either."

That noon Lenore and Alice were having lunch in the hospital cafeteria, and Alice was telling Lenore about her father's departure the next day. "Rush, rush, rush," she said. "Big, big, big. Leave tomorrow. Be in Los Angeles, et cetera, et cetera."

Lenore smiled. "It sounds very jet-set."

Alice made a face. "It's very Steven Frame is what it is." She shook her head. "I still can't understand why he did it. Hired Dad, I mean."

"He needed a good accountant."

"But why pick Dad?"

"Because he's a good accountant." When Alice's expression didn't change, Lenore said, "Why don't you ask him?"

Alice stared at her. "Ask Steven?"

"Well, you are on speaking terms, aren't you?"

"Barely," Alice said. "But all right. I will ask him. As soon as I get back up on the floor."

Calling him at his office, Alice asked if she could meet him there when she got off work, but he said he would be tied up in a series of meetings until after six o'clock. Would she come to his apartment at six thirty? She agreed to do that so long as he understood that she wouldn't be staying for dinner.

On the dot of six thirty she got off the private elevator. Unlike Rachel, Alice didn't seem to notice any-thing about his apartment, let alone comment on the elevator or how it opened into his foyer.

In fact, she wasn't like Rachel in any way. Fair, ethereal, lovely, she made him want to wrap her in silk or velvet—whatever would keep her safe from the world. And safe in his arms.

With almost the force of a physical blow, it struck him what a fool he had been over their broken date. Alice had been absolutely right, and he had been ab-solutely wrong. And he was going to tell her so.

Only he didn't get the chance.

After the barest exchange of pleasantries she said, "Why did you send my father on that business trip?"

He frowned at her. "I don't understand what you're talking about."

"I just want to know why you picked my father to go off for heaven knows how long practically to the ends of the earth."

He was still frowning. "I needed an expert account-ant. And your father is a very knowledgeable man. Very astute." Despite himself, he was beginning to get angry. "You don't understand that, do you? To you he's dear old Daddy. You haven't got the faintest idea how he's managed to do all those things he's done for you."

From the look of her, she was beginning to get angry too. Lord, couldn't they say two words without being in disagreement about something?

"And did you have to spend his whole last evening at home talking business with him?" she snapped.

"Yes, I did."

"Even though his family might want to spend some time with him?"

"That's too bad," he said, trying to control his tem-per. "You're making me pretty angry, Alice. You know that?"

"And does he have to be gone for so long?" she asked, ignoring what he'd said.

"Because he has to," Steve answered. "That's why. That's how long I expect the job to take. Your father understands that. Why can't you?"

"The whole thing just seems—" She broke off and started over. "Steven, did you pick my father to impress me?"

"What kind of businessman do you think I am? I picked your father because he's good. I wasn't trying to do you or him a favor." He was boiling inside now. "I don't know why—"

The intercom buzzed, and he went over to speak into it. "Yes?"

"Miss Joan Shaw," the doorman said.

"All right. Send her up." He replaced the receiver and turned back to Alice. "I want you to meet a friend of mine. A very nice girl, who doesn't find hidden meanings in every little thing I say, who doesn't look for ulterior motives behind everything I do. A girl who just likes me. Rough, tough old me, the way I am, the way I've always been, and the way I'm going to go right on being."

The elevator door opened, and Joan stepped out. "Oh," she said. "I didn't know—"

"It's all right, Joan," Steve said. "I'd like you to meet Alice Matthews. Alice, Joan Shaw."

Alice said a stiff hello, then turned to him. "May I have my coat, please?"

"Certainly," he said and got it for her.

She put it on and with barely a glance at either of them—himself or a now somewhat bewildered-looking Joan—she said goodnight and stepped into the elevator and closed the door.

At about the same time, give or take a few minutes, Russ was discovering that Rachel had left him again—this time for good.

The previous night Russ had tried to talk to her once more about her father, saying he realized how much her father meant to her, how much he had always meant to her, even though she never knew him, how much she felt she needed him, and how he wanted to help her find him. But Rachel claimed she didn't need any help, and when in a further attempt to patch up their faltering marriage Russ wanted to make love to her, she put him off by saying she had taken a sleeping pill and was too sleepy.

The next day Russ came home from the hospital at noon to say that he'd taken some time off because they had to talk.

Rachel, still not dressed, said, "What was the idea of leaving me out here on the couch all night?"

"What was the idea of taking a sleeping pill?"

Instead of answering, she complained about how uncomfortable the couch was.

"I was trying to tell you," he said angrily, "that I'm beginning to understand you a little better. You have to give me credit for trying. But you don't want to understand. You don't even want to listen. I want to understand what your father means to you, what all your problems are—you know, against children, against moving, all that stuff. At least I did want to understand all that. Now I just don't know. Rachel, when a man wants to understand everything there is to understand about a woman, when he wants to help her solve every little problem, when he wants to know her the way he knows himself, so he can keep her safe from harm, that's when a man loves a woman. But I can't do it alone. It's just not possible."

She tossed her dark head. "Oh, I see. You think you're being understanding."

"I want to be," he answered. "But I've got to have help."

She frowned at him. "Are you trying to tell me our marriage is over?"

"I'm not sure we ever had a marriage."

"Oh, come on," she taunted him. "Tell me. You don't have to be afraid."

He shook his head. "I think that's up to you. I've tried to explain to you what I think a marriage should be, and I'm willing to make ours that kind of marriage. The rest is up to you. So think about it. I'll be home around six thirty, and when I get here I'd like to have some kind of answer."

The answer was there when he got home that night and found all her clothes and toilet articles gone, and a note that read: "I've thought it over, and this is the answer."

Rachel had gone to the home of her mother and Ernie Downs and moved in with them.

In some ways Russ was relieved. In telling a friend that Rachel had left him for good, he said he wasn't sure he wanted her back. "For one reason, I'm a doctor. People depend on me. I need to have my mind on my work. It hasn't affected me so far. I've been pretty careful. But I've got no guarantee how long I can keep that up."

Rachel stayed at her mother's house barely long enough to unpack. Then, showering, putting on black lingerie and the clingy black cocktail dress with the low-cut front—though it was long past the cocktail hour—applying lipstick and mascara with extra care, she headed for Steve's apartment, where he was just saying good night to Joan Shaw, the date who had interrupted his quarrel with Alice earlier that evening.

Steve introduced them, saying, "Joan, this is Rachel Matthews, who isn't going to get a chance to talk to me, because I'm a tired businessman who hasn't time for pretty girls who have to talk to him. Anyway, not this week."

He held the elevator door for both of them, but only Joan stepped into it. Rachel whispered to him, "I've left my husband." And when he said nothing: "Please, Steve. I've got to talk to you."

He sighed. "All right," he said. "Good night, Joan." He closed the elevator door, then led Rachel into the living room. "Come on. I'll get you a drink."

While he made the drink Rachel started blathering on again about what a marvelous place he had here and what fantastic taste he had, until he cut her off by saying a decorator had done it—and done it on his own. "You said you had to talk to me, Rachel." He handed her the drink. "What about?"

She held the drink up to him in a silent toast. "About leaving Russ. You told me to leave him, you know."

"I did no such thing." He tried not to look at her, but it was almost impossible. All of her clothes seemed to fit her like skin. "What I said was your marriage seemed to be very shaky at the moment, and you must admit your marriage has been looking pretty

shaky for quite a while. Even to the most casual observer."

Rachel curled up on the couch. He chose the chair
farthest away from her. "Is that what you are, Steve?"
she said. "A casual observer?"

He shrugged. If that dress was cut any lower in
front she'd be arrested for nudity. "Well, I'm an observer."

"But never casual." She smiled her Cleopatra smile,
and he began to feel uncomfortable. "You did tell me
I had to make up my mind. And so I did. I left Russ
for good. You're not sorry I did that, are you?" And
when he made no answer, she smiled again. "I even
hope you're a little bit pleased."

He finally found his voice. He never should have
permitted her to stay. He would ask her to leave. But
he found himself saying instead, "You left Russ even
though it means risking everything?"

Rachel made a face. "Risking what? A chance to
be part of the great Matthews clan? Steve, they look
down their noses at people like you and me."

He could still hear Alice saying, "Steven, did you
pick my father to impress me?" He got up to freshen
his own drink. "Maybe," he admitted.

He might have known Rachel wouldn't let it go at
that. She read him about as well as he read her.
"Nothing you and I could ever do would please them,"
she went on to say. "Look at all the money you've
spent on Alice. Look at what you've done for her father. Do you think she appreciates it?"

"No," he said. "No, I know she doesn't." On his
way back to the chair with his freshened drink, he
stopped by the sofa and looked down at Rachel. "Alice
was by here earlier tonight."

Rachel frowned. "She was? What did she want?"

From where he stood he could look right down her
front, see her curving flesh. He told himself to move,
but he stayed where he was. "It doesn't matter what
she wanted. The important thing is the whole thing is
over and done with." He took a swallow of the drink,
then set the glass down on an end table. "I guess you

could say it's been a good night for getting rid of Matthewses."

Rachel smiled and settled back against the sofa pillows, reminding him, as she had before, of a lithe and graceful cat. And—he further reminded himself—a scheming one. Still, he stayed where he was, looking down at her, reveling in the look of her.

Rachel was still reading him well. "Alice doesn't know what she lost, Steve. You're very special, you know that?"

And she wasn't the least bit subtle. He laughed and sat down on the couch beside her and kissed her on the cheek. She pulled him to her, twisting his face so they were kissing mouth to mouth. Then she pulled away far enough to say "Is this going to be like all the other times, when the kiss didn't mean a thing?"

"I don't know," he said, wanting to kiss her again. Wanting to do more than kiss her.

"Because it should be different now, Steve. I'm not a married woman any more. Not really."

"No," he agreed. "And maybe it is different." The desire to take her, to have her, was almost overpowering. He kissed her again, harder and harder, feeling her body strain against his, feeling her breasts against him, hearing his heart pounding.

"Oh, Steve," she said. "Please. Please."

"Yes, Rachel, yes." He picked her up in his arms and took her into the bedroom. Putting her on the bed, he stood looking down at her, his heart still pounding. She lay back against the pillows, stretching her arms toward him, her dark eyes shining, her mouth glistening, everything about her inviting him, asking him, urging him.

He wanted her. Yes, wanted her. As much as he had ever wanted anything or anyone.

"Rachel, Rachel." He knelt down beside the bed, gathered her into his arms, and kissed her.

And this time didn't stop at that.

He woke up the next morning with a sour taste in his mouth. Rachel was already awake, and she snuggled against him, making it clear he could have her again if he wanted her. He didn't. Showering, shaving, dressing, he tried not to think about her—and for the most part succeeded. When he emerged from the bedroom, she was dressed and waiting for him in the living room.

"You don't get up this early every morning, do you?" she asked, coming up to him and kissing him. It was not quite eight fifteen.

"Why not? I've got to work, you know."

Her coquettish glances didn't do a thing for him in the cold light of day, and he began to wish that last night hadn't happened. Collecting papers from his desk, putting them into his briefcase, he became aware she was talking about something. "I'm sorry," he said. "You were saying . . . ?"

She smiled. "I was saying what a special morning this is."

"Oh." He was sorry he'd asked. He went back to putting papers in his briefcase. "I've got to get to work, Rachel."

"Can I make you breakfast?"

"I don't eat breakfast."

The smile again. And again he was conscious of the sour taste in his mouth. "Isn't this an exception this morning?"

"Maybe," he agreed, "but at the office they don't know that."

"So you don't eat breakfast," she said. "I'll have to remember that. I'll have to learn a lot of things about you, won't I. The kinds of food you like, the names of those wines you once told me about."

He was beginning to feel depressed.

She came over to the desk. "When was the last time you had a vacation?"

Wondering what had brought that on, he said, "Not in a long time."

Her eyes sparkled, and she clapped her hands together in that childish way she had. "Oh, Steve, why don't you do it now? Why don't we just take off for some place together?"

"It's out of the question, Rachel."

"Why?"

"Because I say it is. Because I'm planning to take a business trip any day now."

"Then take me with you."

"Oh, sure," he said dryly. "It happens to be out to the West Coast to meet with Jim Matthews."

"So?"

He stared at her. "Rachel, are you out of your mind?"

The smile again. "Well, Steve, darling, they have to know about us sometime, don't they?"

"Know what?"

"About us."

"I've got to get to work." He headed for the coat closet in the foyer, but she took him by the arm.

"Can't you stay a while just this one special time? Take some time off?"

He unwrapped her fingers from his arm. "Rachel, if you really think you have to learn things about me, there's one very important lesson. It's not last night any more. It's now the old cold light of morning, and I've got to go to work. It's where I belong."

She looked distressed. "But what about me?"

"I don't know," he said, getting their coats out of the closet and handing hers to her. "But you must belong somewhere too, daytimes."

He rang for the elevator, and they both got into it. Leaving the building, he hailed a cab for her and gave her a five-dollar bill and a perfunctory kiss on the cheek. "I'll see you around," he said, helping her into the cab. Then he shut the door and, as the cab took off, went back into the building and up to his office.

Because she had nowhere else to go, Rachel went back to her mother's place. Now that Ada was married to Ernie, she no longer worked at the beauty parlor, and so she was there when Rachel arrived. In fact, she had waited up all night, and now she lit into Rachel about where she had been and what she had been doing.

Rachel refused to tell her. "I'm free," she snapped. "I'm not going to answer to anybody else's rules."

Wounded as always by Rachel's spite, Ada said she had been worried, that was all. Then she tried to talk

Rachel into going back to Russ, patching things up with him, but Rachel was just as unyielding about that.

"But, honey, you can't just walk out on a marriage," Ada said.

"Why not? My father did, didn't he?"

Ada had no answer to that. Instead, she tried once again to find out where Rachel had been all night, and finally Rachel said, "All right, if you must know, I was with Steven Frame, the man who someday is going to give me everything I want."

Maybe someday. But later that day, when she called him at his office to ask if she was going to see him that night, he informed her he had a business conference to attend and would be unavailable. And when, a couple of nights later, he took her out to dinner, it was to say that he regretted what they had done in his apartment.

Rachel stared at him. "But, Steve, that night was perfect!"

"It was perfectly foolish."

"Oh, darling," she said, her voice low and intimate, "don't try to spoil it. It was perfect. You know it was."

He shook his head. "That's the main reason I wanted to talk to you. I don't feel happy about what happened. After all, you're married to Russ."

"But I'm not," she protested. "We're separated. I moved out."

"That doesn't change the fact that you're still married to him. You're not divorced from him, and I'm not very proud of what we did."

"I don't see why," she said.

He gave her that brooding look of his. "Rachel, there are a lot of things you don't see. You really think you know all about me, don't you."

Up went the chin. "Yes, I do. We react the same way to things. And to people. We don't like people looking down on us. We both believe in knowing what we want and going after it." She gave him a triumphant smile. "I learned that from you. I'm not stupid. I learn fast."

But he was unmoved, and after he took her home she got into it again with her mother, who warned her she was screwing up her life and pleaded once more for Rachel to make things up with Russ.

"Look, Mom," Rachel said coldly, "it's my life, not yours. You've had your chance. Now I'm going to have mine. I'm going to have the kind of life I want, not the kind somebody else thinks I ought to have."

Ada told her she was selfish and stupid. Worse than stupid. "You spent the night with Steve Frame. That was worse than stupid. Much worse. And you'll regret it."

The next afternoon Rachel went to see Steve in his office and got a welcome that was far from warm.

"Steve," she said, "you could at least act a little happy to see me."

"Why should I pretend?" he retorted. "I don't know how many times I've tried to tell you this is my office, not some hangout to drop into every time you happen to be in the neighborhood. Next time make an appointment."

"I didn't think I had to make an appointment."

"Well, now you know."

She looked at him as if he had struck her.

"Rachel," he said in a more moderate tone, "I don't want to be this rough, but you've got to stop playing games. All this poor-little-Rachel-that-nobody-loves."

"Well, that's what I am," she said, sounding as offended as she looked. "I came here for advice, but if you're too busy, well, I guess that's it. At least I know where I stand."

He let out a sigh and opened the door to his inner office. "All right, Rachel. I'll give you ten minutes." He ushered her in and indicated a chair, then went behind his desk and sat down. "And let's not waste any of it. If you've got a problem, tell me."

Rachel sat down in the chair. "It's Russ. Should I divorce him?"

Steve shrugged. "Rachel, that's up to you."

She eyed him for a moment. "You mean to me alone and nobody else?"

He nodded. "Yes. Either you want to divorce him or you don't."

"I don't want to do anything that drastic until I know where I stand."

He shrugged again. "You stand on your own two feet. You've left Russ. You're a free woman. Free to do whatever you want."

Again she eyed him. "Steve, you could be a little more encouraging about us."

"About us, Rachel? Oh, now wait a minute. Let's get our signals straight. I like you a lot, Rachel. You know that. But this idea that there is very much going on between you and me is—" He broke off, eyeing her. "I don't know what you think about the other night."

Her answer was surprising—and disarming. "I think one thing, and one thing only," she said. "I was lonely and upset, and I needed someone, and I think you did too."

He nodded. "All right. Maybe you're right. But that doesn't mean—"

She cut him off. "It's a start anyway. A start for whatever we want it to be." Getting up from her chair, she came over to him and tried to embrace him, but he got up too, pushing her away from him.

"All right, Rachel. That's it. Time's up. Discussion's over. I can't give you advice. Besides, this isn't the place to discuss what you want to discuss."

"Will you take me to dinner tonight, then?"

He shook his head. "I can't. Not tonight."

"You have another business conference?"

"Maybe."

She arched her eyebrows. "You mean it isn't a business conference?"

He sighed. "Rachel, do you see what you do? I don't want to hurt you, but you push me into a corner and I have no choice."

"In other words, you have a date tonight. With Alice?"

"I told you, that's finished."

"With somebody else?"

"Maybe."

"Who is it?"

"Rachel, it's none of your business."

"I see," she said with a sulky look. "Oh, sure. I see very clearly now. But that doesn't mean I have to like it. That doesn't mean I have to like it one little bit."

For answer he held open the outer office door for her and closed it after her.

When Steve told Rachel that he and Alice were finished, he believed it, just as he believed that Alice's attitude toward his hiring her father was unreasonable. What he failed to take into consideration was that, given time to calm down, Alice would see how wrong she had been.

Telling Lenore that same afternoon how she had gone to see Steve at his apartment, Alice said, "I distrusted his motives. I thought he was exercising his ego. And, more than that, that he thought he could impress me by doing this thing for my father. I told him all that. He let me tell him off, and then he told me off. And you know what, Lenore? I deserved it."

Encouraged by Lenore not to let foolish pride stand in her way a second time, Alice called Steve at his apartment that evening to apologize.

After a stiff exchange of pleasantries, she said, "The truth is, I'm not fine or happy or anything. I'm wrong. At least, I was the other night. That's why I'm calling. I wanted to apologize for the things I said."

"I want to apologize for what I said, too," he answered.

"It was nothing I didn't deserve, Steven."

"All right," he said. "But I'm glad you called. Maybe this time we can get something straight from the beginning. The basic fact that you're you and I'm me. We may not always agree, but let's talk it over. May I take you to dinner tonight?"

"No, Steven, I couldn't. I *am* me, and if I accepted your invitation and went out with you as a result of this call, I'd just distrust my own motives for calling."

Somewhat to her surprise, he said, "I understand. I even respect it. Just as long as you understand that I'll be calling you soon."

"I'd like that very much."

"Sooner than you expect," he said. "So maybe I should just hang up and call you right back."

Alice laughed. "Not that soon."

"All right," he said. "But anyway, I'm glad you called."

Both hung up considerably happier than they had been a few minutes earlier.

Alice's happiness lasted longer than Steve's. He had no sooner hung up the phone than his intercom buzzed and the doorman informed him that Rachel was downstairs. "All right," he said. "Send her up." That was something else he would get straight now.

When Rachel stepped out of the elevator she looked around her and then at Steve. "I thought you had a date."

"That's what you assumed."

She slipped out of her coat and handed it to him. She was wearing the same black cocktail dress she had worn the other night, but this time it did very little for him. "That's what you wanted me to think, isn't it?" She smiled at him. The Cleopatra smile. But that, too, did little for him.

"Rachel," he said, "I don't care what you think. I also told you I don't appreciate you always showing up unannounced."

"I tried to call you but the line was busy. Was it business or pleasure?"

"That's none of your business."

She smiled again. "You told me a lot of things this afternoon, but I don't think you really meant them all, and that's why I'm here. I'd just like to find out once and for all exactly where I really stand with you."

He hung her coat up and walked over to the bar. She followed and, standing behind him, slipped her arms around him, laying the side of her face against his back. He stiffened, and she said, "Steve, why do you have to make everything sound so cold and business-like?"

Disengaging himself from her, turning around to her so she couldn't make the same move again, he said, "You did that, with all this talk about trying to find out where you stand. Now go sit down, and I'll fix us a drink."

He waited until she walked into the living room and curled up on the couch. Then he turned back to the bar, made the drinks, gave her hers, and sat down in a chair with his.

"The other night you weren't cold," she said. "So why act that way now?" And, when he didn't answer: "We're not at the office now. You don't have to pretend. Steve, what's wrong?"

"We are. Rachel, I want you to listen. You're an attractive girl, and I'm tempted. But I'm a big boy, and I learned how to handle temptation long ago. Which means that while you've done a lot of thinking about where you'd like this whole thing to go, I've done some thinking too. And I've been trying to give you the answer for a couple of days now. I don't know whether it would work or not. All I know is that to go on from here just wouldn't be practical."

She looked distressed. "You're making it sound like a business deal."

"I'm sorry, Rachel, but I think you're a practical girl."

"Maybe. But when it comes to caring about another person, Steve, the way I feel about you—"

He cut her off with a laugh. "You're not going to start talking about love, are you?"

"Well, I know it's too early yet, Steve, but—"

"But you're thinking of chasing me the way you chased Russ?"

"That's not true. He chased me."

"Now, Rachel." Steve shook his head. "You and I shouldn't try to kid each other. You chased after Russ because it was the practical thing to do. You thought he was the answer to all the things you wanted, so you baited your little hook, cast it out, and caught him. I'm not saying I blame you. I can even feel sorry for you that it hasn't worked out."

"If it didn't work out," Rachel said, "there are reasons, and you're one of them. From the moment I met you—"

He put a hand up to stop her. "Oh, look out. The

old practicality is showing through. Rachel, let's face it. I've never kidded myself about why you're attracted to me. You certainly know I'm not a guy with just an ordinary job. You know. Find out what you want and go after it. I'm flattered to have you look into my eyes the way you do, but I don't kid myself for one minute as to what it means. You and I think the same way— that what you do in life should move you up the ladder. Now, I might do that for you, but—"

"I could do a lot for you," she said, the chin up again in that defiant manner of hers. He was sorry she had to be the way she was, and yet he supposed that was the very thing that attracted him to her.

"Sure," he said dryly. "You could spend my money with the best of them."

She looked hurt. "Don't be cruel. You don't know what I've given up."

"No, you're wrong," he said. "I do know."

She started to get up from the couch, but he stared her back down. "Please, Steve. You can't say it won't work without even trying."

"I could wish it would," he admitted.

A mistake to have said that. He should have known that all you had to give Rachel was an inch. This time she did get up. And came over to him. "It would, Steve. I know it would. You do like me, don't you?"

He got to his feet, partly out of self-defense, and partly out of he wasn't sure what. But he kept his hands away from her. "I never said I didn't."

The atmosphere was getting tense. He moved away from her and walked to the bar.

"Then why?" she pleaded, following him.

He turned to face her. "Because it just wouldn't work."

Abruptly she threw her arms around him and kissed him, but he didn't respond. At last she broke away from him, tears in her eyes. And a look of fear as well.

"You'd better go, Rachel," he said. "You can't stay here, and you know it." She started to cry. "I'm sorry," he said, "but you can't."

"But where can I go then?" she asked through her tears.

He shook his head. "I don't know. I wish I could help, but I can't. There's just nothing I can do." He opened the door to the elevator, and she stepped in and pulled the door to after her.

Hearing the whine of the motor as the elevator started down, Steve stood where he was for a bit, wondering if Rachel had finally gotten the message—if he had seen the last of her.

When the next day passed, and the next, and the next, without further word from her, he began to believe he had.

A week later, on the last day of February—and a bitterly cold day it was—Dr. Richard Benson finished examining a young woman who had come to him for a checkup, a woman he did not know, who seemed to have picked him at random from the telephone book, and who had given her name to his nurse as Mrs. Gerald Ketchum Davis. From the stricken look on her pretty, heart-shaped face when he told her she was pregnant, he doubted she was Mrs. anybody.

"Are you afraid?" he said gently, thinking maybe he could draw her out and try to help her if she needed help.

She sat for a moment, clasping and unclasping her hands. Then the stricken look became a look of confidence. "No," she said. "I know exactly what to do."

That afternoon Steve called Alice to invite her out for dinner the following night, and she accepted.

"You're not going to change your mind this time, are you?" he teased.

Alice laughed. "No. I won't do that. I promise you."

A surge of pleasure swept through him as he hung up the phone, and when it rang again a few seconds later, he didn't wait for his secretary to pick up, but answered it himself.

It was Rachel, saying it was imperative that she see him.

He sighed and glanced at his desk calendar. He hadn't really thought he'd seen the last of her. "Okay. At two forty-five. For fifteen minutes. No more and no less." He wondered what she wanted. Imperative.

He wouldn't have thought the word was known to her.

At two forty-five Rachel was ushered into his private office, and the moment the door closed on his secretary Steve found out what she wanted. She told him she was pregnant.

"It's not so bad," she went on to say. "I mean, I don't think it's the best way to start and all that, but it isn't as if we exactly hate each other, is it?"

For a moment he just sat there behind his desk, marveling at her. She was really something, this one. What a pity her talent was so misdirected. "Rachel," he said, "you're a born scrambler. For most girls that would be a terrible blow—finding out she's pregnant. Especially under the circumstances. I imagine it even was to you—for about a minute. But then you started scrambling, because to you scrambling is like breathing. You said, wait a minute. That isn't so bad. It's good. The baby is Steve's. I bet you even persuaded yourself it's true."

She was staring at him bug-eyed. "But, Steve, it is true. You are the father. I know the way Russ and I were living together."

He raised his eyebrows. "And you expect me to believe that? When you found out you were pregnant, you scrambled. You turned a deficit into an asset. You're attracted to me because of my money. And I like you a lot. But I'm not going to let you parlay that into something else. You have a husband, and now you're going to have a child."

She was shaking her head. "There's no possible way it could be Russ's child."

"Rachel, he's your husband, and you lived with him right up to the very night you stayed in my apartment. I'm sorry. I really am, but I'm just not going to believe it."

Rachel started crying.

He was fishing in his pocket for a handkerchief for her when his intercom buzzed, and his secretary told him a Miss Matthews was on the line.

"Well, hello," he said, picking up the phone. "What a nice surprise."

"I hope I'm not interrupting anything."

"You're not."

"I couldn't remember whether you said seven or seven thirty."

"Seven thirty, if that's all right with you."

"That's fine, Steven. I'll see you then. Good-bye."

"Good-bye."

"Who was that?" Rachel asked in a sulky tone as he cradled the phone.

"If you must know, it was Alice."

She wiped her eyes with the back of her hand. "So," she flared, "we're back with dear old Alice, just like that. Now isn't that just too convenient? I'm pregnant, and you're suddenly too busy. It's your baby, but you don't want to admit it. "And besides, Mr. Can't-be-bothered Steven Frame has a date—an elegant little evening planned with Alice." She beat the air with her fists. "Are you going to acknowledge your baby?"

Steve shook his head. "I'm sorry. I'm not."

"Do you think I'm going to keep it a secret?" She tossed her head. "Well, don't you believe it. I'm going to tell. I'm going to walk right out of here and tell."

"You could do that, Rachel, and I'll admit it might do me some harm. But have you thought that you'll also be hurting yourself? You'll be advertising your outside interests in ten-foot flashing neon letters."

She made a face. "I get your message."

"And?"

"And never you mind." She picked up the coat she had taken off and stormed out of his office, leaving him to marvel again at what a scrambler she was.

Back at her mother's house, Rachel started packing a suitcase. Coming into the bedroom to see what she was up to, Ada said, "What are you doing?"

"What does it look like?"

"Well, then, where are you going? And why?"

"Mom, I'm pregnant, and it's Steve Frame's baby, but he's not in the market for any babies today. Isn't that just real nice?"

Ada was staring at her in horror. "Rachel—"

"There isn't anything more to say." Rachel grabbed

a skirt and sweater from the closet, stuffed them into the bag, and closed it.

"But where are you going? What are you going to do?"

"I don't know. But I've got to get away from here and think. Because I for sure have to go somewhere and do something." And she stormed out of her mother's house the way she'd stormed out of Steve's office a short time earlier.

Chapter Twelve

WHEN RUSS came home from the hospital that evening, he found Rachel sitting on a suitcase in the hall outside their apartment. Astonished, not quite believing his eyes, he said, "Rachel?"

She looked up, her face tear-stained. "Russ, I've come back."

For the last few weeks—ever since Rachel had left him, at the end of January—Russ had tried to persuade himself, as well as his family and friends, that he didn't love Rachel any more. Only that afternoon, when Ada came to tell him Rachel had run away, he had said he was sorry but he didn't feel he could afford to be concerned about her any longer. He had gone on to say Rachel would have to learn on her own that the world she lived in was full of people, that her little world seemed empty because she was the only one in it.

Yet the sight of her now—the vulnerability of her —touched him as it always had, and he took her into the apartment with him. He could at least listen to what she had to say. He owed her—and their marriage —that much.

Hanging her own coat as well as his in the hall

closet, Rachel said, "I missed you, Russ. I wanted so much to be back here with you."

He probably sounded as puzzled as he felt. "Honey, there's nothing to hold you here that wasn't here before."

Ignoring that, she came up to him and said, "Have you missed me?"

He nodded. "Yes, I have. But—frankly—is that going to be enough?"

She put her hands on his arms. "It will be enough, Russ, because there is something to hold me here. I found out what it's like to be without you, and I never want to be away from you again." Her hands tightened their grip. "I couldn't stand it. Believe me, Russ, darling."

Desire stirred in him, and he did as she was doing, putting his hands on her arms. "I believe you, Rachel." Then he disengaged himself from her. "But we have a lot of other problems that need working out, too, and I don't know. I just don't know."

He had turned and walked away from her. Now she came up to him and put her arms around him, her face resting on his back, and once again desire stirred in him, more strongly than before. He had missed her more than he would ever say—even to himself.

"Don't you want to try?" she murmured. "Darling, it was so awful without you."

Turning to face her, holding her a little away from him, searching her eyes for the answers he so desperately wanted—and had been wanting for a long time now—he said, "If it doesn't work, I don't know if I could stand that."

She moved closer to him, her eyes never leaving his face. "It will work," she said. "I'll make it work. I promise."

He pulled her to him. "Oh, Rachel. I missed you so much."

"I know," she answered, in a voice so low it was almost a whisper, and he tightened his grip on her, the desire a fierce need now. "But you'll never have to miss me again," she said, "because I'll never leave you again, Russ. I promise." She pulled back a little—to look at him, to touch his face, to trace her fingers on his lips. "Oh, Russ, I love you, and I'm going to be a real wife to you. If you'll let me. Loving you the way a real wife should."

"Oh, Rachel." He pulled her to him again and kissed her—again and again, until the passion inside him became almost unbearable, and then he took her into the bedroom.

The next morning was in many ways as remarkable as the night before. In the two years of their marriage Russ had grown accustomed to getting up alone in the morning, while Rachel went on sleeping—sometimes until noon or after. This morning she was up before him. Heading for the shower, he could hear her out in the kitchen. When he emerged from the bedroom, showered and shaved and dressed, she was putting breakfast on the table for them.

She greeted him with a smile and a kiss, and though it seemed to him that she was under some kind of strain, that there was a too-bright quality about her, nothing she said gave any indication of it. Quite the contrary.

"Last night was wonderful," she said. "Wasn't it?"

"Yes," he said. And she was right. It had been.

She sighed. "It was so good to be back with you and have all our troubles over at last."

He gave her a wondering look. "You think they're over?"

She nodded. A bit vehemently. "After last night, Russ? Of course they are." He must have looked as doubtful as he felt, because she went on, "When we were lying there together, I felt everything was just the way it should be."

He wanted to agree with her, to believe—as she seemed to—that all of their troubles were indeed over, but common sense prevailed. "We still have a lot to talk about, Rachel. Why you left me, what made you want to come back."

Something flickered in her eyes. He would have said fear, but that was ridiculous. Whatever their problems, fear was not one of them. "Well, sure," she said, but without enthusiasm. "If you want to. If you think we

have to. I just don't know that talking does any good."
She smiled then, a rather forced smile, it seemed to
him. "But whatever you say. Only now we have to eat
breakfast, okay? We can talk later, can't we?"

He nodded. "Yes, of course."

Still, he couldn't remember her talking as much
through a meal as she did through that breakfast. Not
about anything of any consequence. Chattering,
mostly. About what a terrible winter it had been, and
how spring was only around the corner now, and she
could hardly wait for it, and how the apartment
needed attention, how neglected it looked, and how he
must have been working too hard, because he looked
tired. But now that she was here to take care of him—
and she was really going to take care of him now—he
would get rested, and life would be good to them, and
they would have fun. No, no, she hastened to add, she
didn't mean running around—not that kind of fun.
That was for kids. But staying at home having-a-family
kind of fun. That was what they were going to do.

And though she seemed wound up tight as a ball,
she was all smiles and wifely concern, and when he set
off for the hospital he was ready to believe that
Rachel's nervousness was merely the result of her apparently sincere desire to have him indicate that all
was well now, all forgiven—and ready to be forgotten,
too. And maybe fear, yes—fear that he would refuse to
take her back, to let her stay—when he was certainly
as ready as she was to work out their differences, to try
again.

Back in the apartment, Rachel's wound-upness
lasted for about two minutes after Russ set off for
work. Then she burst into tears—tears of release, of
sorrow, of bewilderment and helplessness.

After a while she stopped crying. Crying, after all,
would accomplish very little. And there was something
she had to do.

Not bothering to phone for an appointment, she
went to Steve's office, where she had no trouble getting
in to see him. He offered her a chair, but she shook her
head. "I won't be here that long. You may not believe
me, Steve, but I never wanted to make any trouble for

you. It was just that I was very unhappy with Russ, and you were very kind to me. I thought you understood me."

Although he was listening attentively—or seemed to be—he said nothing, so she went on. "Well, I guess I sort of began to rely on you—too much, as it turns out. I admired you, and I kind of waited for you to tell me what to do. It's a wonderful feeling to have someone to turn to—to tell you what to do."

The last thing in the world she had intended to do was to cry again, yet she started crying now, unable to help herself. She took the handkerchief he held out to her and wiped her eyes, swallowing until she had herself under control again.

"Anyway," she said, a little shakily, "it's wonderful to think you have someone."

"I'm sorry," he said, "but—"

She shook her head to cut him off. "Don't feel sorry for me. Nobody's going to have to feel sorry for me. I'm going to be okay. You were right when you said if I made trouble for you I'd only be making trouble for myself." She managed a smile. "May I use your phone?"

"Yes, of course," he said, looking puzzled.

She dialed the hospital and asked for Russ. When he came to the phone she told him she thought she ought to go see her mother and tell her where she was last night, so would he pick her up there on his way home from work.

When she cradled the phone, Steve said, "You were with Russ last night, I take it."

"That's right. I was." She gave him a cold look. "I'm carrying your baby, and you don't want me. But I told you I'd be all right."

A feeling of helplessness washed over her again, and again she had to swallow for control. "It was the only thing I could think of to do. I didn't even know if Russ would want me. But, Steve, that doesn't mean I don't love you, because I do. I love you very much."

"Rachel," he said, "don't say that."

"What's more," she went on, "I think you love me. No matter what happens to either of us, you're going to go on loving me and wanting me—until one day, maybe when you least expect it to happen, you're going to find out you can't stand being without me, that you love me so much you just can't stand it. It's true. You wait. You'll see."

And while he stood there staring at her, a stunned look on his face, she turned and walked out.

But if she left Steve stunned and silent, her mother had a far different reaction.

After explaining to her mother what had happened, Rachel admitted that she hadn't told Russ she was pregnant. She couldn't.

"You'll have to tell him sometime," Ada said. "Unless you're planning to—to—"

"Have an abortion?" Rachel shook her head. "No, Mom. No way. At least not now, now that Russ has let me come back to him. No. I mean to have this baby. I even look forward to having this baby."

Her mother frowned. "And what are you going to say to Russ?"

Rachel lifted her chin. "I'm going to let him think it's his."

"Rachel!" Her mother looked horrified. "You can't do that."

"I can, and I will."

They were in her mother's kitchen; Ada was drying some dishes. Now she shook out the towel with a snap. "I'm ashamed of you, crawling back to your husband, telling him you love him and you want to live with him and be his wife again, when all the time you're pregnant by another man."

Furious, Rachel screamed at her, "Well, what else could I do? I didn't notice you coming up with any great ideas yesterday about how to get me out of this jam. There wasn't any talk about abortion then—or the money to pay for it. You can stand there now and criticize me and tell me I'm no good, but I didn't see you offering to help."

Her mother folded the dish towel and hung it up. "I could talk till I'm blue in the face before you'd listen to me, Rachel."

"Oh, sure, Mom, sure. That's all I ever get from you

—how awful I've been all my life. Well, I'm sick of it."

Ada sighed. "Maybe you're right. Maybe it's my fault. I expect it is."

Rachel went to her mother and put her arms around her. "Then you'll stick with me, Mom? Stay on my side? Please? Please, Mom."

"You mean not say anything to Russ?"

"Yes."

"Promise?"

Ada sighed again. "All right. I don't like it, but . . . all right."

And when Russ arrived to pick Rachel up, and Rachel kissed him and snuggled up to him in front of Ada, saying they were being given a second chance, and wasn't it wonderful, Ada said nothing.

The reaction in the Matthews household—the Jim Matthews household—to the reconciliation of Russ and Rachel was something else again. Jim was still away on his travels for Steven Frame, Incorporated. And Mary, trying her very best to be pleased for Russ's sake, had very little to say. Alice was more outspoken.

"I can't see how Russ could forgive her so easily," she said to Mary. "I suppose it's a terrible thing to say, but when she left him I was glad—glad it was finally over. And now here she is back again. Just like that." Alice shook her head. "I don't know, but there's something about this that doesn't seem right to me."

Mary frowned. "What do you mean, darling?"

"I don't know," Alice said again. "It's just that I don't think she would have come back to Russ without some . . . well, hidden motive."

Her mother was still frowning. "Motive for what?"

"I don't know that either. But Rachel never does anything without having a reason for it. And I think there's some reason for this. For coming back to Russ. Not that I suppose we'll ever know what it is."

Any further speculation by Alice and her mother as to why Rachel had come back to Russ was cut off by the arrival of Steve to take Alice out to dinner—and to what each hoped would be the beginning of a new and easier, more understanding relationship between them.

It was a quiet dinner and a quiet evening. When he brought her home, they didn't get out of the car immediately, but sat talking together.

"Do you realize," Alice said, "we've spent a whole evening together without a quarrel or even a difference of opinion?"

He put an arm around her and hugged her. "I've missed you."

She turned her face to him. "I've missed you, too."

They were silent a bit, and then he said, "Alice, why has it taken us so long to be—not honest, because, Lord knows, we're both all too honest—but open with each other?"

"I don't know," Alice answered. "Maybe it's because when I tell you something I want it to mean something. So many people tell you the things they think you want to hear."

He touched her face with his finger. "You're different from anybody I've ever known, you know that?"

She smiled. "Is that good or bad?"

He smiled back at her. "You're very special. That's why I don't want to have any difficulty getting through to you again. Okay?"

She nodded. "Okay."

He took her in his arms and kissed her, until finally she broke away to say, "I think we'd better go in. Before the firecrackers start going off that somebody's lighted up inside me."

At the hospital the next day, running into each other outside a patient's room, Alice and Russ spoke briefly about his reconciliation with Rachel. Or Russ did, mainly. He said he and Rachel were working things out together, and he had the feeling now that Rachel was really trying. Maybe for the first time. And he was trying, too. "Let's face it," he went on to say. "I'm in love with her. And that's worth hanging on to."

Alice merely said she was pleased for him and she hoped it worked out. She was too fond of Russ to want to hurt him, and maybe she had been wrong about Rachel's having some hidden reason for coming back to him.

The following day Russ went to Chicago for a medical meeting and took Rachel with him. They were gone two weeks, and when they came back Ada was at their apartment to greet them, having cleaned house for them and brought in some flowers. As soon as Russ left to check in at the hospital, Ada turned anxiously to Rachel to ask how things had gone between her and Russ.

Rachel shrugged. "What do you think? It's all love and kisses."

"You mean you're still going through with the deception?"

"Yes, Mom. And drop it. Okay?"

Ada sighed and said nothing.

"I don't suppose," Rachel said, "you've heard anything about Steve."

"Would I be likely to?"

"No. But I thought maybe he might call. To ask about me. It's the least he could do."

"Well, he didn't. And is that all you can think about—Steven Frame?"

Rachel shrugged again. "Considering the way things are, it's pretty hard not to think about him now and then."

Ada made a face. "What you ought to be thinking about is telling Russ the truth."

"Oh, sure, Mom. And be left to raise the baby all by myself? No thanks. No. Lying to Russ is the solution. For the time being."

Ada stared at her. "You're still scheming, aren't you? You're thinking you can buy a little time, that there might be some way you can still get Steve Frame after all."

Rachel smiled. "Oh?" she said innocently. "Is that what I think? Well, Mom, I don't know. Maybe you're right. But in the meantime my husband is coming back soon, and his loving wife wants to change into something pretty for him, so if you'll excuse me . . ." And she showed her mother the door.

That night Rachel began paving the way, as it were. Lying in bed with Russ, she brought up the subject of having a baby. Even as he tightened his grip on her, he said, "I can wait until you're ready."

She answered him by kissing him and saying, "I want you to get your wish." She snuggled against him, running a hand up and down his back. "I was foolish before, Russ. I really do want a baby now. And that's why I know I'm going to have one—because I want it so."

Then, as she had every night since coming back to him, she submitted to his lovemaking, trying to act as if she wanted him just as much as he wanted her.

Because Alice and Steve were dating regularly now, and because Alice wanted Russ to like Steve—to smooth out any hard feelings Russ might have harbored toward him for giving Rachel advice and taking her to lunch—the two couples spent an evening together at the Top of the Tower. Rachel was delighted at the prospect of seeing Steve, but not so delighted at seeing him with Alice. And she was not at all pleased when Russ quietly but firmly laid down the law for her regarding Steve, saying they would be friends with him as a couple but she was not to see him alone under any circumstances.

A few days after the double date, happening to be alone with Alice for a few minutes—and unable to resist making a few digs—Rachel commented that one couldn't expect Steve Frame to abide by the rules as ordinary people had to. "Steve didn't get where he is today," she said, "by sticking strictly to the book. And whatever he did, I bet he covered himself but good."

Alice frowned. "I don't think you have any grounds for hinting at something like that. You're saying he's a cheat when you don't know that."

"Oh, I don't?" Rachel came back at her. "There are lots of ways of cheating. I know there's a lot to admire about Steve. He's very smooth and charming. But if somebody gets in his way—well, watch out."

To celebrate the first day of spring—or so they told themselves—Russ and Alice stopped in a bar near the hospital for a drink after work one day later that week. Noting that Alice had been going out with Steve practically every night, Russ asked her if things were getting serious between them.

"Maybe," Alice said. "I don't know. I'm not sure yet how I really feel about Steven." She stirred the ice in her drink. "He's changed a little the last few weeks."

"Changed how?" Russ asked before taking a swallow of his scotch and soda.

"He's quieter."

Russ grinned. "That doesn't sound like much of a change."

"Maybe not. But I like him better. And it's more than quieter, I guess. Anyhow, he's different."

"Maybe you're different," Russ observed.

"Maybe. Anyhow, we've been getting along awfully well together. Things are so much nicer than they were before. Cheers," she added, almost absently, before taking a swallow of her whiskey sour.

"Cheers to you, too," Russ said. "And could it be that you're nicer—to Steve, I mean?"

She nodded. "Possibly."

For some time there was silence between them, until finally Russ said, "A penny."

Alice smiled. "I was just wondering if Steven is beginning to mean too much to me."

"I hope you're not looking to me to answer that," Russ said, "because there's no way I can do it."

That night Rachel again brought up the subject of having a baby. After being assured by Russ that she was being a good wife to him, Rachel promised to be an even better one and then went on to say "Once we have our baby it will be wonderful." She looked earnestly at Russ. "I know I have your child inside me. I know it, because I want it so. Why don't you set up an examination for me at the hospital?"

"Honey," he said, "there's no hurry."

"No," she agreed, "but wouldn't it be wonderful if we found out I'm pregnant? It would make you happy, wouldn't it, Russ?"

"Yes, but I wouldn't want you to be disappointed."

"Oh, I wouldn't be," she answered. "And neither will you. I'll go there tomorrow, and they'll tell us we're going to have a baby. And we are, Russ. I just know we are."

He agreed to make an appointment for her.

Not surprisingly—not to Rachel, anyhow—the pregnancy test was positive.

When Rachel announced her pregnancy to Walter and Lenore and, a day or two later, to Russ's sister, Pat, and her husband, it so happened that Steve was present on each occasion, and Rachel took pleasure in what she regarded as making him squirm.

But a far more disturbing announcement was in the making for Rachel—one she first heard inklings of from Walter and Lenore.

"I understand," Walter said, "Steve may be a part of your family pretty soon."

It was a balmy April afternoon, and Walter and Lenore and Rachel were having a drink on the patio at the Curtins' house, waiting for Russ to arrive from the hospital for an early evening out together.

Rachel frowned at Walter. "What do you mean?"

He smiled. "It's not as if Alice were going to refuse."

"Walter," Lenore chided him. "Steve hasn't said he's going to ask."

Walter settled back in his chair, stretching out his long frame, a mischievous look in his eyes. "He will, believe me. And we've seen how Alice feels about him."

Rachel was looking from one to the other of them. "You mean Alice and Steve?"

Walter nodded. "Everybody can see it coming any day now."

"Well," Rachel said, bridling, "he hasn't done it yet. You know how men are. He probably isn't really serious. And anyway—my goodness, who knows what might happen in the meantime?"

Neither Walter nor Lenore happened to be looking at Rachel at that moment. Walter was taking a swallow of his gin and tonic, and Lenore was looking at her row of irises, wondering how they were going to do this year. If they had been looking, they would have been shocked to see the jealousy so nakedly displayed.

It was true that in the weeks since their own reconciliation Alice and Steve had been moving closer and closer together. In particular, Steve had begun opening up more to Alice, revealing more about himself.

One evening while they were eating in the little French restaurant down along the wharves, Steve talked—for the first time—about his childhood. "In my family," he said, "if you ever wasted time talking at the supper table, you'd never get your share of the stew. My father decided he was a failure at about the age of twelve. My mother, my brothers, my sister— well, I don't know whether my father's attitude was catching, but they hugged failure to their bosoms too."

"Do you ever see your family?" Alice asked.

He shook his head. "No. I used to, but it just never worked out. I've taken care of all of them for about the last five years. The truth is, my accountant knows them better than I do. Maybe that's why I didn't understand the way you felt about your father being sent away, Alice."

"No, Steven. I was wrong in the things I thought and said."

He smiled. "But at least it got us back together. If that's what it takes, you can tell me off any time you please."

This conversation was taking place the evening of the day Rachel had gone to the hospital for her pregnancy test, and Alice began to speak of that, saying she didn't trust Rachel.

Steve looked up from the salad he had been concentrating on. "Has she said anything—or done anything?"

"No. As a matter of fact, she's trying to convince Russ she's pregnant." Alice shook her head. "Her reason is she wants to be. They've been back together only a few weeks, yet she's insisted on having an examination. And the thing is, she never wanted to be pregnant before. I don't know. I find it hard to believe her. How can she have changed her mind so quickly about wanting to have a baby?"

One night in early April, bringing Alice home from an evening out, walking with her to the front door, Steve was so quiet—and had been all evening, really —that Alice commented on it.

"I guess I have been," he admitted. "Sorry. It's because I've had a lot of things on my mind."

"Business things?" she asked.

"Only partly." They had reached the steps to the front porch, and he stopped and took her by the hand. "I've wanted to talk to you seriously for a long time, Alice, but I made the mistake of letting other things get the best of me. Interfere. But that won't happen again." He drew her to him. "I want you to know how wonderful I think you are."

"Steven," she protested, "I'm not wonderful."

His eyes were intent on her face. "Do you mind if I say you are?"

"No. In fact, I like it very much. If you mean it."

"I mean it," he said. "Alice, you mean more to me than I ever thought it possible for anyone to mean."

For a few minutes they simply stood where they were at the foot of the steps, looking at each other. Then he took her in his arms and kissed her—so passionately, and with such passionate response from her, that when they finally broke away they looked at each other in wonderment.

Steve had meant it when he told Alice he wasn't going to let other things interfere with their relationship, but some things were beyond his control. Only a few days later an automobile accident injured a young woman who was close to Alice and Walter and Lenore, to all the Matthewses, and to most of their friends—in fact, to everyone except Steve. The young woman's hospitalization and—five weeks later—her death interrupted and even shadowed the growing intimacy between Steve and Alice.

Meeting with Walter one afternoon at the end of May to go over some legal matters, Steve said he was very depressed by the young woman's death—depressed and a bit confused.

Walter looked at him, surprised. "This is a Steve Frame I've never met before."

Steve nodded. "Yes, I know. The truth is, Walter, I guess what's really got me down about her death is that it's affected the lives and emotions of almost everyone I know or care about. And I feel left out. There. That's more like the old Steve, isn't it? Always looking out for himself. Always asking, what's in it for me?

Always wanting to be in, instead of on the outside looking in. Only this time I am on the outside. Way outside."

Walter looked at his friend in silence for a moment, then said, "You want to be part of Alice's group, is that it?"

"I didn't say anything like that."

"You don't have to," Walter countered. "I'm saying it for you. The depression, the uncertainty, the feeling of being left out—isn't it because of Alice?"

Steve nodded. "Yes. And I guess that's really why I'm here. You're the only member of that group I felt I could just drop in on and say these things to. It doesn't make any sense, does it."

Walter cocked his head. "Doesn't it?"

At that moment another member of the law firm came into Walter's office. He apologized for interrupting them. Steve gave him a rueful smile. "Don't apologize," he said. "You were indeed interrupting something, and just in the nick of time, too, I might add. I was about to give myself away."

A few nights later the matter of the young woman's death came up again—this time between Steve and Alice. Alice's father was still away on his auditing trip for Steve. After having dinner with Alice and her mother in the Matthews home, Steve took Alice for a drive along the bay. Referring to what had happened, Steve said, "I didn't quite know what you and your family would think was right and proper as far as I was concerned. I only knew what I wanted. And that was to see you. To be with you as soon and as often as I could."

It was a warm June night. The car windows were down, and the breeze off the bay whipped through the car, smelling of sand and pine.

Alice nodded. "I felt like that about you. But it—well, it didn't seem right. And there were other people —people in the family I had to be with. But I'm glad Mother asked you to dinner tonight."

He took one hand off the steering wheel long enough to squeeze her hand. "So am I."

They were approaching the Mount Pleasant lookout

point. Steve slowed, then pulled into the lay-by and stopped the car. They got out and walked over to the stone wall at the edge of the bluff and stood looking out over the bay and at the lights from that part of Bay City they could see from there.

"Mom misses Dad very much," Alice said. "Especially now, with this happening. She depends on him so. And she didn't have Dad to turn to." Alice was silent a few moments, then said, "So many people don't seem to have anybody to turn to—to lean on when they need them. Maybe we're luckier than we know, Steven."

He put his arm around her. "Then you do feel you have me to turn to?"

She turned her face up to his. "May I?"

He drew her close. "That's exactly the way I want you to feel about me."

She smiled. "Then I'm glad, because I do feel that way."

He studied her face a moment. "Is this the time to tell you I love you, Alice? Because I do, you know. I don't say it very easily. But I love you."

"Oh, Steven," she said.

Again he studied her. "Is that all you can say? You can't say 'I love you too'?"

"I don't mean to be hesitant," she said. "It's just that . . ."

"It's just that you like to be sure, is that it?"

"Doesn't every girl?"

He smiled. "You want the future all mapped out?"

"You make me sound terrible," she said, "but in a way I guess that's it. I'm a dreamer, really."

"If you want to know," he said, "so am I. I just don't tell anybody."

She rested her head against his shoulder. "You told me."

"That's because I love you," he said softly. "I trust you implicitly with my dreams. I don't think you'd ever betray them."

"I promise I won't," she answered. "And if I confide in you?"

He squeezed her arm. "Try it."

"All right," she said. "But it takes a little time for me to feel confident."

"Are you beginning to feel confident with me?" he asked, looking down at her.

"Yes, Steven. Yes, I am."

But if Alice was hesitant with Steve, she wasn't hesitant about him. Only a few days later, when Lenore was at the hospital for her regular volunteer stint, she and Alice had lunch together in the hospital cafeteria, and Lenore asked Alice point-blank if she loved Steve.

When Alice admitted she did, Lenore said, "That's nice. Or at least it is if Steve also loves you. And that I don't even have to speculate about. Even if I didn't already know it, I can see it all over your face."

A few minutes later, talking about love, Alice said, "I think love is always real, at least for one of the two persons involved. And when it's real for both of them at the same time, then I guess it would be lasting. Unless, of course, something happens that they can't predict—something to change things between them."

Chapter Thirteen

ONE night toward the end of June Alice and Steve were once again driving along the bay, and once again he pulled into the lay-by at the Mount Pleasant lookout point and they got out of the car and walked to the stone wall edging the bluff.

It was a mild, windless night, starry and clear, a quarter moon high in the sky, the Big and Little Dippers easy to find.

"To tell you the truth," Alice confided to Steve, "they're the only ones I can ever find."

He nodded and smiled. "I know what you mean. In the picture books, with all the lines drawn in, Pegasus looks like a winged horse—at least, more or less. But up in the sky, without the lines, I can't put him together at all."

Alice laughed, and for a few minutes they looked at the stars, enjoying the brilliant clarity of the night and the balmy summer air. Then Steve turned serious.

"I've been giving you time to think, Alice," he began.

"Yes," she said. "And I've needed it."

"But now?" he asked, and when she said nothing, "Don't think any more, Alice. Just love me. Want me. Trust me."

She looked at him, then went into his arms.

"Darling," he said, and kissed her, at first tenderly, then with more and more passion, until they broke away to stare at each other, shaken.

"Oh, Steven," she whispered, going back into his arms.

He held her tight. "I need you so."

Her face was buried against his chest. "And I need you." She lifted her face to him. "Oh, Steven, I do love you. I love you very much."

"Darling," he said again, and once again they kissed as before. Then he said, "Marry me, Alice. Will you marry me?"

"Yes, Steven. Yes, I will."

"Oh, Alice." Again he drew her to him, and again they kissed, and, as she had another time, she broke away from him "before the firecrackers started going off."

When Alice came home, her mother was sitting in the living room, reading—and guessed from the look on Alice's face what she was going to say even before she said it. She hugged Alice and said how happy she was for her. And she was. But she was also a little troubled—as she had been from the start by Steven Frame.

"I wish your father were here, so he could talk to you," she said. She smiled to hide her doubts. "Just to make sure you're sure. That's all."

"Well, of course, I'm sure," Alice answered. Then, trying to make a joke of it, as was her wont, she said,

"Are you worried or something? Do you think at my age I should have said to him, 'Well, Steven, I'll have to ask my mother'?"

"No, of course not, darling, but . . . well, it's just . . . Are you sure you'll be happy with him?"

Alice beamed. "I'm already happy with him. I still can't quite get used to the fact that he loves me, but he really does. And, oh, Mom, I can't wait to tell everybody!"

"I know how you feel," Mary said. "But there might be a point in waiting."

"For what?"

"I was just thinking you might want to hold off telling anybody until we can have a formal engagement party."

"Mmm," Alice said. "That would be fun. But, still, can't we do it both ways? I mean, I don't see why all our friends can't know about it ahead of time. There isn't any reason for it to be a secret, is there?"

"No," Mary said.

Alice beamed again. "Good. Because I can hardly wait to get to the hospital tomorrow and start spreading the news." She hugged herself in her excitement. "And, oh, Mom, won't Russ be surprised when I tell him!"

"Yes," Mary agreed. "And Rachel too, I imagine."

When Alice told Russ the next morning at the fourth-floor nurses' station, he was both surprised and pleased, and gave her a big bear hug, saying what good news it was.

"Are you really pleased?" she asked, a little anxiously. And when he assured her he was, she said, "Then you do like Steven after all."

"I never did not like him," Russ replied. "I just didn't care much for the idea of him handing out advice to my wife about our marriage."

"But, Russ, it wasn't his idea. I mean, I don't mean to blame Rachel, but—"

"No, you're quite right to blame her. I know she forced Steve to give her advice. The trouble is, she's too impressionable. I guess Rachel liked the idea of having a successful, all-powerful executive type taking time out from his business affairs to discuss her personal problems with her. It made her feel important, sought-after. And Rachel needs to feel that way."

Alice agreed. "Only she should look for it from you, right? Well, I think she understands that now."

"I do too. At least, I hope so. You know, I think being pregnant has helped Rachel. That and now this. Your engagement. It's going to make Rachel see that somebody else has first claim on Steve's time and on his interest. I'm really very pleased about this."

The doubts that Mary didn't voice to Alice she did to her other daughter, Pat. "He's too successful. I mean . . . well, he's so high-powered. Maybe too high-powered for Alice. I know my feelings are somewhat influenced by the time when Rachel used to rush to Steve for advice, and by how much Russ resented this. Now, with Steve in the family, Rachel might feel she has more of an excuse than ever to go running to him, and I can't help feeling that marriage is shaky enough at best."

"You're not being truthful, Mother," Pat said, with a shake of her elegant blond head. "It's not Steve you have doubts about. It's Rachel."

Pat's husband, John, put his two cents in. "Russ will straighten Rachel out," he said. "She's difficult, but he obviously loves her and is willing to be patient with her."

Russ had to exercise some of that patience just in breaking the news to Rachel that Alice and Steve were going to get married.

"Well," Rachel said, not at all pleased and not trying very hard to hide it, "so Alice got Steve, huh?"

"He asked her, Rachel," Russ replied. "Which isn't surprising, since everybody knew he would."

"Oh, did they?" she flared. Then, fearful that she had gone too far, she said, "Well, it doesn't surprise me either. Not for a minute. Though I'm not certain they'll be happy together."

Russ frowned. "Why not? He loves her. She loves him. They're an even match."

She made a face. "How sweet you make it sound."

His frown deepened. "What is that supposed to mean?"

"Oh, nothing. I was just thinking of all the arguments they've had already. But you're probably right." And she changed the subject to something else before Russ could probe more deeply.

But she was furious. And she lost no time in heading for the place to vent that fury.

The next morning, unannounced, she went to Steve's office. Not at all pleased to see her, he told her she was stupid for showing up there when Russ had expressly forbidden it, and where any one of a number of acquaintances and friends in common might also turn up and see her there.

"What's the matter?" she snapped at him. "Are you afraid people will talk about us?"

"I'm not exactly crazy about the idea."

"Well, I don't care," she said.

He nodded grimly. "That's because you're fundamentally stupid."

Rachel gave him an ugly look. "I'm getting pretty sick and tired of hearing that from you."

"Then stop coming here."

She didn't answer him immediately, but stood in front of his desk, clenching and unclenching her hands. Finally she said, "Are you really going to marry Alice?"

"Yes, I am."

Her eyes were blazing. "How can you do a thing like that?"

He had been standing behind his desk. Now he sat down in his swivel chair. "I'm in love with her."

She stared at him. "In love?"

"Yes, Rachel. In love."

She laughed—a sharp, angry laugh. "That's the funniest thing I ever heard."

He smoothed a stack of papers on the desk top. "Really?" He glanced up at her. "I'm pretty serious about it."

"And I suppose," she said, running a hand through her thick dark hair, "you've told Alice the story of your life up to now?"

"Alice knows me pretty well."

"Does she know you're the father of the baby I'm going to have pretty soon?"

"No," he said, hitting the desk top with the flat of his hand, "she doesn't know that, because I'm not the father."

"But you are," Rachel said. "I told you."

"Your telling me doesn't make it true. Rachel, we spent one night together. That's all."

"That one night was enough to make me pregnant, and it did."

"Oh, come on, Rachel," he countered with an angry, brushing movement of his hand that sent the stack of papers he had just been smoothing skittering across the desk. He set himself to straightening them again. "Until the night we spent together you'd been living with Russ."

She shook her head. "Not as his wife. If you think I went back to him because— Steve, I had no place else to go. What did you expect me to do?"

"I didn't expect you to do anything, Rachel. If you want the honest truth, I didn't care what you did. All I cared about was that you shouldn't try to talk me into believing I'm the father of your child. I didn't believe you when you first told me, I've never believed you, and I don't believe you now."

She had the ugly look back on her face. "But it's true."

He sighed. "Rachel, your saying it over and over doesn't make it true."

She turned until she had her back to him, and she stayed that way for several moments. Then she turned around again to face him. "But it could be true. At least you'll admit that. That it's possible."

He sighed again. "All right. It's possible. But that doesn't make it true. On the contrary, it's very unlikely."

For the first time since coming into his office there was a glimmer of a smile on her face. "At least I got you to admit it's possible. That's something."

He had been toying with a letter opener. Now he put it down. "Rachel, I've never pretended we didn't spend that one idiotic night together. But that doesn't mean—"

She cut him off. "It wasn't idiotic to me. It was the most wonderful night of my whole life. The most wonderful and the most important. I think about it all the time. Don't you ever think about it, Steve?"

"No, I don't."

"I don't believe you. You wanted me a lot that night, Steve." Again her eyes were blazing. "You do remember. Don't tell me you don't remember."

"All right," he said, exasperated, "I won't tell you."

But still she persisted. "You wanted me a lot. You still do. Right this minute you want me, not Alice. The only reason you're marrying Alice—if you marry Alice you'll be respectable for once in your life. Marry a Matthews and get instant respectability. That's what you figure is going to happen. Be a pillar of the community. Good for business, good for your social standing, everything nice and proper." Her voice was heavy with sarcasm. "Lovely wedding, lovely reception, lovely bridesmaids, lovely bride, lovely honeymoon. Then you'll move into a lovely house in a lovely neighborhood, have lovely children and send them to a lovely school. I'll bet if you play your cards right you could get to be mayor."

He got to his feet. "And you had better shut up."

She stood her ground. "You can't stand to hear the truth, can you."

"Rachel," he said, coming around the desk toward her, "you wouldn't know the truth if you fell over it."

"Well, I know one thing that's true, and you know I know it. Even if you don't want to admit it, I know I'm having your child. And I know one other thing. You don't love Alice. You love me."

He took her by the arm and led her to the door. "Get out or I'll throw you out."

"All right," she said, shrugging out of his grasp. "But you'd better think things over, because you're the one who doesn't want to admit the truth, not me."

And out she went.

If Steve had wounded Rachel, Mary now rubbed

some salt in. Rachel was barely back in the apartment from seeing Steve—and in a rotten mood from seeing him—when her mother-in-law stopped by to visit. Only, as it turned out, not just to visit, but to discuss an idea that had occurred to her regarding the engagement party she wanted to have for Alice.

"Of course," Mary said, "we'll have the party at our house. Maybe in the yard. But since there will be so many young people there, I thought it would be nice if you would be the hostess. We'd try to make it very young, very gay, very modern. If you would invite the people, plan the decorations, greet everybody when they arrive. Naturally I'd help out. I'd see that the food got on the table, and I'll cook it, of course. But you could be the hostess. Wouldn't you like that?"

Cornered, not knowing what to say, Rachel seized on the idea that Russ wouldn't approve of her hostessing the party—because she was pregnant, and he was always telling her she was overdoing.

Thinking she was safe now, warming to her theme, she said, "He'll say no. I'm sure he will. Myself, I'd just love it, but I don't think I'd better, because it would upset Russ. It really would. So I'd better not."

Unfortunately, Russ thought his mother's idea was a splendid one—if Rachel wanted to do it. Backed into a corner, what could Rachel say except yes, of course she wanted to.

Mary's motive in asking Rachel was the best-intentioned in the world. As Mary said to Ada—the two women having become good friends since the marriage of their son and daughter—"You know we've talked before about how important it is to make Rachel feel she's really part of our family, and I think having her plan and give this party will do a lot toward giving her that feeling of belonging."

But Mary also had a favor to ask. Jim was at long last coming home, after a second stop at Tokyo. And he wanted Mary to join him there for the ten days or so he had to be there. After their long separation, Mary wanted very much to go, and she and Jim would of course be back in time for the party itself, but her going would mean that Rachel would be left alone to make most of the party plans. Would Ada give her the help Mary felt she would need?

Ada readily agreed to give Rachel whatever help she needed. But when she went to see Rachel to offer her help, Rachel blew up at her.

"Do you actually believe I'd want to be the hostess for a party like that? That I'd want to stand up there in front of everybody and say, 'Oh, I have the most exciting news for you! Dear, darling, sweet little Alice-blue-gown is going to marry Steven Frame. Of course, she has no business marrying him, because he's the father of my baby, but boys will be boys and all that.'"

Ada literally wrung her hands. "Oh, why did you ever have to get mixed up with him in the first place?"

"Because I love him."

Ada's jaw dropped, and she stared at her daughter in horror. "You what?"

This time there was a little space between each word. "Because I love him."

Ada went on staring at Rachel, but she said nothing. She couldn't find anything to say. There wasn't anything to say.

There was still, however, the matter of the party, and neither Ada nor Rachel could think of how Rachel could now get out of what she had so enthusiastically proclaimed she wanted very much to do.

"I can't do it all by myself," Rachel grumbled. "Even if I wanted to give the party, I wouldn't know where to start."

"That's what I'm here for," Ada said. "To help."

Rachel grudgingly accepted her mother's offer, but over the next few days she went on making frantic little efforts to get out of the spot she was in—efforts that were futile as well as frantic, because in typical Rachel fashion she chose the wrong way to go about it.

Instead of going straight to Mary to say she had changed her mind, she didn't feel up to giving the party, she wasn't experienced enough, or she just plain didn't want to, she found excuses for not getting started with the planning. She tried—unsuccessfully— to avoid her mother-in-law. And she spoke to other people about hostessing the party, in the vain hope that one of them would come up with a reasonable-sounding excuse she could use for getting out of doing it.

And then, of course, Mary left for Tokyo, and it was too late to go to her.

But Rachel still did not give up.

She called Steve and told him he had to get her out of giving the party. He told her he didn't want her giving the party any more than she did, but there was nothing he could do about it.

"How do you think I feel," she said, "being the hostess at a party for you and Alice? I hate it."

"I'm sorry," he said, "but as you once so wisely pointed out to me, we all have to put up with things we don't like in this world. I think those were your exact words."

Fuming at him again for marrying Alice when he was the father of her baby—and, as usual, getting nowhere except to be told he wasn't going to get into that again—Rachel said, "We'll go into that again and again and again—any time I feel like it, and any place, too."

But if Rachel couldn't persuade Steve that he was in fact the father of her unborn child, neither could he persuade her that he loved Alice. "You do not love Alice," she stormed at him. "You love me. You couldn't love anybody like Alice. All that sweetness, and all that niceness. All that respectability. What you're hoping is that some of that respectability will rub off on you, but it won't work, Steve. You're not sweet, and you're not nice, and you're certainly not respectable, and being married to Alice can't make you something you're not. You're ambitious and you're ruthless, and you're cruel, and that's the way you're going to stay, so you might as well make up your mind to it."

How much, if any, of the impending disaster Rachel anticipated and planned for is questionable. She wanted to prevent the marriage, there was no question of that. But though other people saw Rachel as always getting what she wanted, she saw herself as never getting it. If pinned to the wall, she might have said she was going to do something, she just didn't know what.

In any event, she had both a convincing cover for the torture she was going through and a possible escape from the doom that lay ahead. The cover and the escape were one and the same: her long-lost father.

It occurred to Rachel that there was available to her a more recent record of her father's whereabouts than his birth certificate. She wondered why she hadn't thought of it before. Her mother's divorce papers. And sure enough, the divorce papers gave his address as 109 Main Street in the town of Mount Holly, about three hundred miles north of Bay City. Of course, as her mother pointed out to her, that address was where he had been when the papers were served on him twenty years before, and he had never been a man for staying in one place a week, let alone twenty years.

Still, it was a start.

The trouble was—to what?

When Rachel told Russ about the address, he suggested that they dial Information to see if there was a phone listing for her father there, but she wouldn't let him do it, admitting that she was afraid to make the call.

"I don't know what I'm afraid of," she said. "Maybe of my father. Maybe I'm afraid he really will be there."

Russ gave her an understanding pat. "It would be easier, wouldn't it, to go on dreaming about him. If you see him, then he wouldn't be a dream any longer."

Rachel contended that she didn't want her father to remain only a dream, but Russ disagreed. He also doubted that her father was still living in Mount Holly, figuring, as Ada had, that he had probably left there years ago.

In a rare and rather touching display of candor, Rachel admitted that Russ had been right, she did prefer dream to reality. "I guess," she said, "I wanted to go on dreaming about him sitting there at 109 Main Street just waiting for his little girl to call him. A pretty silly dream, isn't it?"

"But understandable," Russ said, putting a comforting arm around her. "Honey, it's a universal failing to cling to a dream rather than face the reality. We all do it at one time or another. It's only when somebody does it all the time that it becomes a problem."

As the time for the engagement party grew nearer, Rachel's tension mounted. After being thrown together with Steve and Alice for dinner one night—and having to listen afterward to Russ exclaiming over how much in love the two of them were—Rachel abruptly announced that she was going to bed.

Concerned about how withdrawn and preoccupied she had been all evening, Russ asked her what the matter was, then concluded it was her father.

Maybe in an attempt to do as her mother had recently advised her—to put Steve out of her mind and her life—Rachel used Russ's erroneous conclusion to vent her frustration. She announced that she had decided not to do anything more about looking for her father—in Mount Holly or anywhere else.

"After all," she said, "he knows where to look for me. He's known for twenty years where to look for me. If he wanted to see me, he knew where I was. He could have gotten in touch with me any time he wanted to. If he doesn't care about seeing me, why should I care about seeing him?"

And then when Russ was summoned to the hospital a few minutes later, she did an abrupt turnabout. In an action maybe also related to Steve in her mind, Rachel dialed the Information operator in Mount Holly and was told that yes, there was a listing at 109 Main Street in her father's name.

The next afternoon Rachel made still another unannounced visit to Steve's office, this time to complain about having to watch him and Alice carrying on right in front of her the previous evening, pretending he was so in love with Alice, complaining, too, that Alice had arranged for a group of her friends to go out together the following night, including Russ and herself, and how did Steve think she felt about that? Was she supposed to enjoy seeing Steve and Alice fall all over each other again for another whole evening?

"What do you want from me?" Steve asked.

She tossed her head. "A little consideration and understanding."

Steve shrugged. "What good would that do? Suppose I did have a whole bunch of consideration and understanding to give you, what good would it do you? It wouldn't change one single thing about your life or mine. Now I'm going to have to ask you to leave. I have work to do. And if you don't want to go out with all of us tomorrow night, why don't you just stay home? Did you ever think of that? Just stay home."

To everyone's surprise, the party-loving Rachel did exactly that. Then she took her frustration out on her mother, who had come over to help Rachel with the party plans.

Ada cut short Rachel's insistent claims that Steve had no business marrying Alice. "He's marrying her because he loves her," Ada said. "I don't like the way you're acting. You talk about Alice as if she'd done something wrong. You're carrying Steve Frame's baby, and then you make judgments about other people."

"I don't care," Rachel said. "I don't want to see Alice and Steve together—ever."

"You're going to have to see them together," Ada reminded her. "You're married to Alice's brother. You may not like it, but you'll see them all the time. And remember, you don't have anybody to blame for all this but yourself."

Nor was Ada any more comforting in her predictions about what Rachel would find when she found her father, if she ever found him.

"I think I ought to warn you you may be in for a shock. All these years you've been building him up into some hero. Well, he's not."

Rachel sniffed. "You haven't seen him for more than twenty years."

"Well," Ada admitted, "he might have changed

from when I knew him. Might have. But I doubt it."

Rachel glared at her mother. "You'd rather cut your tongue out than say one nice thing about him, wouldn't you."

"No, that's not true. I never told you your father was a horrible man. He wasn't. But he was selfish. He never had a thought that wasn't about himself." She shook her head. "I know you've got some kind of notion that he thinks about you because you think about him, but he hasn't bothered to get in touch with you for over twenty years."

Rachel shrugged. "Maybe he's embarrassed."

"Nothing ever embarrassed your father. Your father wasn't a bum, you know. I mean, he was never down and out. He managed to make a living. But that wasn't enough for him. He wanted a lot of money. That's all he ever talked about or thought about—making a lot of money. Buckets of it. I never could understand how a man who talked so much about it and thought so much about it couldn't ever make it. But he couldn't, and that soured him on the world. And me. And you. And family life in general. So he walked out on it and never looked back."

Working with her mother on the guest list over at the Matthews house, Rachel had to listen to Alice enthuse about buying her trousseau—something denied to Rachel in her hasty elopement with Russ—and to the even more discomfiting statement that Alice didn't believe in long engagements, so she and Steven would probably get married the following month.

After thanking Rachel for hostessing the upcoming engagement party, Alice said, her eyes shining, "Love makes the whole world beautiful, doesn't it? It makes it exciting to open your eyes in the morning, and it makes it beautiful to close them at night."

Turning to Lenore, who was going shopping with her, Alice said, "Let's make me beautiful for Steven."

And off they went, leaving Rachel clenching her hands and saying, "I hate her."

Because of the intimacy of the occasion, Rachel was spared the agony of seeing Steve give Alice a diamond engagement ring, and the pledges of love that went with the ritual of giving it, but she wasn't spared the agony of seeing the ring—a solitaire so large and so magnificently faceted and set that it made Rachel's ring seem paltry by comparison.

And so the days passed, and the date for the party drew nearer and nearer, and Rachel's tension and frustration grew greater and greater—mainly because there didn't seem to be anything she could do to prevent what was going to happen from happening.

Grumbling to Russ one day about how her pregnancy was making her fat and ugly, and how everybody was snapping at her, and how she had to give the engagement party, Rachel said, "Sure I want to give the party, Russ, but it's such a big responsibility. If the party's a flop, it'll be all my fault."

It was one of the great understatements of all time.

Chapter Fourteen

THE day of the engagement party dawned bright and clear—a beautiful summer day with very little humidity and a temperature predicted to climb to the high seventies, and then to cool off that evening to the upper sixties.

Alone with her father after breakfast, Alice told Jim how much she loved Steve. "It's funny," she said. "I love him so much now, and six months ago I think I almost hated him. I guess he frightened me a little. I loved him, but I feared him, too."

"And now you don't?" Jim asked.

Alice shook her head, smiling. "No. He's sweet, you know that?"

Her father smiled too. "I agree he's changed. Even

his business associates say he's mellowed. You did that, Alice."

"I trust him, Dad, and he trusts me. We're keeping each other safe."

Over at the other Matthews household—the Russ Matthews one—the atmosphere was somewhat different.

Among the presents Jim and Mary had brought back from Tokyo was a stunning multicolored Japanese-style hostess gown for Rachel. She had been delighted with it until Mary said they had bought it for her to wear at Alice's engagement party.

Before going to the hospital the morning of the party, Russ went to the dry-cleaner's to get Rachel's gown, where it had been altered to fit her. Returning to the apartment with it, Russ told Rachel she would be a smashing hostess. "You won't be nervous once people start coming," he said. "And don't tell the bride-to-be I said so, but you'll be the prettiest one there."

"Oh, sure," Rachel said, miserable.

But it was her mother she snarled at when Ada came by later that morning, as she ran through her usual list of gripes about Steve and Alice.

"You'd better get in a better mood," Ada warned her. "If you're in a rotten mood, it will be harder to pull off."

Rachel made a face. "Oh, don't worry. I'll be all pulled and pasted together when the time comes. It's just too much work to fake it until I have to."

Admiring the Japanese hostess gown, Ada said, "Mary's very sweet."

Rachel made another face. "All the Matthewses are sweet, aren't they," she said sourly. Then, in an abrupt change of subject, she said, "Has my father ever got married again?"

Ada turned from the gown to stare at her. "Rachel, you know very well I haven't heard one word from that man since he walked out on us. If he did get married again, I don't know anything about it."

"I just thought you knew and never told me. Just like you didn't tell me you had his address."

"I didn't tell you because it never occurred to me, that's all. Even now I find it hard to believe he's still at that address."

"Well, he is," Rachel said. "Not that it matters anyhow, since I'm not going to chase after him."

"If you're not going to chase after him," Ada said, "why do you keep asking me questions about him? You've been dying to find him. When did you change your mind?"

"Oh, stop it," Rachel muttered. "You're just trying to give me a hard time."

"I'm not trying to give you a hard time, Rachel. I'm trying to make sure you're going to be a charming, well-behaved, pleasant hostess tonight."

"And what if I'm not in the mood, Mom?"

Her mother spoke firmly. "Well, you just get in the mood. Rachel, you can't ruin this party for Alice. You just shape up, and don't try anything funny, because I'll have my eye on you every minute. And you remember that."

That evening, as Russ and Rachel were dressing for the party, he teased her about being a Japanese doll, and she snapped at him, "Don't tease me. I don't feel well." Then, trying to pull herself together, she said, "Oh, I don't know what it is. I'm fat."

"You're not fat," Russ responded. "You're pregnant. Cheer up. You look gorgeous."

But she wouldn't cheer up. "I don't want to go to the party," she said.

"Sure you do," he said encouragingly.

"I just said I didn't, Russ."

He looked concerned. "But, honey, you're the hostess. You have to go."

"That doesn't change the fact that I don't want to."

Russ rolled his eyes. "Being the husband of a pregnant lady is not easy."

"It's easier than being the one who's pregnant."

"You're just uncomfortable and irritable," he said soothingly. "But it'll be over in a few months. Think of all we have to look forward to."

Rachel had been fastening the front of her gown.

Now she stopped and turned to Russ, who was tying his tie. "If I don't want to go, why should I have to?"

He stopped, too, and gave her his full attention. "For the simple reason that you're committed to. Rachel, you chose to do it. You could have refused, but not now."

"But could I have refused when it was your mother asking me to do it?"

He looked at her with some confusion. "I don't get the point. Why did you feel forced to do it—since that's the way you seem to feel?"

"Well, I would have looked pretty silly refusing."

He shook his head. "Then how can you even consider backing out now? Come on. Finish fastening that, and let's go."

Rachel finished fastening the gown, but then sat down on the side of the bed. "No," she said. "I don't feel good."

"You feel fine," he answered. "Let's go." He held out a hand and pulled her to her feet.

"I'm nervous," she said.

"You won't be for long."

"I won't know what to do. I won't know what to say to people."

"Honey, everyone will help you. And we're not going to disappoint Alice and Steve on account of anybody's mood. Why should you be nervous and mopey? When I talked to Alice a few minutes ago she sounded as cool as ice cream. And if she's not nervous, why should you be?"

Rachel made a last desperate attempt to avoid the party altogether. "Because she doesn't have to do anything, that's why. Russ, I can't do it. I can't."

It was no use. Putting a firm hand on her elbow, guiding her out of the bedroom, he said, "We're going to the party, and we're going right now. Just like this." He guided her through the living room, held the door for her, and gave her a little push out into the hall.

"Oh, all right," she said. "I'm going, I'm going."

When Russ and Rachel pulled into the driveway of

his parents' house, he drove all the way to the back, as he always did, and after parking the car they went in through the kitchen entrance, as they almost always did.

Alice and Steve were there, kissing, and when Russ commented on it, Steve looked around at him in mock disgust, waved his hand, said, "Go away," and returned to the kiss.

That upset Rachel, but what happened next upset her more.

Taking his mother aside a few minutes later, Russ asked her to give Rachel something to do until the guests started arriving.

Mary protested. "But Rachel's pregnant, and she's going to be a very busy hostess in a little while now, and I don't want to overburden her."

"You don't understand, Mom," he said. "She's awfully tense and nervous. I don't know why exactly, except she's been worried all along about hostessing this party. So if you could give her something to do to take her mind off it."

Mary nodded. "All right, darling. Don't worry about it. I'll find something for her to do."

And Mary did. Unfortunately, she went about it in the most disastrous way imaginable. Taking Steve aside, she said, "Russ just told me, Steve, that Rachel seems—I don't know—upset, nervous, tense. I'm going to give her a couple of little things to do here, and I wish you'd help her."

Steve now began to feel a bit nervous himself, but he had no choice but to accede to Mary's request.

"There are some platters here in the kitchen and a few other dishes that I was going to wash. But now, if you'll do them for me, I'll ask Rachel to help by drying them. All right?"

"Yeah, sure," he said.

Mary called Rachel and explained what she wanted. Then she went upstairs to dress, and Rachel and Steve were alone in the kitchen.

To Rachel's angry look Steve said, "Look. You're stuck. We're both stuck."

"Steve," she said, "never mind these silly dishes. I have to talk to you."

For answer, he poured detergent into the sink, ran water into it, and began washing the first platter.

"Steve," she begged him, "you've got to get me out of here. Out of this house, this party. Don't you see what this is doing to me?"

"Don't overdramatize," he said, handing her the platter and picking up the next one. "You don't like it, you don't like being here at this party, because it's for Alice and me. And you don't like being hostess for it."

"You should have gotten me out of that long ago," she said, drying the platter and setting it down on a nearby counter none too gently.

"You know I couldn't get you out of it." He handed her the second platter and picked up a third one. "I don't like your being here any more than you do, but there's nothing either of us can do about it."

Rachel dried the second platter. "I'd like to know why not." She set it down beside the first one.

"You already know why not," he said, handing her the third platter, then starting to wash some small bon-bon dishes.

"Because I got stuck with the wrong man?" This time she slammed the platter down so hard that it was a wonder it didn't break.

Steve sighed. "Rachel, Rachel. You roped Russ in. You wanted him, and you got him to marry you."

"He wanted to marry me," she said. "Anyway, that was before I met you. Before I knew what love was."

"Cut it out," Steve said sharply, rinsing the small dishes and putting them in the dish drainer. "Don't you talk to me about love. You don't know what love is. You've got a wonderful husband that you don't deserve, and—"

"And," Rachel cut in, "I'm carrying your baby."

Steve unplugged the drain. "I deny that again. But I'm not going to argue with you. The party's going on. You're the hostess. You've got to shape up. Stop whining, paint a smile on your face, and laugh, clown, laugh. Okay?" When she didn't answer, he went on. "Grow up. You've got to go through with it, so go on."

Rachel had finished drying the bonbon dishes. Now she shook out the dish towel and hung it up. "Listen to the great Steven Frame," she said, sneering. "The man who can take care of all those big businesses, all those big deals. The man who made so much money, and you can't even solve a little problem like this."

"I can live with it," he said.

"Oh, can you?" she came back at him, getting more and more exercised now. "Can you even live with yourself, play-acting all the time? Every time I walk into a room, there you are nibbling at Alice's ear or something. You don't call that play-acting?" Rachel made a face. "Alice, sweet Alice, namby-pamby Alice."

For the first time, she had gotten to him. "Don't you talk that way about Alice, Rachel," he said, his voice low but harsh.

"Why shouldn't I? Marrying her to get the social position of the Matthewses, you're giving me up."

He shook his head. "I never had any serious or honorable intentions toward you, Rachel."

That remark should have angered her. Instead, she started to cry. Probably she hadn't heard what he said, convinced as she was that he did love her, not Alice, that he was in fact marrying Alice only for the reasons she had accused him of having.

"Please forgive me, Steve," she said, trying to control her tears. "Please forgive me. You don't know how hard it is for me. You don't understand, because you don't want to understand, but, Steve, I love you."

It got her nowhere. "I don't want to hear you say that, Rachel."

"But it's true," she said. "I love you. When I see you with Alice, I just want to die." She wiped her eyes, then returned to her earlier theme. "You're just play-acting with Alice. I know it."

"I love Alice," he said.

"No you don't."

"Yes I do. And get that through your head."

But she couldn't. Or wouldn't. "I know better," she insisted. "How can you love that sticky-sweet namby pamby, when I know what you and I meant to each other?"

"We meant nothing, Rachel. Nothing. Rachel, listen to me. I don't want to talk. I didn't want to get into this with you, but you insist. All right. We meant nothing to each other. You and I meant nothing to each other. I say it because it's true. I never said you meant anything to me. That night in my apartment I acted the way any man would act. Remember what you were like that night in my apartment, Rachel? You came there—and not for the first time, either— and you flung yourself at me. Look, Rachel. You're a good-looking young girl, and you could go out on the street and fling yourself at a total stranger with the same result. That's exactly what I'm saying about you, Rachel. Love you? Nobody who knew you could love you. You're not fit for Alice to wipe her shoes on."

Rachel had been staring at him, a stunned look on her face. The look turned to one of cold hatred. "You'll regret this," she said. "You'll be sorry you ever said this to me, Steven. You'll be sorry."

"Tough," he said, and turned and walked out of the kitchen, leaving her standing there staring after him.

She hesitated only a moment, then left the kitchen and went upstairs to Alice's room, where Alice was getting dressed for the party.

Alice showed Rachel the dress she had bought for the party—a frothy light blue evening gown. Alice blue. Just the sight of it made Rachel sick, but Alice didn't seem to notice.

"I'm terribly excited," Alice said, beaming. "It isn't every evening a girl gets her engagement announced, and what a lovely way to do it. All my family, friends, people I've known gathering here—"

Rachel cut in on her. "To hear that you're engaged to marry Steven Frame, right? You like having it announced."

Alice looked puzzled. "Well, of course. Rachel,

is something wrong? The way you're talking. And you look drawn and pale. Come on, Rachel. I didn't mean anything critical. You're all right, aren't you?"

Rachel gave Alice an arch look. "Being pregnant, you mean?"

"Yes."

Rachel nodded. "Yes, I am pregnant, right?"

Alice frowned. She still looked puzzled. "Well, I mean—"

Again Rachel cut in on her. "There isn't any question about it, is there?" She laughed—a bitter little laugh. And answered her own question. "No, there's no question about it. I am pregnant. Pregnant, pregnant, pregnant."

Alice looked more confused than ever. "Rachel, is there something on your mind?"

"What makes you think that, Alice?"

Alice shook her head. "I don't know, but—well, you seem different. Something, anyway."

"How different?"

"Rachel, I don't know."

"Happier?"

Alice frowned again. "Rachel, what is this?"

"Sadder?"

"Rachel, please. Is there anything I can do?"

Rachel smiled. "That's a good question. But I asked first. How am I different?"

Again Alice shook her head. "I don't understand what you're talking about, Rachel."

"You will. I'll tell you how different I am, Alice. Not happier. Not sadder, for that matter. Madder. Angrier."

Alice's confusion mounted. "Rachel," she said, "I think you ought to explain yourself."

"Don't worry," Rachel said. "I intend to."

"If there's anything I can do to help you . . ."

"You said that before," Rachel answered. "And maybe there is something you can do to help me. Or to help yourself."

"Rachel, please. What's this all about?"

Rachel smiled again—not a very pretty smile. "All this is just leading up to the fact that I have something to tell you, Alice. I don't think you're going to like it, but you have to be told."

"Well, Rachel," Alice answered, still without the remotest idea of what this was all about, "whatever it is, go ahead and tell me."

Rachel nodded. "All right. I will. The man you're going to marry, Alice, is the father of the child I'm going to have."

"Now, Rachel," Alice said, wondering what sickness had got into her sister-in-law, "are you all right?"

"I'm fine. Perfectly fine. Of course, I'm pregnant. Pregnant with Steve Frame's baby."

"Now, Rachel, you'd better not say that, because——"

Rachel cut in on her. "There's no reason not to say it. It's true. It can be true, and it is true. Steve Frame is my child's father. Alice, I'm trying to tell you a simple fact of life, and you'd just better face it. You want to know how it happened? Well, you remember when I left Russ for a while there at the end of January? I went to Steve's apartment, and I spent the night, and I got pregnant. Now, I'm just telling you plain, simple facts, that's all. Well, after I spent that night with Steve, I went to live with my mother for a while. You remember that. Do you? And while I was living at my mother's I found out I was having Steven's baby. You see, Alice, I love Steve. Do you understand? I've loved him for a long time—a lot longer than you have. And I told Steve I was going to have his child, but he wouldn't admit what was perfectly obviously true. I don't know why he wouldn't, because I know he loves me."

Alice had been listening to this outpouring in an almost catatonic state, thinking that Rachel herself had gone mad. Now she found her voice. "Rachel!" But she got no further than that.

"Oh, yes," Rachel said. "He loves me just the way I love him, but maybe he didn't like the idea of my having his child while being married to Russ or anything. Anyway, he wouldn't take any responsibility for the child or for me or for anything, so I went back to Russ."

This time Alice simply continued to stare at Rachel, unable to find anything to say.

Rachel shrugged and looked defensive. "Well, there wasn't any place else for me to go. Nobody wanted me except Russ. Nobody cared what happened to me except Russ. I had to go back to him. There wasn't anybody else. And since we've been back together we've been happy. Well, anyway, he's been happy. And that's because I've nearly broken my back to make him happy. But he *is* happy, and he thinks the baby is his, and he's very happy about the whole thing."

"Rachel," Alice said—heard herself say—"you can't really expect me to believe any of this."

"Oh, Alice," Rachel answered, "you never want to believe anything that isn't all sunlight and roses and sweetness and light." She made a face. "You're so stupid. You're so sweet and sanctified. You think everything's easy for everybody, just because it's easy for you. Well, it isn't. Things are very different for other people from what you think they are. Alice, I'm the one Steve Frame should be marrying. I'm the one he loves. I'm the one who's carrying his child. I'm the one who's absolutely sick with loving him. For months and months and months now. I'm the one who's had to stand around and watch him make a fuss over you."

Rachel had gotten an ugly look on her face, and now it intensified. "Yes," she said contemptuously, "and you falling all over him and kissing him and making a big spectacle of yourself—talking about love and how wonderful it is, and how happy you are and he is, and isn't life grand, and wearing that big diamond on your finger and showing it off to everybody like you'd won first prize. All that—the ring and this party and all that kissing and carrying on—all that belongs to me, not to you, because I love him, and I'm going to have his child."

Alice still couldn't believe what she was hearing or even why she was hearing it. "Rachel," she said, "you just don't know what you're saying."

It did no good. "I know perfectly well what I'm

saying," Rachel retorted. "And there's nothing wrong with what I'm saying, either, because it's all true. What's wrong is you don't want to hear it. And most of all, you don't want to believe it. But it's true."

It suddenly occurred to Alice that she didn't have to go on listening to this insanity. Getting a tight grip on herself, she said, "All right, now, Rachel, you've had your fun. I don't think you're kidding. Not even you would kid about a thing like this. What I do think is you'd make up a little fantasy about what might have happened but didn't. You distort things, Rachel. Whenever things don't go the way you want them to, you take them and twist them around so they're more to your liking. And sometimes I even think you get to the point where you believe them yourself. You've made up everything, because this crazy story you've just told me couldn't be true. Not possibly. Not any of it."

"It is true," Rachel said vehemently. "All of it."

Alice shook her head. "I've known you a long, long time, Rachel. You used to live in this house. I've gotten to know you pretty well since you married my brother. And because of Russ I've tried very hard to like you, because Russ is absolutely, totally in love with you, and it was very important for me to get along with his wife. And to like her if possible. Well, I've tried, and I can tell you now it's not possible. If it ever was possible, certainly it isn't now, after what you've tried to do to me. As a matter of fact, maybe it wasn't ever possible, because the truth is I never liked you. Never. Right from the beginning I thought you were selfish and self-centered and conniving and greedy and jealous and a spiteful, rotten person."

Rachel looked back at her as if she were totally unmoved. "You don't think I'm going to burst into tears because you don't like me, do you?"

"I don't much care what you do," Alice said.

"Because I'm not," Rachel said. "I know why you're going on about how selfish I am and all that. It's just because you know that everything I've just told you about Steve and me is absolutely the truth."

"It's not the truth."

Rachel laughed. "Oh, Alice," she said, "you're funny, you know that? You're just plain funny. You just don't want to believe that anything could happen to spoil Alice Matthews's happy life with Steven Frame. Little Miss Alice and big handsome Steven— that marvelous couple."

Alice sighed. "Rachel, in about two minutes I'm going to throw you right out of this room."

"Oh, I don't think you will," Rachel answered her. "How would it look to Russ and your family and all your dear, devoted friends downstairs who are waiting to hear that you're going to marry Steve? And how would it look to Steve, Alice, if you threw me out of your room?"

"Then why don't you just leave by yourself? Nothing in the whole world can make me believe you've been telling me the truth."

Whatever Rachel might have said to that went unsaid as Mary and Ada came into the bedroom looking for both of them. "People are here," Mary said. "It's time to come downstairs."

"Rachel," Ada said, "you're supposed to be receiving people."

Rachel smiled at her mother. "Alice and I have been having a little talk."

Ada immediately looked stricken, but she tried to sound as if nothing were wrong. "Rachel," she said. "You come with me. I want to talk with you."

"Sorry, Mom. I don't have time. You heard what Mrs. Matthews said. Guests are arriving, and I'm the hostess. See you at the party." And off she went.

If Ada feared that something had gone wrong, Mary did too, but, unlike Rachel's mother, Alice's mother didn't have any idea of what it could have been. She only knew that Alice looked pale and a bit distraught, and that on an occasion when she ought to have been bubbling over with excitement, she was quiet to the point of being withdrawn.

When Alice finally came downstairs—after asking to be alone for a few minutes—Steve came up to her to greet her and put his arm around her. Without intending to, she stiffened, and when Steve led her off to dance, she said she wanted to have the first dance with her father.

While Steve was standing on the sidelines, watching Alice dance with Jim, wondering why she had been so cool and distant to him, Rachel came up to him. "Enjoying yourself, Steve?" she asked.

"Yes," he said curtly.

Rachel smiled. "This is your big night. Make the most of it."

He frowned at her. "What do you mean by that, Rachel?"

Her smile brightened. "I think you'll find out. See you around." And she slipped away.

He found out. He tried to find out during the party —the party that had started out so gaily but now seemed to be falling to pieces. When he finally had Alice in his arms on the dance floor, he said, "Alice, what's troubling you?"

"Nothing," she answered.

"Something is," he insisted.

She didn't answer him.

And she seemed—not only to Steve, but to many others at the engagement party—to want to spend as little time with him as she could get away with.

After the party was over, and Steve was alone with Alice on the porch, he said, "You didn't seem to enjoy the party. Any of it."

"Yes I did," she said. Not very convincingly.

He shook his head, his eyes intent upon her. "You're always the gayest girl in the room at any party. What was the matter tonight?" And when she said nothing: "Darling, don't try to fool the fellow who loves you. Now what's the trouble?"

Alice shook her head. "Nothing. There's no trouble."

"I know there is," Steve said. "You're still acting the way you did all evening. Off somewhere. Not here. Worst of all, not with me."

She smiled—a very faint and little smile. "I'm sorry."

"Don't be sorry, Alice. Just tell me what's wrong."

She shrugged. "I guess I'm tired."

"Were you tired all evening—even when the party started? Alice, I don't believe that. There's something you're not telling me."

She nodded. "Yes, that's true. There is."

"What is it?"

"Not tonight, Steven. Please. Not tonight."

He gave up finally. "You're very dear to me, you know," he said. "The dearest person in the whole world—beyond anything I could ever tell you. Beyond words, beyond deed, beyond anything."

"Oh, Steve," she said, tears glistening in her eyes, but when he bent to kiss her she averted her face, so that the kiss landed on her cheek.

The next afternoon she called him to ask if she might come to his office when she got off duty, at seven. He offered to pick her up at the hospital and take her out somewhere for dinner, but she said she would rather go there.

She arrived a little after seven, and he fixed drinks for them, and they exchanged small talk—but not in the relaxed and carefree way that was customary to them. She still looked pale, and she still seemed quiet and withdrawn—if anything, more withdrawn than on the previous night.

The small talk finally turned to the party, and from out of nowhere, it seemed to Steve, Alice brought up Rachel, going on and on about her—how she had looked, whether or not she was happy with Russ—until finally, with a sinking feeling, Steve said, "Is it Rachel who's got you all upset?"

"Who said I was upset?" Alice countered.

"I did. And you are. Look, Alice, you're not the same with me as you were before the party, and you know it. Now why aren't you? Alice, you never horse around with me. You never have. If there's something on your mind, you always come right out and say it. Now what is it?"

When he still couldn't get an answer from her, he put his hands on her shoulders. "Alice, it's me. It's Steve. It's the guy who loves you. Quit treating me like somebody you just met."

She would not look at him, but at least he got a

response from her. "Is that the way I'm treating you?" she said.

"Worse than that," he told her. "Like somebody you just met and took an instant dislike to. Alice, tell me what the trouble is. Have I done something?"

Now she looked at him. "That's what I have to find out," she said, in a voice so low that he could scarcely hear her. "Steven," she continued, "Rachel says you're the father of the child she's going to have. Is that true?"

He stared at her in horror. He might have known that stupid, self-pitying, spiteful— "No," he said, "it's not true."

"Then why does Rachel say it is?"

"Because she's envious—jealous, greedy—always wanting what other people have."

"Yes," Alice agreed. "I told her that myself."

"And besides, Rachel's basically a very unhappy person."

"Yes," Alice agreed again, "I know that, too."

He began to feel a bit better. "Alice, let's not let Rachel make trouble for us."

"She's already done that, Steven. Steven, Rachel never used to want a baby. Russ did, but she didn't. Did you know that?"

The little-bit-better feeling faded quietly away. "I got that impression, yes."

Alice was looking squarely at him now. "Didn't she ever tell you how she shouldn't have a child— because of how sick she was the time she lost her first one?"

"She may have. I don't remember."

"Steven, when Rachel left Russ at the end of January and went to live with her mother, you saw her a few times while she was living there, didn't you?"

The sinking feeling was back, stronger than ever. He nodded. "She kept calling me up and asking my advice about what she should do."

Alice frowned. "Do about what?"

The office was air-conditioned, but he was sweating. "I don't know. About Russ. About her life. I don't know. So I took her out to dinner a couple of times."

"Is that all?" Alice asked. "You just took her to dinner a couple of times?"

The trouble was, he couldn't lie to her. He never had been able to lie to anybody, and he most especially couldn't lie to Alice. "Alice, Rachel came to my apartment a few times. Just showed up. Uninvited. I had to throw her out once or twice."

"What about the other times?"

"What other times?"

"The times you didn't throw her out."

He was cornered now, and he knew it. "There was only one time."

She looked at him in silence for a long time. "Only one time. When you didn't throw her out."

"That's right."

She had gone paler than before. "But there was one time."

"Alice," he begged. "That doesn't mean I'm her child's father. You know that."

"No, it doesn't mean you're her child's father, Steven. But it means you could be, doesn't it?"

He sighed. "Yes. I suppose so."

She gave him a cold look. "And even if you're not, there was that one time when you didn't throw Rachel out—when Rachel stayed. Isn't that right?"

"Alice," he pleaded, "you and I hardly knew each other then. And I thought we were all washed up. It wasn't anything like it is with us now."

She was still looking at him coldly—and with distance. "I don't know how it is with us now."

He said the only thing that mattered to him. "I love you, Alice."

And she said what he might have expected her to say. "Steven, Rachel is my brother's wife."

"I love you," he said again.

"Did you hear me?" she asked. "Rachel is my brother's wife. And whether you're the father of her child or not, how do you think I can . . . be with you? How can you think of being with my family after what you've done to Russ?" She looked at him again in silence. "I'm sorry, Steven. I think you'd better take this."

She took off the ring he had given her, and when he would not take it from her, she put it on the desk, picked up her purse, and walked out of the office.

Chapter Fifteen

ALTHOUGH the strain between Alice and Steve at the party indicated to her family and their friends that something was awry, the news that Alice had broken their engagement stunned everyone except Rachel. And no one except Rachel knew why she had done it. Alice's sister, Pat, was sure it was only a lovers' tiff. Their father, Jim, was just as sure it was more serious. Mary decided that Alice had decided that, much as she loved Steven, his world was too high-powered for her, but Mary's theory was not very convincing even to herself.

As for the formerly engaged couple, neither of them would say anything at all—beyond stating that they didn't wish to discuss it.

A furious Steve went to see Rachel, to tell her that nobody had ever done as bad a thing to him as she had done, that he would be watching her, and that the first chance he had, he would louse her up and louse her up good.

More alarming to Rachel—because it was more immediate—was Alice's threat. She also came to see Rachel, saying she hadn't made up her mind yet whether to tell Russ that Rachel had spent the night with Steve, but when she did decide it would probably be to tell him.

Although Alice said nothing to Russ, he was suspicious on his own that Rachel had had something to do with the breakup, primarily because of her tense, nervous behavior the night of the party. Russ's probing on top of Steve's and Alice's threats was enough to make Rachel leave town again on the part-pretext, part-genuine search for her father. This time she did have a definite address to go to, but when she reached Mount Holly she learned that 109 Main Street was not a residence but a storeroom, where her father kept machinery and tools, and where apparently he turned up only very occasionally. She couldn't find anybody who knew him or knew much of anything about him. The rent for the storeroom was paid by check in the name of some company and was sent by mail. Still, she resisted Russ's telephoned entreaties to come home, saying she wanted to stay there awhile in the hope that her father would show up—and in the further hope, though she said nothing of this to Russ, that Alice's attitude toward her would soften in the weeks she was away.

Rather than soften, Alice's attitude toward Rachel hardened—if any further hardening was possible. On occasion Alice showed a hardening attitude toward life as well. Taut, brittle, flippant toward her family and her friends, she boasted to a date one night that she had once been sweet and nice, and where had it gotten her? No, one should be hard, selfish, greedy. And so far as happiness was concerned, why should anybody expect to be happy?

She didn't fool the date or her family or her friends. It was doubtful that she even fooled herself.

After making her father promise he would say nothing to her mother, Alice finally told him why she had broken her engagement. Jim understood why Alice didn't want Mary to know. They were both afraid Mary wouldn't be able to hide her knowledge from Russ—or her hatred of Rachel—and they both believed it was extremely unlikely that Steven was the father of Rachel's baby. Believing this, Jim felt he should not come between husband and wife, that it was up to Russ to find out what kind of wife Rachel had been to him.

One thing Jim could do—and did—was to stop handling Steve's accounting work, though Steve urged him to stay on. And as the weeks went by, and summer turned to fall, Jim decided that, despite the risk, Mary had to be told why Alice had broken her engagement, that it wasn't fair to her not to tell her, and that if he told her when Russ left for Mount Holly to bring Rachel home, Mary would have time to get her emotions under control. Alice reluctantly agreed, and then went on to have an exchange with her father about something that had begun to trouble her.

"How do we know," she said, "that Steven isn't the father of Rachel's child?"

"Darling," her father answered, "she stayed with him only one night."

Alice nodded. "I know. But why was she so positive to me the night of the party?"

"She wanted to hurt you. She wanted to keep you from marrying Steve."

"But that's just my point, Dad. She didn't have to tell me she was having his baby to do that. Just the fact that she stayed with him that one night—that would have been enough. And she must have known that. But, Dad, she went on and on. She kept saying Steven belonged to her—that that engagement ring was really hers. Why would she go on like that if he isn't the father?"

Jim shook his head. "I think she wants to think it's Steve's baby." He shook his head again. "It doesn't make sense. She stayed with him only one night. She's married to Russ. No, I think it's Russ's baby."

"Maybe," Alice said. "And maybe not."

"Anyway," Jim said, returning to their earlier conversation, "I've got to tell your mother. She's got to know. Besides, she can listen to you and understand. And if necessary you can cry on her shoulder."

"I don't need any shoulders to cry on," Alice said, starting to get taut again.

Her father put his arm around her. "Yes you do, honey. You cried on my shoulder, and it helped. She'll talk to you and help you, and things won't seem quite so dark."

Alice's fears that Mary wouldn't be able to hide her feelings once she knew about Rachel and Steven were justified. After Jim told her, Mary brooded about it for a couple of weeks and then decided Russ had to be told. She called him one day near the end of September and asked him to come over, saying she had something to say to him about Rachel. He had arrived, and she was on the point of telling him when he got an urgent call from Ada saying that Rachel had started into labor, and would he meet them at the hospital. A few hours later, Rachel was delivered of a three-pound-four-ounce boy named James Gerald Matthews, in honor of Russ's and Rachel's fathers, a boy presumably two months premature, in actuality one month premature.

The next morning, at breakfast, Mary confessed to Jim that she had almost told Russ about Rachel and Steve.

"I'm glad you didn't," Jim said. "There's no question in my mind that the baby is Russ's, and you certainly can't tell him now."

"But, Jim," Mary protested, "Russell has a right to know."

"It's not a question of right," Jim said. "Russ loves Rachel a great deal, and there's no way of telling what it might do to him if he ever thought there was even a chance this isn't his child."

Mary started to say something, but Jim went on before she could. "You know, Mary, it would destroy him completely. He's very happy about the baby and about the way Rachel has finally started to be a good wife to him."

"That's the way she's made it appear," Mary cut in bitterly. "A good wife."

"Nevertheless," Jim said firmly, "Russ is probably happier right now than he's ever been in his life. Maybe happier than he ever expected to be. And neither you nor I can do anything now to destroy that happiness. And what's more, my dear, very soon—tomorrow or the next day at the latest—you and I are going to have to go see Rachel and her baby in the hospital."

Mary stared at him. "No. I can't. I can't bring myself to do it, Jim."

Ballantine Books of Canada Ltd.

5390 Ambler Drive, Mississauga, Ontario L4W 1Y7

25859

REVIEW COPY

Title   ANOTHER WORLD

Author   KATE LOWE KERRIGAN

Publication Date   CURRENT   Price   1.95

Please send us two tearsheets of any review you may publish

"Darling," he said, "we have to. Staying away from the hospital, not going to see Rachel, would be the next thing to telling Russ, don't you see? He'd be bound to wonder why."

And so they went, though it was all Mary could do to be civil to Rachel, and it was hard to say which of the two women was the more nervous, since Rachel had no guarantee that Alice hadn't told her parents of Rachel's one-night stand, or would not at any moment.

Ada was also nervous. She believed—and with reason—that Rachel's marriage to Russ was the only real thing Rachel had, and that she had better hang on to it. In her mother's presence Rachel was contemptuous about Ada's fears, confident that the Matthewses had not been told and suspected nothing, offering as proof the handsome tote bag Jim had brought her for a present. And offering, further, her own rationale as to why Alice would continue to say nothing.

"She wouldn't want anybody to know," Rachel said, "because she'd hate to have anyone realize Steve ever loved somebody more than he loved her."

Ada shook her head. "Alice isn't like that. She cares about people. She's not like you."

Rachel made a face. "You bet she's not like me. For one thing, she couldn't hold Steven Frame. She couldn't get his love in the first place. I'm the one he always loved, and that's the truth."

"Did Steve Frame love you well enough," Ada asked harshly, "to admit this baby was his?"

"How do you know he won't do that someday?" Rachel flared back at her.

Now it was her mother who made a face. "That's what I mean," Ada said. "Rachel, don't think like this. You haven't called Steve, have you?"

Rachel didn't answer.

"You're here in this room, and there's a telephone, and it would be just like you to call him. Did you?"

"What if I did?"

"You did, didn't you."

Rachel's chin went up. "Why not? I mean, after all,

he is the father of my child. He certainly had to know it was born."

"And did he care?"

Rachel looked away from her mother's probing gaze. "I don't want to talk about it."

"Well, I do. Rachel, don't see him or talk to him or even think about him. You just remember you're married to Russ, and you're a very lucky girl to be married to him. Keep away from Steven Frame."

"I'll do what I want," Rachel answered. "And you can't stop me. Maybe I've got plans for Steve and me, and it's none of your business."

But Rachel's cockiness fled the moment Alice set foot in her hospital room. And if she expected forgiveness, she was far from getting it.

"You've hurt me pretty badly," Alice said, "I can't deny that. And you've done something even worse to my brother. Even if he doesn't know it. Yet."

Rachel gave her a fearful look. "What do you mean, he doesn't know it yet? You don't mean you'd tell him?"

"I didn't say I'd tell him, but I might. That's something you'll have to live with, Rachel, isn't it?"

And there was something else she had to live with. When Rachel called Steve to say he had a son, he denied it again and hung up on her. Nor did she fare any better in their first face-to-face confrontation. At the hospital to visit an employee, Steve happened to encounter Russ, who insisted that he go with him to see Rachel and the baby.

He went reluctantly, and when Rachel smiled at him and said—in Russ's presence—"Have you seen James Gerald, our son?" her inference wasn't lost on Steve.

It was lost on Russ, who explained that the baby was premature. "But he's healthy and strong," he added.

Rachel smiled again. "Just like his father."

When Russ had to leave to see a patient, insisting that Steve stay and visit with Rachel, Steve said, "You're treading on thin ice, aren't you?"

She shrugged. "I'd say you are, Steve."

"Listen, Rachel. Get off my back."

"Does the truth hurt?"

He shook his head at her. "What are you, Rachel?" He might have expected how she'd answer that one. "The mother of your child, right?"

"He's not my child. You can forget that nonsense."

"Nonsense, Steve? I'm talking about your son—the tiny little thing in an incubator down the hall. Your son. Go see him. Look closely—and think again. Afraid to do that?"

"You're the one who should be afraid," Steve said to her. "What more can you do to me? You already did your damage. There's nothing left to destroy, Rachel."

"Oh, you mean Alice." Rachel shrugged again. "I just told her the truth, that's all."

"You told her a lie. I'm the one who has nothing but the truth to tell, Rachel, and it would be a pleasure telling it. Look what you're doing to Russ—making a fool out of him every chance you get. Somebody ought to do something about that."

"You wouldn't dare," Rachel said.

"You watch your step, Rachel," he answered her, "and don't ever mention Alice's name to me again." And without waiting for her to respond, he turned and walked out of the room.

Waiting for the elevator at the nurses' station, Steve ran into Alice, who accused him of coming to see Rachel. He explained how the visit had come about and that he had gotten out of there as fast as he could.

"How like you," Alice said coldly.

"Stop it, Alice," he said. "I can't take any more snide remarks today from anyone—even you."

"Did Rachel have a few for you?"

"Yes, but it doesn't matter." His spirits had lifted at the sight of her, but they were sinking rapidly. This encounter was not going to be any different from any of the others he had had with her since she had broken off with him last summer. He might as well talk to a stone wall—with pieces of glass cemented into it.

"It doesn't matter," she was saying now, "that Rachel just had a baby, and the baby might be yours?"

He sighed. "The baby isn't mine."

"How can you be sure?" She shook her head. "Have you seen the baby?"

"No, I haven't, because it doesn't interest me in the least."

She pointed toward the premature-baby nursery. "Well, go and look at it, why don't you."

Steve frowned. "Are you trying to tell me it looks like me? If it did, would Russ be walking around crowing the way he is?"

Alice shrugged. "I look at that baby, Steven, and I see you."

"But nobody else does, do they?"

"No," she admitted.

He eyed her. "I think you want it to be my baby. Oh, Alice, if only I could talk to you. If only we could have a rational discussion."

She searched his face. "Steven, I have a rational question. How will you ever know for sure the baby isn't yours?"

Although Jim and Mary did go to the hospital to see Rachel and the baby—as Jim had insisted they must in order not to arouse Russ's suspicions—they didn't go as often as they would have had there been no question that the baby was their grandchild, nor did they make the kind of fuss over the baby that not only Russ but others expected of them.

Worse, a matter they had discussed with John Randolph some months earlier and had forgotten about was now brought to their attention.

Stopping by their house one morning on the way to his office, he said, "You remember you wanted me to look into trust funds—find out the best way to establish trusts for the grandchildren as they came along."

Jim and Mary exchanged glances as John bent to set his attaché case down, and Jim gave a little warning shake of his head. "Yes," he said, "I remember we talked about it."

John accepted Mary's offer of a cup of coffee, then said, "Well, I think the simplest thing, Jim, is for you to open a savings account in the baby's name, with you as trustee. Or Mary. Or both of you. You just specify 'in trust for James Gerald Matthews' and that does it. Of course, you add to it as you see fit from time to time, and James Gerald will be given access to the money when he's eighteen or twenty-one—whatever age you decide on. That's really the simplest way to do it."

Jim cleared his throat, and avoided looking at Mary. "Well, thanks very much, John, for looking into it for us. It does seem the simplest way."

John finished his coffee and said he had to be going and could he give Jim a lift to his office, but Jim declined, saying he wasn't quite ready to leave the house yet. After John had gone, Mary gave her husband a troubled look and said, "Is it always going to be like this?" Then she answered her own question. "It is going to be like this. Little things like setting up a trust for the baby. Things we're supposed to do for our grandchild, who isn't our grandchild at all."

"Mary," Jim said, "the baby probably is our grandchild."

"Maybe," she agreed. "But we can't go through with this, can we?"

"You mean the trust fund?"

She shook her head. "Not only the trust fund. It seems so wrong to live with what we know."

Ignoring the wider implications of what she was saying, he simply said, "Maybe Russ and Rachel have forgotten we ever talked about a trust fund. At least we can hope so."

Rachel went home from the hospital less than a week after the baby was born, but the baby had to remain in the premature nursery until his weight could be brought up to five pounds. The day Rachel came to take him home, Steve was once again in the hospital to see his employee, a Mr. Olcutt. He wanted Olcutt to go over some papers if he was sufficiently recovered from his appendectomy to do it, so he stopped at the nurses' station to ask Alice what condition Olcutt was in. Before Alice could answer him, an elevator door opened and out stepped Rachel, with the baby in her arms.

Her eyes lit up on seeing the two of them. "I brought

the baby up to show Alice," she said to Steve, "and lo and behold, you're here too." Turning the baby to them, holding back the blanket that was partially covering his face, she said, "Isn't he just beautiful? Isn't he the handsomest thing you ever saw in your whole life?"

Noting Alice's distress, her inability to come up with anything, Steve said, "He looks fine."

He had hoped that would put an end to it, but of course he should have known that Rachel wasn't about to make anything less than the most of this unexpected opportunity. "Alice," she went on, "don't you think he's adorable?"

"I think all babies are adorable," Alice said stiffly.

Rachel's smile widened. "Yes, but James Gerald is really adorable, don't you think so?" She laughed her self-deprecating little laugh. "Oh, listen to me, going on like a mother. Stop me, somebody."

"Why don't you stop yourself?" Steve asked.

Rachel gave a little shake of her dark head. "Well, because I can't. I really can't. I know I sound silly over this baby. You know, I never knew it would be like this—having a baby. I guess I never thought much about it, but it's wonderful, really it is. It's just wonderful. Alice, you've no idea how wonderful it is."

"No," Alice said, looking increasingly pale and drawn. "I've no idea."

"Well," Rachel said, "take my word for it. It's the most wonderful feeling in the world."

Rachel's attention was momentarily distracted as a nurse came along and stopped to admire the baby, and Steve suggested to Alice that he go along and see Olcutt, but Alice begged him to stay, saying she didn't want to be left alone with Rachel, for fear of what she might do to her.

Turning back to them, Rachel said, "Alice, you haven't really seen the baby."

"I've seen the baby," Alice replied.

Rachel held the baby out to her. "Go ahead, Alice. You can hold him if you want to."

"Rachel," Steve said curtly, "cut it out."

"Well, she can," Rachel insisted. "He's tiny."

Alice had been holding herself in. Now she let go. "Rachel, that's enough." Ignoring Steve's plea to take it easy, she said, "I thought I knew every rotten thing about you, Rachel. How you lied, how you cheated, how you took whatever you could from everybody and gave nothing back. I thought I knew all your silly little vanities, your silly little ambitions, your silly little connivings. I knew you were stupid and selfish and faithless and ungrateful and absolutely incapable of one single thought that wasn't about yourself. I knew all about that and a lot more. But this is something new. Today I'm seeing something else, Rachel. I'm seeing another side that's vindictive and cruel, that takes pleasure in hurting and humiliating. Get out of here, Rachel. Get out of here. I can't bear to look at you."

And Rachel got.

Before Rachel's return from Mount Holly, Alice had moved out of her parents' house to an apartment she shared with another nurse at Memorial Hospital. She made the move partly to reduce to the absolute minimum her contacts with Rachel and partly to get away from talk—or nontalk—about her broken engagement to Steven Frame.

Yet one night when Russ came by to see her, it was Alice who brought the subject up, saying she'd like to stop and start all over again by falling in love with somebody else.

"You're still in love with Steve, then," Russ said.

"No," Alice replied. But then in the next breath she said, "Yes. Yes, I am."

Distressed by Alice's distress, Russ put an arm around her. "Maybe you can get back together with him, Alice."

She shook her head. "No. Never."

He frowned, puzzled, as most people still were puzzled, without any idea of what had come between the two of them. "Would he reconsider?"

"That question does not arise," Alice said.

His frown deepened. "And there's no way you can reconsider?"

"No way."

"Alice, is there anything I can do?"

She looked at him with tears in her eyes. "No, Russ. Thank you. But no."

"Time will help," he said, not knowing what else to say.

She wiped her eyes. "You mean it will help patch things up?"

"No. I meant help you get over the pain."

The look she gave him tore at his heart. "I'll never get over it," she said. "Never."

Rachel hadn't been home from the hospital more than a day or two before she started bugging Russ about moving into a two-bedroom apartment, insisting that the baby needed a room of his own. Russ was agreeable, but said they could wait until the lease on their present apartment expired, in six months. Without saying anything further to him, Rachel started looking for an apartment, getting her mother to baby-sit for her.

One day she came home with the floor plan of a chic two-bedroom apartment with a terrace in a building that was being put up in the Prospect section of Bay City, a section with several expensive new highrises. When she told her mother the rent was $425 a month, Ada was aghast.

"Russ can't afford a rent like that," Ada said. "How do you expect to pay it?"

Rachel shrugged. "Never mind. I'll think of something. I want to live well for a change. I don't want my baby living in some junk heap like this."

"Rachel," Ada said, "Russ isn't Steve Frame, you know."

"No, he isn't," she agreed, the hard look in her dark eyes, bitterness in her voice. "Russ is only a resident. But he's going to earn money one of these days—the way all doctors do."

Ada nodded. "And in the meantime, how are you going to pay the rent?"

"Well, the apartment is for the baby as much as anybody else. I don't see why Steven shouldn't help pay part of it. After all, it *is* his baby."

But when she went to his office to make her appeal, Steve refused. "Now get this straight, Rachel. Don't

push me—not an inch further. I have no intention of
giving you money for any reason. I am not that baby's
father, and I am most certainly not going to support
him. Is that absolutely clear? Now get out."

Rachel had never been one to give up easily, and
she didn't give up now. She simply channeled her
energy in a different direction. At breakfast one morning she said, "Russ, there's something I've been wondering about. What bank is the trust fund going to be
in?"

Russ gave her a blank look. "What trust fund?"

"Why, the one your parents are setting up for the
baby. When I first got pregnant, they said they'd set
up a trust fund for each grandchild, and ours is the
first. Haven't they mentioned it to you?"

"No."

"Well," she said, "you'd better ask them about it
then." She smiled. "Other people might want to contribute to the fund, too."

Russ frowned and put down the paper he'd been
trying to read. "Other people contribute to a fund set
up by my parents? Rachel!"

"There's no law against gifts to someone else's trust
fund, is there?"

"No. But it's a little unlikely. And besides, I don't
want to ask Mom and Dad about it. That's their business. I'm sure they haven't forgotten. They'll get around
to it."

After breakfast, preparing to leave for the hospital,
Russ spied the floor plan and asked about it. Rachel
extolled the apartment and the building—with door-
men and elevators, and a laundry facility on every
floor—as being just right for them, but when she told
him what the rent was, he said he didn't earn that
kind of money, they couldn't afford the apartment,
and forget it.

One day right after Christmas Alice stopped by her
parents' house to pick up a gift that had been mailed
to her there from a college roommate. Seeing some
baby things on the sofa in the living room, she asked
what they were. Mary explained that Russ had dropped
them off that morning. Rachel was coming by later

with the baby to have dinner with them, and then later still Russ would join them for a little while before taking Rachel and the baby home.

Alice raised her eyebrows. "She's coming alone? To have dinner? Then watch out, Mom."

Her mother looked puzzled. "What do you mean?"

"Only that Rachel wouldn't come here simply for the pleasure of it. She's up to something. You'll see."

That evening, after a somewhat strained meal, Rachel began going on and on about the baby, upstairs sleeping, and how Jim and Mary hadn't seen much of him, had never held him, and how they would have to get to know their grandson better.

"Why," said Rachel, looking at them with wide-eyed innocence, "I can already tell what the baby's going to be like. He's going to be determined—and a scrapper. Very strong. And he'll be smart, too. We'll help him along, of course—good schools, everything he needs. We have lots of plans."

She beamed at each of them, and because somebody had to say something, Jim said, not very enthusiastically, "We'd like to hear them."

"Well," Rachel responded, not needing enthusiasm from anybody else to generate her own, "you should just hear Russ carry on about what that boy is going to have."

"A lot of love, one would hope, first of all." That from a very uncomfortable, forewarned Mary.

"Well, my goodness, of course. I mean, besides that." Rachel beamed at them again. "First, enough room to grow in. Jamie will have his own room just as soon as . . . well, pretty soon anyway." She waved a hand airily. "And those wonderful educational toys. And everything. He's going to have the very best. And we have to do everything we can to see he gets it. Don't you agree?"

Mary tried to keep her voice calm. "Within reason. Whatever one can afford, of course."

Rachel rolled her eyes. "Oh, Russ—my goodness, Russ doesn't make enough money for us to afford anything. Not yet, anyhow."

"He'll be going into private practice before long," Jim reminded her.

"I know," Rachel said. "But it will be a struggle."

"We all had to struggle, Rachel," Mary said. "None of us had it easy."

Ignoring her mother-in-law's comment, Rachel said, "Russ and I think it would be a good idea for the baby to have some money just for himself. Don't you think so? I mean, what you talked about before. The trust fund."

At that moment Russ arrived, putting an end to any further discussion of the trust fund. But Rachel had made her point, and they were scarcely gone from the house when a fuming Mary turned to him, saying she would not be blackmailed by Rachel. Uneasy with the word "blackmail," Jim did have to admit that Rachel's brazenness surprised him.

"After what she's done?" Mary retorted. "You're surprised at one more proof of her character?"

"Well," Jim said, unwilling to believe he could have been so totally wrong about Rachel, "let's keep our perspective. Her interest in a trust fund for the baby is quite natural, and it might be innocent enough."

But Mary wouldn't buy that. "Innocent? Not for a minute." She shook her head. "I refuse to let her worm a trust fund out of us."

"It would be the baby's, darling, not hers."

"I don't care," Mary said. "I'm not going to let her use us."

Jim sighed. "I'm not so sure we can avoid it. It might be rather obvious to more people than Rachel if we refuse this trust fund we've promised to set up. As far as everyone else is concerned, there is no before and after. It's all just Russ and Rachel and their baby—our grandson."

"But is it our grandson?"

He sighed again. "I think it is, darling, and we can't suggest anything else by suddenly canceling our plans to set up a trust fund for the baby."

"I see," Mary said bitterly. "Shame and deceit, months and years of hypocrisy. Somewhere along the line I see my son destroyed."

"Mary," Jim said, "I know how you feel. But I still believe the baby is Russ's, no matter how doubtful it seems. And the fact is, we promised to open a trust fund for that baby, and I'm afraid we're going to have to go ahead with it."

At the same time that she was working on getting the Matthewses to set up the trust fund, Rachel wrote a letter to her father at the Mount Holly address, telling him about herself and that she was married now and had a baby, and could he send some money to her.

When Ada heard what Rachel had done, she was —as usual—appalled. "You think your father's going to send you money when all these years he hasn't even sent a single word? When are you going to come to your senses and start facing facts? Forget your father, forget the Matthewses, forget Steve Frame, forget the apartment. Settle for what you've got before you end up losing that, too."

Now that Russ was nearing the end of his residency at Memorial Hospital, Jim and Mary met privately with him to offer to give him the money he would need to set himself up in private practice. When he was reluctant, they insisted, urging him to let them do this one last thing for him. Finally he agreed to take the money he would need to buy all his medical equipment, if he could do it on the basis of a loan. Jim then raised the matter of the trust fund, but Russ insisted that they were doing more than enough as it was and they should hold off on that until after he was in private practice. Relieved, Jim and Mary agreed.

When Rachel heard that Russ had told his parents to forget about the trust fund, at least for now, she was furious. Since the birth of the baby Rachel had astonished everyone, her husband included, by taking to motherhood with a vengeance. She bought a convertible couch and slept in the living room with the baby—on the pretext that the baby needed someone with him continuously, and that Russ needed his sleep undisturbed by her having to get up to feed the baby at night. On the further pretext that Jamie was premature and needed extra protection from germs, she wouldn't let anyone else—including Russ—hold the baby for more than a few minutes.

Although Russ was dissatisfied with their current domestic arrangement, Rachel was careful not to provoke him to anger, sweet-talking him, letting him make love to her, and—when all else failed—reminding him that it was only temporary.

But in her fury about the trust fund's being dropped in favor of "a lot of old machines" for Russ's private practice, she went too far.

"What the baby needs," she stormed, "is some money of his own. The baby needs money in the bank, not a bunch of equipment."

"I'll be the judge of what the baby needs," Russ said, turning on her at last. "Now, I've put up with a lot from you, Rachel, your little whims and fancies. I've put up with your monopolizing the baby, shutting me out of his life and out of your life. I've put up with all that because I love the baby, and I love you. But when it comes to deciding how we spend the money, what we buy and what we do without, what's important materially for our child, then I am the head of the family—your husband and Jamie's father—not just a man who happens to live here. Do you understand?"

Rachel said nothing more, but she very quickly made it clear in other quarters that, so far as she was concerned, neither her quarrel with Russ nor his conversation with his parents had ever taken place. When she was asked by Liz Matthews to model in an upcoming fashion show at a benefit luncheon sponsored by the Bay City Women's Club, Rachel agreed to do it, then went on to enthuse to Liz about the baby's trust fund that Russ's parents had promised to set up, saying they were making a point of having it be a savings account so that anybody else who wanted to could also put money in it. Unfortunately, she didn't know yet what bank the savings account was going to be in, but as soon as the Matthewses let her know, she would let other people know. About as subtle as a brick, Rachel was.

While Rachel was spreading the word about the trust fund to everybody who would listen to her, she received help from an unexpected quarter. Russ was selected to take part in a medical study being conducted in Houston at the space center—a study that was expected to go on for several weeks. And since he couldn't afford to take Rachel and the baby with him, they stayed behind in Bay City.

As Rachel had figured, Liz lost no time in repeating their conversation about the trust fund to Jim and Mary. Mary was so enraged that she refused to have anything more to do with it, leaving it all to Jim, who in turn decided that since he, too, wanted to have as little as possible to do with it, he would make Russ and Rachel the trustees, and then he and Mary would be out from under.

"I'll try to get to the bank today," he said, "and get the papers for them to sign."

"But Russ isn't here," Mary said, frowning. "He's in Houston."

"I know. But I want to get this whole thing over and done with. I'll get the papers to Rachel. She can sign them, and we can wait for Russ's signature until he gets back."

"Wait a minute," Mary said. "That means Rachel will have access to the money."

"Well, yes," Jim admitted, "so long as she's sole trustee, but that will only be until Russ gets back and we add his name."

"That money is for the baby. I don't trust Rachel."

"Now, Mary," Jim said, "whatever else you may think about Rachel, you have to admit she's pretty devoted to that baby."

Mary was adamant. "I don't trust her. Don't set up the trust fund until Russell gets back. Please wait until he gets back, and he can sign the papers and be a trustee along with Rachel."

But Jim was just as adamant as she was. "Mary," he said, "I've waited too long. I'm tired of hearing from everybody about the trust fund. Regardless of what's happened, I'm going to go ahead with it."

Unable to get to the bank that day, Jim went the following day, taking Rachel with him. "For the time being, Rachel," Jim said to her as they rode downtown, "you're in sole charge of this money we're going to put in the bank today. You understand the responsibility, don't you?"

Rachel nodded. "Well, sure. This money's for Jamie. It's for his future and everything."

"That's right," Jim replied. "And even though you and Russ are the parents, you're in the same position as a lawyer holding money for a client."

"Well," Rachel said, "you keep making me feel more and more important. Look, Mr. Matthews, I understand that the money is going to be used later on, when Jamie maybe goes to college or something. But . . . well, I mean, is there any restriction? I mean, if something happened and we needed money for Jamie for some other reason . . ."

"If that happened, Rachel, then naturally you'd be able to draw on it. An illness or something like that."

Rachel nodded again. "Things do come up sometimes," she said, "and I wanted to know. I mean, you never can tell, can you?"

And, looking away from him, she beamed in triumph.

Chapter Sixteen

WHILE Rachel was manipulating the baby's trust fund into existence, there were two important developments in Alice's life. The first concerned Steven Frame directly, the second indirectly.

One night around midnight toward the end of January Alice was on duty in the Emergency Room at the hospital when an automobile-accident victim was brought in by ambulance. The man was apparently not badly injured, because he was on his feet, being helped into the Emergency Room by an attendant, but when he looked up, and Alice saw that the man was Steve, her heart contracted.

"He's pretty knocked out," the attendant said, "but he said he could walk."

Alice scarcely heard him. "Steven," she said, pulling a chair up for him, helping the attendant lower him into it.

"It happened over at that big intersection on Grove Street," the attendant said. "Somebody rammed into him. About twenty minutes ago. The guy in the other car called the ambulance."

"Steven," she said again. "Steven."

He raised his head to give her a bleary look. "Why, look who's here," he said in an unsteady voice. "It's the Angel of Mercy. Hello, Angel of Mercy."

He tried to get up, but Alice held him down, saying, "No. Stay where you are. You're too weak to stand. One of the doctors will be with you in a minute. Where does it hurt, Steven?"

"In my shoulder." He gave her another bleary look. "Alice, you look beautiful. But blurry. And you keep getting blurrier. Alice, why is that?"

"Steven, just sit quietly and don't talk."

"Al—" His head dropped sharply as he passed out, and Alice had to grab him to keep him from slipping out of the chair onto the floor.

"I think he's been boozing it up," the attendant said.

"Well, think again," Alice said sharply. "He isn't drunk."

The attendant raised his eyebrows. "Excuse me for living. And if you don't need me any longer . . ."

"No. I don't. Thank you."

As the attendant walked off, Steven came to. "Alice, I had an accident." His voice still wavered.

"Yes," she said. "I know you did. And the doctor's here now, Steven." She turned to the staffer. "He's complaining of pain in his shoulder, Doctor. And he passed out just now for a few seconds."

The doctor started looking him over. "No cuts, apparently. Can you sit up all right?"

Steven nodded. "And I can walk, too." He winced. "It's my shoulder."

Alice helped him take off his jacket and shirt, and the doctor examined his shoulder. "It looks as though you've strained a ligament. Torn it, maybe. We'll go over you thoroughly before we let you out of here, but I think that's all. Let's get that shoulder taped."

As it turned out, the doctor was right. A torn ligament in Steve's shoulder was his only injury—that, and a bit of shock. A couple of hours later he was released.

The next day a dozen roses were delivered to the apartment Alice shared with her fellow nurse, Muriel Burke. When told they were from Steve, Muriel said, "You mean Steven Frame, ex-fiancé?"

Alice nodded. "That's the one."

"Well, well, well. Look. I'll get that big crystal vase. They'll be gorgeous."

"Don't bother, Muriel. I don't want them. I'm going to throw them down the compactor chute."

Muriel frowned. "What did he say on the card?"

"He just said sorry and thank you." She explained about the accident.

"It seems a shame to throw them out," Muriel said. "I mean a dozen roses is a dozen roses is a dozen roses, no matter who sends them."

Alice reconsidered. "I guess you're right, and I am being silly. Leave them then."

Muriel smiled. "After all, it's not their fault they came from Steven Frame. And, by the way, I already knew about the accident. I heard about it this morning from Dr. Mercer."

"Why didn't you tell me?"

Muriel's smile became a grin. "I wanted to hear what you had to say about it. It was awfully nice of him to send roses, I think. Especially when he didn't have to." She eyed Alice a moment. "I think he didn't want to let it go at just saying thank you and walking out of the Emergency Room." When Alice said nothing, Muriel went on. "Dr. Mercer told me you were pretty shook up last night when they brought him in. Were you?"

Alice nodded. "I guess I was. A little."

Again the eyeing. "A little or a lot?"

"Well, all right. I thought for a minute there—I thought . . . but then I knew almost right away he wasn't badly hurt."

"If he had been badly hurt, how would you have felt?"

"I don't know." After a moment she said, "Pretty awful, I suppose. Yes. Awful. I'd have felt awful."

Muriel took a breath. "Because you still love him?"

Alice nodded again. "Yes. I still love him. I still love him a lot."

"Apparently he still loves you."

"It doesn't matter whether he does or not," Alice said.

Muriel frowned. She knew no more about why Alice had broken her engagement than anybody else. At least not yet. She had made up her mind to try to find out. And toward that end she said now, "But it has to matter."

"No, it doesn't," Alice answered. "Not after what he did to me. It makes absolutely no difference at all." She stopped and frowned and shook her head. "I didn't mean to say that, Muriel. I can't talk about it. Do you mind?"

"I guess not, no."

Alice sighed. "I wish I could talk about it, but I can't."

And that, for the time being, was that.

The second development in Alice's life, the one that concerned Steven indirectly, took place one evening the following week.

Alice's brother-in-law, John Randolph, had just brought a young man named Chris Tyler into his law firm, and he and Alice had taken an instant liking to each other. Only a few months out of law school, Chris was twenty-four years old, very tall, and slender to the point of being thin, with dark brown hair so curly and worn so full as to make his face look gaunt.

When Pat Randolph met Chris, he reminded her —despite their physical differences—of Steven Frame. He had that same brooding quality, and the same outspokenness and independence of spirit. And he asked and took no favors.

Though she said nothing, Pat thought Alice felt the same way about Chris—which explained her attraction to him. In any event, when Chris asked Alice out to dinner, she accepted, suggesting they meet at the Tallboys Restaurant in downtown Bay City.

Alice arrived first, and as the headwaiter escorted her to the table Chris had reserved, she noticed that Steve and some girl were seated at an adjoining table, just finishing their meal. Pretending not to see him, she sat down to wait for Chris, and when Chris arrived she made quite a fuss over him, saying she couldn't wait for him to get there, and if she was turning his head, it was because she intended to.

Chris was puzzled—bewildered even—until Steve Frame and the girl passed by their table, and Steve paused to ask Alice how she was.

"Why, hello, Steven," Alice said brightly—too brightly. "How are you?"

"I'm okay," Steve answered; then, after giving Chris a curious, hostile look, he followed the girl out of the restaurant.

To Chris's question as to who that was, a suddenly very subdued Alice said it was merely someone she knew.

Chris looked at her for quite some time. "I think we're going to have to talk about him."

She shook her head. "No. I don't want to."

"Because you like him?" Chris asked. When there was no answer, he said, "Okay. You don't like him. Same thing, didn't you know that? Love-hate. The two sides of the same coin. I am right, don't you agree?"

Alice nodded. "Well, in a way. Steven and I used to be engaged."

"I see," Chris said. "And why did you want to come here for dinner?"

Alice gave him a puzzled look. "Why? Because it's a nice place."

"Did you used to come here with Steven Frame?"

"Sometimes."

"Lots of times?"

"All right," Alice said. "Quite often."

"And you thought if we came here tonight you might run into him?"

Alice looked offended. "That wasn't why—"

Chris cut her off. "There he was, right at the next table, and when I came in, bright-eyed and bushy-tailed, you start to make a big fuss over me, and I get all pleased and bothered. But Steven Frame isn't pleased at all. Just bothered."

"Chris," Alice said, "I never meant—"

Again he cut her off. "Oh yes, baby, that's just what you meant. You meant for Steven Frame to see you with another man, having a high old time. That would show him, wouldn't it? That you don't give a hoot where he goes or what he does or anything. You've got your life, and you're leading it to the fullest."

"Chris," Alice protested, still looking offended, "do you think I would do a thing like that?"

"You just did a thing like that." He put on a mock smile and said in a falsetto voice, " 'Why, hello, Steven, how are you?' " He made a face. "And the minute he's gone your temperature goes down, your blood pressure goes down, the lights go out, and you're sitting here with just an ordinary guy. Me. Well, I don't much like that, Alice. I don't like being the ordinary guy you go out with just to show Steven Frame you're not sitting home alone."

Alice was shaking her head. "But I didn't mean—"

Again he cut her off. "Yes you did. And, Alice, if that's the game you want to play, okay. Just don't play it with me, that's all."

She looked at him earnestly. "I don't want to play any game with you, Chris."

"So don't. From here on in, any time you want to go out with me, it's got to be because you want to go out with me. Understand?"

She nodded. "I understand."

Chastened by her one, rather feeble attempt at game-playing, Alice should have stayed around to watch an expert. She might have felt better.

With Russ out of town—and out of the way—Rachel bent all her efforts toward securing the fancy apartment she wanted in the building Ada referred to as the big glass cookie box. The problem was, the rental agent would not hold the apartment for her without the payment of one month's rent and one month's security—a total of $850. Rachel's first thought, of course, was the baby's trust fund, which Jim had put $4,000 into and she hastened to the bank, only to be told that no withdrawal of any amount could be made for thirty days.

There was still no letter from her father in answer to her appeal to him for money. In fact, after making inquiries at Rachel's behest through a legal contact in Mount Holly, Walter Curtin had learned that an assistant of her father's had come to the storeroom there and cleaned out most of her father's belongings, informing the landlord that the lease would not be renewed when it expired the end of February.

With only a handful of apartments left unrented in the G line—the kind Rachel was set on having—and learning that Steve ate lunch frequently in the Tallboys, Rachel maneuvered Ada into baby-sitting for her several days in a row, maintaining that she had a lunch date with this person and that one, so that she could scout for Steve. She finally found him there one day alone, and she walked over to his table and sat down.

Looking up from the salad he was eating, he said, "I can't say I really want you at my table, Rachel. Come to think of it, that's the last thing in the world I want."

Rachel smiled. "Not the very last. I mean, the last thing you'd want would be to have me make a scene right in the middle of the Tallboys Restaurant at high noon, right?" Taking his menu, she said, "What's good here? I understand you eat here all the time."

"Uh-huh. And you've been here too, Rachel. The headwaiter said some young woman has been in here asking about me."

Told what Rachel wanted of him and why, Steve said, "You're trying to use me to get money for an apartment you shouldn't have."

Up went her chin. "I think I should have it. I know I should have it for my baby."

"Your baby," he said, with a shake of his head. "All you know is *you* want it. All you know in this whole world is what you want. That's all you ever think about—what you want, what you need, what you haven't got, what you must get. And everybody else can roll over and play dead, as long as you get what you want. Well, good luck. Only you're not getting it from me." He eyed her a moment. "Nice try, Rachel. Do you want half a lobster? I'll order one for you. Coffee? Chocolate eclair? I'll tell them to put it on my bill. You're getting a free lunch from me, Rachel, and that's all." Then he got up and walked out, leaving her sitting there.

Doubly fearful now of not getting the apartment, Rachel used every ruse she could think of. Telling the rental agent that her husband was wiring her the money but the bank had their account mixed up and would he please hold the apartment one more day, she wormed a hundred-dollar check out of Liz as a contribution to the baby's trust fund, then took it to the rental agent as proof that she could come up with the rest of the money. Another friend of the Matthews family's gave her another hundred dollars for the trust fund. It also went to the rental agent. Pretending to have lost her wallet with fifty dollars in it, she managed to get fifty dollars in cash from Russ's sister Pat. Pretending that Russ had left her short of money, she got twenty-five dollars out of Ada's husband, Ernie, then denied doing it when her mother asked her about it. And eventually the thirty days went by, and she got the balance she needed from the baby's trust fund, finally securing the apartment for herself.

Unaware of what use Rachel had put some of the trust-fund money to, Jim and Mary's prime source of distress in that matter was having to admit to Alice that they had set up a trust fund at all. Alice was appalled.

"How could you do that to me?" she said. "How do you think I feel seeing Rachel rewarded? It's ridiculous. It's absolutely ridiculous. It started when she was living in this house. She decided she wanted my room—the room I'd had ever since I was a little girl. And she got it. Nobody stopped her. And then when I found a man I could love and who loved me, she couldn't wait to spoil that for me, too. Do you think it was an accident she waited for my engagement party to tell me she was having his baby?"

There were tears in Alice's eyes, and they started to roll down her face, but she ignored them, putting a hand up to her forehead. "I think I'm going out of my mind," she said bitterly. "I'm sure I am. I'm crazy, because now that Rachel has taken everything and I've got nothing, you're rewarding her by giving her some money."

"Darling," Jim said to her, "that money's for the baby."

She gave him a tortured look. "Is there any sense to anything? Russ gets to go to a prestige study group, Pat tells us she's having a baby, Rachel's got money in the bank—well, when is it my turn? When am I going to have something? Something I can keep?"

Both Jim and Mary went toward her to console her, but she brushed off their attempts, said, "Leave me alone," and rushed out of the room.

For what it might have been worth to Alice, everything wasn't coming up roses for Rachel either. Telling her that he had received another letter from his colleague in Mount Holly, Walter explained to Rachel that the colleague had left word for her father's assistant to get in touch with him on Rachel's behalf the next time he came to town. One day the previous week, the assistant had come to town, packed up what was left in the storeroom, turned the keys over to the landlord, with whom the message had been placed, and left town without getting in touch with Walter's colleague.

"Maybe he didn't get the message," Rachel said.

Walter shook his head. "No. He got it all right. The landlord gave it to him, and the assistant said it would be taken care of. Unless, of course, you've heard directly from your father."

"No," Rachel said, looking despondent. "I haven't

heard anything. Not even an answer to my letter telling him about the baby and everything." She had been looking down at her hands, twisted together in her lap. Now she looked at Walter, her eyes wide and wistful, and he felt a stab of pity for her. "What if I never find him?" she asked.

Walter tried to sound as kind as he could. "You had better prepare yourself for that possibility, Rachel. Try to put him at the back of your mind if you can."

The only thing that could put Rachel's father at the back of her mind was necessity, and necessity did it. Russ called to say he would be home in three days, giving Rachel exactly that amount of time to pull off her *fait accompli*. She called the moving company to arrange the move to the new apartment, and then she called Mary and Jim to beg off from dinner at their house that evening on the grounds that she had to clean the apartment for Russ's return. The excuse sounded fishy to Mary, and that, combined with other bits of news that had filtered back to them— Rachel borrowing the fifty dollars from Pat and the twenty-five dollars from Ernie—convinced her that Rachel was up to something.

When Jim tried to calm Mary's fears, she accused him of taking Rachel's side, and before they knew it they were quarreling, which stunned them both—and led Jim to speak of what Mary's bitterness toward Rachel was doing to the two of them. "I don't want to hear any more about it," he said. "About what you think Rachel is doing or not doing. I just don't want to hear any more about it."

At that point Alice walked in, guessed that they were quarreling about Rachel, and agreed with her father that there was no use in talking about the matter. "What's the point," she said, "in talking about what Rachel does or doesn't do or says or doesn't say? What good can it possibly do? Especially when what you or I think doesn't matter one bit to her. If Rachel is up to something, as I assume she is, since she always is one way or another, then she'll do whatever she has in mind, and someday someone somewhere—probably Rachel herself—will let us in on it. Especially if letting us in on it serves Rachel's purpose."

But neither Jim nor Mary nor Alice heard what Rachel was up to from Rachel. Not this time. They heard it from Russ, who was so stunned at what Rachel had done that he couldn't believe it. Meeting him at the airport, she drove him to the new building, then rode with him up in the elevator to 15G—her "surprise" for him.

It took him a few minutes to take it all in. Looking around at their familiar things in this unfamiliar place, his head still reeling, Russ said, "You moved us in here without consulting me? Without saying a word to me?"

Rachel said it wouldn't have been a surprise if she'd said anything to him and tried to deflect his questions about what the rent was. When it finally got through to Russ that this was the very apartment he had told Rachel they couldn't afford, she tried to justify her action on the ground that now that he and an obstetrician/gynecologist he'd met in Houston—a former Bay City resident named Dan Shearer—were going into private practice together, they could easily afford this apartment.

Russ stared at her. "Are you out of your mind? In the first place, it's not definite that we're going into practice. We're still exploring the idea. And in the second place, if we do go ahead, we're going to be in more of a jam for money than ever, because we'll need every cent we've got for office equipment and rent. Speaking of which, where did you get the money for the move and the first month's rent for this place? How much did all that come to?"

"What's the difference?" Rachel said. "I got it, and we're here, and I must say you're not being very nice about it."

But Rachel's blandishments had lost whatever force they once had. "Did you borrow it?" he asked.

"Of course not. I just had it."

"What do you mean, just had it? Don't you think I know how much money we have?"

"I'm not talking about that money," Rachel said. "I'm talking about . . . well, like I told you on the phone a few weeks ago, your father finally set up that trust fund for Jamie, and I took some of the money from that."

He was staring at her again. "You took Jamie's money—your own baby's money—for this ridiculous, extravagant—"

Rachel cut him off. "It's not ridiculous. It's a beautiful apartment, and besides, I didn't take all that much, because in the meantime your Aunt Liz and another friend of your parents each gave me a hundred dollars for the trust fund, and I used that money."

He couldn't believe his ears. "And don't you realize that's even worse? Because if that money was supposed to go into the trust fund, then you were not only taking money from Jamie but you were using gifts from relatives and friends for a purpose for which it was never intended." He shook his head. "You've done some pretty strange things since we've been married, Rachel, but this . . . How could you do it?"

She was frowning at him. "Do what? I really, honestly don't know what you're making such a fuss about. So I didn't tell you about it because I wanted to surprise you, and so what if I used Jamie's money? After all, the apartment is for him. I wanted him to live in this kind of place."

"You're a liar," Russ said, and when she gave him an unbelieving look, he repeated it. "I said you're a liar. Jamie? You didn't do it for him. You did it for yourself. Because for some idiotic, childish reason this is where you wanted to live. And I think it's the absolute bottom, the most outrageous, despicable thing I ever heard of."

Nor was that the end of the matter. After conferring with his father and with his prospective medical partner, Russ came home one evening, sat Rachel down, and laid a few things out for her. Understanding that it would be costly to break the new lease, move out, and find a less-expensive apartment somewhere else, Russ had agreed to let Jim help him with the rent until he and Dan Shearer were established in practice together. So he and Rachel would stay where they were—under certain conditions.

First, her name would be removed from the baby's trust fund. Russ would be the sole trustee. Second, he would give her a household allowance for basic expenses, and each week they would go over it together and she would account to him for every penny spent. As for anything other than basic expenses—clothes for herself, furniture, whatever—she was to spend nothing without discussing it with him first.

"Is that understood?" he asked.

She frowned. "No, it's not. I mean, well, if you insist about the trust fund, okay. But the rest . . ."

He stood his ground. "Rachel, that's the way it's going to be. Not just about the trust fund, but about everything. If you don't agree to it, say so right now."

She made a helpless little gesture. "And if I don't?"

"You wanted this apartment, Rachel. And you wanted it badly enough to lie about it and take the money from our own child to get it. Well, if you don't agree to the ground rules I laid down, you can have it —all to yourself."

And that was that.

For the time being, anyhow. When Rachel's mother said she was surprised that Russ hadn't kicked her out, Rachel tossed her head and said, "He was only a little upset, that's all. And he'll get over it. You know how crazy he is about me. In a day or so everything will be fine. And meanwhile, I got what I wanted, didn't I?"

While Rachel had been busy arranging her surprise for Russ, Ada was trying to cope with a surprise that had been handed her. Her younger brother Sam, a lawyer, moved from Bay City to the town of Somerset, about an hour's drive west, and there ran into a man he thought was Ada's former husband, a man with the same name, certainly: Gerald Ketchum Davis.

This Gerald Davis owned and operated a restaurant in Somerset called the Riverboat that had an illegal gambling room in the back equipped with slot machines, roulette wheels, and the like—maybe the "machinery and tools" that had been stored at the address in Mount Holly.

Wanting to make certain of the man's identity before saying anything to Rachel, Ada went to Somerset. The man was indeed her former husband.

Surprised to see her, and not exactly overjoyed, Gerald made polite inquiries as to where she lived and how she was, apologized for never having gotten in touch with her, and couldn't remember Rachel's name, though he claimed to have thought about Ada a lot, and offered her some money now to make up for never having sent her any after walking out on her all those many years ago.

Ada said she didn't want money from him. It was Rachel she had come to see him about. "Rachel's got this idea about you," she said, "that you're some kind of a god. That's the way young girls feel about their fathers, in case you didn't know—especially when their fathers aren't around. Anyway, that's how Rachel feels about you. She thinks if she could just get together with you, you'd take care of her—solve all her problems, straighten out her life. Be the magic father, in other words. Rachel has a husband—and a nice husband—but she has problems her husband doesn't know about. And I've got the feeling she's going to bring those problems to you and dump them in your lap. And when she does—"

Gerald had been listening in silence, but now he interrupted her. "Hey now, I'm no high-class problem-solver. I've got my own problems."

"And when she does come to see you," Ada repeated, "be nice to her."

"Well, of course I'll be nice to her," he protested. "What do you think I am?"

Not bothering to answer that one, Ada said, "She's going to come running to you when I tell her where you are. The kid is mixed up, and . . . well, she isn't always nice. But, like I said, she thinks you're a god, she thinks you can straighten everything out for her. And what I want from you, Jerry, is plenty of help for that girl. You've never done anything for her—ever—but now you can come through for her. Isn't that right?"

Gerald sighed. "I understand," he said. "If she does

come to see me, I'll help her all I can. But I've got something to tell you, Ada, that may make you decide not to tell Rachel I'm here—or may make her decide she doesn't want to come see me after all. You see, I got married again after our divorce. And I have another daughter—Pamela."

Ada left Somerset and made the trip back to Bay City as uncertain as she had been on the way over. As she said to her husband that evening, "Rachel might go into a tailspin if she knew that this man she thinks is so great gave everything to his other daughter and in all that time sent absolutely nothing to her." Ada paused to consider, then went on to say, "On the other hand, maybe it would do her good to know." She considered some more. "He might give her money. He offered me some."

"Ada," Ernie said, "Rachel doesn't need money from her father. Russ can support her."

Ada gave her husband a bleak look. "Yes, I know, but the question is how long is he going to be willing to do it. I'm afraid for that marriage. I mean, how long is Russ going to stand for it? If she pulls just one more thing, I think Russ might walk out on her. Or if she pushes him too far." Ada shook her head. "If she gets in that kind of trouble, it might be fine if she could go to her father. I don't think much of him, but he might welcome her, you know. Even that half sister might turn out to be a friend to her."

While Ada was reporting on her trip to Somerset, her former husband was explaining to his daughter Pammy that she had a half sister named Rachel. "I'm pretty sure," he said, "that when Ada tells her where I am, Rachel will come over here to see me. After all, I *am* her father."

Pammy made a face. "Well, isn't that just fine and dandy."

Her father gave her a comforting pat. "I figured I'd better tell you about her in case she does show up here, but I wanted you to know she doesn't mean a thing to me. After all, I haven't seen her since she was a baby. The only person in the whole world who means anything to me is you."

Ada's uncertainty about whether she should tell Rachel about her father was not resolved that evening. Or ever, actually. When Rachel finally learned of her father's whereabouts, Ada had nothing to do with it.

And Rachel had one more problem to dump in his lap.

Rachel had believed it when she told Ada that Russ would get over his anger in a day or two and everything would be fine again, but Russ didn't, and everything wasn't. Not that he stayed angry, but he didn't return to the kind of affectionate behavior she had become used to. He was polite but cool, civil but indifferent, and though he said nothing to her about his feelings, he confided to his parents and to Alice that the only reason he was staying with Rachel was because of their son.

And he was absolutely unyielding about the ground rules he had laid down for Rachel. She literally did have to account for every penny she spent, and he refused to give her permission to buy any extras.

The fashion show Liz had spoken to Rachel about took place on April 3. All of the young women who modeled were told that they could buy their dresses at forty percent off, and Rachel very much wanted to buy an evening gown. Russ said no.

Rachel fumed at him. "How much longer is this going to go on? This new kick we're on about not spending any money. Here it is spring, and I haven't gotten a single new dress or anything."

"And you aren't going to for some time," Russ said.

"Why?" Rachel asked. "After all, you're going to be opening your own office soon."

"That's right," Russ said. "And in case you've forgotten, we're already in hock for this apartment you moved us into, and I'm going to have to go even deeper into debt to pay for my share of the clinic with Dan Shearer."

"I know that, Russ, but you'll be able to pay that off in no time. Look at all the money you'll be making."

Russ had been trying, not too successfully, to read some medical journals that had been stacking up on him. Now he put the article he'd been reading aside.

"What makes you think I'll be making a lot of money?"

She gave him a bewildered look. "What do you mean? I thought the whole idea of opening your own office—"

Russ finished the sentence for her: "Was not to make money but to practice medicine—the kind of medicine Dan and I are really interested in. Sure, I'll be making more than I do now as a resident, but not an awful lot."

She still looked bewildered. "But, Russ, of course you will. I've been asking around, and do you know what doctors get now for just an office visit?"

He nodded. "Yes, I know, but Dan and I won't be getting anything like that."

"Why not? I mean, even though you're just starting out you've got a right to charge as much as anyone else."

"We probably could if we wanted to," Russ agreed, "but that's not what Dan and I are interested in. There are enough high-priced doctors in Bay City already. What we want to do is concentrate on patients who haven't been able to afford it. And our fees will be scaled accordingly."

She was now staring at him open-mouthed. "You mean," she said, "things aren't going to be any different for us then—that we aren't going to have any more money than we have now?"

"Very little more. Is that a big disappointment to you?"

Without thinking, Rachel said, "Yes, it is. I thought that when you finally—" She broke off, realizing what she was saying and where it could lead. "Why, no, Russ, of course not," she amended. "I mean, if that's what you want to do."

"It's what I want to do, and it's what I'm going to do." And he went back to his magazine, not the least bit fooled by her sudden sweet reasonableness.

At the fashion show earlier that day Rachel had got into an argument with Alice, who was also modeling for the benefit luncheon. Alone together for a few minutes in the dressing room, Rachel started complaining about Alice's attitude toward her, saying, "Alice, just because you feel you have to be angry with me—I mean, is there any reason to—"

Alice cut her off. "To ruin your life the way you ruined mine?"

Rachel sniffed. "I don't see how you can say your life was ruined. I mean, my goodness, Steve was only—"

She didn't get to finish that sentence either. Alice turned on her. "Don't you ever say that name to me. Ever. Do you understand that? Don't say anything at all to me, because there's nothing you have to say that I want to hear. Now or ever, Rachel."

Yet less than a week before that, in talking to her father about Rachel and her one-night stand with Steve, Alice herself had said what she wouldn't allow Rachel to say or even imply. "I may have been pretty upset about it once, Dad, but now I'm beginning to think it was a good thing. Steven means nothing to me now—absolutely nothing. I ran into him a while ago at Walter and Lenore's, and whatever I may have felt for him once was gone. He could have been a complete stranger. But when I'm with Chris Tyler—well, that's something else."

Jim nodded and said nothing, but he was not convinced. It hadn't been all that long since Alice had said to him, "When you've gone along for quite a while believing everything is just fine, that everything is settled and happy, and there are things to look forward to and then all of a sudden there's nothing at all to look forward to . . . and it isn't because you've done anything wrong or mean or malicious—you haven't done anything at all—except love and be loved and look forward to being happy. And then all of a sudden that person you loved and who loved you simply isn't there any more."

Pat Randolph wasn't the only one to see resemblances between Steve and Alice's new boy friend, Chris Tyler. A number of Alice's friends had commented on them, too. Like Steve, Chris seemed terribly sure of himself. He was determined to make his own way in the world. And, also like Steve, he had a gruff exterior, but underneath it he was not as tough as he liked to make out.

Some of Alice's friends thought she was simply being consistent in what she liked in men—that the qualities the two men shared were qualities Alice found appealing. Others felt that Alice was dating Chris because he reminded her of Steve—that when she was with Chris she could fantasize being with Steve.

Chris himself had suspected in the beginning that he was only a substitute—the classic rebound—but he swore he would make Alice forget Steven Frame, and she was willing enough to let him try. As she said to her roommate, Muriel, she couldn't spend the rest of her life going into a tailspin every time she ran into Steve, whether he was with somebody else or was alone.

One evening shortly before the fashion show, Alice and Chris had dinner at her parents' house. They insisted on doing the dishes for Mary, and when they were alone in the kitchen Chris said, "I'm getting very serious about you, Alice. You know that, don't you?"

Suddenly uncomfortable, Alice said she didn't know it and tried to change the subject, but to no avail.

"You don't believe me?" he asked. "Well, there's an easy way to prove it." He looked about him. "A kitchen isn't exactly the place for it. I always figured there'd be soft lights and a band playing when I got around to it, but . . . Alice, will you marry me?"

She stared at him.

He now stared at her. "I said, will you marry me? What is it?"

Alice shook her head. "Nothing. Not a thing." She turned to busy herself at the sink.

Chris took her by the arm and turned her so that she was facing him again. "Don't give me that. I know that look. Your Steven Frame look. I've told you before, Alice. I'm not Steve Frame. I'm me. And one of the things I'm trying to do is make you forget about him—that you ever knew him."

She nodded—an eager little nod. "And I have forgotten about him," she said. "At least, he doesn't mean anything to me any more."

"Good," Chris answered. "Then will you marry me?"

She chose to believe he was only joking, and responded accordingly. "Stop that, Chris. You know you're not serious."

He had a most serious look on his face, and what he said was "The whole point of this was to prove that I was, but if you don't believe me, okay, Alice. Maybe this wasn't the place for it, but I'm not through yet. I'll ask you again. And if it's necessary, again and again."

One evening shortly after the fashion show, Chris and Alice were alone in her apartment. The record player was on and playing the ballad "Yesterdays." Alice and Chris were dancing to it in the middle of the living room, but when she started humming along with the record, he stopped dancing, and accused her of thinking of Steve. "Is he ever very far from your mind?"

Alice gave him a troubled look. "Do you want me to be honest? All right. I think of him. But I would, wouldn't I, sometimes?"

Her answer didn't satisfy him. "I gather you think of him often enough that you can't take me seriously when I propose to you. Because you didn't, you know."

"I wasn't sure you were serious," she said. "I'm not even sure you are now. I mean, all this humbleness all of a sudden. That's not like you."

If she had expected to draw a laugh or a smile or any acknowledgment that she was kidding him, she was disappointed. He said, still looking serious, "I want to change for you."

Now Alice became serious too. "Aren't we getting into pretty deep water?"

"Alice," he responded, "I'm proposing again. I want to marry you. You can't make any mistake about how serious I am."

She kissed him—a very gentle kiss—then said, "That was to let you know that I do think a lot of you—and more tonight, I think, than ever. I like you very much, but I just want us both to be awfully sure, that's all."

"I am sure," he said. "We don't have to be married right away. What I'd like to know is that we will be someday."

The troubled look was back on her face. "Not now, Chris."

"But maybe?"

For a few minutes Alice said nothing. Then, finally: "Yes, maybe. Yes, Chris."

He took her in his arms and kissed her.

The following evening Chris stopped by the apartment to take Alice out to dinner. They were just leaving the apartment when the phone rang. It was Russ calling from the hospital.

"I'm covering Emergency tonight," he said, "and we're in a bit of a jam. Miss Richards phoned in sick, and I ordered a replacement, but she won't be here for about forty-five minutes, and in the meantime we've got an accident case coming in that sounds as if it might be serious. Head injury. The man's in a coma. Since you're so nearby, Alice, I wondered if you could come over and give us a hand until the replacement gets here."

Alice looked from the phone to Chris. "Well, I do have a date, Russ—a dinner date with Chris—but . . . well, sure, I'll be right over."

She explained the call to Chris, who said, "I thought we'd eat at the Blue Bell, here in the neighborhood, so I'll tell you what. I'll drop you off at the hospital, go on to the restaurant, and when you're relieved you can join me there. Okay?"

"Fine," she said.

The accident case arrived in Emergency before Alice did.

To the attendants, who brought the man in on a litter, Russ said, "How's he doing?"

"Not too good, Doctor," one of them answered. "He hasn't stirred since we picked him up. Pulse and respiration both irregular."

Russ turned to call to another resident. "Ready with an airway. We may need oxygen, too." Then he took his first good look at the accident case and saw that it was Steven Frame.

Chapter Seventeen

MOMENTS later Alice came into the Emergency Room, fastening the cuffs of her uniform, a somewhat harried look on her face. Nodding to the other resident to take over for him, Russ hurried over to her and took her out into the corridor.

The harried look gave way to one of bewilderment. "What's the matter, Russ?" she asked. "Don't you need me any more?"

"Yes, we need you. But the thing is, there are complications."

"You already said he was in a coma."

Russ nodded. "Yes, but that's not the kind of complications I'm talking about. It's Steven Frame." She gasped and stared at him in horror, and he went on. "I'm sorry, Alice—sorrier than ever now that I asked you to come over to help—but . . ." He put a hand on her arm. "Are you all right?"

She was white-faced, but she nodded. "Yes. Yes, of course I'm all right. Let's get back in."

Together they hurried back inside, and after taking a quick look at the unconscious Steve, Alice went to the supply cabinet, pulled out what she needed, and returned to his side, where Russ and the other resident were conferring.

"It's a skull fracture." Russ was saying. "Not much doubt about it. It looks depressed, too. And with the nasal and oral bleeding and the leakage of fluid, I think there's a chance of an intracranial hemorrhage. So we'll check for blood traces in the spinal fluid, then get an arteriogram. And I'm going to call upstairs to see if there's a neurosurgeon in the house. We'll know for sure about operating when we get the test results, but I'm almost sure he'll have to be operated on."

Sponging the blood from Steven's head, helping the other resident do a spinal tap, Alice felt as if she were doing all this under water—that she could only move slowly, clumsily, when she should be moving with the speed of light.

She heard Russ on the telephone, talking to Dr. Cameron—and she allowed herself one little sigh. Dr. Cameron was the best neurosurgeon in the state.

"We've got a serious head injury down here in Emergency," Russ was saying. "It looks like a depressed fracture of the left parietal, with some bleeding and some leakage. I've ordered a tap and an arteriogram. I thought it would be better than a straight X-ray. We should have the results in twenty minutes."

When he had finished his phone call Russ came back to tell her what he knew about Steve's accident. "He was at one of his construction sites—the one at Riverview—going over some plans with the foreman on the job. They were doing some blasting, and a beam fell and struck him on the head."

Alice looked from Russ to Steve's inert form and back to Russ again. "But when you're on a construction site, aren't you supposed to wear a hard hat?"

"He was wearing one," Russ answered. "But the beam knocked it off as it knocked him down, and it was the fall that did the damage."

Alice looked again at Steve. She hardly dared to breathe. "What do you think his chances are?" It came out almost in a whisper.

Russ touched her shoulder. "We'll know better after we've seen the test results." When she looked at him through tear-blurred eyes, he said, "I really feel bad about this, Alice—that I had to call you on this —but the relief nurse should be along any minute."

Alice stared at him. "Do you think I'm going to leave here? Now?"

He was searching her face. "Well, I know this is kind of rough on you, and I thought—"

She cut him off. "I'm staying."

Russ nodded. "I thought you might." He turned. "Oh, Dr. Cameron. Good. I'm glad you're here."

Russ explained what had happened while Dr. Cameron examined Steve, who still had not stirred or shown any sign of life beyond breathing. Dr. Cameron began testing Steve's deep reflexes: biceps, triceps, wrists, knees, ankles.

"I didn't like the ones on the right side," Russ put in.

"No," Dr. Cameron said, nodding his agreement. "I'd proceed with the X-rays, Dr. Matthews, but I don't have any doubt about what you'll find. I'm sure we're going to have to go in. In fact," he added, straightening up from the examination, "I'm going to call the O.R. right now and have a team standing by."

The Emergency Room's replacement nurse arrived a few minutes later, so when Steve was taken upstairs to the operating room, Alice was free to follow—to stand in the corridor outside saying over and over, "Don't let anything happen to him—please, please. What he did doesn't matter. Just don't let anything happen to him."

At some point during the long surgical procedure, Walter and Lenore appeared at her side, saying that the foreman on the construction site had called Steve's office, and the office had called Walter, and they had gotten there as soon as they could.

Alice described the injuries. "There was a possibility of a clot forming, so they decided to operate immediately. There's no great problem about the fracture itself once the pressure is relieved. The rest depends on what they find—how much brain damage there is. The thing is, even if he pulls through, there's no telling what the results might be—either temporary or permanent. Partial paralysis, or loss of memory or other functions. There's always a chance of it."

When the operation was finally over, and Steve had been taken to the Recovery Room, Alice went back to her customary station on the fourth floor to await further word. She had been there maybe an hour when Russ came by looking for her.

"Go on home," he said, "or you won't be fit for

anything tomorrow. That's when you can really be useful." Seeing her give an anxious start, he turned. Dr. Cameron was coming toward them.

As he came up he said, "He's resting comfortably. We'll probably be bringing him down from Recovery in about an hour. The operation was successful. We relieved the pressure, stopped the intracranial bleeding, and removed the clot." Alice gasped, and Dr. Cameron nodded. "Yes. One had already formed." He patted her shoulder. "We can hope for the best. He's young and he's strong."

After a few more comforting words, Dr. Cameron went on his way, and Russ turned to Alice. "Let me take you home."

"It's all right, Russ. You don't have to."

"I'm not going to let you go home alone. You're beat."

Somebody said, "I'll be glad to take her home, Doctor," and Alice and Russ both turned. It was Chris.

"Oh, Chris," she said. "I'm sorry. I completely forgot about you, but . . . well, you see, something happened."

"I know," he said. "They told me downstairs. Is he going to be all right?"

"We don't know yet," Russ said. "Maybe tomorrow."

Chris nodded. "Then let me take you home, Alice. I'm sure you'll want to be here early."

"Yes, I guess I will. All right, Chris."

Although Alice was exhausted, she wanted to walk the few blocks, and Chris said that was all right with him. Walking along in the stillness of the night, he said, "It's going to be hard, because you still love Steve, don't you?"

"No, no," she said quickly. "No, I don't. I guess I feel something for him. The question is, what?" They walked a few steps in silence, and then she went on. "I certainly did love him once, but that's all over with. That's why I broke our engagement."

He glanced at her. "Is that why you broke it—because it was all over? Or did you break it and then try and convince yourself it was all over? There's a big difference."

"Chris, I'd really rather not talk about it, if you don't mind. Not tonight."

"Okay," he said. "Tell me about the accident. How it happened and exactly what happened to Steve."

She told him, and by the time she had finished, they were at her apartment. Agreeing with him that she could use a drink—one, anyhow—she invited him in, and he fixed one for her.

When he handed it to her, she smiled at him—a tired smile, but a friendly one. "Your whole attitude," she said, "not being annoyed with me for not showing up at the Blue Bell, letting me talk about what happened—how I feel about it— Oh, Chris, I'm not clear about that myself yet."

He nodded. "You know I care about you, Alice."

"Yes, I know. And I haven't forgotten what you said last night."

"This isn't the time to talk about it, Alice."

"No, but, Chris, I do think a great deal of you—especially after the way you've been tonight."

He nodded again. "All right. But let's leave it at that for now. You get some rest, and I'll talk to you tomorrow."

Chris left, and Alice finished her drink, telling herself how calm she was—and in the next moment she burst into tears.

At the same time, in Steve's room at Memorial Hospital, he had still not regained consciousness, but he was beginning to get restless, tossing and turning, and when the night nurse came over to his bed to make sure he was all right, she was startled to hear him calling Alice's name.

The next morning Alice was at Steve's bedside by seven thirty. He was quiet now, his eyes still closed, his head bandaged. She had taken his blood pressure and was taking his pulse when he opened his eyes and looked at her.

"Steven," she said, but almost before she had

finished saying his name he had closed his eyes again, and she wasn't at all sure he had recognized her.

The door opened, and Dr. Cameron came in. "Well," he said. "Good morning."

"Good morning, Dr. Cameron."

"How's our patient?"

"That's what I'm waiting for you to tell me. He opened his eyes just now—but only for a second—and without any sign of recognition."

Dr. Cameron nodded and began checking the deep reflexes as he had done the night before. But with far more satisfactory results. "Fine," he said. "Very different from last night." Then he examined Steve's eyes, and as he was doing so, Steve opened them again. "How are you?" Dr. Cameron said.

There was no response, and an instant later the eyes were closed again.

"That's the same way he did it before," Alice said.

Dr. Cameron nodded again. "It's only to be expected. He's a strong young man in very good physical condition, but his system has had quite a shock. Not just the original injury, but over two hours of surgery as well."

The door opened again, and Russ came in, his face lighting up at sight of Dr. Cameron. "Good prognosis, I hope," he said.

"Yes, I'd say so," Dr. Cameron replied. "There's no sign of any neurological impairment. Reflexes normal, no sign of paralysis. The night nurse reported that he mumbled several times—called out someone's name—so it's not likely his speech has been affected. Of course, there's no telling yet whether there might be some traumatic side effects, such as loss of memory. Not necessarily permanent or complete."

Steve opened his eyes and blinked a few times.

Dr. Cameron looked from Steve to Alice. "Are you going to be taking care of him?"

She nodded. "Yes. For a while, anyhow."

"Then I'll talk to you later." He and Russ went out, leaving her alone with her patient.

A few minutes later Steve opened his eyes again and looked at her. "Hello, Steven," she said. To her surprise—and great relief—he nodded slightly. Encouraged, she said, "Do you know where you are?"

"Hospital?" he said in a shaky voice.

Still more encouraged, Alice said, "Yes. And do you know who I am?"

A faint smile suffused his features. "Of course," he said in his wobbly voice. "You're Alice?"

She smiled back at him. "Alice who?"

"There's only one Alice. My Alice. My darling." He made some sort of motion under the bedding. "Hand?"

"What?" Alice said, still trying to absorb what he had said before that.

It was an effort for him to speak, and it took a bit of time, but finally he said, "Your hand."

She held out her hand to him—her left hand, as it happened—and he brought his own hand out from under the bedding and squeezed it, smiling. Then he frowned—a kind of woozy frown. "Where's your ring?"

Alice was bewildered. "Ring? What ring?"

"The one I gave you," he said, still with some effort. "Your engagement ring. Why aren't you wearing it?"

She stared at him, not knowing what to say. Or what to think, for that matter.

"You told me—you said you'd never take your ring off."

"Yes, I know," she said, wanting above all not to upset him, not when he was in this fragile condition.

"Then where is it? Have you lost it?"

"No. No, I didn't lose it." She tried frantically to think.

"Then why aren't you wearing it?"

"I . . . uh . . . I found that I have to take it off sometimes, after all. I mean, in spite of what I said. I . . . uh . . . you see, I've been working a strong antiseptic solution, and I didn't want to risk damaging the diamond."

He smiled and squeezed her hand again. "My sensible Alice. My own girl, Alice?"

She smiled at him, her throat choked. "Yes, Steven. Yes, your girl."

He let go of her hand. "I love you," he said, and drifted off again.

She was standing at one of the windows in his room, trying to get control of herself, when Russ came back. There were tears in her eyes when she turned to him, and he gave her an anxious look. "What's happened? Has he had a relapse?"

"No, no," she said. "It isn't that. He's the same as he was. A little better, actually."

Russ frowned. "Then what's the matter?"

She took him outside into the corridor. "After you and Dr. Cameron left, Steven opened his eyes and looked at me, so I asked him if he knew who I was, and he smiled and nodded at me."

Russ was still frowning. "So what's wrong with that?"

"I was just getting to it. He asked me why I wasn't wearing my ring—my engagement ring. He thinks we're still engaged. He doesn't remember what happened."

Russ let out his breath. "Oh. The lapse of memory. Well." He gave a shake of his head. "Alice, you've never told me anything about why you broke your engagement"—he put a hand up—"and I'm not prying now. But could you tell me this much—did Steve want to break it?"

"No," Alice said.

He spread his hands. "Well, then, there's your answer. The blow on his head blotted out the memory of something he'd like to forget. Breaking off with you has apparently caused him a great deal of mental anguish—so much so that now his mind refuses to accept it at all."

"But he'll have to remember it sometime."

"Yes, I'm sure he will when he gets stronger and more oriented. A lapse of memory like this is rarely permanent. At least for the most part. It's possible he'll never remember certain things—the accident itself, perhaps, the events leading up to it—a day here and there. But what usually happens in these cases is that the memory comes back bit by bit, until most of the pieces are there."

"And in the meantime?" Alice asked.

"I'd say that depends on you," he answered her. "Dr. Cameron told me that if Steve continues to progress without physical setbacks, without any psychic disturbances, he may be in the hospital a relatively short time. Two or three weeks."

"In other words," she said, "you want me to play along with him, let him go on thinking we're still engaged."

Russ looked at her with tender concern. "There's no question in my mind that that would speed his recovery, but there's got to be some question in your mind."

"Oh, Russ," she said, "you know I want Steven to get well as soon as possible."

"I didn't mean that. I meant what playing along with him is going to do to you."

"Never mind me," she said with a little shake of her head.

Russ frowned. "I have to mind you. And so do you, for that matter. It's going to be very hard. Look what it's done to you already." He considered a moment. "I could have you taken off the case—make some excuse to Steve. Think about it."

"No," Alice said. "I don't need to think about it. In the first place, he wouldn't understand. The way Steven feels about me. I mean," she hastened to add, "the way he thinks he feels about me. If you told him I was sick, then he'd worry. And that wouldn't help, would it?"

"No, it wouldn't," Russ agreed.

"And besides, if it makes him happy to have me there with him, especially thinking what he does, then that in itself will help him get better, won't it?"

"Yes, I would think so."

Alice put a hand on Russ's arm. "I'll be okay. I mean, I know it was hard just now, but that was mainly because it came as a shock to me. Now that I'm prepared for it, now that I understand, it won't be as hard."

Russ searched his sister's face. "Do you honestly believe that?"

Alice didn't answer him, but said, "I have to get back to Steven."

Back inside the room, Alice found him awake again. He gave her his somewhat woozy smile and said, "You were gone a long time."

She smiled back at him. "No, Steven. Only for a minute or so."

"It seemed like a long time." His voice was getting a bit stronger, but now a distressed look came over his face. "Alice, you won't leave me?"

"No."

"Never?"

"No," she said again, as firmly as she could. "Never."

He smiled. "You'll live with me and be my love?"

"Yes."

"Just as you promised?"

"Yes, Steven, just as I promised." She put her hand on his forehead. "Try to get some sleep now. It will help you get better."

He closed his eyes, and in a few minutes he had drifted off, but Alice sat on by his bedside, blinking, trying to keep the tears from coming.

That evening her father stopped by her apartment on his way home from the office, and she told him everything that had happened. When she explained how she was having to pretend to Steve that she was still engaged to him, her father said, "Darling, what a terrible strain it must be on you."

The tears she had more or less held back all day started streaming down her face now. "It isn't pretending for me to tell Steven I love him, Dad. Because I do love him. I always have."

The next morning when she walked into Steve's room he was awake and waiting for her. Waiting to take her in his arms.

She told him he wasn't strong enough, then bent and kissed him gently. "As soon as you're well," she said to him. "There's all the time in the world."

He nodded. "A whole lifetime, Alice. A whole lifetime."

"Yes, Steven." Then she spoke more firmly. "Now, Steven, I'm your nurse, and if you don't want to—"

"You're my girl," he said, cutting her off. "My nurse is my girl."

She tried to ignore him. "If you don't want me to take your temperature, all right, we can wait. But you'll have to take this." She held out a tiny paper pill cup and poured water into a glass from the pitcher on his bedside stand. "Something the doctor ordered. Take the pill, Steven."

He took it, then held out his hand to her. "Please sit beside me, Alice. Just for a little bit."

"All right," she said, and pulled a chair up to the bed.

He took her left hand in his. "I love you, Alice." He brought her hand to his face and pressed his face against it. "Funny. It took me a long time to admit I loved you. We wasted a lot of time, didn't we?"

"Yes, Steven, we did."

He gave her a somewhat anxious look. "But no more wasting time, Alice. No more, right?"

She nodded and bit her lip. "Right, Steven."

He seemed to be struggling with something. Maybe the medication was beginning to take effect. "Engaged, right?"

She nodded again. He was still in such fragile condition. "Yes, Steven. Engaged."

He frowned down at the hand he was still holding. "Why don't you wear your ring?"

She caught her breath. "I can't, don't you remember? I told you I can't wear it here at the hospital because of the antiseptic solutions."

He considered that, then said, "Put it on a chain and wear it around your neck."

What was she going to do now? "Maybe," she said. "I—I'd have to find just the right chain. We'll see." She gently disengaged her hand and stood up. "Steven, I have to go down to the nurses' station for a few minutes." What she had to do was get herself under control.

But he wouldn't let her go. He reminded her that

she hadn't taken his temperature, and then, when she started to, he said, "Put the thermometer in and then talk to me. Talk about the house we'll have—the life we'll have. Please, darling."

Alice sat down again and let him take her hand in his again. How often they had talked about their dream house. She swallowed a couple of times and looked not at him but over his head, into the faraway distance. "We'll have a nice house in the country—a nice, old-fashioned house with an upstairs and a downstairs, and with Early American furniture, and a wood-paneled room for you to have an office in. A den. A house with many windows—big windows—and drapes that go from ceiling to floor. And when you pull them back, there's the countryside. Elm trees and hickory, I think. And I'd like a row of poplars."

She swallowed again—two or three times—and tried to keep her expression perfectly calm. "Poplars are kind of formal-looking, but I do like them. Maybe right on the border of our property, Steven, so that when we look through that big picture window after we pull the drapes back . . . Oh, Steven."

She couldn't go on, but he nodded to her to do so, and so she swallowed yet again. "We'd have a fireplace. A stone fireplace. And it would be quiet where we live. So quiet. With just us there together."

With a shake of her head, she stood up and took the thermometer out of his mouth, looked at it, and jotted his temperature down on the chart. But if someone had come into the room at that moment and asked her what his temperature was, she couldn't have said.

Putting the thermometer back in the solution-filled glass, she said, "I have to go now. For a few minutes."

He reached for her hand and caught it. "Just tell me one thing, Alice. Tell me you love me."

"I love you, Steven." Quickly she turned and walked out of his room, closed the door behind her, leaned against the corridor wall, and cried.

Beyond the emotional strain, Alice was putting in a twelve-hour day nursing Steve. That evening she called Chris to break a dinner date she had made with him before Steve's accident, explaining that she was completely exhausted. Chris said he wasn't surprised, only disappointed.

After arranging a new date for two nights later, Chris asked how Steve was.

"As well as can be expected," Alice said.

"There's something about the way you said that. Is there something you're not telling me?"

"Yes," Alice admitted. "But I don't want to go into it now. I'll tell you when I see you Thursday night."

After hanging up, Alice turned to her roommate, Muriel. "He was disappointed but very nice about it. I think he kind of expected it."

"Does he know what happened to Steve's memory?" Muriel asked.

"No. That's what I was referring to when I said I'd tell him Thursday." She sighed and sat down on the sofa. "Today was particularly bad. He keeps asking me why I'm not wearing the ring. If I had it, I suppose I would wear it—just to keep him happy."

"Let me fix you a drink," Muriel said.

Alice shook her head. "No thanks, Muriel. I'm too tired even for that. He was off on something else today, too. Our honeymoon. He wanted to know if we'd made any definite plans for it. I said no, and he said there were two places he'd always wanted to go to—really spend some time in with someone he loved. Paris and Venice. And he started pressing me, telling me we should set the date as soon as possible, because the time to go there is the spring." She sighed again. "I told him we'd better wait and see when he was discharged—how long he'd have to convalesce."

Muriel had been listening sympathetically. Now she said, "Pretending about the way you feel about him—that isn't really pretending, is it?"

For a moment Alice didn't answer. Then she said, "All right. No. It's not pretending. I still love him. I never stopped loving him. That's what makes it so awful. Like a nightmare. Because there are times when I forget what happened myself—when I feel we're back there again last summer, when we were going to get married and I was happier than I've ever been in my life. And then I come out of it again, and I remember where I really am." She gave Muriel an agonized look. "Oh, Muriel, what am I going to do when he finally does remember, and it's all over again?"

Chapter Eighteen

ALTHOUGH Russ told Rachel about Steve's accident the morning after it happened—and said it was clear to him that Alice still loved Steve, making their break-up even more puzzling to him—Rachel was unable to go to Steve at once. He wasn't allowed any visitors.

As soon as he was, she began casting about for some plausible reason for visiting him, since there was always the possibility that she would run into Russ—and every certainty that she would run into Alice.

And then one morning in mid-April her mother came by after talking to Jim and Mary Matthews, and she dropped the little bombshell that Steve had lost his memory and thought he was still engaged to Alice.

"Why didn't Russ tell me?" Rachel demanded, furious.

"It's none of your business," her mother said. "But there's something else that is. Tell me. Why is it Russ all of a sudden prefers eating breakfast at his parents' house instead of with his loving wife?"

Rachel started making excuses, then suddenly changed her tune. "I'm sick and tired of having to fawn over him day and night, when all I can think about is Steve. It's Steve I should be married to."

"Well," her mother said, "you're not. You listen to me, Rachel. You went after Russ because you wanted him. Now, whether you want him or not, you'd better hang on to him, or you'll end up with nothing."

But, as usual, Rachel paid no attention, and, no

longer caring whether she had an excuse, she hotfooted it over to the hospital to see Steve. To her great
relief, there was no one in the room with him.

She smiled and said, "I'd have been to see you long
before this, but——"

He cut her off, not the least bit happy to see her
there. "Forget it."

Her dark eyes went wild. "Forget it? Steve, sweetheart, you know I love you, and people who love each
other . . . well——"

"Stop it, Rachel," he said harshly. "My fiancée is
taking care of me, and that's all I need."

Rachel arched her eyebrows. "Your fiancée? Alice?
Is Alice saying she's your fiancée?"

Steve frowned. "What is this? Alice is the girl I'm going to marry."

The eyebrows were still up, and now the voice was
arch. "Marry? Marry Alice? Steven Frame, do you
really think that? Or is this some kind of game you're
playing?"

Steve gave her a bewildered look. "I don't play
games, Rachel. You play games."

"Me?" she replied with an innocent look. "I don't
know what you're talking about."

He grunted. "What about the game about the
baby?"

"It is your baby. Your child."

"Rachel, I'm tired, and I'm not going to play that
game, so you might as well forget it."

Her expression hardened. "Steven, look here. Somebody ought to tell you——"

But before she could say more, Alice came into the
room, and Rachel started dissembling at once. "I was
just telling him how worried we were about him. Russ
and me and everybody. Russ gives me a report about
him every night—about how he's getting along. But I
had to come see for myself."

His distaste for Rachel plain on his face, Steve said,
"I was just telling Rachel no one has to worry, because
what better medicine could there be than to be nursed
by the girl I'm engaged to."

Steve took Alice's hand and asked for confirmation,

and Alice gave it to him. But Rachel had never been easily daunted, and she hadn't changed. "Alice," she said, "wait a minute. You have no right to let this go on."

Alice turned to her. "Rachel, I think you'd better go."

"You can't let Steve think that," Rachel said, not stirring.

Alice stirred for her. Taking Rachel by the hand, pulling her to her feet, she forced her out of the room, and closed the door behind them.

Rachel jerked away from her. "Don't you push me around."

"I'll push you around as long as you upset a patient of mine. Now let me tell you something, Rachel. Steven is a very sick man."

"Sick?" Rachel said. "He's out of his mind. Those fantasies about the two of you."

"Exactly," Alice said. "Fantasies. That's what they are. And until he gets well, we're all going along with him. You understand? Everyone. Including me. The doctor doesn't want any psychological disturbances. Steven's physical condition is bad enough. And you're going to go along with this, Rachel, by staying away from Steven. Do you understand?"

Rachel tossed her head. "I don't see why."

"I don't care whether you see why or not. I'm telling you to stay away, Rachel, and if you don't, I'm going to tell Russ what happened between you and Steven."

Under ordinary circumstances Rachel might not have paid any more attention to Alice than she had to Ada. After all, eight months had gone by since the engagement party, and if Alice had said nothing thus far, was she likely to say anything now? But beyond the fact that Steve was badly injured, the circumstances in Rachel's life were far from ordinary.

That same evening Russ told Rachel he didn't think their marriage was working out, that his idea of a happy marriage, in which two people who loved each other worked together for mutual fulfillment and understanding, was far different from hers, which consisted of a fancy apartment, fancy clothes, and a rich

husband. It continued to distress him that she had sad-
dled him with an apartment they couldn't afford—and
used the baby's money to do it—and, to top everything
off, her attitude toward the clinic was that it was stupid and would deny her the life of luxury she had obviously married him for.

Frightened, and badly so, Rachel really poured it
on, swearing that she loved Russ and couldn't live
without him. It got her nowhere, so she played the only
trump card she had: Jamie. If Russ wasn't willing to
try harder to make a go of their marriage for her sake,
wouldn't he at least do it for his son?

Russ agreed to that, and Rachel stayed away from
the hospital. With candor rare for her, she even admitted to her mother that her marriage was in trouble.
"And," she went on, "since Steve won't admit the baby's his, and I can't find my father, I've got no one else
to turn to. But don't you worry, Mom, I'll hold on to
Russ. I may not be so crazy about our marriage, but I'll
make it work, because it's all I've got right now."

Ada was still agonizing over whether she should tell
Rachel of her father's whereabouts—and circumstances. Tempted to do so now, but fearful of Rachel's
reaction to the news that she had a half sister, Ada
kept silent.

It was through Lenore that Rachel found out about
her father. Walter and Lenore drove over to Somerset
one evening toward the end of April to have dinner
at the Riverboat, and Lenore took home with her a
couple of matchbooks as souvenirs. She gave one to
Rachel, who had heard about the Riverboat and ex-
pressed a wish to go there. Inside the matchbook cover
was printed, "Gerald Davis, Proprietor."

Stunned to see the name, convinced that this was her
father, Rachel decided to go to Somerset that very day,
despite the fact that Russ and his new partner, Dan
Shearer, were holding a reception at the clinic that
night to celebrate its opening the following day.

Lenore protested the decision. "Your father will be
where he is tomorrow and the day after that, Rachel.
And opening the clinic is a very big step for Russ—
the beginning of a whole new part of his career. How

do you think he'll feel if you're not there with him at a time like this?"

Rachel shrugged. "He won't care."

"You're wrong," Lenore said. "He will care. And even if he doesn't, don't you? Isn't Russ more important to you than a father who deserted you years ago— who never made any attempt to get in touch with you?"

Russ, of course, did care, but he saw no point in arguing with Rachel about it. "I would have thought you'd be interested enough in the clinic to come over tonight, no matter what. But there have been other things in the past I've minded even more, so just forget it."

So Rachel set off to Somerset, only to be told when she arrived at the Riverboat that Mr. Davis had left for the evening and wouldn't be back until morning.

Early the next morning Rachel was back again, asking the bartender for Mr. Davis. The bartender said he had someone with him in his office, but if she'd sit down and wait he'd tell Mr. Davis she was here to see him.

Rachel sat down and looked at a girl seated at another table, leafing through a magazine, apparently also waiting to see somebody. After several minutes a man came up to her and said, "Are you the young lady who was asking for me?"

Almost breathless with excitement, a hollow feeling in the pit of her stomach, Rachel said, "Are you—are you Gerald Davis?"

He nodded. "Yes. Can I help you?"

The girl at the other table had now come over to Rachel's table. "Excuse me, Pops," she said, "but I have to see you about that new swimsuit you promised me."

Rachel scarcely heard the girl. She was still trying to absorb the unbelievable news that she had at long last found her father.

"Pammy," she heard him say, "this young lady is here to talk to me." He turned back to her. "The bartender told me he thinks you're here about a job. You a singer? We've already got a singer."

Rachel stared at him, bewildered. "I'm not a singer."

He shrugged. "And we don't have waitresses here. We use waiters."

"I'm not a waitress."

He shook his head. "The only other job is the hat-check girl, and the girl we got has been here since we opened."

"You don't understand," Rachel said. "I'm your daughter. I'm Rachel."

The girl named Pammy turned to stare at her. "Hey, Pops," she said unhappily.

Rachel frowned at her father. "Why does she call you Pops?"

"Well," her father said, "I . . . uh . . . she . . . uh . . ."

Pammy answered for him. "Because he's my father, that's why."

The hollow feeling in the pit of Rachel's stomach became a big, gaping hole. "He's your *father?*"

Pammy nodded. "Well, yeah. I mean, what'd you think?"

Rachel didn't know what to think about anything at that moment. She was still trying to sort things out a few minutes later, when, after some polite chitchat, her father said he was all tied up with deliveries just now, and could she come back around four o'clock?

When she came back at four o'clock, he wasn't there. She waited for him in his office, looking at photographs on the wall of Pammy at various stages in her life. Finally her father came in, apologizing for keeping her waiting. When Rachel showed him a picture of the baby and said his middle name was Gerald —for him—he was astonished, and then he looked at the picture more closely and found nice things to say about the baby before handing it back to her.

He asked her about her husband and where they lived in Bay City and how she was—things like that. But it was hard to keep the conversation going, because every time they got started on something her father was interrupted by the bartender about a delivery of one kind or another.

Finally he said, "I'm sorry, Rachel. This is a busy time around here."

"Oh, that's all right," she said. What else was there to say?

He tried a smile. "Rachel, I'm sorry about—you know—about not having looked you up all these years. I meant to, but . . ." His voice trailed off.

"Why didn't you?" Rachel asked.

"Well," he said, "you know how it is. I was on the bum for a while there, when you were little. And then I got married again. And Pammy was born. And I had Marsha to think of—that's my second wife—and then Pammy. Say," he went on, brightening a little, "I hope you and Pammy get to be friends. You're a little older than Pammy, and you're married. You could sort of be like a big sister to her. Sometimes Pammy thinks she's more grown up than she really is."

"Does she?" Rachel said. She said it only to be polite. She wasn't the least bit interested in Pammy.

"Well, you know how girls are," her father said. "I mean, you're a girl too, but you're married, and you've got a baby."

"Your grandson."

He nodded. "Yeah. My grandson. James Gerald Matthews. Well, well. Makes me an old man, doesn't it."

"It makes you a grandfather," Rachel said.

He looked a bit flustered. "Yeah—well—that sounds kind of old, don't you think?"

"I'd like for you to see the baby."

Her father smiled and said vaguely, "Well, I will. One of these days I will. Sure."

Once again the bartender stuck his head in the door about a delivery problem, and after conferring with him, her father turned to her to say, "Rachel—honey, I'm afraid you'll have to excuse me. This is really important."

Rachel nodded. There was no hollow feeling and no hole any more. There was nothing. "Yes," she said. "I can see it's important."

Her father looked relieved. "You understand, don't

you?" He was already ushering her out of his office.

"Yes," she answered. "I understand."

"But any time you want to see me—well, you know where I am. I mean, drop in any time. We can always have a talk." He bent to give her a little kiss on the cheek, then straightened up again. "So long for now." And he closed the office door.

Her father's polite indifference was the most supreme test of her staying power Rachel had ever come up against, but she passed it. She called Russ to say that her father had been as excited to see her as she was and she would be staying on another day in Somerset, so she could have still another talk with him.

And at least this time they came to grips with things. Rachel asked her father if she should call him Daddy or Pops. He suggested Jerry.

Rebuffed, she nevertheless pushed on. Telling him how she had dreamed about him as a child—and how she told her schoolmates he was away on secret missions for the government, to explain his absence—she said, "In my dreams you sent me presents. The card always said, 'To my little sweetheart. Someday we'll be together.'" Rachel laughed her little self-deprecating laugh. "Those were little-kid dreams. My grown-up dream has always been looking for you, and in this dream you were looking for me, too. And it always ended with our finding each other, and everything being beautiful. You would help me, give advice. You know, it's very important for a daughter to have a father to talk to. Just being able to talk to a father about a problem might help make it go away. I have a lot of problems, Daddy, and I need your help."

Her father shook his head and gave her a kind of beseeching look. "You've got me all wrong," he said. "I'm not this guy you've been dreaming about—the guy who can do everything, take care of everything. If you want to know what I really am, I'm a heel. Do you think I would have walked out on Ada and you if I wasn't?"

Dismayed, Rachel said, "There was a reason. There had to be. Maybe you had problems."

He nodded. "Sure. And the way I handled them was

to put them behind me and never once look back, never once try to get in touch with either of you. Because if I did, there would be the problem again. I'm not saying I'm not ashamed of what I did, but you see, I'm so stupid about handling the things that bother me, I won't be much good to you with the things that bother you."

Unwilling to believe what he had told her, Rachel made still another try. "How about talking things over? I mean, if I could just tell you about some of the things."

He patted her hand. "I'm sure everything will turn out all right with you and Russ." He smiled—the same smile he'd given her the day before when he started ushering her out of his office. "You know, I'm real pleased to find I have a daughter like you. Such a pretty girl, married to such a fine husband—a doctor—and with such a beautiful baby. I sure hope Pammy does as well as you have, Rachel. Do you think you and your husband could ever come to Somerset some night for dinner?"

Rachel's floundering hope rallied a little. "Oh, yes. I'm sure we could."

He smiled again. "And if I ever get to Bay City, I'll look you up."

The hope died altogether. "I guess I'd better be going," she said. She stood up and picked up her purse.

"I have something for you," her father said, and gave her what Ada subsequently described as advertisements for himself: a bottle of cheap perfume, a couple of Riverboat ashtrays, a lobster bib for the baby. "And don't forget," he added. "If you and your husband do get over, everything's on the house. Okay?"

Unable to speak, she nodded and left.

As soon as Ada had heard the news that Rachel had gone to Somerset, she hurried after her, and after learning from Rachel what had transpired between her father and herself, she went to see her former husband a second time.

Gerald tried to defend himself. "Those crazy ideas she had about me—those fairy tales—who put all that in her head?"

"She made it all up herself," Ada said. "Because she couldn't face the truth—the fact that she had a father who didn't care whether she was alive or dead."

He tried to change the subject by telling Ada what a fine job she had done with Rachel. "She's a beautiful young lady," he said expansively, "with nice manners. She seems a lovely person."

But Ada wasn't about to let him off the hook. "She may seem so, but she's not. Your daughter is a liar and a cheat. You could even call her a thief. All she cares about is money. What Rachel wants, Rachel goes after. So far she's lied her way into marriage with a nice guy by pretending she loves him when she doesn't. She's stolen her own baby's money to move into an apartment her husband can't afford. And there's more, too. She even broke up an engagement trying to get what she wants."

Gerald was staring at her. "Do you think telling me all these things is going to make me want to take her in my arms? Try to be that superman?"

Ada gave him a sour look. "I'm not doing that. I know you could never be to Rachel what she's dreamed of. I just want you to know what you did when you walked out on her. If she'd had a father to grow up with and talk to, she wouldn't have had to lie. She wouldn't have had to make up those fairy tales. She would have been a different kind of person. I don't know what kind, but different. More satisfied. She wouldn't be reaching for the moon and trying to get it any way she can. That's what I want you to know, Gerald Davis. To know and to live with."

Going home to Russ, Rachel at first maintained that everything had been splendid between her father and herself. Then she admitted that it hadn't, but claimed it wasn't his fault, it was Pammy's. Finally, looking at the assortment of giveaway junk her father had pressed on her, she broke down and cried, saying, "Junk! It's all junk! My father loves me so much he gives me junk!"

At about the same time that Rachel's illusions about her father were being shattered in Somerset, Alice was going through the equally painful process of watching Steve regain his memory—while having to maintain to almost everyone that it would be a relief to her when she no longer had to pretend.

The process began one afternoon in his hospital room when Alice was given a message to call Chris Tyler about a dinner date. Steve asked who Chris Tyler was, and she explained that he was a lawyer working in John Randolph's firm. Steve had, of course, met Chris many times, but he couldn't remember having met him at all. Nor could he remember what he himself had been doing prior to the accident at the construction site.

"It's kind of scary," he said now to Alice. "Do you realize that? If I've forgotten what happened right before the accident, then think of how many other things I must have forgotten—really important things."

Trying to reassure him, Alice said, "It won't do you any good to worry about it."

He stirred restlessly in bed and asked for another pillow. "Why are you having dinner with him—this Chris Tyler?"

"He wants to talk to me about something personal."

Steve lay back against the extra pillow and smiled at her. "It's bound to be about a girl, and he couldn't have picked a better person to talk to than you. If you want to talk about a girl in love, you talk to a girl who's *in* love. And you are, aren't you?"

Alice smiled back at him. "Do I really have to answer that? You know I am."

He reached for her hand. "I wanted to hear you say it. I love you so much, Alice."

At dinner that night, Chris asked Alice what she was going to do when Steve regained his memory.

"I won't have to do anything," she told him. "When Steven gets his memory back, he'll not only remember that we're not engaged any longer, he'll remember why, and that will be that. Everything will be back to the way it was."

Chris didn't believe her. "Things won't be the way they were again. They can't be. I don't know what happened between you—why you broke the engagement—and there's no need for you to tell me—but if you still love him, and he still loves you, then is whatever came between you going to be such an insurmountable barrier?" He eyed her a moment. "You don't have to give me the answer to this, but I think you should be very clear about it yourself. Why is it? Why does it have to be?"

"Because it is," Alice said. "I wish it didn't have to be, but it is."

At dinner with her parents the following night, Alice said that her playing along with Steve was helping him. "His memory is coming back gradually," she went on. "He seems to remember the past as hazy pictures. First he thinks perhaps something has happened. He just has a vague feeling about it. And then he begins to fit it together bit by bit—like a puzzle. He's working hard at it. It exhausts what little strength he has right now. It's like exercising a broken limb. Today he remembered just a little bit more. He remembered having a talk with you, Dad, about his accounting work, but he can't remember what it was about."

"You think it was the day I told him I wouldn't handle his accounting any longer?" her father asked.

Alice nodded. "Yes, I'm sure it was."

"It looks to me," her father said, "as if you won't have to pretend much longer."

He had meant to be comforting, but Alice started to cry, distressing both her parents. "I'm not pretending," she said, taking the handkerchief Jim offered her. "That's the trouble. Everything I tell him is true. I do love him. I love him more than anything."

The next morning while Russ was making rounds he went into Steve's room to check him over, then told him he could go home in a couple of days if he had somebody there to take care of him. Russ offered to round up a couple of practical nurses, then mentioned that he too would be leaving Memorial Hospital in a couple of days, to open a clinic with Dan Shearer.

Surprised to hear that Russ's residency was coming to an end, Steve said, "It seems so sudden. I don't know. I get the feeling every once in a while there's some sort of time gap in my life."

"What brings on the feeling?" Russ asked.

Steve shook his head. "I'm not sure. People. Pieces of conversations." He frowned in concentration. "And Alice does. It's when she leaves the room, as she did just before you came by. I get to feeling uneasy. I get the feeling she'll never come back again." He shook his head again. "I know it's ridiculous, but that's the feeling I get. When she goes out that door even for a few minutes I get the feeling she's lost to me forever."

Russ tried to reassure him. "She'll be back, Steve."

Steve nodded. "Part of my head knows that. But the other part—I don't know. I seem to be out of touch in some funny way."

At that moment Alice returned. Taking her aside, Russ told her what Steve had just told him.

"Then he's remembering, isn't he?" Alice said. "His memory is coming back."

Russ nodded. "I think so. I think a memory breakthrough is imminent."

The next morning Alice told Steve that Dr. Cameron had okayed his dismissal for the next day and that practical nurses had been engaged for him.

"I'll go home only on one condition," he said. "That you promise to come see me every night after you get off duty."

"All right," Alice said. "I promise."

"Every night—and your days off?"

"I promise." Then, as a shadow crossed his face, she said, "What is it, Steven?"

"I don't know. I keep getting this bad feeling, and I don't know why. What is it I've forgotten?"

"Don't worry about it, Steven," Alice said.

But he continued to. "My memory seems . . . things seem to be lost to me. You know how you can have a feeling you've forgotten something, and you try and try to come up with it, but you can't remember what it is. And the harder you try, the further away it slips. It's odd. These bits and pieces that I have remembered, I've wondered whether they were things I

dreamed. I've had some of the darndest dreams.
There's one about blasting. And one about a party.
And something about after the party that I didn't like."

He was getting more and more upset, and Alice
tried to calm him, but he went on worrying the subject like a dog worrying a bone. "And there was a
time when I ran into you at someone's house. There
was someone else. You were there, Alice. And Walter
and Lenore. I don't know. Alice, Alice." He reached
out for her hand, and she took it, trying to comfort
him.

"Please, Steven. Don't. Don't upset yourself."

"I'm all right," he said. "It was just for a minute
that I had this feeling. That I hurt you. Terribly—in
some way. And you didn't like me any more." He
gave her an anxious look. "You do like me, Alice,
don't you? You do love me, don't you? And even
though you can't wear your ring here at the hospital,
we are engaged, aren't we?"

She squeezed his hand, then held it against her
face. "Yes, Steven, of course we are. You mustn't
get so upset."

A short time later a package arrived from Steve's
office containing the clothes for him to go home in.
As Alice hung up his shirt and jacket and trousers,
he said, "Did the secretary bring my cuff links?"

Alice looked in the box. "No. Unless maybe she put
them in the pocket of your suit. Here. I'll look." She
went through his pockets, found a small jewelry box,
and handed it to Steve. "That must be what this is."

"Thanks," he said, taking it from her. He opened
the box. Inside were his cuff links and Alice's engagement ring. He stared at the ring, then looked at Alice
in bewilderment. "It's our engagement ring. But you
said—" He broke off, and the look of bewilderment
turned to one of horror. "Oh, my God. I remember
now." He buried his face in his hands. "I remember
everything."

"Steven," she said.

He looked up at her, in such misery that her heart
went out to him. "Alice," he said, "I don't know what
to say."

She gave him an understanding smile. "Why do you feel you have to say anything, Steven?"

"Because now that I do remember, I'm beginning to realize what these last three weeks must have been like for you. Being here with me day after day, having to pretend— Oh, Alice, can you forgive me?"

"There's nothing to forgive you for. I mean, you didn't do it intentionally. You didn't deliberately forget what had happened."

"No, I didn't," he agreed. "It was just all gone. But, Alice. There's no question that I forgot a lot of things —everything that had happened for about a year— but I never forgot that I loved you." He looked away for a moment. "I'm sorry. I probably shouldn't have said that." Then he looked back at her, his dark, brooding eyes intent on her. "Why did you do it, Alice? Why did you pretend—and go on pretending that things were the way they used to be?"

"Steven, you're forgetting something else. I'm a nurse. I was taking care of you. And the doctors didn't want you upset. You were too weak, too sick. They were afraid of what the additional shock might do to you. Russ and Dr. Cameron both said if I possibly could, I should go along with you. They thought it would be only for a little while."

Steve twisted his mouth in a wry grimace. "And it went on for three weeks. And all during that time I talked about when our marriage was going to be, when we were going on our honeymoon. It must have been agony. And talking about the house we were going to build. Now I do remember." He shook his head. "I certainly can't expect any more from you."

"You're still sick, Steven," Alice said. "You still need special care. And you're going to need it for quite a while yet—even at home."

He looked at her in wonder. "Alice, are you saying you'd still be willing to come and see me and take care of me?"

"I am a nurse."

"Meaning you'd do it for anyone?"

She shook her head. "No, of course I wouldn't. Steven, it must be obvious that . . . well, if I didn't

have some sort of special feeling for you, do you think
I'd have done what I did? Pretending that nothing
had happened between us?"

"Then you will come see me and take care of me?
Alice, I'd like you to very much."

"All right, then. I'll do it."

He smiled. "I appreciate that—as much as I appreciate everything you've done for me. But there's
one thing that puzzles me. While my memory may
have been gone, and I may have forgotten what happened, there was nothing else wrong with my head.
And I remember asking you several times if you loved
me, and you always said yes."

"Because I had to, Steven."

He nodded. "I can understand now that you had
to do it. The thing is, I think I would have known if
you were pretending. And I don't think you were pretending, Alice."

Alice neither denied nor confirmed what he believed.

Steve brought the subject up again the first evening
she went to his apartment to see him after getting off
duty at the hospital. But he approached it a different
way. Through Rachel.

"We're going to have to talk about Rachel sometime," he said. "So we might as well do it now. She's
the key to everything that happened to us."

"Yes," Alice agreed. "I guess you could say that."

The day nurse had let Steve get up and come out
into the living room, where she had settled him on the
couch. Telling the evening nurse she could go out for
her dinner, Alice asked Steve if he wanted to go back
to bed, but he said he was fine where he was. At least
for a little while longer. So Alice straightened the pillows behind his head and smoothed the blanket covering him.

"How do you think I feel about Rachel?" Steve
asked when Alice had finished and sat down in a
chair beside the couch.

Alice shrugged. "I don't think you like her very
much."

"I never did like her," he said. "I felt a bit sorry

for her—for a while. But after what she did to us I could wring her neck."

"But you did have an affair with her."

"I didn't have an affair with her. I was with her one night. One single night. I've admitted that to you before. And I'm not excusing myself. It was a terrible thing to do. I'd give anything not to have done it. But you can't call that an affair, can you?"

Alice gave him a troubled look. "I don't know. And I don't see that it matters. The important thing is you were with her for one night, and she claims her baby isn't Russ's child—he's yours."

Steve made a face. "She claims. How do you think she feels about Russ?"

"I certainly don't think she loves him."

He grunted. "The only person in the world Rachel cares about is Rachel. Outside of the baby." He reached behind him to adjust a pillow. "There's something she wants—enough so she'll do anything. Lie, cheat, destroy a dozen lives to get. And that's money. Alice, I happen to be rich. Don't you realize what Rachel's been trying to do? If she could get me to believe the baby's mine, she thinks, I'd marry her. Well, I wouldn't—no matter what. I can't stand the sight of her. But even if I didn't marry her, I'd be obligated to take care of the child. And of her. Which means she'd still be better off than she'd be married to a doctor who cares more about caring for people than he does about money. Doesn't that make sense to you?"

"I suppose in a way it does," Alice answered. "But even if it's true, it doesn't solve our problem."

"Maybe not," he agreed. "But if you admit it makes sense, don't you feel that that might be at least a beginning—a first step?"

The troubled look was back on Alice's face. "A first step to where, Steven? After what happened, where can we possibly go?"

Steve looked at her in silence for a bit, then changed the subject. "What's Chris Tyler to you?" he asked.

Alice was looking down at her hands clasped together in her lap. "I've been out with him pretty often."

"Do you like him?"

She nodded. "Yes."

"How much?"

"Quite a lot?"

"Alice, look at me." When she did so, he said, "And he likes you. A lot."

She frowned. "How do you know that?"

"I don't. I've just got a feeling he's in love with you, that's all. But what counts with me is whether you love him. Do you?"

Alice looked away from him again, not answering.

"You don't love him, do you. Because you love me."

Abruptly she got up from the chair she'd been sitting in, saying it was time for his medicine. He reached out and grabbed her hand to keep her from leaving his side.

"You love me, Alice."

"Steven. Please."

"Does Chris Tyler want to marry you?"

She nodded. "Yes. He does." He waited for her to go on, and finally she did. "But I couldn't say yes to him."

Steve pulled Alice down beside him on the couch. "You couldn't say yes because you love me."

"Steven, please," she said again, and made a little move to stand up again, but he wouldn't let her go.

"Has he asked you more than once?"

"Yes."

His voice had gone husky. "But however many times he asked you, you didn't say yes. And the next time he asks you, what then?"

"Steven, I don't know." She wouldn't look at him.

He put his hand under her chin and turned her face to him, but she cast her eyes downward. "I'll tell you why you don't know," he said. "It's because you love me. Nobody else. Am I right? Look at me, Alice. Am I right? You're damn right I am." He pulled her to him and kissed her, and when she responded, he kissed her more passionately than before, until finally she broke away.

"No, Steven, no. It's no use."

"Alice, can't we at least talk about it?"

She shook her head. "Hasn't everything been said already?"

"Alice, those weeks in the hospital proved something —that you and I both love each other. As much as ever."

"But there's still the fact—"

"I know," he said, cutting in on her. "I spent one night with Rachel." He sighed. "I regret a lot of things I've done. I've made a lot of mistakes. But the worst thing I ever did—the thing I regret most—was that. Because it hurt you." He took one of her hands in his. "But, destructive as it was, can't you ever forget it? Can't you ever forgive me?"

She squeezed his hand. "I forgave you a long time ago. But can't you see? I can forgive you for my sake. I could forget it forever, if only you and I were involved. But there's Russ."

Steve frowned. "You're thinking about Jamie, but I swear to you, Jamie is not my child." And still another time he pleaded his case—that logic dictated that Russ had to be the baby's father.

Alice agreed, and further admitted that her father felt the same way. "But Russ is my brother," she went on to say. "I love him very much. He's been so miserable, because Rachel has done such terrible things to him."

Steve frowned again. "I don't understand what you're getting at."

"What I'm getting at is that Russ is the only person who has the right to forgive what happened. And he doesn't even know about it. That's what makes it so awful. Because if he ever did find out what you and Rachel did to him, it would just kill him. So he mustn't find out—ever. And not just because it would destroy his marriage, but because he loves Jamie so much. Jamie means everything to him. And in divorces the mother always gets the child. So if that happened he would be left with nothing."

"Alice," Steve said, "there's no need to make Russ more unhappy. But how can you destroy yourself because you can't tell him something he's better off not knowing?" He brought her hand to his lips and kissed it. "I know you can't forget it now. Neither can I. But in time—in time we'll forget all that happened. It will be as if it never were. Alice, you do love me, don't you?"

"Yes, Steven, I do."

He kissed her hand again. "And I love you. I'll never love anyone else."

Her eyes filled with tears. "I want to believe you. I want to be able to forget what happened. But—oh, Steven!" The tears streamed out of her eyes, and she buried her face against his shoulder. He put his arms around her, holding her close.

Chapter Nineteen

A few nights later Alice went to her parents' home when she got off duty. It was a balmy evening in the middle of May, and her father was sitting on the front porch, reading the paper. Her mother had gone to the store for some last-minute item for dinner.

"It's all right," Alice said. "I really wanted to talk to you alone, Dad."

He put his paper down, and patted the space beside him on the swing. "You look upset, darling."

Alice sat down. "I am upset. Steven and I had a long talk the other night. And do you know what we were talking about? Us. The two of us. He loves me, Dad. He loves me very much. And I love him. And he wanted to know why we couldn't get married in spite of what happened. And—well, why can't we, Dad? Tell me, why?"

Then, not giving her father a chance to tell her anything, Alice went on to plead her case—the case that

only a few nights before had been Steve's. Steve and
Rachel had only been together that one night—and
only then because Rachel had thrown herself at Steve.
Steve had never cared for Rachel, and now he despised
her. Other single men had had affairs, and what Steve
had done didn't even qualify as that. So if what he
had done wasn't so awful, why shouldn't she be able
to forgive him, and why shouldn't the two of them
get married? Especially since everybody—except her
mother—was convinced that Russ was the baby's father.

Jim listened in silence to her outpouring; then he
said, "You still haven't mentioned one important ele-
ment—maybe the most important. What happened
and to whom it happened."

Alice swallowed. "You mean Russ."

Her father nodded. "If Russ ever found out, how do
you think he'd feel? That his sister had married the
man who betrayed him with his wife—and did it after
she knew what had happened?"

Alice sighed. And made the same point that Steve
had made to her—why should Russ ever find out?
Why would anybody want to tell him something he
was better off not knowing?

"You're leaving out the fact that you know, Alice,"
Jim said. "You're a grown woman, capable of making
your own decisions. If you decide to marry Steve, we
wouldn't dream of trying to talk you out of it, but the
question is, what would it do to you—to your marriage?" He searched her face. "Can you really forget
about what happened—what Steve did to your
brother?"

For a long time Alice said nothing at all. Finally
she said, "I don't know, Dad. That's what I'm trying to
decide. And I don't know."

Mary didn't share her daughter's doubts. Not only
was she convinced that the baby was Steve's—because
Rachel had claimed it was—she was distraught at the
prospect that Alice might marry Steve anyhow.

The next time Alice saw Steve, he made one last
appeal to her. "I was hoping," he said, "we could start
all over—from the beginning. Go back to where we

were before. Forget everything that's happened. Forgive first. Forgive me for being a fool. And maybe
after a while forget. Can't we do that? You know I
love you, Alice."

When she didn't say no, it encouraged him, and he
went on. "Please, can't we just try, Alice? Let's have
some good times together, the way we used to. Let's
try to love each other again."

This time she answered him. "I want to say yes,
Steven, but it may not work out the way we want it
to."

"But at least we can try, can't we?"

She made her decision. "Yes. We can try."

He took her in his arms and kissed her.

Although Rachel had boasted to her mother that she
would hold on to Russ, that she would make her marriage work, she was doing a poor job of trying. And—
to Rachel—for the best of all possible reasons. Just as
Russ had never been able to get over the move to
the new apartment—and the use of the baby's trust-
fund money to do it—Rachel couldn't get over Russ's
decision to set up the kind of clinic he had with Dan.

Going to the clinic one evening to try to persuade
Russ to take some time off to go to a movie with her
instead of working late, as he had been every night,
trying to identify an illness plaguing one of his patients
—a project that he admitted might take days or weeks
—Rachel said, "And meantime what am I supposed to
do? You've been at this precious clinic of yours day
and night ever since it opened. Maybe it would make
sense if you were making some real money out of it,
but no, you're not interested in that. All you're interested in is taking care of charity patients—patients
who can't even afford to pay you."

"I told you that's how it would be," Russ said when
she finally ran out of breath.

"I know what you told me, but I didn't think it
was going to be quite like this. Not only not having a
cent so I can buy a decent dress once in a while, but
not even going out to a movie. Is this how our whole
life is going to be from now on?"

"Very likely," he said curtly. "And I don't expect a thing out of you, Rachel. Not a thing."

And he slammed back into his laboratory, leaving her standing in the waiting room.

Later that night, discouraged at his lack of progress in identifying the disease his patient had, frustrated by his deteriorating marriage, Russ locked up the clinic and started home, then changed his mind and went instead to see if Alice was at her apartment.

She was, and she invited him in, curious as to what had brought him there at that hour of the night.

"It's Rachel," he said. "I've just about had it with her—and our marriage." Telling Alice about their fight earlier that evening, he went on to say, "The point is, it's one more fight in a series of fights between us." Russ shook his head. "It's funny. Except for the very beginning, we've really only had one happy period in our whole marriage. It was when Rachel came back after leaving me that second time— when she went to live with her mother. Everything seemed fine. She even seemed eager to have a baby. Remember I told you she insisted on the test for pregnancy before she'd scarcely had a chance to get pregnant?"

"But she could have gotten pregnant before she left you," Alice said.

Russ shook his head again. "No. I told you our marriage had been hell, and I meant it. Why, before she left that time we hadn't lived together as man and wife for weeks on end."

Alice stared at him, suddenly realizing what that meant.

Russ in turn stared at her, seeing the blood drain from her face, knowing he had upset her, but not, of course, knowing how. "I'm sorry," he said, supposing that Alice was distressed simply at hearing about his marital problems. "I forget the strain you've been under since Steve's accident. And I know what you're thinking. You're wondering how this kind of thing could happen between two people who once thought they were so much in love. You're wondering if it can happen between two people as much in love as you and Steve, isn't that right?"

"Yes," she said, too disturbed to know what else to say. "Yes. That's what I was thinking."

"Well, don't worry," he said in a soothing tone of voice. "You and Steve aren't Rachel and me."

"We're not so different," she replied, this time believing she spoke the truth, though she hardly knew what she was saying—or whether she was making sense. "After all, you and I are brother and sister."

Russ nodded. "Yes. You and I are similar. But Rachel and Steve—I can't imagine two more opposite kinds of people. At any rate, my point is that if you and Steve can get over whatever obstacle there is to your marriage, I know you'd never have the troubles Rachel and I have had."

That wasn't all Russ said to her. There was more. But she couldn't absorb any of it, and finally, believing he had overtired her—and of course, it was late—he took his leave. For a long time she just sat where she was, not moving, not thinking, hardly breathing. And then, when the enormity of what Russ had told her finally penetrated her spinning brain, she burst into tears.

The following night Alice was to have dinner with Steve. On and off all that day she considered calling him to break the date. But what would be the use? It would only postpone what had to be said. And done. So she didn't call him, and promptly at six thirty he rang her doorbell.

As he walked into her living room he handed her a small box. "A little present," he said. Then, when she just stood there looking from the box to him, he said, "Open it."

It was a tiny jeweled heart on a delicate gold chain. "It's very nice," she said, trying to smile. "Thank you."

He beamed. "Do you really like it?"

She swallowed. "Yes, I do. But we have something to talk about."

"Can we talk about it at dinner?"

"No. I think here will be better. It's important."

He gave her a quizzical look. "Alice, are you all right?"

She swallowed again. "Yes. I'm fine. But, Steven, we have to talk. Something has happened. About you and me and my parents and my brother and everything."

The quizzical look became a frown. "You mean your parents don't like it that you're seeing me? Alice, at this point I think we have to put our feelings about each other first."

She shook her head. "That's not what this is about."

He was still frowning. "Is it something about how you feel about me? Have you stopped loving me?"

"No," she said.

"Do you still want to see me? Do you still want us to try to be as we were before?"

She suddenly covered her face with her hands. "I don't know. Steven, please stop asking me all these questions."

He came up to her and gently took her hands from her face. "Alice," he said with deep concern, "what is it? What's happened?"

She told him.

And now the blood drained from his face. He turned and walked away from her. "I can't believe this whole thing," he said in a tight, choked voice. "I never believed Rachel when she said she and Russ hadn't been living together."

"Rachel told you that?"

"At least a dozen times. But I thought she was just trying to make me think I was the father. I simply didn't believe her." He turned back to Alice. "But if Russ says—" He broke off.

Alice nodded. "Then it's so. Then you are the father of Rachel's child."

"Alice, I swear to you I never believed it. I never thought for a second I was the baby's father."

"I believe you, Steven. But the fact remains that you are."

He was still trying to absorb what she had had so much trouble absorbing the night before. "Rachel was living with her mother. She had just left Russ. She came to my apartment, and that one night she stayed. And then she went back to her mother's, and a couple of weeks later she showed up again and told me she was pregnant." He spread his hands, his face still white and drawn. "Alice, how could I believe her? I mean, she'd been married to Russ. She was only away from him less than three weeks. How could I believe she got pregnant on that particular night? She kept telling me she and Russ hadn't had anything to do with each other for a long time, but I didn't believe it. How could I? Knowing Rachel, how could I? I simply thought she was trying to trap me. She wanted to get a divorce from Russ, marry me. Alice, it sounded so contrived. Like a plot. And I wouldn't play along with it."

Alice nodded again. "So she went back to Russ."

"And made him think the baby was his." He frowned. "But then why, if she'd made up her mind to deceive Russ—why did she tell you the truth?"

"Can't you see why? Steven, she told me on the very night you and I were to announce our engagement."

He sighed—a long, drawn-out sigh. "She couldn't stand it that you and I were happy. In love and happy and going to be married. Is it possible for one woman to be so jealous of another woman that she'd wreck her own life?"

"I don't think Rachel was thinking about wrecking her own life," Alice said. "Only about wrecking ours." She, too, sighed. "And now there's Russ's life to think about. He's been trying to hold that marriage together somehow because of Jamie. If it weren't for that baby, he'd have left Rachel a long time ago. Instead he's gone on living with her for the sake of his son—who turns out not to be his at all."

The next day when Russ came to the hospital to make rounds Alice avoided him, and as soon as she got off duty she went to her parents' home to tell them what had happened.

At the same time, Ada was with Rachel, worried as usual about what was going to happen to her daughter. Rachel pooh-poohed her mother's fears. "I've got nothing to worry about, Mom. You're forgetting about Jamie. Russ has always been crazy about him."

Ada sighed. "What you're saying is what's holding your marriage together is Jamie. So what's going to happen if he finds out Jamie isn't his child?"

"That's crazy," Rachel said. "The only ones who know about what happened between Steve and me, outside of you, are Alice and Steve. Alice doesn't believe Jamie is Steve's child any more than Steve does. And even if she did know, do you think she'd tell Russ, when she knows how much Russ loves Jamie? Forget it, Mom."

The phone rang, and Rachel went to answer it. It was her father-in-law, asking for Russ. Rachel said he was at the clinic. Not wanting to interrupt Russ's work, Jim left a message with Rachel to have Russ call him, but by the time Russ got home it was too late to call, so he went over to his parents' house the next morning to have breakfast with them, as he had gotten into the habit of doing lately.

Less than an hour later, he was back in the apartment. Rachel was up, wearing a housecoat and moving about the living room, making a halfhearted attempt to straighten up the usually untidy room. She looked up in surprise when Russ came in, and when he told her to sit down, he wanted to talk to her—and told her in a very stiff tone—her eyes went wide with fright.

"What's this all about—the way you're acting?" she asked.

"You've no idea?"

"No, of course I haven't."

"You're a liar, Rachel. You've always been a liar and a cheat and a selfish little conniver. I've known it for a long time, but I kept closing my eyes to it, trying to ignore it, because I felt there was one thing that made our marriage worthwhile—one thing that made it worth trying to save. Jamie. But now I've discovered that's the biggest lie, the biggest cheat of all. How could you do it, Rachel? How could you be so low, so completely without conscience as to pass off Jamie on me as my own son when you've known from the beginning he was Steve Frame's baby?"

"That's ridiculous," Rachel said. "How can you say that?"

"Rachel, stop lying, because it won't work."

"Russ," she pleaded, "I've tried to be a good wife to you."

He was totally unmoved. "Rachel, do you remember what our marriage was like before you left me the last time?"

She shrugged. "I guess maybe things weren't so great between us."

"Great?" His eyebrows shot up. "It wasn't a marriage at all. I hadn't been near you—you hadn't let me come near you for week after week." He made a face. "You went after me in the first place because you thought you'd be marrying money, getting status, social position—all the things you really wanted."

"No," she protested. "I love you."

"No you don't," he said coldly. "You couldn't love anyone. And when you discovered it was going to take a long while before I went into private practice—and even then I'd never make the kind of money Steve already had—you went after him."

She was like a juggler who suddenly sees everything getting out of control. "That's not so. We're just friends."

Russ shook his head in wonder. "Friends. That's a very polite name for it. You spent the night with your friend, and when you discovered you were pregnant, you found out he didn't want you. Oh, he didn't believe the baby was his, but he didn't want you anyway. So you came back to me. You threw yourself all over me, so you could pass off Jamie as my child."

"Russ, that's not true!"

"It doesn't matter whether you admit it or not, Rachel, because I know it's true, and I know what you did to Alice, because you wanted to wreck her whole future. You wanted to see that she didn't marry Steve. That was one of the most vicious and despicable things I've ever heard of."

"Russ," she protested again, staying in there in spite of everything, "you're not giving me a chance."

"A chance to what?" he asked. "To do more lying?"

Do you think I'd believe anything you say to me now? It won't work. There's only one person you've ever cared about, ever considered in all the time I've known you. And that's yourself. You even used Jamie—the baby you claim you love—as a weapon. You used him as an excuse to move us into this fancy apartment. Well, now you can have it all to yourself, because I'm leaving you, Rachel. We're through."

And he went into the bedroom to pack his bags, leaving her standing where she had been in the living room, staring after him, not quite believing yet exactly what had happened.

After dropping his bags off at his parents' house, Russ went on to the clinic and tried to lose himself in his work there, but the shock of what he had been told that morning was still rolling around inside of him, and when the day was over he left the clinic, not knowing where he was going or what he would do. He walked around aimlessly for a while, and finally wound up at Alice's apartment.

Steve was there with her. He had been pleading with her not to consider their situation hopeless, reminding her that the big obstacle in the way of their getting together had been Russ—the fact that Russ didn't know what had occurred. Well, now he knew, and however strongly he might react now, in time he would be bound to get over it, to see it in perspective.

"How can he have any perspective about it?" Alice asked.

"Because he's a fair and intelligent man," Steve answered. "I'm not trying to excuse what I did, but eventually he's bound to realize that if what happened hadn't happened with me, it would have happened with some other man, because of the way Rachel is. All I'm asking of you, Alice, is that you don't close the door. Not consider our relationship hopeless. It's going to take a while for all of us to make an adjustment to the fact that everything's out in the open now. It's not going to be an easy time for any of us."

Before Alice could respond, the doorbell rang.

It was Russ, and whether or not Steve had been accurate in saying Russ would get over this in time and see it in perspective, he had been right on target in predicting Russ's reaction now.

"This is a bit of a surprise," Russ said, eyeing Steve. "I guess it was dumb of me not to realize you might be here, but then, I've been kind of dumb about a lot of things. It must have seemed very funny to you at the time."

Steve shook his head. "It never seemed funny to me, Russ. Believe me. Look, I know how you feel."

"How can you?" Russ replied. "You're a rich man, Frame. You have almost anything anybody could ever want. But that wasn't enough for you. You still couldn't say no to my wife."

Alice had been looking from one to the other of them, not knowing what to say, or whom to say it to. But so far as the two men were concerned, she might as well not have been there.

"I'm not going to defend myself, Russ," Steve was saying now. "Or even try to defend myself. There's nothing you can say to me that I haven't said to myself already. I'm sure you know it wasn't anything I wanted."

Russ gave him a scornful look. "Don't you think I know that—that Rachel was the one who was chiefly responsible for what happened? All those times when she went running to you supposedly for advice, we know what she was really after. But Rachel is a child —emotionally, at least. And not very bright. A very selfish, spoiled child. You're a man—a mature, responsible man. Couldn't you have seen what the consequences were going to be for all of us? Or didn't you care?"

"Of course I cared, Russ. I cared very much."

If Steve had thought Russ's opinion of him might soften a bit from their exchange, he was wrong. "As far as I'm concerned," Russ said, "Alice's breaking her engagement with you was the only good thing to come out of this whole mess. Because it gave her a chance to find out exactly what sort of person you are. I wouldn't blame her if she wouldn't have any more to do with you than I'm going to have to do with Rachel."

And without another word he turned and left, leaving a shaken Steve and an agonized Alice. Where now was there any hope that Russ would forgive if not forget?

The next morning Rachel admitted to her mother—since she had no choice—that Russ had left her. "It's hard to believe my own husband would talk to me the way he did," she said in an injured tone. "He called me a cheat and a liar. He said I'd gone after him for his money and social position." Rachel tossed her dark head. "Huh! You'd think he had money. And he said that was the reason I slept with Steve, too. But it's not. I love Steve. I loved him then, and I love him now."

But Rachel was talking to the wrong person. Her mother scoffed at the notion that Rachel loved Steve any more than she had ever loved Russ. "You brought this all on yourself," Ada said. "You were unfaithful to one of the finest guys there is anywhere, and you tried to ruin Alice's life as well. Russ was right in everything he said to you."

Furious, Rachel accused Ada of being against her the way everybody always was against her. Nobody ever cared how she felt about anything—what she wanted, what she needed, what mattered to her.

In the middle of Rachel's tirade, the phone rang. It was Steve saying he wanted to talk to her about Jamie, and would it be convenient if he dropped by early that evening—about six thirty?

Rachel said that would be fine, and she hung up the phone, her fury dissipated, a smile on her face, a jaunty air about her as she walked back to where her mother was standing. "You want to know what I'm going to do now, Mom?" she said, plopping down on the sofa. Her smile broadened. "I'm going to do what I've wanted to do for a long time now. I'm going to marry Steven Frame."

That evening when Steve arrived, Rachel was all dressed up in a green velvet pant suit and a silken blouse in a lighter shade of green with a big floppy bow at her throat. She had very carefully washed and set and combed her hair, and she was wearing mascara and a bright lipstick. The finishing touch had been to dab a good French perfume at her wrists and in the hollow of her throat. She looked lovely, and she knew it.

After taking him into the baby's room to see his sleeping son, Rachel led Steve back out to the living room, saying, "Isn't he a handsome little fellow?"

Uncomfortable, trying to be polite, Steve agreed that he was.

Rachel smiled at him. "He looks just like you."

Steve shrugged. "If you say so."

Rachel asked him to sit down on the sofa; then she posed for him. "Do you like my outfit?"

"Yes," he said—again politely. "It's very nice."

She smiled again. "It's new. I'm wearing it for the first time tonight—in honor of a very special occasion. Your coming over here. I wanted to look my best for you."

He nodded. "You do look very nice." He cleared his throat. "Rachel, I came over because I wanted to talk to you about Jamie."

"Yes, I know. But about us, too." She sat down beside him.

He frowned, moving away from her. "What about us?"

She smiled more brightly than before. "I know it's been a long time, Steve, but all this time I've felt a closeness to you."

She moved closer toward him, and he stood up and went to sit in a chair. "That's very kind of you, Rachel."

"I know how you are, Steve. You're slow to talk about things like this, but you can to me. Or wait. No. I'll say it for you. I know you love me and want to marry me. I love you, Steve. I want to marry you. I'll get my divorce from Russ and—"

"Wait a minute," he said, putting a hand up to stop the flow of words. "You've got the wrong idea, Rachel. I did want to see you tonight, but only about Jamie. I accept the fact that Jamie is my son—that in this one instance you told me the truth. And I'm willing to pay child support. I'm even willing to pay for you to stay in this apartment, if that's what you want."

She was looking at him in bewilderment. "Steve, I'm talking about love. Marriage."

"Well, I'm not. I'm not going to marry you, Rachel. I have no intention of marrying you, now or ever. I love Alice. I always have. She's the only woman I've ever wanted to live with."

Rachel made a face. "Alice? That whining little nothing?"

Steve got to his feet, his face a thundercloud. "Cut it out, Rachel. And get this through your head. I love Alice. But even if she never marries me, I'd never marry you. Is that clear?"

"But I always thought you loved me." She looked and sounded hurt. "All the time I was with Russ I thought you loved me."

"I'm telling you I didn't. I'll have my lawyer work up a generous money settlement. I owe that to you and to Jamie. But one thing I want very clear. In the future I want nothing—absolutely nothing—to do with you. And now if you'll excuse me, I can find my own way out."

And out he went, and for the second time in as many days Rachel could not quite believe—not yet—exactly what had happened.

By the next morning she was ready to believe it—more or less. She admitted to her mother that Steve had said he wouldn't marry her, and she blamed Alice for his attitude. "Who do you think poisoned his mind against me?" she charged. "But just you wait. I'll get him to marry me yet. You'll see."

While Rachel was making her prediction, Russ was seeking Alice out at the hospital, finding her at last in the cafeteria in the basement, where he joined her for a cup of coffee.

He apologized for speaking to Steve the way he had in front of her, aware now of what she had—had to have—been going through, saying he didn't like to add to her problems.

"It's all right," Alice said. "You had to see Steven some time, and you certainly had to say what you wanted to. I want you to know that the worst part of this whole mess was what to do about you."

But Russ brushed that aside, saying that was his problem and he would handle it. "What about you?" he asked. "Anyone can see you still love Steve. And it's just as obvious he still loves you."

Alice agreed but admitted she didn't know what she was going to do, saying she'd been over it a dozen times, with Steve and by herself. And she still didn't know.

"If you really do love him . . . Look, Alice, if you're thinking about how I feel toward him—what he's done to my life—"

Alice cut in on him. "Don't tell me to forget it, Russ, because I can't. I can't forget any part of what happened. I just don't know what I'm going to do."

By the time she saw Steve again, she did know what she was going to do. She called him and asked him to come to her apartment the next night, after dinner.

He looked anxious when he got there. "You haven't decided to cut me out of your life completely, have you?"

"No," she said.

"Don't shut me out," he pleaded. "You don't even have to say you love me. Just say you'll give me a chance to prove how much I love you—a chance to win you back. I know it will be hard after all that's happened, and it may take a long time. But I don't care how hard it is or how long it takes, because I feel that somehow, in some way, I will be able to convince you we belong together, like we used to."

She gave him that troubled look that had become so familiar to him—and that tore at his heart. "Steven, how can things be the way they used to be?"

He took her hand and held it between both of his. "We had so much. There was so much love between us. I used to feel we could change the world, you and I. And that love is still there, Alice. I've never stopped loving you for one second of one hour of one day, no matter what you may have felt about me." He shook his head. "Whatever bad things you've thought about me, you were right."

"That's not the point, Steven."

He pressed her hand more tightly. "Please, Alice. I'll do anything."

"The point is, I'm so mixed up I feel as though I don't know anything any more. I wanted to see you tonight because I've decided to go away. To Europe. England, France, maybe Spain. Travel till I find a place I like and then stay there for a while."

He had not released her hand. "But, Alice, why?"

She shook her head. "I don't know. I just want to get away from Bay City and try to decide what to do with myself."

"Will you let me know where you are?"

"Maybe, Steven. I don't know."

He kissed the hand he was holding. "Because I'm going to wait for you to come back, you know."

She shook her head again. "You don't have to promise anything."

"I know I don't have to," he said. "I want to."

The troubled look again. "But I can't promise anything."

He kissed the hand again. "It doesn't matter. I'll wait."

"I got an indefinite leave of absence from the hospital."

"Do you have money?"

She nodded. "Yes. My savings account."

For a few moments they stood looking at each other. Finally Steve said, "What else is there to say?"

"Nothing really," she told him. "Except good-bye."

He shook his head. "I'm not going to say that. You're not going to get me to say that, because however long it takes, I'm going to be right here in Bay City waiting for you to come home to me."

Nor would he let her leave without promising him that he could see her one last time before she went away.

Rachel meanwhile was being Rachel—with a vengeance. Before Russ walked out on her she had made a date with Lenore to go to an auction. Stopping by Lenore's house to pick her up, she tried to maintain that her breakup with Russ wasn't permanent, but Lenore wouldn't buy that, saying that she knew exactly what had happened.

"Then I'm glad," Rachel said with a sniff. "I don't like to have to go around blaming other people for what happened if it's not really necessary."

Lenore was looking at her in bewilderment. "Blaming who?"

"Steve Frame. If you know what happened, you probably know how it happened. I guess maybe I was a little weak, but I really couldn't help myself. I mean, it's kind of flattering to have a man so crazy about you, and Steve kept after me and after me, and when he finally got me to come to his apartment that night, we got to drinking, and then he took advantage of me—"

Lenore cut in on her. "You forget Steve is a friend of mine."

"Well," Rachel said defensively, "it was all Steve's idea."

"Was it Steve's idea," Lenore said coolly, "that you pass Jamie off as Russ's child?"

"No," Rachel admitted.

"Then I think we'd better drop it, Rachel."

But Rachel couldn't drop things when they weren't going her way, so she tried another tack. "I know," she said. "It's because of Alice. She's been going around poisoning everybody's mind against me, because she's jealous. She knows Steve really prefers me to her."

This was too much even for the kindhearted Lenore. "I heard it all from Steve, not from Alice. And he said he's not the least bit interested in you and never has been. On the other hand, he loves Alice very much, and she loves him, and they've both been absolutely miserable for over a year now because of what you did. I don't like hurting anyone's feelings, Rachel. Even yours. But I can't go on with this. I think maybe we'd better forget our date."

And she showed a now fuming Rachel to the door.

From Lenore's, Rachel went to the clinic to see Russ —and saw Alice instead. "Well," she said, still fuming, "I'm glad I ran into you. I've been hoping I would. Because I want to tell you exactly what I think of you."

The look Alice gave her was as cool as Lenore's had been. "I'd be very interested to hear it."

Taking her literally, Rachel plunged ahead. "Well, I think you're too much. You always hated me from the very beginning. And the reason you hated me was because you were jealous of me—because Steve loved me more than he did you. And you're so jealous you had to tell Russ about Steve and me. You broke up our marriage and left Jamie without a father. And now you're going around telling everyone else about it, too. Poisoning their minds and turning them against me."

"I see," Alice said. "Now would you really like to know what happened?"

Rachel made a face. "I don't want to hear anything from you."

"I'm sure you wouldn't," Alice agreed, "but I'm going to tell you anyway. I didn't hate you. Not at the beginning, anyway. I didn't like you much, because I didn't trust you. But I also felt sorry for you. Well, you taught me what a mistake that was at my engagement party. But I didn't tell Russ about you and Steve. I didn't tell Russ because I knew how much Jamie meant to him, and I couldn't be sure he wasn't Russ's child."

Going on to tell Rachel how she had found out the truth and what she had done about it, and that it was her parents who had spoken to Russ, she said, "And I'm glad they did, because when they told him, he was through with you. And if everyone else is through with you, if everyone wants no part of you, it's for only one reason—because they finally discovered what I've known all along—that you're a scheming, selfish, lying cheat, who's finally gotten exactly what she deserves."

Alice had come to the clinic to tell Russ good-bye. Now she went to her parents' house to do the same. When her father took her in his arms, she started crying, saying she was leaving because she didn't know what else to do.

"Where are you going?" Jim asked. "And for how long?"

"I'm not sure," she told him. "I'm going to London first to see a few people there. And then to Paris. I'm just going to stay away for as long as I need to." She shook her head. "I'm not even sure what it is I hope to find."

Her father held her close. "Peace of mind, darling. Or at least putting behind you everything that's happened, so you can see it in perspective and make some decisions."

"I guess so," Alice said.

He looked at her, his face full of love and concern. "I hope and pray you'll find what you want—and sooner than you think."

Alice's last good-bye was saved for Steve. That night he came to her apartment.

"May I write you?" he asked.

She shook her head. "The whole point of this is to have a chance to think. If I get letters from you . . ."

He understood. "Okay. Will you write me? It doesn't have to be a letter. Just a postcard to let me know how you are."

"I'd rather not make promises," she said.

He reached into the pocket of his jacket. "I brought you something, Alice. A going-away present. I figured you wouldn't wear that other ring I gave you at this point—the engagement ring—but I hoped maybe you'd wear this one." He held out an old-fashioned wide gold band etched with flowers. "It's old and very simple. You can think of it as kind of a friendship ring." He took her left hand in his. "Will you take it and wear it?"

"Yes," she said, looking at him, her eyes filled with tears.

"I hoped you would," he said, slipping the ring on her finger. "I wanted you to have something to remind you of me."

She tried a little smile—not very successfully. "Do you think I need this, Steven, for that? Don't you think I'm going to be thinking of you too much of the time as it is?"

He put his hands on her arms. "I love you, Alice. I love you very much."

"I love you, too," she answered in a choked voice.

"Oh, Alice," he said. "This is the worst moment of my life. There have been other terrible ones before this—when you broke our engagement, and when I saw you afterwards and you acted as if you barely knew me. But this. To have everything out in the open, to tell you I love you, and have you say you love me and still . . . Do you really have to go away, Alice?"

She nodded, her eyes still filled with tears. "Yes, I do. I've got to get this straightened out in my mind. Try to decide whether we can do anything about this —the way we feel about each other."

For a long moment they stood as they were, and then he took her in his arms and kissed her—a long kiss, more desperate than passionate. And when at last Alice pulled away from him, the tears were running down her face.

"I think I'd better go," Steven said. "I'm not going to say good-bye, because it can't be good-bye. I'll just say till I see you again." He kissed her gently, tenderly, and left.

Chapter Twenty

THE plane carrying Alice to Europe had hardly left the ground before Rachel was back at Steve's office, saying she had something very important to talk to him about: her love for him, and, whether he would admit it or not, his love for her.

He wouldn't admit it and wouldn't discuss it.

"Well, then," she said, "if you don't think about me, what about Jamie? A little boy needs more than money. He needs love, attention. He needs a father.

Steve, you've at least got to come and see him sometimes. You can't just let him grow up alone."

"He's got you," Steve said.

"He needs a father," she repeated. "Come see him
once in a while, won't you?"

"We'll see," he said. "But I don't think so. And now
I think you'd better get out of here."

She looked at him in dismay. "You mean you
aren't even going to talk to me. For goodness' sake,
Steve. All I'm asking you to do is be a father to your
own child."

Steve grunted. "All you're asking me to do is spend
a lot of time with Jamie, so you can try to change my
mind about you. Well, it won't work. I'll never change
my mind. Now get out of here."

Still, Rachel had the last word. "All right," she
said. "But you'll change your mind. I know you will."

And she believed he would.

Steve understood this. As he had said earlier that
day to Walter, a pathological liar like Rachel could
come to believe her own lies. That was why he wanted
Walter to handle all of the financial dealings with
Rachel—draw up the terms of the settlement for the
baby and the allowance for Rachel, plus a separate
trust fund for the baby that Rachel couldn't get her
hands on. Steve himself wanted no part of it—or her.

But—not surprisingly—it wasn't that easy.

First she balked at signing the financial agreement
Walter drew up, saying she didn't think Steve was offering her nearly enough money. "He's a very rich
man," she said. "A millionaire. And after all, Jamie is
his son."

"Legally," Walter pointed out, "Jamie is Russ's
son."

Rachel frowned. "Steve has admitted Jamie is his."

Walter nodded. "He's admitting it in the most con-
crete way possible—by providing for Jamie's support
and by including him in a new will I'm drawing up
for him. In addition, he's giving you an allowance—
separate and distinct from the money he's giving you
for Jamie—which I think is more than generous. If
you're not satisfied with the amount, I suggest—as I

did when I called you to come in about this matter—
that you retain a lawyer."

At first she claimed she couldn't afford a lawyer,
but when it became clear to her that Walter was no
more sympathetic than Lenore had been to her version
of what had happened—she claimed Alice went to
Europe because she couldn't get anywhere with Steve,
and after the way she'd been carrying on about him,
she just couldn't face everybody—Rachel announced
that she would indeed get a lawyer, and that wasn't all
she was going to get. "I'll get more money, too," she
said, her face flaming. "And you'll see, and Steve
will see, and Lenore will see. You'll all see."

And she flounced out of Walter's office.

When Walter told Steve Rachel was hiring a lawyer
to get a bigger settlement, Steve burst out laughing.
Then he shook his head. "I'm laughing at the absolute
ridiculous irony of the whole thing. For one idiotic
mistake, one night out of my whole life, I lose the girl
I love, I ruin her brother, and now the girl that
brought the whole thing about wants more money."
He shook his head again. "It's unthinkable. Walter,
Rachel's not going to get one penny more out of me
than what I've offered. Not one penny. I've already
offered her more than she deserves. I mean, for herself. For her own use. That's the most I'll pay, and you
can tell her that."

But he ended up telling her himself. He went to see
her one afternoon toward the end of June, angry that
the matter was still hanging fire.

"The amount I told Walter to offer you for Jamie's
support was almost double what he thought was fair.
And not only that, I'm offering you a living allowance
for yourself completely apart from what you'll need
for Jamie."

When she brushed it aside as not being enough, and
said her lawyer agreed with her, Steve said, "Then tell
him to take the whole thing into court, because I'm
not going to give you one cent more."

Rachel laughed. "You wouldn't do that—let it go
into court, Steve. Why, the papers would get hold of

it, and everyone in Bay City would hear about what happened between us, and how Jamie's your son."

"And you think I care about that, Rachel? There's only one person in the world whose opinion matters to me. Alice. And she already knows."

Rachel stared at him. "You can't mean it, Steve— that you'd let it go to court."

"I'm afraid you don't know me very well, Rachel. I won't be pressured into anything. If you want the settlement, fine. If you don't, then you're going to have to go to court to get anything."

"I think you're being unfair. Since you never spend any time at all with Jamie, never even want to see him, the least you can do is give me enough money to take care of him properly."

"I'm offering you more than enough," he countered. "As for seeing Jamie, he's too young to even know who I am. But give me a few weeks to make some arrangement at the office, and I'll start spending some time with him."

Hardly daring to believe she had heard him right, but quick as ever to seize any opportunity handed her, Rachel beamed and said, "That's great. If you're too busy during the week, we can make it Saturday or Sunday. We can go for a drive in the country and—"

"Just a second, Rachel," he said, cutting her off. "I'm talking about seeing Jamie, not you. When I see him, it's going to be without you."

She was back to staring at him. "Do you think I'm going to let you take him without me around to look after him? You're his father, but that doesn't mean you know how to take care of him. Either I go along or you can forget it. And since you're acting this way, I'm not going to sign the agreement, either—at least not for that amount."

"Okay," he said. "Then that's that, because I told you I'm not going to give you any more."

While she was trying to get more money out of Steve, Rachel was also trying to get money out of Russ—or his family. Russ had offered to pay for the divorce, but that was all. No alimony and no child support.

When John Randolph, who was representing Russ in this, explained the terms to Rachel, she objected. "But I was his wife." she said, "I should get alimony." And, remembering what Walter had told her regarding Jamie, she went on, "And Jamie is legally Russ's son."

"That's true legally," John agreed, "but I'll simply repeat that Russ is willing to pay for the divorce even though he's letting you file for it, and that's all he's willing to pay for. And, under the circumstances, I think he's being generous."

Rachel made a face. "He'll let me file, and then he'll let me starve. Everyone in this town is on the side of the Matthewses. But there's one little thing I plan to do about that. Fight them. I'm not going to let the Matthews family walk all over me. I'm Russ's wife. I've done his cooking and his cleaning and other things, too. When I ask for alimony, all I'm asking for is my back pay."

As somebody who knew Rachel well observed, she did have some problems, but too many scruples was not one of them.

When John told Jim and Mary Matthews about Rachel's intransigence Mary said, "Rachel hasn't conceded anything. I think she's already building up a case for her own innocence. It just goes to show you the kind of scheming mind she has."

Inevitably the baby's trust fund—the one Jim had set up for Jamie—intruded into their lives again. Fearful that Rachel would try to get her hands on the money, and in any event feeling that they owed Steven Frame's baby nothing, Mary wanted it dissolved and said so.

"There's no way you can do it," John said. "That's the purpose of trust funds. To protect those under trust. That's why they're set up in such ironclad fashion."

"But Russ is the trustee," Mary said.

John nodded. "Yes, I know he is. But as the trustee he has only limited powers. And abolishing the fund isn't one of them." He considered a moment. "There is one thing he could do. As trustee he could write a check out for the full amount of the fund—which to all intents and purposes would abolish it." He considered some more. "But the check would have to be justified as an expenditure for Jamie."

"Justified to whom?" Jim asked.

"To the person the court would regard as Jamie's legal guardian."

"But isn't that Rachel?" Mary said, frowning.

John nodded again. "Exactly. If Russ withdrew the funds without Rachel's okay, she could accuse him of misuse of funds—violation of the trustee agreement —and sue him."

Jim was already shaking his head. "I've been reluctant all along to get into this, and now I say forget it."

But Mary was adamant. Pointing out that Jamie's father was a millionaire and didn't need any of their money, she reminded him that they had a responsibility to their other grandchildren—their oldest daughter, Pat, having given birth to twins a few months earlier.

"Well," John said, "the only other thing is a public hearing. You established the trust fund in the belief Jamie was your grandchild. This has proved to be fraudulent. On those grounds you sue to get your money back. I do have to add that the only person you can sue is the trustee, and that's Russ."

"Oh, dear," Mary said, and sighed. "How I wish we'd never come up with the idea in the first place. Or that Rachel hadn't remembered we had and practically browbeaten us into going ahead with it."

"It's not as bad as it sounds at first," John said. "There are certain understandings that can be made with the courts, where even though it's a suit of law, it's what you might call a friendly one. The judge and everyone involved would be aware of protecting both Russ and Jim. It's even possible the case can be heard in the judge's chambers instead of in open court."

Jim was shaking his head again. "But if something did go wrong, it could hurt Russ's career and my business. I want to think this over."

"It's also possible," John added, "that Rachel might decide to be cooperative. She must know Jamie isn't entitled to that money—and in fact doesn't need it. I think she might be persuaded to agree on Jamie's behalf that the money should be returned."

"You don't know Rachel," Mary said.

And indeed he didn't.

The lawyer Rachel had hired to represent her was a swinger in his early thirties named Brian Blake. Slick, smooth, sophisticated, Brian was a tall, good-looking man with flashing dark eyes, straight dark hair, and an aquiline nose. And he had one of the best wardrobes in town. He was smart, competent, and—as he remarked to Rachel early in their acquaintance—he didn't mind an interesting lie sometimes. He also had a penchant—though he didn't remark on this to Rachel—for bedding down his female clients until such time as it suited him not to.

Brian had several meetings with Walter about Steve's financial settlement for Rachel and Jamie. True to his word, Steve refused to increase the overall amount, but Brian did manage to persuade Walter to have the trust for Jamie end at age twenty-one instead of age twenty-five, which meant a slightly larger annual income over a shorter span of time.

Rachel grumbled but signed the agreement, then told Brian to get more money out of the Matthews family since he had been unable to get more out of Steve.

"I don't think there's much chance," Brian said, reminding her of the circumstances that had ended her marriage and the fact that Steve was paying both child support and an allowance for her.

"I don't care," Rachel said. "I deserve some money from them for all those years."

He shrugged. "We've got one thing—a little leverage in the fact that it's your husband who wants the divorce. If he wants it badly enough, he may be willing to pay to get it."

"I want him to pay," Rachel said. "And I want him to pay a lot. Not just because I want the money, but because of all the things the Matthews family has done to me."

Brian gave her an appreciative look. "You're really a good hater, aren't you?"

"Is there anything wrong with that?" she flared.

He smiled. "On the contrary. Good haters usually make good lovers, too. That's been my experience." Then he made a date with her for dinner that night.

She was preparing for her dinner date—and having another argument with her mother—when Brian telephoned to say he had met with John, and not only were the Matthewses unwilling to give her any alimony, they wanted her to sign an agreement abolishing the trust fund Jim had set up.

Slamming down the phone, Rachel stormed at her mother, "What is Russ trying to do to me? They're trying to take the trust fund away from me—my baby's trust fund! It's Russ who's making them do it. I know it is. He's the one who's putting them up to it. Well, he's not going to get away with it. He left me. He left the baby. And he made all my friends hate me. He won't give me any money, and now he's making his parents take away my baby's trust fund. Well, I'm not going to let him do that to me and Jamie. And I'm going to tell him so!"

The next morning she was at the clinic almost before it opened. Bursting into Russ's office, where he was going over some case histories, she started storming at him. Without so much as a hello-how-are-you, she said, "Nobody's going to get that trust fund back. That's Jamie's money."

"Rachel," Russ said, putting down the folder he'd been looking through, "to use a nice impersonal legal term, a fraud was perpetrated on me by you. You told me Jamie was my child when you knew quite well he was Steve's child."

She tossed her head. "I don't care. The money is still Jamie's."

"You have no legal claim."

"I'm not going to sign the statement you want me to. I'm not going to sign anything giving up what belongs to my son, and you can just tell that to your father and mother."

"Okay," Russ said with a shrug. "We thought this would be the simpler way, but if you're not willing . . ."

"You mean I get to keep the money then?"

"No, Rachel. I don't mean that at all. We'll be in touch with your lawyer. And now, if you'll excuse me . . ." He picked up another folder and started going through it, and eventually she walked out of the office, not knowing what he meant or what would happen, feeling unloved and put-upon, convinced that everyone was out to make her life just as mean and difficult as they could. And that included her baby's own father.

She was sure she had Steve right where she wanted him when she informed him that without her along to take care of Jamie he could forget about seeing the baby. And then her mother informed her that Steve had come up with an idea of his own. He would come to see Jamie if Ada was there to take care of him.

"He doesn't want you to be here," Ada said. "He wants you out of the apartment before he gets here. And you're not to come back until he's gone."

Rachel stared at her mother, open-mouthed. "Well, of all the nerve," she said at last. "I won't go for it. Not for a minute. What right has Steve got to tell me I can't come and go at my own apartment when I feel like it!"

"You might bear in mind," her mother said, "that he's paying the rent on it."

"I don't care if he is or he isn't. He's not going to order me out whenever he wants to."

Her mother shrugged. "You want me to tell him that? I will, but I can tell you right now what his answer will be. He won't come to see Jamie. At all."

Rachel sniffed. "I don't believe it."

"You'd better," her mother said. "Because that's what he told me."

"I don't see why he has to be that way about it."

Her mother shook her head. "Because he sees right through you, that's why. He knows that if he comes to see Jamie and you're there, you'll start cooking up all kinds of ways to get him to marry you, and he doesn't want to marry you."

Rachel made a face. "So he says."

"So he means, if you want my opinion," her mother replied.

"Well, I don't."

"Rachel, watch your tongue. Now tell me, what's it to be? Steven Frame wants to visit Jamie on his terms or Steven Frame isn't going to visit Jamie at all."

"Oh, all right," Rachel grumbled. "On his terms. For now, anyhow."

Rachel had given in because she didn't really expect to have to live up to the terms of the agreement, and she wasted no time putting her expectations to the test. The first afternoon Steve was scheduled to come visit Jamie, Ada arrived in plenty of time for Rachel to clear out, but Rachel found excuses for staying.

"You promised you'd be out of here before he got here," her mother said.

Rachel denied that. "I said I wouldn't stay here while he was here. I didn't say anything about leaving before he got here."

"Rachel, will you stop that? He said he didn't even want to see you, and you agreed."

"Okay, okay. So I got held up. What's the big deal? I've got to water the plants, and I've got to—" The doorbell rang. "So let him in, Mom."

Ada did so, and Steve came in with a package, took one look at Rachel, and turned around and walked out again, slamming the door behind him.

Rachel ran after him, catching up with him by the elevator. "Where are you going?"

He rang for the elevator. "Back to my office."

"But you're supposed to spend the afternoon with Jamie."

"And you were supposed to be gone before I got here. That was the arrangement."

"So I was supposed to be gone. Do you have to hold me to the last detail?"

"Yes, I do," he said, "because I had my doubts

about the whole thing from the beginning. If you can't keep your word about it when we're trying it for the first time . . ." He shrugged and didn't finish the sentence.

"Well, you didn't have to walk out just like that," Rachel said. "I was just going. I got held up because there were things I had to do. I had to get Jamie up and dress him."

"Couldn't Ada do that?"

"And I'm not sure I like the arrangement anyway," she said, ignoring his question, as was her wont when the question was one she didn't care to answer.

"Then let's forget about it," Steve replied. "I'll go on back to the office." The elevator door opened.

"No," Rachel said. "I'm going. I said I would, and I will. I just have to get my purse. You can wait here if you want to, or you can come in with me."

"I'll wait," he said.

When Rachel had finally gone and Steve was back in the apartment, Ada apologized for Rachel's behavior, then took Steve to Jamie, almost ten months old now and playing in a playpen in his room.

"He's a cute little boy," Steve said to Ada. Then, feeling a bit awkward and self-conscious, he got down on the floor and said, "Hi, Jamie," to his son. He picked up the package he had brought and unwrapped it. "I brought you a rabbit. How about that?" He held out the woolly animal, and the baby reached out for it and took it.

"I hope you won't mind my saying this, Steve," Ada said. "But I wouldn't do that every time I came here. I know why you want to. But if you keep on doing it, when he gets older, then all you'll be to him is somebody who brings him presents. And he's going to need other things—someone he can count on, talk to, love."

Steve nodded and watched the baby playing with the rabbit. "You've got a point. Bringing presents is the easy way. I'll remember that." He looked from the baby to Ada. "You seem to know a lot about bringing up kids. You've got a real feeling for them.

What I don't understand is how Rachel turned out the way she did."

"I guess part of it," Ada said, "is that she didn't have a father who could love her—and help her do what was right."

When Steve returned to his office later that afternoon he called Lenore to tell her about his visit with the baby and to say he hadn't heard anything yet from Alice.

"She'll write you," Lenore assured him. "There's no question she loves you."

"I feel that way too," Steve said. "And she knows how I feel about her. Things have got to work out for us."

A week earlier Steve had shown Walter and Lenore a picture of some property out in the country that he was interested in. Now he told Lenore that he had bought it and was going to hire an architect to design and build Alice's dream house. "Just the kind of old-fashioned house she's always wanted," he went on to say. "When she comes back I'll take her out to the property and show it to her and tell her it's hers— ours—to share for the rest of our lives."

"You don't think," Lenore said, sounding doubtful, "maybe that's moving ahead too . . . well, too fast?"

"I know," he acknowledged. "Maybe I'm dreaming, but I prefer to think I'm not. Anyhow, I'm going ahead with it."

"Well, if you think so." She still sounded doubtful.

"Lenore," he said, "if I didn't believe Alice will come back to me some day, I don't know what I'd do. I never realized one girl could come to mean so much to a man, but that's what Alice means to me. Without her," he said again, "I don't know what I'd do."

Alice had left Bay City early in June. The third week in August Steve received a letter from her. She was living with a French family in Avignon, and working in a nearby children's hospital. She loved being in France, she felt better than she had when she left home, he was not to worry about her.

Walter came into Steve's office a few minutes later,

and an excited Steve showed him the letter. "She doesn't say when she's coming back," he said as Walter scanned the letter, "but she sounds fine, doesn't she? I'm glad she's having a good time." He beamed at Walter. "The important thing is she wrote to me. I mean, she doesn't hate me or she wouldn't have written to me, right?"

Walter smiled and handed the letter back. "I don't think Alice has ever hated you, Steve."

About a month later Steve was scheduled to fly to London on business, but he decided to send an assistant in his place. As he explained to Walter, "The reason I don't want to go to London is that London is in England, and England is just across the channel from France, and I don't want to go to France. I might not be able to restrain myself. I want very much to see Alice, but in spite of the letter, she's given me absolutely no indication she wants to see me."

"You could be wrong, Steve," Walter said. "Maybe she does want to see you."

Steve shook his head. "No. If she did, she'd have said so. Alice doesn't act cute or coy. She's very straightforward. And I don't want to force myself on her. I don't even want it to look as if I'm forcing myself on her. So that's out."

But events were taking shape that would change his mind. A short time earlier Russ had written Alice to say how sorry he was for the way he'd blown his stack at Steve in front of her that night in her apartment. He hoped that wasn't why she'd gone away— because she was torn between the way she felt about Steve and the way she felt about him.

Her answer was as follows:

Dear Russ,

I'm writing this at a café near the Rhône. I've gotten very French that way. I not only have my coffee here and read the newspapers, but I also write my letters here. I've been wanting to answer your letter for some time, but it wasn't easy, because it touched on at least one point that's been on my mind ever since I left Bay City—and that I still haven't resolved. It was nice of you to apologize for having said what you did to Steven that night, but it was completely unnecessary. You didn't say anything that wasn't true—that I hadn't thought, and that he hadn't said himself. But that wasn't why I went away. I would have gone even if you hadn't said what you did, because the fact is that whether Steven meant to or not, he did something that hurt both of us—you and me—terribly. That's why I had to get away—to sort that all out and decide how I really felt about what happened. Having answered your question, I have one to ask you, and I beg you to take all the time you need to think about it and then to answer me honestly. We've always been honest with each other, Russ. That's one of the reasons we've been so close. My question— how do you feel about Steven now? Do you feel as bitter toward him as you did? And, believe me, I could understand it if you did. More important, how would you feel if Steven and I should get together again, and I married him? Would you feel that, by marrying the man who had hurt and betrayed you, I had betrayed you too? I'm not saying I'm going to marry him. I don't know if I will—or even if I want to. That's one of the things I'm still trying to decide. But what you say will help me make up my mind, so, Russ, please be honest. No matter how painful you think it may be to me, do let me know. You can read this to Mom and Dad if you like, and of course give them my love.

As ever, Alice.

Showing the letter to them, Russ said, "Sure, I still feel bitter toward Steve. I probably always will, even though I know what happened wasn't his fault, but Rachel's. On the other hand, if Alice really loves Steve and thinks she can be happy with him, I think she should marry him. I mean, why should all three of us be miserable?" He shrugged. "The part that's been giving me trouble is the way Alice put it. Because, in a way, she's asking me to decide for her whether she should marry Steve or not, and I can't do that. She's got to decide for herself."

Over the next few days some of Russ's bitterness began to dissipate. Rachel was out of town when Jamie became critically ill with meningitis, and Steve came to the hospital and stayed there until the crisis passed. The baby's regular pediatrician was also away when the illness struck, and Ada asked Russ to take care of Jamie, so the two men saw a lot of each other in and around the baby's room. On one of those occasions Russ told Steve about Alice's letter, and Steve was so encouraged by what she had written that he decided to make the trip to London after all and then fly to Avignon to see her.

They met in a small restaurant, where she told him she was both glad and sorry to see him—because seeing him made her life complicated.

"For me," Steve said, "seeing you makes life simple. I want to keep looking at you—be with you forever."

Alice shook her head and looked away.

At a nearby table were a young French couple, obviously very much in love. Nodding toward them, Steve said, "They seem to find it very simple to be in love."

"Yes, but it's not that way for us, Steven."

Taking her hand, he said, "I think it can be."

She squeezed his hand for a moment, then withdrew hers.

Explaining how he happened to be there, Steve told her he knew about the letter she had written Russ. At first Alice was distressed that Russ had told him, but then she let herself be persuaded that it was just as well that he knew.

Finally she broke down and said, "I love you, Steven. I do. I think of you, I dream of you, if you want to know. But I hope you have to go back to Bay City right away because—"

He cut in on her. "I do have to."

"Good," she said.

"For one thing," he added, "there's something I have to do for you in Bay City. I'm preparing a surprise for you, Alice. For later. And I think you'll like it. At least, I hope you will."

A few hours later he was flying over the Atlantic, more sharply lonely than he had been since the day she left Bay City, but also more filled with hope.

Chapter Twenty-one

INFORMED by Brian Blake that the Matthewses were prepared to sue to have the baby's trust fund dissolved, and that the basis of the suit was fraud, Rachel asked what her chances were.

"Well," Brian said, "it's complicated, but there's certainly the basis for a suit there." And he went on to explain that the suit would be filed against Russ as trustee of the fund.

"You mean if they did go to court they'd win?"

He shrugged. "I'm sure they think they would— not only because there was fraud, but because your husband wouldn't actually fight the case."

"No, of course he wouldn't," Rachel agreed. "He wants to see his father get the money back too." She was in Brian's office, and she got up from the chair she'd been sitting in and went to look out his window —a high, lovely view of the bay, with the tops of other buildings in between. After a few moments she turned back to Brian, seated behind a massive desk that always reminded her of the one in Steve's private office. "I don't care," she said, "what would come out in the trial about me and Steve Frame, because everybody knows about it anyway. But if you think I haven't got a chance—if you think I'm going to lose . . ."

Brian gave her that lazy smile of his—the one he knew turned her on. "Why do you insist on selling me short? I said I'm sure they think they'd win. The fact is, the case isn't quite as clear-cut as the Matthewes seem to think." He got up and came over to join her at the window. "There's a very good chance I can beat them." He took her in his arms and kissed her, then pulled away to say "We shouldn't give in. On the suit, I mean." And kissed her again, long and hard.

Concerned that Rachel was being conned by her lawyer, and doubly concerned that Rachel was running around with him—as Ada put it—while she was still married to Russ, Ada said to Ernie, "What if he's handing her a lot of baloney about what a great lawyer he is and how he's going to get her a whole lot of money she's not really entitled to? You just mention money to Rachel and she lights up like a Christmas tree. If Mr. Blake is handing her a lot of stuff about how she'll get money from Steve and money from Russ and money from everybody, he'll have her eating out of his hand."

But, whatever else he might be up to where Rachel was concerned, Brian was not "handing her a lot of stuff" when it came to the matter of the baby's trust fund. When Rachel admitted to Brian that she was scared of going into court, he told her he wouldn't let her go in if he didn't think he could win. Then he questioned her in detail about her relations with the Matthews family—and, in particular, her relations with Alice—and concluded the session by saying he thought they were going to win.

So certain was he of that, and so careless was Rachel of what damage any bad publicity might do either to Russ's clinic or Jim's accounting firm, that they turned down the suggestion by John Randolph that they apply to the judge to have the suit tried in his chambers instead of in open court. So it was left to John to make the application—on the basis that a trial in open court would be harmful to Jamie's good name. Since the baby's own mother could hardly oppose the application on that basis, Brian made no objection, and the judge approved it.

Round one to the Matthews family.

The first witness at the hearing was Jim Matthews. He explained on direct examination why he and his wife wanted the trust fund dissolved. After he had finished his testimony, Brian reserved the right to cross-examine him later, explaining there was a possibility another witness might appear.

The next witness was Mary. On direct examination she testified that she and her husband had saved money over a good many years, that they had three children and had expected to have grandchildren someday.

"You wanted to secure the future of your children's children?" John asked.

"Yes," Mary responded.

"Your grandchildren?"

"Yes. Our grandchildren. And so we set up this fund for that girl's baby, and she let us do that when she knew it was not our grandchild." Mary was having difficulty keeping her emotions under control. "Not our son's child."

Brian stood up. "Objection, Your Honor. Her answer is argumentative and goes beyond the scope of the question."

"Objection sustained." The judge turned to John. "Do you have any more questions of this witness?"

"No, Your Honor."

"Mr. Blake?"

"I have no questions."

"The witness is excused."

Mary stepped down, and Russ took the stand.

"You are the defendant of record," the judge said to him. "Do you have a lawyer present?"

"No, Your Honor," Russ replied, "but I've consulted a lawyer, and on his advice I plead *nolo contendere.*"

Russ was dismissed, and John had no further witnesses to present. The judge turned to Brian Blake. "I take it you have witnesses?"

"Yes," Brian said, and he called Rachel to the stand. "Your husband is Russell Matthews?" he asked her.

"Yes, but we're going to get a divorce."

"Just answer the question I put to you," Brian admonished her. "He is your husband?"

"Yes."

"Was the infant James Gerald Matthews born to you while you were still living with your husband?"

"Yes," she said, turning to smile at the judge. Rachel was looking particularly lovely that afternoon—and very demure, wearing a pretty little hat that tied under her chin. The judge almost forgot himself so far as to return her smile.

"Mrs. Matthews," Brian went on, "a great deal has been made in this court about the fact that your husband is not the father of your child. Is that correct?"

She nodded. "You see, one time my husband, Russ, got furious at me over nothing at all, and so I left him and—"

"Objection," John said. "This isn't responsive."

"Objection sustained." The judge leaned forward to make a note on the pad in front of him.

Brian used the opportunity to wink at Rachel. Then he assumed a look of grave sympathy and concern. "I know this is very difficult for you, Mrs. Matthews. You're being asked to go into intimate matters that must be very painful."

Rachel nodded and did her best to assume the attitude of one going into intimate matters that must be very painful.

"Now, Rachel," Brian went on. "Yes or no. Was your husband the father of your child?"

"No."

He nodded. "I'll ask you something the plaintiff would undoubtedly want to ask. Did you tell your husband he was not the father of little Jamie?"

"Well," Rachel answered, "it's very hard to tell Russ anything because he doesn't understand. He gets so mad."

Brian interrupted before John could. "Did you keep it a secret?"

She nodded. "From him, yes."

"From everybody?"

"No, not from everybody."

"You told someone?" he said, sounding surprised. "Who?"

"Alice Matthews," she answered. "Russ's sister."

"When?"

"Before the baby was born."

Brian nodded. "And where was this Alice—this sister of your husband's—living at the time?"

Rachel smiled a little. "With Mr. and Mrs. Matthews—her parents."

Brian smiled back at her. "Thank you. No further questions."

When Rachel had been dismissed, Brian called for Alice Matthews. John pointed out that Alice was in Europe and turned to the judge. "I think Mr. Blake knows that."

Brian acknowledged that he did. "I had hoped she would come here for this trial. I've sent registered letters to several addresses, and I've sent a cable, and I have a subpena waiting here for her. But if she's chosen not to come here, and since Rachel Davis Matthews was my only witness, I'd like now to recall Mr. James Matthews for cross-examination."

Jim returned to the stand.

"Miss Alice Matthews is your daughter?" Brian asked.

"Yes."

"At some point during the pregnancy of Rachel Davis Matthews, did Alice live in your home?"

John got to his feet. "Your Honor, I object. This is irrelevant."

"Your Honor," Brian cut in quickly, "I'm simply trying to reestablish that this witness had ample opportunity to talk to his daughter—"

"And the fact," John said, cutting Brian off, "that Mr. Matthews and his daughter are on speaking terms is heartwarming but equally irrelevant. This case is about a trust fund and a fraud—with which Alice Matthews had nothing to do."

"Not so, Your Honor," Brian said with a vigorous shake of his head. "I'll tie these matters up to the issue. I ask that you let me proceed de bene—that is," he said, turning to the few family members in the room, "to so demonstrate."

"All right," the judge said. "De bene."

"Thank you," Brian said. "I'm simply addressing myself to the allegation of fraud—trying to prove there was no fraud." He turned back to Jim. "You did talk to your daughter—much—while she was living in your house and afterward. Isn't that true? And did you ever talk to her about the parentage of your daughter-in-law's child?"

Jim nodded. "We talked about Jamie—yes."

"I asked you if you talked about his parentage."

"Yes, we did."

"Once? Or more than once?"

"More than once," Jim acknowledged.

"Now," Brian went on with a satisfied look, "you've heard Rachel Matthews's testimony. You heard her say she told your daughter that your son was not the father of little Jamie. Was that news to you?" Before Jim could answer, he went on. "Let me put it to you this way. In these conversations you had from time to time with your daughter Alice about the parentage of Jamie, did Alice tell you that Rachel had told her Russ was not the baby's father?"

"Alice did tell me that, but—"

Brian cut him off. "She did tell you that once or more than once?"

"More than once."

"She told you before the baby was ever born, didn't she?"

"Yes, she did."

"And before she left your home?"

"Yes."

"And after the baby was born?"

"Yes."

"And after Alice left your home you continued to speak to your daughter?"

"Yes, of course I did."

"She told you again and again the baby was not your son's."

"She told me," Jim corrected him, "that Rachel had said that."

Brian looked at him a moment. "Well, it's true, isn't it? It's the whole basis of your claim that there was fraud."

"Yes, it's true," Jim admitted. "The baby is not my son's."

"One more question. If you were told over and over again that your daughter-in-law said the baby was not your son's, and if that was the truth, then how has your daughter-in-law committed fraud?"

"Your Honor," John said, getting to his feet again. "I object. He's calling for a conclusion on the part of the witness."

"Objection sustained."

Brian smiled and shrugged. "I withdraw the question. No further questions."

He sat down, and John approached the stand. "Did you believe the baby was not Russ's?"

Brian stood up. "Objection. The issue is whether fraud was committed, not whether the plaintiff held erroneous beliefs."

The judge nodded. "Objection sustained."

John tried a different approach. "Did you have reason not to believe—"

"Same objection," Brian said.

"Sustained."

"When you set up the trust fund did you believe Jamie was your grandchild?"

"Same objection," Brian said again.

The judge thought differently. "No," he said. "I'll allow this. The witness must answer."

"When I set up the trust fund," Jim responded, "I did believe Jamie was my grandchild."

"No further questions."

Each counsel then gave his summation, the judge declared a recess of one hour, the hearing was reconvened, and the judge rendered his decision—that no fraud had been committed.

Round two to Rachel.

Rachel went off to St. Thomas in the Virgin Islands for a vacation—part of which she shared with her attorney—Mary took to her bed with nervous exhaustion, and John gave Jim some gloomy predictions about

Rachel's upcoming divorce action—predictions that were confirmed when Brian returned from frolicking with Rachel and met with John to discuss the case.

"I assume," John began, "that you and Rachel don't want a difficult and probably very unpleasant divorce case any more than Dr. Matthews and I do." When Brian agreed, he went on. "It's my further assumption, since Rachel agreed to file for the divorce, that she wants it as much as Dr. Matthews does."

"I'm afraid that's not quite true," Brian said. "In fact, she doesn't want a divorce. She's willing to agree to one under the proper circumstances. The usual ones. After all, it is usual for a husband to make provision for the support of his wife."

"That's nonsense," John protested. "This isn't the usual case and you know it. The circumstances are very different. Let's not play games. Rachel had a child by another man while she was married to Dr. Matthews."

Brian shrugged. "The grounds for divorce in this case as we've discussed it so far is desertion—desertion of Rachel by Dr. Matthews."

"Because Dr. Matthews is a gentleman, and he wanted to do what he could to protect Rachel's good name and the name of her child."

"Very estimable, I'm sure," Brian said.

"Now," John continued, "that being so, you and I should be even more concerned about it. We're both attorneys, both aware of what the consequences of a contested divorce could be. We should do everything in our power to avoid that."

"I've already agreed to do that," Brian reminded him. "But only under certain circumstances." Adding that he didn't want to be unreasonable, he suggested that they work out a separation agreement—an agreement including alimony.

John didn't consider that reasonable and said so, adding that alimony in any amount was out.

"I see," Brian said. "Well, in that case, Mr. Randolph, you had better prepare your client for the very thing you claimed you wanted to avoid—a very nasty court fight. And as for any unpleasant publicity,

Dr. Matthews has far more to lose from that than Rachel does."

After Brian had left, John sat thinking for a while. Then he picked up the phone and called Steve to make an appointment with him, saying that there was something Steve might be able to do for him—and, incidentally, for the Matthews family as a whole.

When they met, John asked Steve if he would testify that he was Jamie's father—if such testimony became necessary in the divorce case—and further, how much money he was now giving Rachel for herself and for the baby. Steve readily agreed, and he also agreed to have his blood typed, saying that he would back the Matthews side all the way.

It was at this time that Jamie was stricken with meningitis, and Rachel was summoned back from St. Thomas to Bay City, there to hover anxiously over his bed with Steve while Russ devoted himself to saving the baby's life. When the baby had recovered, John remarked to Mary and Jim that out of gratitude to Russ Rachel might now relinquish her demand for alimony, but Mary scoffed at the suggestion.

Steve meanwhile was taking action on another matter. He called Rachel to ask her to come to his office, and when she got there he ordered her to return the Matthews trust fund.

She stared at him. "How dare you? That's my baby's money, and they aren't going to get their hands on it."

He stared right back at her, his dark eyes cold. "The money belongs to the Matthewses. They put it in trust for their grandchild, which Jamie isn't."

She tried her wide-eyed, helpless approach. "But he's a poor innocent little baby."

"Look," Steve said, disgusted. "You're getting money from me—a lot of money. I've provided very generously for Jamie—for his entire life. He will never go hungry. He'll never want for anything. How do you think it makes me feel having part of my son's support paid by a man with much less money—and who isn't even related to my son?"

Rachel's chin went up. "I don't care how it makes you feel. If you're so worried about how people feel, then think about me—how I feel when everyone in Bay City is trying to steal money away from my baby."

"Rachel, for the last time, Jamie doesn't need that money, and the Matthews grandchildren do, and I'm going to see that Jim and Mary get it back."

"I'd just like to see you try," Rachel said. "I've already been to court about it once, and the judge ruled I could keep the money. You can't take me to court again."

"I don't plan to take you to court. It's very simple. If you don't return the trust-fund money to the Matthewses, then I'm going to cut off your personal allowance."

Unable to dissuade Steve, Rachel went to Brian—and got nowhere. She wanted to take the case to court. He tried to explain to her why they couldn't.

"But he's already signed an agreement to give me that money," Rachel protested. "Can he just take it away from me?"

"He can't take Jamie's support money away," Brian said, "but that's not what he's threatening. He says he'll stop your personal allowance. If we went to court we might—*might*—get a little of that restored. Very little. Because no judge would hold him to what he's paying you now—especially when he heard your side. The best that would happen would be that Steve and Walter Curtin would suggest a minimum acceptable limit, and the judge would agree, and that would be that." He spread his hands. "And it would be a lot less than you're getting now—enough less so that you couldn't go flying off to the Virgin Islands or buy new clothes every week. The only thing to do is return the trust fund."

Rachel started to cry. "Are you against me too?"

He got up from his desk and went to sit with her on the couch in his office, putting an arm around her. "I'm not against you—and you know it. I'm your lawyer, and I'm advising you to do the smartest thing possible. You don't need that money. Jamie doesn't need it. And I think if you return it, it might improve your chances of getting alimony."

She stopped crying and turned to look at him.

"Why do you think Russ is refusing to pay you alimony?" he asked.

"Because he's mean and he hates me," Rachel answered without a moment's hesitation. "And his parents hate me. They've always hated me."

Hardly able to keep a straight face, Brian said, "I wouldn't go that far, but the bad feelings between you are certainly one reason why he won't give you support. From their point of view that trust-fund money is theirs. If you return it, they would look on that as a generous gesture, and we might be able to come to a small settlement out of court. That is, of course, assuming you still want alimony from him."

She looked at him in astonishment. "Well, of course I do. I deserve it. He owes it to me."

Brian shrugged. "I thought you might have changed your mind out of gratitude to Russ for pulling Jamie through that sickness."

Rachel, who had practically gotten down on the hospital floor to kiss Russ's shoes after he pulled the baby through, now looked at Brian as if he had taken leave of his senses. "That has nothing to do with this. I'm grateful, of course. But he was just doing his job."

"In that case, Rachel, you'd better go ahead and return the money to the Matthewses. It's the only way to keep your personal allowance from Steve."

Rachel thought a bit, then said, "I'm not promising anything. But I'll think about it."

Before she had time to do that, she came up with another complaint, and this one she took to her mother. Rachel had left Jamie with her mother when she went to St. Thomas, and when she learned that during her absence Ada had given John permission to have the baby's blood typed, she was furious, accusing her mother of siding with the Matthewses against her.

"You bet I'm siding with the Matthewses," Ada said. "After all the rotten things you've done to them— and that includes trying to get alimony out of Russ."

"Oh, you're impossible," Rachel retorted. "Russ owes me that alimony, and you and all your clever little tricks aren't going to stop me from getting it. Everybody in the world is trying to take money away from me. Everybody's against me. Even my own mother."

That night Brian came to Rachel's apartment to discuss the impending divorce action. After explaining the purpose of the blood typing—to try to prove that Russ wasn't Jamie's father—he broke the news that Steve might testify against her.

She was shocked and dismayed. "It would be awful for me if he did that, wouldn't it?"

"It would be awful for him, too," Brian replied. "And that's just the point. He's an important man. Everyone knows who he is, and he has a good reputation. And here we have a nice, messy divorce case involving a fight for alimony and illegitimacy and all sorts of things reporters like to latch on to. If a man in Steve's position testifies in a case like this, all the money he owns couldn't keep some nice scandalous speculation out of the newspapers. How do you think he'd like that?"

"Not much," Rachel said. "But it would be a good joke on him, though."

Brian made a face. "Some joke."

Rachel smiled. "He might appear anyway. He likes to pretend he doesn't like me. It's kind of a point of honor with him not to like me, you know. So he might get on the stand just to prove he doesn't. Prove to himself, I mean. He does like me, though, deep down."

"I don't care whether he likes you or not," Brian said. "All I'm trying to do is keep him off the witness stand. And if things go the way I think they will, I'll keep him off. All this business about blood types. It doesn't matter what they can prove by it. You just watch. It will be entirely irrelevant to the case I'm going to put on, and that's why I'm sure Steve Frame won't appear."

"Whatever you say," Rachel said, "as long as you get me the alimony Russ owes me."

Brian eyed her a moment. "And to that point—have you thought about the trust fund?"

She nodded. "Yes, I have. And I've decided I'm not going to give it back."

He sighed. "Rachel, I've told you before. You have

no choice. And now you leave me with none. Either you give the money back or you get yourself another lawyer to get the alimony for you."

Finally convinced that she had no choice, Rachel returned the trust-fund passbook to Russ along with a signed statement giving up all claims to the money. She didn't mention Steve or Brian but maintained that she was returning the money out of gratitude to Russ, out of concern for Pat's twin babies, out of regret for having upset his parents—in other words, out of the goodness of her heart.

With the agony he and his parents had gone through at the trust-fund hearing still fresh in his mind, Russ was bewildered by this sudden change in Rachel's attitude—that what she had fought so tenaciously for she had now decided didn't belong to her. His mother wasn't bewildered. "I've got this same old feeling again," she said, "that Rachel's up to something."

When the divorce came to trial, John Randolph made it clear in his opening statement that his client did not oppose the petition for divorce brought by his wife, but he did oppose paying alimony—for reasons that would appear in testimony.

Rachel was sworn in as the first witness and questioned by Brian. When he got to the subject of the child, he said, "Is Dr. Matthews the father of this child?"

"No."

"You have no intention of fooling anybody about that, do you?"

"No," she said again.

Brian turned to the judge. "Your honor, my client feels there is no necessity of mentioning the name of the actual father of Mrs. Matthews's child—unless, of course, the other side insists on it. Would it be all right for the purposes of the record here for me to call the man Mr. X?"

The judge looked to John, and he stood up. "We do not object, providing it's understood we are not binding ourselves to codes of courtroom conduct dreamed up by the appellant or her attorney."

"We see no purpose," Brian said, "in subjecting to humiliation the father of this child."

"There's no cause for counsel to argue here," the judge admonished him. "Mr. Randolph does not object to your calling the father of the child Mr. X. Neither does the court."

Brian turned back to Rachel. "You've freely admitted here that Mr. X is the father of your child, haven't you?"

John stood up again. "Objection. We've been over this."

"Sustained," the judge said.

"Specifically, have you admitted this fact in any other court proceeding?"

"Well," Rachel said, "you see, about the trust fund—"

"I'll come to that," Brian said. "Now, Mrs. Matthews, since you admit your husband is not the father of your child, on what basis do you feel you should have alimony?"

Rachel put on her wide-eyed innocent look. "Well, I worked hard all those years as his wife."

Brian now put on his look of grave concern. "Just a minute, Rachel. I know this touches your emotions deeply, and you're not being very coherent. Take a moment to collect yourself, and then tell us in your own words what your marriage to Russell Matthews was like."

"It was awful, if you want to know the truth about it. When I married Russ, he was an intern and didn't make much money. Not that that wasn't all right with me. I mean, I was willing to work hard and to have dinner waiting for him when he came home, and to sew and do the laundry. I mean, I knew an intern isn't a millionaire or anything."

"Would you say you performed your wifely duties?" Brian asked.

"Objection. He's leading the witness."

"Let me caution you, Mr. Blake," the judge said.

"Sorry. How did you behave in your marriage, Mrs. Matthews?"

Rachel smiled a little. "I performed all the wifely duties—cooked, sewed, did the laundry. All that."

The judge cut in. "We've already heard that."

"Well," Rachel went on, "and I waited. For Russ to come home. Sometimes he couldn't. They'd keep him late at the hospital, and he wouldn't call me and tell me until I had the dinner burning in the oven."

"And when he did come home?"

"Well, he was awful. I mean, he'd grump and growl and criticize. And I knew we couldn't go out often, but, I mean, he wouldn't even take me to a movie."

"So you were home alone most of the time. But when he was there?"

"When he was there he behaved like I was a piece of furniture. I'd feel more alone than ever."

"Did that have anything to do with what happened between you and Mr. X?"

"Yes. Russ drove me to Mr. X. He was the only person I could talk to. I found it nice to be able to talk to somebody who understood."

Brian gave her a sympathetic nod. "I think we can all understand what you're telling us. Now. Back to the trust-fund court case mentioned before. What was that about?"

"Russ's parents set up a trust fund for little Jamie and then they sued to get it back, but the court said the money was Jamie's and they couldn't have it." She turned to smile at the judge, who merely looked back at her with no expression. "But then I got to thinking it over and decided the Matthewses should have the money back, and I gave it to them."

"Even though it was legally your child's money—and a court had so decided?"

"Yes."

He nodded. "My last question has in a sense been answered. You don't want any money you aren't entitled to, is that right?"

"That's right," Rachel answered. "That's why I gave back the trust-fund money. But I'm entitled to alimony, and I do want that."

Russ was the next witness, and it was during his

questioning by John that Brian made the point he believed essential to his case.

"When your son was born," John asked Russ, "did you doubt he was yours?"

"No."

"Were you confronted several months later with evidence that he was not your son?"

"Yes, I was."

"What action did you take?"

Russ looked to the table where Rachel was sitting. "I left her."

John returned to his table and picked up some documents, then walked up to the judge's bench. "If it please the court, I'd like to introduce as evidence the blood typings of Dr. Matthews and the child Jamie Matthews."

Brian got to his feet. "My client has freely acknowledged that Dr. Matthews is not the father of her child. Beyond the fact that the child's paternity is already in evidence, it is irrelevant to this case. I would agree with Mr. Randolph that the question of paternity is relevant as an issue for the divorce petition, but defense is not opposing the divorce. Defense is only opposing the payment of alimony, and I submit that the issue of paternity is not relevant to that."

Both attorneys looked to the judge for his ruling. "Sustained," he said.

Brian sat down and leaned over to whisper to Rachel, "That should keep Steve Frame off the stand. How else is he involved in this matter except over paternity?"

John continued his questioning of Russ, drawing from him a description of the marriage totally at variance with the one Rachel had depicted. He told how she had constantly complained, had never tried to adjust to his situation, had looked after him only when it suited her, and how she had been sometimes affectionate and sometimes not, depending on her mood or whether she had wanted something out of him.

"I will ask you now," John said, "to examine your conscience—and remember you are under oath. Did you treat your wife in such a way as to cause her to seek a relationship with another man?"

"I did not," Russ answered. "I loved her, and I tried to make her happy."

All that Brian managed to establish in his cross-examination of Russ was that he had criticized Rachel and had often left her alone at night—out of necessity.

And then, to Brian's surprise, John Randolph called Steve Frame to the stand, where he acknowledged under oath that he was Jamie's father. Instantly Brian was on his feet to object. "Your Honor has already agreed that the issue of paternity is not relevant to the payment of alimony."

John turned to the bench. "It is not paternity per se that I'm getting at. I'm merely establishing it in order to elicit further information that I submit is relevant to the payment of alimony."

Told to proceed, John elicited the information that Steve had set up a trust fund for the baby that paid for his support, and that, in addition, Steve paid Mrs. Matthews's rent and a personal living allowance—all set forth in a document signed both by himself and Mrs. Matthews. And the document was introduced as evidence.

"Now, Mr. Frame," John continued. "The plaintiff has testified she voluntarily returned the Matthews trust fund to them. Is that true?"

"No, it is not."

"Did you have anything to do with it?"

"Yes. I told Rachel to return it. She objected strenuously. I then demanded that she return it, or I would cut off her personal allowance. She then returned it."

In his decision the judge stated that both the plaintiff and her child were being provided for—most generously, he might add—and therefore the divorce was granted without alimony.

Round three to Steve. Or, as he hoped, to himself and Alice.

Chapter Twenty-two

A month after his first visit to Alice in Avignon, Steve returned for a second visit. Because Alice didn't trust herself to see him anywhere except in public, they met in the same little restaurant.

"I'm not hiding anything from you, Steven," Alice said after he had kissed her tenderly—and she had let him do so. "I couldn't if I tried. I didn't last time, did I?"

He searched her face. "If you mean I left here feeling you loved me—"

She nodded. "That's what I mean. And that's why you came back, isn't it? Because you knew I loved you, and I want you. Is it shameless for me to say so?" And then, before he could answer her, she went on. "But that's not all there is to say."

He sighed. "If you're going to bring up Rachel and the baby and Russ . . ."

"No," she said. "I brought those things up before. Long ago. We know they lie between us. Somewhat, anyway. We do know that much, don't we?" Again she didn't wait for him to answer before going on. "But that's not it. I need to be free a while longer."

When Steve pressed her as to why she needed to be free, she told him about her work at the children's hospital. "It's important work," she said. "And it's important to me for something else besides. I'm away from home, and you've got to know what that means to me. When I was a little girl and went off to camp, I always wanted to run back home the first night. But I'm not a little girl any more. I find I like being away from home."

"Then let me move here to Avignon."

Alice shook her head. "You don't understand, Steven. You're home. Wherever you are is home."

It was an astonishing admission, but almost before he could convince himself that she had said it, she destroyed whatever hope he was allowing himself. "And I don't want to be there." This time it was she who searched his face. "For now I don't want to be with my parents or with you but with myself—and the children here who need me."

"Alice," he said, his voice low and intent, "I need you."

She shook her head again. "I need to learn about me. Without my parents and my brother and sister, and without you. Just with the children and myself. My nursing skills. That's all. I have to learn about me, and then maybe I can shake off my hangups."

He took her hands in his. "All right," he said. "Stay here as long as you have to. Find yourself. But then come back. Come see the surprise I have for you."

But it was she who had a surprise for him. Four months later, on an afternoon toward the end of February, Steve's secretary buzzed him to say there was a woman there to see him who wouldn't give her name. Figuring it was Rachel—though why his secretary wouldn't warn him, he couldn't imagine—he strode to the door, determined to get rid of her. When he opened the door, there stood Alice.

He couldn't believe his eyes. For a few moments they stood where they were, each looking at the other, not moving. Then she said, "May I come in?"

Unable to find his voice, he made a sweeping motion with his arm, and she walked into the office, and he closed the door and then turned to look at her again. And found his voice. "Seeing you here," he said, with a little shake of his head. "I mean, seeing you in France was wonderful, but seeing you here—" He shook his head again. "I don't know what to say." He tried a smile. "I'm having trouble saying anything. Whatever I do or say—it has to be the right thing."

Again they looked at each other, not moving. There was maybe a distance of five feet between them, but it could have been fifty feet from the expression on each of their faces. Finally he spoke again. "I could stand here like this and look at you for the rest of my life."

Alice smiled. "We'd both get old and wrinkled, and we'd still be standing here."

He smiled back at her, but the tension in the air was as strong between them as it had been from the moment he opened the door to find her standing there. "That's okay with me," he said.

She nodded. "It's okay with me, too."

"I'd like to have this moment last forever, Alice. I want to tell you there hasn't been one second of one hour of one day that you've been away from here that I haven't wanted you."

"I know," she said. "It's been the same with me."

He longed to take her in his arms—or even to reach out to her. He did neither. "I want to kiss you more than I've ever wanted anything. Do you want me to?"

"Steven," she began, but he didn't let her finish.

He seemed to be afraid she would say no. "It's all right," he said. "I understand. It's been such a long time. And sometimes I thought it would never end, that I'd spend the rest of my life waiting for you. And," he hesitated to add, "I was willing to do that. There didn't seem to be anything else to do, because when you love somebody—" He broke off. "But now you're home."

"Yes," she said. "I'm home for now."

His heart sank. "Only for now? Not to stay?"

"I have to go back to Avignon to finish up a project there. And after that, I don't know. There are still some things I have to work out, Steven."

"I see. But while you're here, Alice, will I see you?"

"As much as you want to."

He felt as though he'd been holding his breath, and now he could let it out. "That's great. That's everything. And when you've got things figured out, then maybe . . ."

She nodded. "Then maybe I'll come home for good."

Again they fell silent, and this time she broke the silence. "Steven, do you know what I want more than anything? I want you to kiss me."

In the next breath he closed the distance between them, taking her in his arms. "My love," he whispered. "My Alice. My very own Alice." For a moment he looked at her in wonder and delight; then he bent to kiss her—at first gently and tenderly, and then with passion.

Back in October, in Avignon, when Alice told Steve about wanting to run home from camp as a child, she had come close to putting her finger on one of the essential truths about her character. In telling her parents now why she had gone to Avignon in the first place, she came even closer.

"You do understand why I had to leave Bay City, don't you?" she said to them. "I couldn't just go on living here as though nothing had happened—when so much had happened. I had to be all by myself and far away—to try to figure out exactly how I felt about it."

"And have you figured it out?" her father asked her.

"I know more than I did when I went away," she answered. "I think I'm closer to understanding myself than I was. And maybe one of these days I'll understand it all."

While Alice was in Avignon Russ had started dating a quiet, gentle, dark-haired girl named Cindy Clark, who had come to the clinic as one of its first patients and who had stayed on there to work as the receptionist. How important Cindy had become to Russ was evident when Alice asked him once again how he felt about Steve, especially now that so much time had gone by.

"I wrote you when you were in France," he said, "saying I'd probably always feel a certain amount of antagonism toward him after what happened. But, as you said, a lot of time has gone by, and some good things have happened to me that kind of balance the bad things. The clinic's been a success. I'm seeing a lot of Cindy. My life has kind of settled down, and things are running pretty smoothly."

He smiled—that same, sweet smile that was so like him—and that she had missed, more than she had realized. "I guess you could say I've turned into sort of a different guy. You know I never did blame Steve for what happened as much as I blamed Rachel. And now I hardly even blame Rachel any more. I blame myself, mostly, for not knowing what kind of a woman I was married to."

He shook his head, looking askance. "I must have loved her. If I didn't, how could I have been so stupid about her?" Then he shrugged. "Oh, well. It doesn't make too much difference any more who was selfish or who was stupid or who was anything. I don't really care any more who was to blame. And anyhow, Alice, none of what happened to me should have anything to do with what you decide about Steve. That's between you and him. If I don't think about what happened any more, you shouldn't either. What's important is what Steve feels for you and you feel for him."

But if Russ was removing himself as an obstacle, Rachel very definitely was not. A few weeks earlier, when Rachel was trying one of her many maneuvers to be at the apartment when Steve came to see Jamie, Ada had accused her daughter of trying to get Steve interested in her. "And he doesn't even like you," Ada said. "There's only one person in the world he really cares about, and that's Alice."

Rachel sniffed. "How long do you think he can go on being in love with her when she doesn't care enough about him to come back here and be with him?"

"Then you admit that's why you want to see him—so you can get some place with him."

"I don't admit any such thing," Rachel snapped back at her. "But I don't like your saying I haven't got a chance with him."

While Alice was in Bay City, she and Steve went to see Lenore one afternoon. Rachel picked the same afternoon to see Lenore—and because Ada had other plans and couldn't baby-sit, she took Jamie with her. Nobody had told Rachel that Alice was in town, so it was just one of those things—until Rachel decided, as might be expected, to take advantage of the situation. "Well, now," she said, after she got over the surprise of seeing Alice there, "what do you think of this young man?" She thrust Jamie toward Alice. "This is Jamie."

Neither Alice nor anyone else responded, but that didn't stop Rachel. She beamed down at her son and then at Alice. "How do you like his new outfit?" Without waiting for an answer this time, she turned to Steve. "Steve, how do you like it? It's very important for you to like it." Now she thrust Jamie toward him. "Jamie, show your daddy how gorgeous you are."

"That's enough, Rachel," Steve said harshly.

Lenore, ever the gentlewoman, tried to rescue the situation. "Rachel," she said, "Alice is only here for a very short time, and we have so much to talk about, maybe if you . . ."

Rachel gave Lenore her wide-eyed, innocent look. "Oh, did I come at a bad time?" She turned to Alice and Steve with a smile. "I'm so sorry, but—look. Can't we all just be friends? I mean, what's past is past."

"Rachel," Alice said stiffly, "I'd really rather not talk about it."

Rachel ignored her. "And here we are all living in the same town. We have the same friends—Walter and Lenore and—well, I mean, like here we all are, and there's no sense in being silly about it, is there?"

"No," Alice said, not having any other choice.

Rachel smiled again. "Well, then, why don't we all just try to be nice and friendly and like that?" She took Jamie by the hand. "What do you think of my beautiful little boy, Alice?"

Steve started to speak, but Alice shook her head at him. "He's very handsome," she said, "and he seems like a very nice little boy, too."

Rachel fairly beamed. "He's very sweet. Anyway we think so, don't we, Steven?"

Steve looked ready to throttle her, but before he could do so, Lenore maneuvered her to the door. At the door Rachel turned back to Alice and Steve. "I just wanted to show you how cute Jamie looks and all, but I guess I'd better be getting on home." And with another brilliant smile directed at both of them, she finally left.

Lenore was full of apologies. She didn't like Rachel, and she certainly didn't count herself as one of her friends. Nor had she invited Rachel over.

"It's all right," Alice said, looking devastated. "I know how Rachel pushes herself on people. And I suppose it had to happen sooner or later, so maybe it's best to have gotten it over with."

In telling her mother about the incident, Rachel defended herself as having handled it pretty well, claiming she didn't like the whole thing any better than Alice did. "And if the rest of us were trying," she went on to say, "why couldn't she?"

"Because she's the one who was hurt, that's why," her mother answered. "Much more hurt than anyone else."

Rachel shrugged. "All I did was tell her Russ wasn't Jamie's father. I thought she ought to know, because Steve actually loves me more than he does her. He did then, and he does now."

"Stop it!" Ada yelled at her, her patience at an end. "Steve never loved you! You threw yourself at him, and the reason you told Alice about it was because you couldn't stand the idea that he loved Alice."

But there was no persuading Rachel. And when she heard that Alice was returning to Avignon, she was, as she remarked to Brian Blake, not the least bit sorry. "Not because I care what Alice does," she said, "but on account of Jamie. Steve hasn't seen Jamie at all since Alice has been in town, and I think that's awful to neglect his own son like that."

During their last evening together Alice and Steve talked about the encounter with Rachel, and Alice admitted it had shaken her. "But Jamie is your son," she went on to say. "That's a fact I have to face—and deal with it if I can. And without any help from Rachel. She has a way of making things as difficult as possible, and she's not going to change. Russ has, though." And she told Steve of her conversation with Russ.

"That's something for our side, isn't it?" Steve asked.

"Yes."

"But not enough?"

She shook her head. "Not quite. Not yet."

"Soon maybe?"

"Yes."

They were dancing at the Tallboys, and now he held her close. "I love you, I love you. How can you go away and leave me?"

"Oh, Steven," she answered, "it's not easy. But I have to." She pulled back to look at him. "I'll write to you."

"Can I call you—say, once a week?"

"All right. Yes."

"Saturday night. Alice, you do love me, don't you?"

"Oh, Steven, yes, I do."

Once again he held her close there on the dance floor while other couples danced around them. "Oh, Alice, I love you so much. Nothing in this world exists for me except you. And everything exists because of you. If I feel the sun, it's because you feel the sun. If I see the snow, it's because you see the snow. If I hear music, it's because you hear music. Everything is you, and you are everything." This time it was he who pulled back to look at her. "I'm just trying to tell you how much I love you—and how much I'm going to love you forever. I want to be sure you know that no matter what you do way off there in France—when you get up in the morning, when you eat breakfast, when you get dressed and go to work, when you come home and go to bed, even when you wake up in the middle of the night—I want you to know I'm here every minute loving you and wanting you and needing you."

Tears had filled her eyes. Now they rolled down her face. He tried to brush them away with his hands, but they kept on coming, so he gave up and pulled her close to him again and kissed her and held her close.

While Steve was driving Alice to the airport to begin the long journey back to France, Rachel was depositing Jamie with Ada for the night—and Ada was wanting to know why.

"What's going on between you and Brian Blake that you have to leave Jamie overnight with Grandma and Grandpa?"

"Nothing's going on, Mom," Rachel said. "It's just

that we're out late, that's all, and it's easier this way on everybody."

Ada gave her a skeptical look. "You think Brian Blake's going to marry you?"

Rachel nodded. "Actually, as a matter of fact, I do."

"Has he asked you?"

"Not in so many words."

Ada grunted. "What other way is there except in so many words? A man doesn't ask a girl to marry him in sign language."

Ignoring her mother's remark, Rachel said, "Brian and I have a really deep understanding. He understands me, and I understand him. He loves me."

Ada remained skeptical. "Has he said so?"

"Mom, I don't want to talk about it."

"Well, I do. There's something about Brian Blake when he's around you that gives me the creeps."

But, as usual, there was no dissuading Rachel. All she said to that was "Why don't you stop worrying and relax? Let me worry about Brian Blake."

Still, it occurred to Rachel that maybe she ought to try to pin Brian down, so that night, after they had had dinner out and had come back to the apartment, where Brian was going to spend the night—and, as Ada had suspected, not for the first time—Rachel snuggled up to Brian, saying, "You know I like you. I more than like you. I think you're the nicest, smartest, handsomest, and most exciting man I've ever known."

Even as he began to caress her he gave her a look reminiscent of the one Ada had given her a few hours earlier. "More exciting than Steve Frame?"

Rachel shrugged, then turned her back to him so he could unzip her dress. "What's Steve got to do with it?"

His hands were cool against her skin. "A good deal, I think."

Rachel pulled the dress over her head and dropped it on a chair. "No, he hasn't. I don't really see him any more. Not the way I see you."

Brian took off his shirt and hung it in the closet. "And is that your choice or his?"

"What's the difference?" she answered, in that way she had of avoiding questions she didn't want to answer. "I don't see him, and I have been seeing you. The important thing is I like you a lot, and I wish we could be together all the time."

She was sitting on the bed, and he came over and sat beside her. "I don't know about all the time," he said, "but we can certainly arrange to see each other more often than we have."

That wasn't exactly the answer Rachel had been looking for.

"At this particular moment," he went on, "I don't feel I can make a firm commitment to anyone about anything. Of course," he added, putting an arm around her and drawing her close, "I could always change my mind about that, and if there's anyone who could make me change it, it's you."

He bent to kiss her, and she responded passionately, clinging to him as his hands began moving up and down her body, urging her as his mouth was urging her to open up to him, to want him, to take him, and moments later they lay back on the bed, desire uppermost in both their minds—and, underlying it, a conviction on her part that he did love her and he would very soon now ask her to marry him.

Especially if she gave him every opportunity to do so.

And so for the next three months—as spring moved into summer—Rachel gave him opportunity after opportunity. Since he seemed to be jealous of Steve, she told him that she and Jamie were going to fly to St. Croix with Steve for a long weekend. All he said, between kisses, was "That's nice."

"I said I'm going with Steve," she repeated. "Steve Frame."

"Yes, I know who you mean," he replied. "That's wonderful."

"It was Steve's idea," she went on, beginning to feel a little desperate. "He said he wanted to spend more time alone with us."

Brian kissed her again. "That must make you very happy," he said in that lazy way he had of speaking

when they were lying in bed together, as they were doing now—as they seemed to spend almost all of their
time together doing.

She pulled away from him and sat up, moving far
enough away from him that he couldn't reach out for
her and pull her back down beside him. "You don't
care if I go away for a few days with another man?"

"Of course I care," he answered, stretching his arms
out to her. "Of course it bothers me. I don't like the
idea one bit." He smiled at her—the lazy smile to
match the lazy voice. "Now. Is that what you wanted
me to say?"

He was maddening. She never knew when he was
serious and when he was only teasing her. "Do you
mean it, Brian?"

He sat up and reached for her and pulled her down
with him. "Of course I mean it. But I can't run your
life for you. You make your own decisions."

She snuggled against him. "If you'd rather I
wouldn't go . . ."

He held her close. "Of course I'd rather you
wouldn't go."

"Good," she said. "Then I won't go. I want you to
help me make my decisions—what you think is very
important to me." She let him kiss her—a long, linger-
ing kiss, their bodies pressed together. And then, as
the kiss became more demanding, more urgent, she
pulled back far enough to say "Is what I think important to you?"

"Uh-huh. Very important," he answered, then went
back to kissing her, and this time there were no more
interruptions.

And so it went, she pursuing, he eluding. When
Brian told Rachel he had an offer from a law firm in
New York City—and took her there with him for a
few days of business and pleasure—she was convinced
that he was going to accept the offer and take her
there with him permanently.

When Steve came by for his next visit with Jamie,
Rachel told him he might have to come to New York
to see his son if things worked out the way she expected them to. "I may be moving there because of

Brian. He got this fabulous offer from a big law firm there, and he didn't know what to do about it, because he was afraid it would mean leaving me, and of course he didn't want to do that." Then, ever mindful of where the real potential lay, she went on to say, "Brian wants to marry me, and I haven't made up my mind yet if I should or shouldn't. What do you think I should do, Steve?"

That gambit proved useless. "If you want to marry him," Steve said with a shrug, "I think it's wonderful."

But if that gambit was useless, the next one was disastrous. Brian returned to New York for a few days. Pressed by Rachel in a phone call, he said he missed her and wished she were there. She took that as an invitation and flew to New York to join him—only to discover another woman with him in his hotel room.

Rachel was stunned, Brian disgusted.

"I thought you'd be so happy to see me," she said after he had asked the other woman to wait down in the lobby for him. "I thought it was such a wonderful surprise."

"You thought!" he replied with a shake of his head. "You've got a way of thinking all sorts of things. Why don't you ask once in a while instead of thinking all these fantastic things?"

She was staring at him. "You mean you don't want me?"

"All right, Rachel," he said with a sigh. "I don't want you. That's right, I don't want you. I don't want you here in New York. I don't want you in Bay City from now on. I don't want you in my life. You're a very attractive girl, and we've had a lot of good times together—lots of fun and games and all that. But that's all it ever was."

She was still staring at him, a look of utter disbelief on her face. "That's all? But you loved me. You were going to marry me."

"No, Rachel. I never told you I was in love with you, and I never told you I wanted to marry you. You dreamed that all up by yourself, and once you dream something up, you go right on living as though the dream was a reality. Well, as of right now, stop dreaming. Wake up. Face facts. Pull yourself together. Because I am not in love with you, I never was, and I never will be. And I never wanted to marry you. I don't want to now, and I never will want to. Is that crystal clear?"

Back in Bay City, her mother offered her advice instead of sympathy, telling her she had better stop and look at herself and make some changes, because she would never find a husband as she was now—self-centered and interested in a man only for what he could give her and not for the man himself.

But Rachel already had something else—and someone else—in mind. She would go see her father and tell him what had happened between herself and Brian. Her father would tell her what to do, and he would of course be glad to see her. After all, he was her father, wasn't he?

"Aren't you building something up in your mind again?" Ada asked. "Aren't you doing what you did when you went to New York? You were so sure Brian was going to be overjoyed to see you. Now you're so sure that when you show up in Somerset your father is going to throw his arms around you and tell you how happy he is to see you. It could happen you'd be as wrong about this trip as you were about your trip to New York."

But Rachel was unmoved.

And so, in a manner of speaking, was her father.

Although he said he was glad to see her and—after hearing her story about Brian—felt sorry for her, his judgment of the affair tallied with her mother's and Brian's—that she had brought the disaster on herself by building up in her mind something that was only a fantasy.

"And there's more to it than that," he said. "This is the way you run your life all the time. Steve Frame—the one whose baby you have—you thought there were going to be big things between you and him, didn't you? And that Dr. Matthews you married. You told me yourself he'd disappointed you."

"But that was all a long time ago," Rachel protested.

"I know that," he said, "but you behaved the same way."

Rachel gave him an unhappy look. "I thought you'd comfort me."

Her father bent down and kissed her on the cheek. "I want to comfort you, Rachel. Believe me, I do. But I'd rather have you in good shape ten years from now than have you go on dreaming and dreaming and dreaming."

There was something else she had thought—that he would let her stay with him for a week in Somerset. She had counted on it, made all her plans around it. But when she told him what she wanted, kept pressing him about it, he finally told her no.

"Rachel, look," he said. "I'm in a hurry. You've caught me at a bad time. I've got some people I have to meet—business people who are important to me—so I'll have to say this fast. This week you've got planned —that's a dream too."

"What?" she said, her eyes flying wide. "You mean you're not going to let me stay here with you?"

"Listen. The thing you've got to learn is everybody has troubles, not just you. I've got troubles. I don't want to go into it, but there's a problem I've got with my daughter right now."

Her eyes went even wider, if that was possible. "Your daughter? I'm your daughter."

"Oh. Well, yeah," he said, "but I mean Pammy is the daughter who grew up with me. You know what I mean. Now look. I've got to go. I'd like to stay with you, but I've got to go. If you want to have dinner here, on me, fine, but . . ." He shrugged.

Tears shimmered in her eyes. "But the week together is out, right?"

"I'm afraid so."

"Then don't talk any more," she said. "Just go."

It was at this very low point in her life that Ted Clark came into it.

Ted Clark was Cindy Clark's brother. Dark-haired like his sister, he was of medium height and medium build. He was also handsome, with a well-scrubbed all-American look about him. The look was somewhat deceptive. For the past four years he had been living in St. Louis—and getting into trouble there, though when he returned home he was careful to keep that part of his life a secret, saying only that he had been in the restaurant business. The trouble was drug trouble, and it followed him to Bay City, where, to satisfy threats made against him, he stole Cindy's clinic keys, had a duplicate set made, and then broke into the clinic one night—to make it look like an outside job— and stole some drugs from the supply cabinet.

The take satisfied the man who was making the threats—at least for the time being—but unfortunately Russ happened along while the theft was in progress, and a panicked Ted knocked him out, very nearly killing him. Russ recovered, and Ted stole no more drugs, but the memory of what had happened remained to haunt him.

In an effort to better himself and put the painful memory behind him, Ted got a temporary job in a Bay City restaurant, then went to Somerset to talk to Gerald Davis about a possible job at his Riverboat. It was there that he met Rachel.

She was sitting at the table where her father had left her, and she was crying. After some hesitation, Ted, who had been having a drink at the bar after talking to Gerald, came over to her table.

"You don't have to tell me a thing," he said, "but you're going to feel better if somebody's sitting with you." When she said nothing, he pulled out a chair and sat down. "Maybe the next thing you're going to tell me is get away from you, and if you do, I'll go. But first I'd like to say I'm not trying to be fresh or pick up a pretty girl, but you're crying. You're sitting here all alone, and the worst part of it is I can tell you're feeling all alone."

He tried a smile. She didn't smile back, but then, she hadn't told him to get lost either. "I know that feeling," he said. "I've had it. And no strings attached, please believe me, but I'd like to help. Now, tell me if you want me to leave."

Rachel had taken a handkerchief out of her purse to

wipe her eyes. "You'd like to help?" she said bitterly. "You don't know me."

"I know you're Mr. Davis's daughter," he answered. "But that's not important. What's important is you're feeling all alone."

Encouraged by his earnest manner and needing somebody to pour her troubles out to—and maybe thinking a stranger was easier to confide in than a friend, assuming she still had one—Rachel began to talk to Ted about how she didn't want to go home just yet, since everybody in Bay City believed she would be staying a week with her father—and thus made the discovery that Ted also came from Bay City.

Ted suggested that she take a room in a motel in Somerset for a week, offering to have dinner with her each evening if she wanted the company, admitting that he had things on his mind he'd like to get off it, and that by helping her he'd be helping himself. They'd be helping each other.

Rachel moved into a motel, and when Ted showed up the first night she was surprised. She hadn't thought he had really meant it. He reassured her. "I'll be coming here tomorrow night and the next night and all the nights until you leave here, but you don't have to talk unless you want to. You don't have to tell me a thing."

She sighed. "I don't know if I'd know where to start."

"Don't worry about it," he said. "I know one thing already. What your father did to you."

Defending him, Rachel said, "My father's a nice man. He's got problems, I guess. That's all."

"His problems I don't worry about," Ted responded. "It's your problems that count, and I'll tell you this. If I were a father, and my daughter came to me in trouble and said I want to stay with you for a week, believe me, my problems wouldn't matter. I'd have her stay with me."

Rachel looked at him in disbelief. "Why are you so nice to me?"

He shrugged. "I'm just a guy, Rachel. Nothing special. I've got a job in the restaurant business, and I'm looking around for a restaurant of my own. I had one, but I had to get rid of it. It was a long way from Bay City, and Bay City was where I wanted to be, so I'm glad now I moved. Because you're there."

She liked his saying that and said so. Telling him that she was divorced, she said, "My husband's family never thought it was nice I was in Bay City. They didn't think I was good enough for their son."

"You're good enough for anyone's son."

She thanked him and told him about Jamie—except for the fact that her former husband was not Jamie's father. In telling Ted about Brian, she was more honest. And when it came out that Cindy Clark was Ted's sister—Cindy now being engaged to marry Russ—Rachel told Ted who her former husband was. And then, matters having progressed between them, she said, "What do we do about that?"

"Look, Rachel," he said, "we've found each other—sort of. We need each other. We're helping each other, right?"

"Yes," she agreed. "And nobody has ever been as nice to me as you."

"Then nothing's changed. I don't care who your former husband was. I hope you don't care who my sister is. Rachel, I want to go on seeing you. I don't want any of this to end."

Rachel didn't either. "You're wonderful," she said. "Nobody before ever made me feel like somebody. I mean, in answer to your question, yes. I don't want this to end either."

By midweek matters had progressed to the point that Rachel said to Ted, "You've done a lot more than just talk to me. You've been kind and thoughtful and interested in me. You didn't just listen. You gave me courage. No matter what happens to me from now on, I'll never forget these few days and how wonderful you were. And how you gave me the feeling that you really cared for me."

"I did care, Rachel. And I do. This may sound crazy when we've only known each other for such a short time, but I love you."

Rachel frowned at him. "Ted, please don't say that unless you really mean it."

"I do mean it, Rachel. I love you."

"Oh, Ted," she said breathlessly, "and I love you."

By the end of the week they were married—there in the motel room, with Gerald Davis giving his daughter away.

And at about the same time, over in Bay City, Mary Matthews was saying to Jim, "I feel better about Alice and Steve now that Russ has Cindy. That means Rachel is out of the picture."

"Rachel's been out of the picture for a long time," Jim reminded her.

"Well, out of Russ's mind and heart, yes," Mary agreed. "But—"

"But nothing," Jim finished for her. "Rachel's out of Russ's life. Alice won't have to be reminded all the time of what Rachel did to him. Nobody will have to be."

And also at the same time, in Bay City, Steve received a cablegram from Alice saying she would be home the following night.

Chapter Twenty-three

THE morning of Alice's return, Rachel and Ted came back to Bay City. While Rachel was in Somerset, Steve had been taking care of Jamie. Now he brought him back to his mother, who thanked him effusively.

"I have something to tell you," Steve said, when Jamie had been put in his playpen and they were alone in the living room of her apartment. "Alice is coming home tonight. To stay. That's why I'm glad you're back —because I wanted to see you. I want to marry Alice. I've wanted to for a long time. And, Rachel, from time to time in the past you and I have had some pretty knock-down, drag-out fights."

"Well, we won't any more," she said.

Not believing her, he said, "Let me go on. All those fights were about the effect you had on my relationship with Alice."

"I know," she said, "and I'm sorry."

He stared at her.

"Truly I am, Steve. You see I'm a different person now, I mean it. Things have happened."

"What things?"

She smiled. "I'm married now."

He was back to staring at her. "Married?"

"Yes," she said, and told him all about Ted, including the fact that he was Cindy's brother.

So once again—however differently—Alice's return was marred by something Rachel did.

After the breathless greeting at the airport, after the big welcome-home party at her parents' house, Alice and Steve were sitting alone on the Matthewses' front porch swing discussing this latest turn of events.

"It's awful," Alice said. "It means that when Russ marries Cindy, Rachel is going to be a member of the family again. Sort of, anyhow. By marriage. Aren't we ever going to be rid of her for good?"

"I never have been rid of her," Steve answered. "And I can't tell you how sorry I am I had to spoil your homecoming with news like this."

"It's all right," she answered. "It wasn't your doing. And anyhow, we can't let Rachel continue to affect our lives as she has in the past."

But trying to talk something away didn't always remove it.

"When will I see you again?" Steve asked. "Tomorrow night?"

"I don't know," Alice answered. "I haven't had a chance to catch my breath yet."

"Please," he begged. "We have an awful lot to talk about."

She looked at him, then nodded. "All right."

He put his arm around her, drawing her close. "Alice, my Alice. I can't believe it yet. That you're actually home. And for good." He put a hand under her chin, searching her face. "I love you so." Then he took her in his arms and kissed her.

After he had gone, Alice went back inside the house, where Russ was breaking the news to his parents about Ted and Rachel. "Cindy doesn't think Rachel has told him Jamie wasn't my child."

"No," Alice agreed. "Steve doesn't think she told him that either."

"Of course she didn't," Mary said. "That's why they got married in such a hurry. Rachel wanted to make certain of him—get him to marry her—before he found out." She sighed—a long and troubled sigh. "I thought we were through with her after the divorce, but here she is back in our lives again." She turned to Alice. "What will this mean to you and Steve? I mean Jamie."

"Jamie has been a problem all along," Alice told her. "The big problem is between Steven and me. I don't know how I feel about this. It's all happened so quickly, I haven't had a chance to see it in any kind of perspective, All I know is I love Steven. I love him very much."

Her mother frowned. "But you're going to think seriously about it, aren't you?"

"Of course I'll think about it," Alice said. "I'll have to."

When Steven brought her home from their date the next night, he started telling her what all was happening in the area in the next few weeks—the kind of events they had attended before and had enjoyed: a folk-music performance, the ballet, the series of summer concerts in the park, and so on. But Alice cut in on him.

"Steven," she said, "just a minute. Don't start making too many plans for us. I can't spend every single evening with you."

He turned a troubled face to her.

"Don't you want to see me, spend time with me?"

"Of course I do," she said. "Within reason. But I think we should be sensible about it."

"It's because of Rachel, isn't it? This latest move of hers. You and your whole family must have breathed a sigh of relief when she and Russ were divorced, figuring she was out of your life for good. And now here she is back in the picture again."

He had unwittingly echoed what her mother had said, and Alice replied in the same vein. "Steven, she was never out of the picture as far as you and I were concerned. After all, you are Jamie's father, and you have been seeing him, haven't you?"

"Yes," he admitted. "I even took care of him while Rachel was in Somerset."

For a few minutes they sat in silence on the swing. Then Alice turned to him, and after a moment she said, "Why are you looking so sad?"

"You know why," he answered. "I love you. I've loved you since practically the first time I met you. I'll always love you. These last few months—especially after I went to see you in France—I felt so good about us, so kind of hopeful. I started thinking that in spite of what had happened with Rachel you still loved me—loved me enough to be able to bury what had happened. And maybe someday . . ."

"Steven, don't you think I do love you? Love you as much as you love me? But there are problems— things that happened that I can't forget. At least not yet."

He took one of her hands in his. "Do you think someday you can?"

"I hope and pray I can."

He looked at her a moment. "What you're saying is maybe we should start all over again—the way we were in the beginning—and see what happens."

She nodded. "That's right. And if what we feel for each other is real and strong, then time can only strengthen it. If it's not, the sooner we find it out, the better."

"All right," he said. "Then I'll have to take my chances with you. I won't push you about dates or anything else." He grinned—a sudden, mischievous grin. "But what about tomorrow night?"

She smiled. "All right. Tomorrow night is fine."

While Alice was still in Avignon her mother had told Steve that if Alice wanted to marry him, she and Jim wouldn't dream of standing in their way. But now that Rachel had thrust herself into their midst again by marrying Ted Clark, all of Mary's old doubts began flooding back.

"How do you feel about him?" Mary asked Alice one afternoon when Alice mentioned that she and Steve had another date that night. "If you don't mind telling me."

"I don't mind telling you," Alice answered. "Only I can't. I don't know. Not definitely." She sighed. "I love him, but . . ."

"But you're not sure you want to marry him?"

"No. Mother, look. Tell me how you feel about Steven."

"Darling," her mother answered, "Steven wants to marry you, not me."

"Then how do you feel about that?"

Her mother didn't answer immediately. "First of all," she said at last, "I want you to be sure of your own feelings. And I want you to realize that what happened before—when you found out Rachel's child was Steven's son—that was a pretty awful discovery. I think you should consider the fact that the damage can't ever quite be undone. I know Steven loves you. He's shown you in a million ways how sorry he is for what happened with Rachel. But the fact is, it did happen. And now, to make things even more difficult, Rachel has married the brother of Russ's fiancée. When I think of all the trouble that girl has brought our children." Mary sighed and shook her head.

"I know," Alice said. "And, as you said the other night, there is Jamie to think about. Steven will go on supporting him and seeing as much of him as he possibly can. Of course I'm glad he feels that way. It's the way he should feel."

"But it's going to complicate things for you, Alice. I mean, it isn't simply a matter of Steven and Jamie. It will be Steven and Rachel and Jamie. There will be times—maybe a lot of times—when Rachel and Steven will have to confer about their son."

"Yes," Alice said. "I know."

"That's why I want you to think long and hard

about marrying Steven, Alice. Because of all the complications."

"I have been thinking, Mom. The trouble is, I don't get anywhere. I can't make up my mind. And Steven is so patient, so dear, so willing to wait." Alice's voice broke on the last words, and her eyes filled with tears. "I'm such a fool."

"You're nothing of the kind," Mary said. "Darling, I don't want to stand in the way of your doing whatever you feel in your heart you want to do. You know that. It's just that I want you to be sure."

Alice wiped her eyes with the back of her hand. "That's what's so hard for me—to be sure of anything."

Mary was also worried about how Russ would feel, although he had said more than once that he shouldn't be a factor in Alice's decision. In fact, one evening shortly after Alice's return Russ told his father he hoped things worked out for Alice and Steve, because they deserved it.

"I wish your mother felt that way," Jim said. "She finds it somewhat distressing for Alice to begin all over again with him."

It was a hot, airless evening in the middle of July, and the two men were sitting out on the flagstone patio at the back of the house, trying to catch whatever stray breeze might be around.

"Has Mom said anything to Alice?" Russ asked. "Anything more than her first night home, I mean."

Jim nodded. "Yes. And Alice herself is still undecided."

"Alice has been undecided for a year now."

"I know," Jim acknowledged. "But that simply indicates how deep the problem has been."

"But, Dad. Alice loves Steve. Anybody can see that."

"I know. It isn't me you have to convince, Russ. It's your mother. And she isn't dead set against the marriage. She just wants Alice to think long and hard before she makes up her mind."

The two men sat in silence for a bit, listening to the night sounds of summer.

Finally Russ said, "Steve isn't the same man he

was last year, any more than I am. After all, he's been through a bad time too. And if they love each other, then nothing should stand in their way." He yawned and stretched. He had put in a long day at the clinic, and he was tired as well as hot. "They need time together, that's all."

"You're right," Jim agreed. "Whatever they choose to do will grow out of this second courtship."

The second courtship, as Jim had termed it, seemed to be moving right along. On their way home from the folk-music festival, Alice and Steve were full of themselves and the events of the evening they had so enjoyed. Turning to him, Alice said, "It makes me happy to see you happy."

"You're the one who makes me happy," he answered. "I feel I'm going to burst." He laughed. "A great explosion, and Steven Frame goes all to pieces. And all from happiness." He maneuvered the car into the outer lane, from which he would turn onto the shoreline drive. And that would take them to their favorite lay-by at the Mount Pleasant lookout along the bluffs. "I feel alive again for the first time in months," he said.

"And I've had such a lovely time tonight," she said. "And all because of you."

They were on the shoreline drive now and climbing to the bluffs. "I say things to you I've never been able to say to anyone before in my life. Because you listen to me." He shook his head. "I can't believe you're here at all sometimes."

"But I am here."

He shot a glance at her. "Tell me I won't wake up tomorrow and find you're gone."

"I'll be here."

"You're sure you won't be back in France, and I'll be staring into space, longing to see your face again?"

"No, Steven. I'll be here. I promise." They rode in silence for a bit, and then she said, "I like you so much. Besides loving you. I like you."

They were approaching the lay-by. Steve slowed the car and then swung off the road and into the parking area. He braked the car and cut the engine, and they got out of the car and went to stand at the stone guardrail.

"In Avignon," Alice said, "there was a little old woman who worked in my pension. And every night she waited by the gate for one of the villagers. I'd watch them from my window. They never said anything. He'd take her hand, and they'd walk away —back to their house in the valley—like kids. But they weren't kids. Some nights I'd see him waiting for her—walking back and forth beyond the hedge like a teenager. When I told her that was true love, she smiles and said it was more than just love. They liked each other." Alice turned to him, touched his face with her hand. "He looked at her the way you look at me."

He clasped her hand. "I'll look at you like this forty years from now, too, if you'll let me."

She smiled. "We'll just go from day to day for the time being, but don't stop looking at me like that."

"I won't," he answered. "Not in a hundred years. I like to look at you. I like just to be with you."

"Steven," she said, "do you have any idea how much I like you? Just as much as that little old woman liked her husband all those years."

He put his arm around her, and they walked over to a spot on the stone rail wide enough to sit on. For some time they simply sat there looking out across the bay and up to the stars in the sky. Then Steve began to talk a bit about his childhood.

"I don't know how I come across to people," he said. "I've got a whole building full of employees, and I've made a lot of money. You know that. But earlier this evening—at the festival—you called me a hard-headed realist. Do you remember?"

She nodded. "Yes. I remember."

He nodded, too. "And maybe I seem that way. Capable. In command. I've got some abilities. I know that. And I put them to use. I keep my head. But, Alice, that's surface. External. It's scarcely real compared with what goes on inside. With the things I hope." He turned to smile at her. "When I was a little boy I hoped to have a bedroom of my own."

"You make me ashamed," she said, "because I've been so fortunate."

"Don't wish you weren't," he told her, "because when you're one of a large brood, and your mother calls to you and uses the names of three of your brothers before she hits on your name, you don't like it. You understand it, but you don't like it. You want to become yourself. I suppose that's why I created Steven Frame Enterprises."

She started to speak, but he went on. "I mean Steven Frame Enterprises as an entity. But it's a business entity, Alice. Don't ever think it's the real me. It's a substitute me."

Alice gave him a little squeeze. "Don't worry. I know there's more to you than what sits behind that desk."

He shook his head. "The point is, I don't know it. I thought I might find myself, find out who I was, through you. When I met you I began to think my hopes—all those vague, half-formed hopes—would take shape."

She gave him another squeeze. "It makes me feel responsible."

"No," he said, "I don't want you to feel responsible. What I thought was that knowing you, being with you, would help me understand myself." He shook his head again. "And then I threw everything away, didn't I? Steve Frame, the hardheaded realist, who sits behind the desk in that office. Some hardheaded realist. Some fool."

For answer she kissed him.

"No," he said, "don't pity me. I love you, and I want you to love me. But not out of pity."

She told him then about her conversation with her mother. "Mom blames Rachel much more than she blames you."

"I'm not trying to shove the blame off on Rachel," he replied. "I did a shockingly stupid thing. I know that. I did it, and I can't undo it, as much as I wish I could. But it doesn't change the fact that I love you, Alice." He took one of her hands in his. "More than

anything or anybody on earth. And I always will—
no matter what happens."

"Steven, I believe you. And what's made the whole
thing more difficult for everybody is Rachel marrying Ted."

He turned from her to stare out across the bay.
"Rachel, Rachel, Rachel. Always Rachel." With a sigh
he turned back to her. "Alice, my darling, I'm not
trying to force you to decide one way or the other
—for me or against me. But it means so much to me.
I just can't tell you. It means everything to me to
have you say 'Yes, I'll marry you.' I'll wait as long
as you want me to, but it isn't easy, believe me. Not
when I love you so much."

She was in tears, and he reached in his pocket for
a handkerchief, then gently wiped her eyes. "I didn't
mean to make you cry. I'm not going to tell you I love
you if it makes you cry."

She took the handkerchief from him and dabbed
at her eyes more forcefully. "Oh, Steven, I don't want
to be the way I am—feeling one way one minute and
another way another minute. Never being able to
make up my mind and say yes, I'll marry you, or no,
I won't. It isn't fair or right, and I know that. But I
can't help myself. I do want to marry you, but I don't
want to marry you. I don't want to live with all the
problems and hurts and memories. But I love you.
I do love you. And I want to marry you. Only I
can't forget what happened with Rachel, and I don't
know if I'll ever forget. And if I don't forget, what will
become of us? Of you? Of me? What would our
marriage be like? Steven, help me. Please help me,
because I can't help myself. I'm trying, but I can't.
I just can't."

She was sobbing now, and he took her in his arms
and held her close, wishing that he could help her
come to a decision, but knowing that he couldn't,
that she would have to come to it herself.

The source of their conflict—Rachel—had maybe
half persuaded Steve that she had changed, that she
was indeed a different person now, in love with Ted
and Ted alone, wishing only happiness to Steve and

Alice. But none of the Matthews family was persuaded even a little bit, and Rachel's own mother must have thought she was hearing things when Rachel said to her, "I love Ted, Mom. This is different from Steve and Brian. Everything about it is different."

Well, not quite everything.

As suspected by the Matthewses, Rachel had indeed let Ted think Russ was Jamie's father, but in a matter of days she told him the truth—and promised she would be honest with him from then on. Ted said he hadn't been completely honest with her either. His current job was only temporary, and he didn't have any money outside of what he earned.

Ada would have gasped to hear Rachel's summing up of that exchange of confidences. "Isn't it all wonderful," she said, "to have everything out in the open? Nothing hidden. You know all about me, and I know all about you, and nobody's lying or pretending about anything. I just think it's wonderful. It's the only way to live." She beamed. "And our whole lives together are going to be just like this—loving each other and not ever hiding anything, right?"

Since Rachel didn't know quite all there was to know about Ted, and he didn't see fit to tell her at that time, he only nodded and said nothing.

Nor was Rachel above a little of the old dishonesty when it came to bettering herself, something she had always been devoted to. His temporary job nearing its end, Ted applied for a permanent job at the Fireside Inn on Market Street in downtown Bay City, only to learn that the present owner wasn't looking for an employee but a buyer. Since Ted had no money and no collateral with which to borrow any, he put the Fireside Inn out of his head. Rachel didn't put it out of hers. She went to Steve and asked him to back Ted. Steve told her to discuss it with her father first, since he knew nothing about the restaurant business, and then get back to him.

Rachel's interpretation of discussing it with her father was to tell him Steve wanted to go into the restaurant business with him by being a co-investor in the Fireside Inn. Gerald said he'd have to think about it and do some investigating—that he wasn't promising her anything.

Rachel then went back to Steve. "My father thinks it's a marvelous idea," she said. "And a very good investment. So he's going to invest in it. And now will you help Ted out in it, too?"

"Rachel," Steve said, somewhat taken aback, "I wouldn't even consider the idea until I've had a chance to look into it. With or without your father."

"I don't see what there is to look into," Rachel said.

"The Fireside Inn, for one thing. And your husband, for another."

"But Ted's a wonderful person," Rachel said. "He's smart, and he works hard, and he's honest, and he has great ideas about the restaurant business."

"That may be. But all I know about him—on my own—is that he married you. Rachel, I'm a businessman, and I've got to look at this thing primarily as an investment."

"It's an investment in Ted," she countered. "And it's for Jamie, too. After all, don't you want Jamie's stepfather—the man he's going to be living with—to be a success?"

"Okay, Rachel," he said, putting a hand up to stop her. "I'll look into it and see if it makes sense to give Ted the money. If it does, then I probably will."

Talking the matter over with Walter, Steve acknowledged that there was some merit—considerable merit—to Rachel's argument regarding Jamie. "While I'm Jamie's father," he said, "Ted's his stepfather now, and Jamie's going to be spending a lot more time with him than he is with me. And don't you think it would be a lot better for Jamie if his stepfather is successful doing what he wanted?"

Walter agreed it would.

"And it wouldn't just be better for Jamie," Steve went on. "It would be better for Rachel, too. I've always been concerned about her as far as it affected Jamie."

"Yes, I know you have. And there's more to it than that, Steve. There's you and Alice."

Steve nodded. "Exactly. If Ted does make a go of it, and his marriage to Rachel works out, then there's that much more chance she'll stay out of my life."

"Then you're going to do it?"

"I want to talk to Ted first, but if I'm as satisfied that he can make a go of it as Gerald Davis is, then I probably will."

Walter began putting papers back in his briefcase prior to going back to his own office. "And what about Alice?"

Steve frowned. "What about her?"

"Does she know about this?"

"Oh. No. There's no reason for her to know about it yet. In the first place, it's not definite. And in the second place, things are too uncertain between us. And I don't want to make them even more difficult and complicated. But I can't see why she'd mind, if that's what you were thinking. After all, it isn't Rachel I'll be getting involved with if this does go through. It's her husband."

Walter shrugged. "Well, it's your decision." But he went out of Steve's office not looking altogether convinced. And when Steve phoned him a couple of days later to say he had decided to back Ted, but he still hadn't told Alice—he was waiting for the right time and place—Walter again said nothing one way or the other, but he felt privately that Steve was being unwise.

Steve might have felt that way too had he been privy to a conversation between Alice and Lenore that took place after Rachel had stopped by to see Lenore one afternoon.

"I think marriage has changed her for the better," Lenore confided. As somebody had once pointed out, it was enormously difficult for Lenore to be unkind to anyone. "Not that I blame you for the way you feel about her, Alice," she hastened to add, "but I think she's softer. Less intense and demanding. In love is what I mean, I guess. But I guess I shouldn't talk to you about Rachel."

"I'm sorry," Alice said. "But the very mention of her name gets my back up. I shouldn't feel this way, but I can't help it." She sighed. "I never used to agonize over things much. I accepted whatever came along. But I'm so upset over everything—including the engagement party for Russ and Cindy that Pat is giving next week. You know Rachel will be there."

Lenore frowned. "No, I didn't know."

"Well, she will be."

"Does she have to?"

"I suppose not. No. But how would Cindy feel if her own brother—whom she's very close to—wasn't invited to something as important to her as her engagement party? And Pat couldn't very well invite Ted and not invite Rachel with him. So I told her to invite them."

"Oh, dear," Lenore said, looking distressed.

"Oh dear is right," Alice agreed. "I'm so nervous about the idea of meeting Rachel there I've been tempted not to show up myself. But then how would Russ feel?" She shook her head. "Anyhow, it's not just that. It's the whole idea of Steven and me. When we're together I feel as if Rachel and Jamie and the past are still a part of our lives. And our future."

"But, Alice," Lenore said, "there's no reason to think they will be. Not if you make it so."

"And how can I make it so?"

"By forgiving. Even if you can't forget, you can forgive."

Alice nodded. "In a way I guess I have forgiven, but Rachel had Steve's baby, and she was married to my brother. Those two facts go over and over in my mind. Suppose I married Steven and then became one of those bitter wives who doubt their husbands and never believe them?"

"I think," Lenore said, "you're imagining something that isn't going to happen."

The night of the engagement party, Alice wasn't the only one who was nervous. Rachel was so nervous that she wished she hadn't been invited. And when her mother called, and Rachel said something about thanking Steve again for backing Ted, Ada said the best way she could thank Steve was not to do or say anything at the party she would be sorry for.

It was, of course, asking a great deal from somebody who, on meeting her former mother-in-law at the party, said she was happier now than she had ever been.

The encounter between Rachel and Alice, when it finally happened, took place on the terrace outside the Randolphs' living room.

Ted was with Rachel, and Rachel introduced him to Alice, telling her how she had met him at her father's restaurant and how it was love at first sight.

"I hope you'll be very happy," Alice said politely.

Rachel beamed. "Thank you, Alice. I hope you will be, too. I don't know how things are now between you and Steve, but I can tell you he missed you terribly when you were away."

"I missed him, too," Alice replied and started to leave, but Rachel called her back.

"Can I say something?" she asked.

"It all depends on what it is," Alice answered.

"It's about us. I know I did some terrible things and made a lot of trouble for you in the past. I really am sorry about it. But everything's different now. I love Ted very much, and we're very happy together. I'm sorry about what happened."

Touched in spite of herself, Alice said, "That's a very nice thing for you to say, Rachel."

"I mean it."

Alice nodded. "Yes, I think you do, and I'm glad." She smiled. "Now, will you excuse me? Steven is waiting for me."

When Alice had gone, Rachel turned to her husband. "I can't tell you how relieved I am. I've been worried to death ever since we got here about what would happen when I ran into her. Even if she didn't say something really nasty to me, I thought she might cut me dead or not say anything at all." She shrugged. "I guess she's decided to let bygones be bygones."

Inside the house, Alice was telling Steve and Walter and Lenore about Rachel's apology. "And that's that," she concluded. "I've seen her and talked to her, and now I feel as if I can really start enjoying this party."

Sometime later Alice and Rachel ran into each other again—this time at the buffet table.

This time Alice initiated the conversation. "Ted seems very nice, Rachel."

Rachel beamed again. "He's not just nice. He's wonderful. He's gentle and thoughtful and sweet, and I'm sure he's going to do just marvelously in the restaurant business. You know, Alice, I can't tell you how good I feel about this—the fact that we can talk to each other just like anyone else. I was scared to death about it ever since we were invited here and knew you were going to be here too. I just didn't know what would happen when we met."

"I think," Alice said quietly, "you could have taken it for granted that I'd at least be polite."

Rachel's smile had faltered during her confession. Now she brightened again. "Well, I wasn't too sure. But you've been a lot more than polite. You've been really nice—not just to Ted, but to me, too, and I'd like you to know how much I appreciate it."

Alice smiled, too. "Well, I've been trying hard to forget about things, Rachel."

"I know. And I hope things work out for you and Steve. He really is a wonderful man. I always thought he was, but now, after what he did for us—Ted and me—"

Rachel broke off as Steve came over to get Alice to join him with some friends out on the terrace.

"Before you go," Rachel said, "I'd like to give you a message from my mother. Steve, I mean. I told her on the phone what you've done for Ted and me, and she said to tell you it's just wonderful."

Alice looked puzzled. "What did Steven do?"

"Why, Ted's new restaurant," Rachel said. She turned to Steve. "I know I thanked you once, but I wanted to do it again. Ted had given up on it. There it was. Exactly the kind of restaurant he was hoping to run someday, only he couldn't raise the money to buy it." She turned back to include Alice in her remarks. "And then Steve came along and said, okay, I'll lend you the money."

Alice looked so stunned that Rachel's bright little

smile faded. "Did I say something wrong?" she asked.

Steve was pretty stunned herself. "You said something that's no help at all, that's for sure, Rachel."

Rachel looked from one to the other of them. "I didn't mean to blurt out anything I shouldn't have." She wrung her hands. "Please, Alice. You must believe me."

"All right, all right," Alice said through lips that hardly moved. "I do believe you. All you did was tell the truth."

"But I wouldn't have said anything at all if I didn't think you knew already. I mean—"

Steve cut in. "There's no need of going over and over it. If there's any fault here, it's mine."

"That's right, Rachel," Alice said.

Rachel shook her head vigorously. "Oh, no. No, you don't understand. Steve hasn't done anything wrong, Alice."

"Rachel," Alice said, "I don't think Steven needs a defense from you."

"That's right," Steve said. "Drop it, Rachel."

"But I can't," Rachel countered, wide-eyed. "I caused trouble I didn't mean to. Listen to me. I'm married to Ted now. I want things to go nicely. With Russ engaged to Ted's sister, I want things to be fine, so if you'll just listen, so that you'll know—"

Steve cut in again. "That you didn't mean any harm. Yes, you said that. Let's just drop it."

"It's more than not meaning harm," Rachel persisted. "I want Alice to understand that what you did—my goodness—it was nice and good, not bad."

"Rachel," Steve said, almost at the end of his patience, "Alice can make up her own mind about things."

But still Rachel wouldn't give up. "Alice, listen. I was sure Steve had told you he'd financed Ted. So he hadn't told you yet, and I shouldn't have mentioned it. But the big point is it was just a business deal."

"I'm happy to see Steven is making good business deals," Alice said coldly. "He's always been very clever at that. I'm sure he'll continue to prosper."

"You've got to listen, Alice," Rachel said. "Steve isn't the only one who financed Ted, you know. I mean, I didn't tell you that, but my father put in money, too."

"Fine," Alice said. "Now why don't we all go our separate ways?"

"Alice," Rachel pleaded, "Ted is a very good restaura— However you say it. I mean, he knows how to run a restaurant, and he has very good ideas."

"That's right, Rachel," Steve said, "and it's irrelevant to what's happening here." He tried to signal her to leave, but Rachel went right on.

"My father knows the restaurant business."

Alice turned to her. "I really don't want to talk about it."

Steve also turned to her. "This is between Alice and me."

Rachel looked from one to the other. "But it was what I said that got everybody upset."

At that moment Pat came up to the table, and Alice turned to her. "Is there anything I can do, Pat?"

Pat smiled. "No, Alice. Stay with Steve."

"Stay with Steve," Alice parroted. "No, thank you very much. Staying with Steve and with Rachel is precisely what I don't want to do." And she walked out of the room.

Rachel started to follow her, but Steve grabbed her and told her to stay out of it. Then he took off after Alice.

He caught up with her on the terrace. Taking her to a deserted corner of it, he tried to explain. "Listen, Alice, with everything there is between you and me—"

She interrupted him. "All there is between you and me is Rachel and Jamie and what happened in the past. Now please leave me alone."

Alice turned to leave, but he wouldn't let her. "You won't even let me explain what Rachel meant?"

"I know what Rachel meant. I'm not sure what you mean."

"I hoped you'd say you trust me—that you know I wouldn't do anything to hurt you—ever."

He tried to get her to look at him, but she wouldn't. "I find that hard to believe right now," she said.

"Alice, don't turn me away because I was foolish enough to want to find the right place and the right time to tell you."

Now she did look at him. "Why must you always have the perfect time and the perfect place?"

"Because I love you. Because I want everything to be right for us."

"Everything doesn't work out just the way you want it," she said. "Rachel has seen to that."

"Alice, if you'd let me explain."

"I don't want to talk about it, do you understand?"

It was a rhetorical question, but he answered it anyway. "No," he said, "I don't understand."

But it was no use. She wouldn't talk about it or let him explain what he had done and why. She turned and walked away from him, and a few minutes later she slipped out of the party and went home alone.

Chapter Twenty=four

THE next morning at breakfast Alice told her parents what had happened at the party. To her surprise, her father defended what Steve had done.

"Steve is a businessman," Jim said. "He must get involved in all kinds of projects."

Alice frowned at him. "But why would he want to help Ted and Rachel?"

"Darling," her father answered, "he may feel that now that Ted is Jamie's stepfather, he should help him get on his feet." Mary had gone to the stove to get the coffeepot, and he held his cup out for her to fill. "Or that may have had nothing to do with it. Businessmen often invest money in projects for people they have no personal interest in."

Alice also held her cup out to her mother. "But Steven has a personal interest in Rachel."

There was an awkward pause as Jim and Mary exchanged glances. Each started to say something, then apparently thought better of it, and it was Alice who finally broke the silence.

"I said I didn't blame Rachel. For saying what she did last night. I don't think she was deliberately trying to make trouble. At least, she didn't give me that impression. But the thing is, why should Steven have hidden it from me?" She answered her own question. "Because he knew I wouldn't have liked his doing what he did. And wouldn't have approved of it if I'd been asked." Alice had picked up her cup to drink some coffee. Now she put the cup back in its saucer and buried her face in her hands. "I don't want Rachel back in our lives."

Again Jim and Mary exchanged glances.

"Honey," Jim said, "if she's the mother of Steven's child, I'm afraid she is in his life."

Alice took her hands away from her face and looked at her father. "I was hoping it wouldn't be that way."

Her father looked back at her. "Would you love a man who abandoned his responsibilities to his own child?"

"That's not a fair question, Dad. I've said all along I think Steven should be responsible for Jamie. And not just be responsible for him financially. Spend time with him. Care about him. But this isn't that at all. I don't want Steven going into business deals with Rachel and then hiding it from me."

Jim picked up his coffee cup and drained it. "Rachel and Ted are his son's family."

For the first time Mary spoke. "You can't expect him not to care what happens to Jamie's family, can you?"

Alice sighed. "I don't know what I expect any more. No matter how much Steven says Rachel doesn't mean anything to him any more, he's bound to her through Jamie." She turned to her mother. "That's what you've been trying to tell me ever since I came home from France, isn't it?"

"Yes, darling," Mary admitted.

Alice sighed again. "I thought I was aware of all the complications. But I don't think I really understood what they would mean until last night. Last night brought them home to me rather forcefully, I'm afraid." She picked up a piece of toast and started to butter it, then put the toast back on the plate. "I guess I've been hoping they'd go away all by themselves."

"That's a futile kind of hope," her father said.

Alice nodded. "I know. Like chasing will-o'-the-wisps."

For a few moments nobody said anything; then her mother spoke. "And what are you going to do now?"

"I don't know. I thought I had just about made up my mind, and then this happened." Alice shook her head. "Why do things have to be so difficult? Why can't we have a simple life together, Steven and I, without the problems of the past?"

Neither Jim nor Mary answered her—maybe because neither of them had an answer.

"I just wish," Alice continued, "that Rachel wasn't here in Bay City, where she's a constant reminder."

"This is one complication you may be facing all your life, my dear," her mother said. "If you marry Steven."

"I know," Alice acknowledged. "More than ever now, I know."

After her gaffe at the engagement party, Rachel was afraid that Steve would change his mind and not back Ted after all, but Steve set her fears at rest when he came to see Jamie the next afternoon for his regular weekly visit.

Relieved, Rachel offered to explain the whole thing once again to Alice, but that was the last thing in the world Steve wanted. "Stay away from Alice," he warned her. "Whatever is wrong between us is nobody's fault but mine, and since I'm the one who got myself into this, I'm the one who's going to have to get myself out of it."

But in fact it was Walter Curtin who got Steve out of it.

Walter and Lenore invited Alice over for dinner, and as soon as they were all settled on the patio with pre-dinner drinks, Walter said to Alice, "Why do you think Steve helped finance Ted?"

Alice shrugged. "Because of Jamie, I suppose. And because Rachel was after him to do it, maybe. I don't know."

"Well, I do know," Walter said. "Sure he did it for Jamie. And as far as Rachel is concerned, he feels some guilt, I guess. Any man who fathers an illegitimate child and then refuses to marry the mother is bound to feel some guilt, wouldn't you think?"

"I guess so."

"Oh, Alice," Lenore said, "I'm sure of it. And so would you be if you weren't personally involved."

Alice looked at Lenore, then nodded. "All right. Okay. So he feels some guilt. I can understand that. But—"

Walter put up a hand. "Let me finish. Or continue, at any rate. Then there's the business side of it. Steve looked into the restaurant and decided it was a good business venture—that the restaurant is a sound one with good prospects."

Alice nodded again. "Dad mentioned that aspect of it."

"Well," Walter said, "your father's a businessman too. I'd expect him to see that side of it. But the big thing, Alice—the important thing, after all that's been granted—is that he did this for you."

Alice stared at him. "For me? How can you possibly think that?"

"I can think it because it's true. Look, Alice. What's kept you and Steve apart all this time?"

"Rachel," Alice answered without hesitation. "Mostly Rachel and what she did."

Walter nodded. "And what she might do if you and Steve got married. Isn't that right?"

"Yes," Alice agreed. "All along I've been afraid

of the way she'd crowd Steve. Wheedle him and ask him for things."

"Especially money," Lenore put in, and Walter nodded again in agreement.

"Yes," Alice said. "Especially money. Rachel may have changed somewhat since her marriage to Ted, but she can't have changed that much."

"All right," Walter said. "We're all agreed on that. So now consider something you obviously haven't considered up to now. If Ted made a go of his restaurant, what excuse could Rachel have to come around and ask Steve for anything more? Don't you see? Steve was looking ahead to what it would be like when you and he were married. He was trying to fix it so Rachel would be out of your hair. For good. Financing Ted was an act of love for you."

Alice looked from him to Lenore. "It's true, Alice," Lenore said.

Alice looked back to Walter. "I never thought of it that way. But now that— Oh, dear. Lenore, may I use your phone?"

Lenore smiled. "Of course. Ask him to join us for dinner."

"Well, I—"

"Walter and I will make ourselves scarce for a few minutes after he gets here. Long enough for you to say whatever you have to say."

Alice smiled—her radiant smile of old. "All right." Then she flew into the house to call Steve.

When Steve arrived, he and Alice walked down to the end of the garden in the Curtins' back yard, and he told her what Walter had already told her—as to why he had decided to back Ted in the restaurant.

"I wanted to tell you," he added, "but I wanted to wait for exactly the right moment."

"And when would that have been?" she asked.

"I don't know. I guess when you were a little more relaxed about Rachel. Convinced she wasn't going to be a threat to us."

Alice frowned. "Do you think I feel she is?"

He smiled. "If you don't, then why were you so upset?"

"All right," she agreed. "But it wasn't only that. It was because you didn't tell me what you'd done. You didn't trust me to understand."

"And would you have understood?"

She didn't answer him immediately. "I think so," she said at last.

He took her hands in his. "Well, I said the other night it was a mistake. It's funny. All my life I've taken long chances, but the one thing I was afraid to gamble on was anything that has anything to do with us, because I love you too much."

"And I love you, Steven."

She moved toward him, and he took her in his arms and kissed her.

Finally she broke away to say "I've been wanting you to do that for days."

He searched her face. "Does that mean you've forgiven me?"

"I'm the one who needs to be forgiven, Steven. For not believing in you. For not giving you a chance to explain."

"No," he said. "What happened was my fault. When you called me a little while ago, I was afraid you were going to tell me it was all over—that we shouldn't see each other again."

"I couldn't do that even if I wanted to," she said. "Every day since that party has been like a nightmare to me. Even if Walter hadn't talked to me—even if you hadn't explained—I don't think I could have gone on much longer without you."

Later that evening, when Walter and Steve were off together at one end of the living room, looking at something, Lenore took Alice out to the kitchen to talk to her. It had been obvious to all of them through drinks and dinner that the lovebirds were reconciled, but Lenore wanted to know more than that. She wanted to know precisely how Alice felt about Steve.

Alice smiled. "I adore him, if you want to know." Then she sobered. "I've made a little progress, Lenore. I really have."

Lenore raised her eyebrows. "Meaning . . . ?"

"We were apart all too long after the engagement

party. I know I don't want to be apart from him again. I'm just going to have to remember about Rachel and about Jamie—remember that that's what drove us apart. And see that it doesn't happen again. I think I've come to grips with the fact that Jamie is important in Steve's life—and that Rachel is Jamie's mother, and we'll have to deal with her."

"You said 'we,' " Lenore remarked.

"I mean Steven and I."

"Oh, I knew who you were referring to," Lenore said. "It was your use of the pronoun that intrigued me. When you're thinking and talking that way, I'd say you're really answering the question I asked you." She smiled. "So, Alice, let me know when you and Steven name the date."

Later still, when Steve was driving Alice home, she said, "I'm not going to be silly again, Steven."

He glanced at her. "What do you mean by silly?"

"I mean I'm not going to imagine things. I'm going to let you explain things. When you call me and leave a message, I'm going to call you back right away. I'm going to acknowledge that the things in your life are things in your life, and I'm not going to get in the way of them."

He glanced at her again and smiled. "Alice, you're moving a long way toward me tonight, the way you're talking. Do you know that?"

She nodded. "Yes, I know that."

"We also have some lost time to make up for."

"I know that, too."

He pulled up in front of her parents' house and cut the engine. "May I see you tomorrow night?"

Now that he was free of driving, she moved closer to him, and he put his arm around her. "Tomorrow night and every night you want to," she said.

"Then every night it is." He hit the steering wheel with his free hand. "I forgot. Thursday night is out. I have to go to the opening of Ted's restaurant. Or at least I'm supposed to go."

"I think you should go," Alice said. "Considering you helped him buy it."

"I know," Steve said, "but I'd rather be with you."

She smiled up at him. "I wonder why you didn't think of asking me whether I'd like to go with you."

He stared at her. "Go with me? To Rachel's husband's restaurant? Rachel will be there."

Alice shrugged. "If you don't want me there, I understand. It's all right with me."

"That's not the point. I didn't think you'd want to be there."

"If you're going, then I'd love to go with you." She smiled again. "Wherever you are is where I'd like to be."

"Rachel or no Rachel?"

She nodded. "Rachel or no Rachel."

"Well, hallelujah," he said, and took her in his arms and kissed her, then gave her a big bear hug.

At the opening Rachel was graciousness itself—both to Alice and Steve and to Russ and Cindy. Of all of them, Steve was the most nervous. He probably had the most reason to be. But the evening went off without a hitch.

"What are you doing Saturday morning?" Steve asked Alice as he was driving her home.

"Putting my hair up in curlers, I expect."

"Will you go on a picnic with me around noon?"

"A picnic? Where to?"

"Out in the country."

"Where out in the country?" she wanted to know.

"Just out in the country." He smiled at her. "It seems to me—of course, my memory could be faulty —but it seems to me something was said only a couple of nights ago about trust."

She smiled back at him. "That's right. You were supposed to trust me."

He sighed an exaggerated sigh. "My memory is faulty, then."

"So where out in the country?"

But he wouldn't say. "Come with me on Saturday, and you'll find out."

Each time Steve had visited Alice in Avignon, he had spoken of the surprise he had for her when she returned to Bay City, but since her return he had said nothing more about it, although the surprise—

the house he had designed and built for her—was finished and had been for some time.

He explained why one day to Walter after telling Walter that he hadn't shown the house to Alice yet.

"I'm not going to show it to her or tell her about it. She still hasn't made up her mind whether she wants to marry me or not. And while it's her house— I mean, no matter what she decides to do, I've built it for her with no strings attached—I'm afraid if I showed it to her now, she might think I was trying to pressure her."

Now he felt the time had come to give Alice her surprise. Thus the Saturday-morning picnic.

As they pulled up to the property late Saturday morning and Steve brought the car to a stop, Alice looked around her. "Why are we stopping here?" she asked. "It doesn't seem exactly like the place for a picnic."

"Patience, darling, patience. Will you hand me the picnic basket, please?"

She did so, and they got out of the car. Once again Alice looked around her—more dubiously than before. "Steven, this is all private land. Or it looks as if it is, anyhow. It probably belongs to whoever owns that house over there."

"That's who it probably belongs to all right."

She stood looking at it. "It's a beautiful house."

And it was, even from a distance. A two-story white frame house in the Colonial style, it stood at the top of a small rise. A circular drive led to and away from it in the front. In back was a flagstone terrace, and along one side meandered a small brook. The grounds around the house had been landscaped to blend with the small woods that began at the rear of the back yard.

Alice turned from looking at the house to Steve. "But what are we doing here?"

He beckoned her over to the shade of a tall maple tree. It was a hot morning at the end of August, but it was measurably cooler under the tree. "I stopped here, Alice," he said, "because I want to talk to you."

They had brought a blanket along, and now he

spread that on the grass and set the picnic basket down at one corner of it. "Come," he said. "Sit down."

She sat down, and he sat down beside her.

"It couldn't wait another second," he continued. "This is very definitely the time for me to say what I have to say." He was grinning, and his voice had an ebullient tone to it. He cocked his head at her. "You know why this is the proper time?"

She shook her head.

"Then I'll tell you. Number one, it's a glorious day. Number two, it's the first free day I've had in a long, long time. Number three, you're here beside me. Number four, there's a bottle of wine in that picnic basket."

"Oh ho!" Alice exclaimed. "Is that why you said you'd take care of the picnic? I hope there's food there, too."

"I'll have you know, madame, we have the finest roast beef and Swiss cheese sandwiches you'll ever taste."

"For breakfast?" she said in mock alarm.

"Breakfast, lunch, or dinner. Now where was I? Oh, yes. Number—whatever number it is now—I feel wonderful because I'm in love with you. And I know you're in love with me."

For answer she leaned over and kissed him.

"Alice," he said, all seriousness now, "I want you to marry me."

She, too, turned serious. "You mean you want an answer today, don't you?"

He nodded.

"Steven, you know very well there are problems."

"Rachel?"

"She's one problem, yes."

He nodded again. "And, more to the point, Jamie."

"He's your son. As I said the other night, I don't want to get in the way of your obligations. But the very fact of it might get in our way, Steven."

"Only if we let it," he said. "Alice, why don't you let me deal with it? You do love me, don't you?"

"You know I do."

"Then trust me to take care of anything I have to take care of. To keep us together and happy. Forever."

She put a hand against his cheek. "Steven, when you talk like that I believe you can deal with anything."

"Darling," he answered, "when you trust me I can deal with everything, I'm sure. Just look at us. You love me, and the day is beautiful, and I've asked you to marry me, and you're going to say yes." He took the hand she had put against his face and kissed the palm of it. "You *are* going to say yes, aren't you?"

"Oh, Steven," she said tremulously, "yes, yes, yes."

He took her face between his hands and kissed her —very gently, very tenderly—then pulled her to him and kissed her with passion, until they both broke away simultaneously to stare in wonder at each other.

He stood up and held a hand down to her. "Come on, I want to show you something." Taking her outstretched hand, he pulled her to her feet, and they started walking to the house.

"Show me what?" she said.

"You'll see." They were walking up one side of the driveway. Now he led her across the grass to the flagstone terrace at the back.

"I still think we shouldn't be here," Alice said. "I wouldn't like to get shot at for trespassing."

"I think they have to warn you first. Or post a sign or something. Well, now who's getting curious?"

She had stopped to peer in one of the large picture windows at the side. "It isn't even finished," she said. "Or at least there isn't anything in it. It must be brand new."

"It does look that, yeah."

"Oh, and, Steven, look at that fireplace." She drew her breath in. "I've never seen anything so magnificent."

"You like it, then?"

"It's beautiful."

The terrace was raised, and he led her up the two steps to it and to the low stone fence that bordered it on three sides. They sat down on the fence.

"I want to talk to you," he said. "I want to tell you how it's been for me since you left Bay City and went off to France. It left me here lonely for you, thinking of you all the time, and planning."

She gave him a quizzical look. "Planning?"

"I had to plan, Alice. After all, planning is my profession. I plan in my business all the time. The only thing is that in this case I didn't plan very sensibly."

"Steven," Alice said, looking bewildered now, "I don't have any idea of what you're getting at."

"You will. I made no plans for what I would do if you didn't come back. Or if you came back, but not to me. I had no plans for that. I don't know what I would have done if it had worked out that way."

"Well, it didn't work out that way," she said, putting a hand on his arm. "I came back, and I'm going to marry you."

He covered her hand with his. "That's what I dreamed of."

"And what you planned? Is that what you've been trying to say?"

"Yes. But not just that. In more detail."

She was back to looking bewildered.

"Is it all right with you," he went on, "if we get married very soon?"

"I'd much prefer it. I don't think I can stand very much more waiting, Steven."

"Good," he said. "And when we've set the date, perhaps then, Alice, perhaps you'd like to unlock the door of this house, and wander through the rooms." He took a key out of his pocket and put it in her hand. "That's what I've been trying to tell you. That's what I dreamed about when you were away. And I made my dreams come true. I built this house for you."

She stared from him to the house to the key in her hand and back at the house again. And back to him. "You built this house? You built this house for me?"

He nodded. "Yes, I did. But something else I never planned was what I'd do if you decided you didn't want it. I certainly wouldn't have liked the idea of anybody else ever living here."

She still had an incredulous look on her face. "Steven—this house—it will be ours?"

"It's yours."

She stood up and looked at the house again from where she stood. Then she ran to the back door and peered in through the window next to it, touching the window frame as if caressing it.

"Do you want to go in?" he asked.

She spun around to him. "Yes!"

He joined her at the back door, and she unlocked it, and they went inside. Immediately inside the back door was a small room for removing muddy boots and shoes and leaving rainwear and umbrellas. Beyond that was the kitchen—bright and airy and large. And though it gave the impression of being old-fashioned, it was complete with every modern appliance and convenience.

"And, oh, the cupboards!" Alice exclaimed. "How did you know I love cupboards?" She went from one to the next, opening doors, pulling out drawers. "Oh, Steven."

And that was mostly what she said throughout the tour of the house: "Oh, Steven."

A center hall divided the front of the house and gave onto a wide, sweeping stairway. To the left of the hall was a formal dining room, and to the right was the living room, with a massive fireplace and floor-to-ceiling windows.

Upstairs were four rooms—three bedrooms and a study for Steven. And all around the house, upstairs and down, was a view of the countryside: the woods in back, the small stream along one side of the house, the graceful driveway in front bordered by small flowering shrubs.

Back outside again on the terrace, Alice said, "Can we get married here? Here on the terrace?"

"We can get married wherever you want," he said.

She gave him a radiant smile. "Then it will be here. Oh, Steven, how can I ever thank you?"

"Very simply," he said. "By marrying me."

When Alice returned home from the picnic she told her parents about the house and that she and Steven would be married there the third week in September. Jim and Mary each embraced her and wished her happiness, but when she had gone upstairs to change her clothes Mary admitted she still had reservations about the marriage.

Jim tried to reassure her. "Mary, it's all in the past. Jamie now has a stepfather who's apparently a fine young man. He can take Steve's place in the child's affections."

Mary wasn't convinced. "You neglect one thing," she countered. "Steve's feeling for that child. He's not simply going to turn Jamie over to Ted Clark and forget about him."

"No, I suppose not," Jim admitted.

"And," Mary continued, "do you think for a minute Rachel is ever going to forget who the real father is?"

"Well, of course not, but I don't see what that's got to do—"

Mary didn't let him finish. "Do you think she's going to let Steve forget he's the father?" She shook her head. "There's Steve—torn between his love for Alice and his loyalty to Jamie and constantly badgered by Rachel. You ought to know Rachel better than that."

"Maybe you're right. But everybody says how Rachel has changed since she married Ted. And she does seem different, even to me."

Myra gave him a withering look. "You always were soft on Rachel. And I don't believe in this so-called change. Not for all the tea in China. You wait. You'll see. Remember, Steve is very rich, and Rachel won't forget that. Every time something goes wrong she'll call on him. And if something doesn't go wrong all by itself, she'll see to it that it does. And don't think she won't. And how will Alice feel about that?"

"Mary," Jim said, "you're talking about things that both Alice and Steve are both aware of—and have been for a long time now. Why don't you let them work it out?"

Early the following week Alice stopped by Steve's

office to invite him to come to dinner that night at her parents' house. He was reluctant, saying that Mary was uncomfortable with him.

"Darling," Alice rejoined, "she'll welcome you into the family. I want you to get to know her as I do. She's always been the most generous, most loving mother anyone could wish for. And not just to me, but to all of us."

Steve shook his head. "You think I don't know that? Someone who's never had the kind of family you have realizes how special yours is as soon as he sees it. And envies it." He smiled. "Alice, will you tell your mother something for me? I'm marrying you, and that matters more to me than anything in the world, but in marrying you I'm becoming a member of your family. Tell her I think nothing nicer than that could ever happen to me."

"You can tell her yourself," Alice said. "Tonight at six."

That night after dinner—a dinner at which Mary had done her best to put Steve at his ease—they drew up the wedding list, and Mary asked Steve about his family.

He was reticent, saying only that both his parents were dead and that although he would write his brothers and sister and tell them he was going to be married, he doubted that any of them would want to come to the ceremony. "I'm afraid we aren't much of a family," he said. "We have very little to do with one another."

Mary found that odd but said nothing.

She would have found something that was taking place in another household at that same moment considerably odder.

"Steve and Alice are engaged," Ada said to Rachel.

Rachel's eyes flew wide. "No kidding, Mom? They really are?"

"Yes," Ada said dryly, "they really are. Why should that surprise you so?"

Rachel shrugged. "I knew Alice was crazy about Steve, but she couldn't seem to make up her mind whether she really wanted to marry him or not. And I didn't think she ever would."

"Well, she's going to—on the terrace of a house he built for her out in the country. Over toward Danville."

"A house? He built a house for her?"

"That's right."

"I never heard anything about it."

"Why should you?" her mother said. "It's no concern of yours. And anyhow, he kept it a secret. He wanted to surprise her. Mary Matthews showed me some pictures of it. It's gorgeous."

"If Steve had it built, I'm sure it would be." She smiled. "I think it's just marvelous they're getting married. I hope they'll be very happy."

Ada had as much trouble believing that as Alice's mother would have. "Do you really mean that, Rachel?"

"Yes, of course I do. I have Ted now, and he's all I want. In fact, as soon as Ted makes a go of the restaurant and pays Steve back the money he put into it, we'll never have to think about him or have anything more to do with him—ever."

Ada gave Rachel a long look—and a searching one. "When you talk like that, Rachel," she said at last, "it makes me wonder."

Rachel shrugged again. "You can wonder if you want to, Mom. I stopped wondering when I married Ted."

"And what about Jamie?" Ada asked.

"What about him? After Steve and Alice are married, she'll see to it that Steve has as little to do with his son as possible. You can count on that."

That, at least, sounded more like Rachel.

Later that same evening, alone with Alice on the Matthewses' front porch, Steve asked her about a ring.

"I don't want another engagement ring," she said. "We both want to forget we were engaged before and how that ended, don't we?"

He agreed to that.

"Can't we just have traditional gold bands?" she went on. "Very plain, very simple."

"Okay," he said. "One for you and one for me."

"We can pick them out tomorrow if you want to," Alice said. "There's a jewelry store on Main Street where I saw a whole tray of gold bands in different widths." She smiled. "Good, honest gold bands."

Steve smiled too. A sardonic smile. "Yeah. My mother had one of those good, honest gold bands. It was the only piece of jewelry she ever had. She never even owned a wristwatch, and here I am—"

Alice cut in on him. "Steven, don't make yourself suffer for things you can't help."

"I guess it was your mother asking about the wedding invitations that got me started thinking about my parents and the rest of the family." He shook his head. "My brothers and sisters are all scattered now. I'm not even sure where some of them are. I guess you could say I abandoned them. Certainly I've never seen any of them since I left home." He shook his head again. "Some family you're marrying into."

"Steven, it's you I love. It's you I'm marrying. Not your family. No matter who your family is or where any of your brothers and sister are, it's you I love."

The next evening Alice came home with the ring she had bought for Steve. Showing it to her mother, she said, "You should have seen him at lunch today. He was like a little boy." She laughed. "He tried to act tough, but he was so sweet. He said he was such a bungler, he didn't know a thing about weddings, and he was afraid he'd do something wrong."

"Did you remind him he'll have a chance to rehearse everything first?" Mary asked.

"Yes. And I told him about some of the wedding ceremonies I'd seen in Avignon. They weren't off-beat —just simplified. Beautifully dignified. I liked them a lot. They exchanged the vows very simply and directly. And there was no processional or recessional."

"And is that what you're planning for Steven and yourself?"

Alice nodded. "More or less. At least we'd like to make it our own ceremony. So it won't be the usual service. Well, some of it will be the same, of course."

"I'm glad to hear that," her mother said. "I think I'd like just a touch of convention, but then, maybe I'm hopelessly old-fashioned."

Alice smiled and gave her mother a little hug. "All Steven and I want is a marriage as good as yours and Dad's, that's all."

"And that's all your father and I want for you, darling. But you are starting out with a problem we never had."

"I know," Alice acknowledged, "but Steven has promised to solve that problem, Mother, and I know he will. I know he will."

Shopping with her sister, Pat, for her wedding clothes, Alice recounted the conversation with their mother. "All you're doing," Pat remarked, "is joining the club. John and I started with problems. Walter and Lenore started with problems. And I bet Mom and Dad did, too. She just doesn't remember, that's all."

Planning for the wedding, getting the invitations out, shopping for wedding gowns and a trousseau, going to showers, getting presents, the bride buying her gift for the groom, the groom buying his gift for the bride . . . so the days went by, and almost before anyone realized it, the wedding day was upon them. September 23. The day Alice Matthews was finally going to marry Steven Frame.

Chapter Twenty-five

THE wedding day dawned bright and clear—a mild September day, still more like summer than fall.

Early that afternoon Walter Curtin, in his role as best man, stopped by to pick up Steve and drive him to the wedding. Steve admitted to being a nervous wreck.

"You're a man now putting away childish things," Walter commented. "That's enough to make anybody nervous." He smiled. "You're starting to make sense of your life—real sense. And you can only do that with the woman you love. That's what it's all about, I think."

"Is it?" Steve asked.

Walter shrugged. "What other security is there?"

There was nothing particularly surprising in the fact that Steve was nervous. Or that Alice was, either. But Rachel was also nervous. And despite the fact that she was not invited to the wedding—nor had she been included in any of the pre-wedding parties—she was perfectly aware of what was taking place today.

"Do you think Ted and I should have sent a present?" she asked her mother.

"It depends on how you and Ted feel about Alice and Steve," Ada answered. "I got them a present."

Rachel was at her mother's house, having a cup of coffee with her in the kitchen. Now she got up from the table and went to stare out the back window. "I wish them all kinds of happiness," she said in a bleak-sounding voice. "And I know Ted does, too."

After a few moments she turned to face her mother, a smile on her face. A rather forced smile. "Ted is such a wonderful person, Mom. There's just no comparison."

Ada raised her eyebrows. "Comparison with Russ or comparison with Steve?"

Rachel turned back to the window. "Oh, why are you bugging me? Today of all days."

"Honey, I'm not bugging you. Today two people you tried to break up are getting married."

"So? I told you, I want them to be happy." She was still staring out the window.

"I remember not too long ago," Ada went on, "you wanted to marry Steve yourself."

"Well, sure," Rachel said, coming back to the table and sitting down again. "When I was pregnant with

Jamie. Wouldn't any woman feel the same? Wanting to marry her baby's father?"

"Not if she was married to another man at the time. And it wasn't just when you were pregnant with Jamie that you wanted to marry Steve. You wanted to marry him afterward as well. Even when he made it clear to you he wasn't interested and never would be."

"Never is a long time," Rachel said.

"Meaning?"

Rachel sniffed. "Meaning nothing. Anyhow, everything is different now. I'm not going to do bad things any more. I've changed. I've been different ever since I met Ted and he asked me to marry him. He loves me a lot, and he's good to me."

"Russ loved you a lot and was good to you."

"Russ never needed me. Not the way Ted does."

Her mother gave her a skeptical look. "And is that what's made the difference?"

"That's right." The famous chin went up. "If it wasn't for Ted and the way he feels about me and the way I feel about him, I'd be nothing. Like I used to be. Leading that kind of dumb life and doing all the dumb things everybody hated me for. That they still hate me for. But all that's over now. It is. It is."

Ada said nothing. And believed nothing. Whatever she might hope, did hope, she would wait and see what came to pass.

Out at the new house in the country—upstairs in the bedroom she would share with Steven—Alice was getting dressed for the wedding, and Pat was helping her.

"Just think," Pat said. "This time tomorrow you'll be on the beach at St. Croix with your husband."

"Mmm." Alice pulled her wedding gown over her head and turned to Pat so she could zip it up the back. Then she turned to face her sister. "How does it look?"

Pat beamed. "Beautiful."

Although Alice and Steve had planned a contemporary wedding ceremony, Alice's wedding gown was traditional. Made of white crepe, it had long sleeves and a flowing, floor-length skirt. The bodice was fitted and covered with tiny seed pearls, and the neckline was heart-shaped and accented by a pearl necklace—the groom's gift to the bride.

"It seems foolish, doesn't it," Alice said, "to spend so much money on a gown I'll wear for maybe an hour."

Pat beamed again. "But what an hour."

Mary came in with the bridal bouquet—white chrysanthemums and daisies—and a companion bouquet of yellow chrysanthemums and daisies for Pat, Alice's only attendant. "Darling," she said to Alice, "you look lovely."

Alice sighed. "I wish I felt lovely. I feel funny. Like this is all happening to somebody else, and I'm on the outside looking in."

"That's the same way I felt on my wedding day," Pat said. "Mom too, I bet."

Mary nodded. "That's right. And so does almost every bride. At least, every one I ever heard of. Here, Alice, let me help you with the veil."

"I don't know why it is," Alice said, "but I keep thinking of the night of our engagement party. And Rachel coming to my room with her little bombshell."

"Well, she's not coming with any bombshell today," Pat said firmly. "She's not coming period."

Now Jim joined them. "Alice, my darling," he said, smiling, "you look positively radiant."

Alice sighed. "I don't feel radiant."

"She feels funny," Pat said. "Like every other bride there ever was."

Alice shook her head. "No. More than that. It's all the problems. I can't seem to get them out of my mind."

Her father took her by the arm. "Then you'll simply have to put them out," he said. "There's no room for them now. You're beginning a new life."

"I know that," Alice told him.

He patted her hand and smiled at her. "And you're going to be happier than you've ever been before, Alice. You'll see." He turned to Mary and Pat. "You two had better get on down to the terrace, or you'll miss the wedding. I was sent up here to fetch the bride."

And, indeed, drifting up to them from the terrace below, came the pre-wedding music, played by a string trio.

After a final smoothing of her own gown—a pale yellow chiffon—Pat took her mother by the arm, and they went downstairs to join the others. In a couple of minutes Jim and Alice started down the stairs.

Because there was no processional, as such—just Alice and her father coming out to the terrace together—Walter and Steve and Pat approached the space for the ceremony from the side and waited there for Alice to join them.

When she had, the minister stepped forward and began to read the ceremony that Alice and Steven had written for him.

"Alice," he said, looking at her. "Steven," he continued, looking at him. "Surrounded as we are here by the beauty of God's nature, and by those we most love, let us turn our hearts and minds to the two before us, who wish to bind their lives together in peace and in love.

"Our world is not an easy one. We have much pain to answer for from day to day, and we have tragedy that seems to strip us of all hope again and again. But we are together through all of this in love. As it has been said, no man is an island entire of itself. Every man is a piece of the continent and a part of the main. We are involved in all mankind, and each time two people come together before God to bind their lives as one, it is a reaffirmation for all mankind—a reaffirmation of human faith and courage.

"The human heart is boundless and God's love for us eternal, imperfect as we are. The courage to love is the greatest of all mankind's strengths—and the most difficult. And now we have Steven and Alice before us, who wish to take their place among those who have said yes to living, yes to the hard task of loving, yes to all the best that mankind stands for.

"Steven, do you love this woman?"

"With all my heart," he answered.

The minister turned to Alice. "And, Alice, do you love this man?"

"Yes, I do," she answered. "Very much."

"Steven, will you care for Alice with gentleness and strength and understanding—to the very best of your own human capabilities?"

"I will."

"Alice, will you match Steven's gentleness with gentleness, his strength with your own strength, his understanding with yours—to the very best of your own human capabilities?"

"Yes, I will."

"And will each of you deal with each other honestly and with compassion?"

Both of them answered that they would.

"And leave room for joy to flower in your growing love?"

Again they answered in the affirmative.

The minister looked out at the assembled guests, then looked down at the paper he was reading from. "I see no reason before God or man that these two young people should not be joined in marriage. If any man or woman feels strongly otherwise, let him speak now or forever hold his peace."

If anyone was thinking of Rachel, nobody gave any indication of it.

The minister looked at Alice and Steven. "The rings, please."

The rings were produced by Walter as best man and Pat as matron of honor.

"With God as our witness," the minister intoned, "place the rings on each other's hands."

They did so.

"Since you love each other in your heart of hearts and have promised to help each other live and grow in wisdom and compassion, may God bless this union. With these rings, you, Alice, and you, Steven, bind your lives and loves together forever. I now pronounce you man and wife."

Steve and Alice turned to each other, looking at each other in that breathless way they had. Then he lifted her veil and kissed her, and the string trio struck up a merry little air.

And now everybody began to surge forward to congratulate the bride and groom. First were Jim and Mary.

"Welcome into the family, Steve," they both said, Jim shaking hands with him, Mary kissing him.

"Thank you both," he said, smiling, hugging Alice to him at his side. "I'll make her happy, I promise you that."

From the way she looked, he had already done so. She was radiant.

"Alice will never want for anything," Steve went on. "I mean love, first of all. But she'll have the security of a good home, too. I'm going to take care of her in every way I know how."

"I'm sure you will," Jim said, and turned to kiss his daughter. "All the happiness in the world, darling."

"Thanks, Dad."

And suddenly they were surrounded by family and friends, many of the women smiling through tears of wiping their eyes, everybody offering a kiss or a handshake.

And then, as the reception got under way, and champagne was served, Walter proffered the best man's toast.

"We've just seen two of our most favorite people tie the knot," he proclaimed with a broad smile. "They're beautiful. We love them. There's not too much to add to that ceremony. I think everything's been said, except to say we're here, we're your friends, we love you, and may your marriage be as truly happy as the ceremony that began it today."

Everyone applauded, the trio struck up a dance tune, the waiters finished clearing the last of the chairs off the terrace, and the bride and groom began to dance, followed shortly thereafter by other couples.

More toasts, more cheering, more applause, more dancing—and drinking and eating—and an hour or so later Steve and Alice drove off in a shower of rice.

That night, as they stood on the balcony of his house in St. Croix, looking at the starlight reflected in the Caribbean Sea—a sea so calm that night as to be almost silent—Alice squeezed Steve's hand. "How perfect everything is," she said.

He gave her hand an answering squeeze. "I want it to be that way for you always."

Alice smiled. "I think that's one of the reasons I love you so much. You always seem to be thinking about me and about what I'd like."

"Darling," he said, holding her close, "you're the most important thing in the world to me. You always have been, and you always will be."

"Oh, Steven," she said. "I love you so."

"And I you," he answered.

He bent to kiss her—a kiss that began with love and turned into passion as each began yearning for the other, their bodies trembling as they pressed together in an intensity of wanting—a need to seek, to take, to give, to surrender. But this time they didn't have to break away and stare at one another in breathless wonder. This time they could consummate both their love and their passion.

Afterward they lay in bed talking about their wedding and about the dream house Steven had built for Alice.

"I wouldn't have it different in any way," Alice said. "Only I wish I'd been there to help you plan it."

"It's still got to be furnished. I thought you'd like to do that yourself."

She smiled at him. "We'll do it together. I'd like to furnish it with antiques, I think. Except for the children's rooms. How many children shall we have, Steven? Two? Three?" In the half-light it seemed to her a shadow crossed his face. "Steven, what is it? What's wrong?"

"Nothing."

"Is it Jamie? Were you thinking about him because I was talking about children? Our children?"

Steve put an arm around her, drawing her close. "Darling, Jamie's no problem. I told you that before you married me. He may have been once, but he's not going to be ever again."

"All right," she said. "I believe you." She reached up and kissed him, then lay back in his arms. "Oh, Steven, it's so beautiful here. The sea and the beach and everything."

"It's one of my favorite places in the world," he said. "Beautiful and peaceful and serene." He held her close. "I want us to stay exactly as we are at this moment. Just the two of us alone together." He kissed her forehead. "Don't ever leave me, darling. I'm only half alive without you."

"I won't, Steven. I won't leave you."

"Promise?"

"I promise."

And once again, as starlight filled the room, and the sea below whispered against the shore, they made love.

Back in Bay City a storm was building, and as an angry wind tore against the trees outside, Rachel lay in bed unable to go to sleep, thinking about Steve and Alice being together in his house in St. Croix.

She was also thinking about the time last March— only six months ago—when Walter and Lenore were vacationing in Steve's house there, and Steve arrived at Rachel's apartment for his weekly visit to their son. Because Jamie had a cold at the time, Rachel had refused to go out and leave Ada in charge as she was supposed to do.

Explaining this to Steve, she said, "Jamie's still sleeping, and I don't want you to wake him up."

"What am I supposed to do in the meantime?" Steve retorted. "Sit around here with you?"

"Is that really so awful?" she asked.

"Yes," he said without hesitation.

Rachel sniffed. "That's not a very nice thing to say." He shrugged. "It happens to be true."

"And besides," she said, ignoring him, "there's something I want to talk to you about."

"Well?" he asked when she didn't go right on. "What is it?"

"It's about Walter and Lenore being in your house in St. Croix."

Again she waited, and again he said, "Well? What about it?"

She smiled. "I just thought of something. Your house down there is pretty big, isn't it? Don't you think it would be a marvelous idea if we flew down there some weekend soon—you and me and Jamie—and spent it with them?"

He was frowning at her. "I think it's a terrible idea. Forget it."

She persisted. "There's plenty of room in the house, Steve, and getting out in the sun would be the best thing in the world for Jamie's cold."

Steve shook his head. "You know, sometimes I think you're not all there in the head, Rachel. In the first place, if I don't even want you around when I come to see Jamie, why should I want to spend a whole weekend with you?"

"Well, it wouldn't really be with me. It would be with Jamie. And I bet Walter and Lenore would love it."

Steve made a face. "Walter and Lenore would hate it. They went down there to get away from everybody for a while."

"Well," Rachel said with another sniff, "I was thinking about Jamie more than anything. It's a crime his father should have a house down in the Virgin Islands and everybody should go down and use it except him."

"When he gets older I'll take him down there. Without you. And by the way, Rachel, I won't be here to see Jamie next week. I'm flying to France to see Alice."

Rachel frowned. "Why are you doing that? She just left here a few days ago."

"What business is that of yours?"

"I guess you didn't get very far with her while she was here, then, did you? I mean, she didn't stay very long, and I haven't heard anyone say she was coming back and marrying you or anything."

"I don't care what anybody said or didn't say," he answered. "I'll tell you this. I'd rather spend five minutes with Alice than be married to anybody else in the world. She's the only woman I have ever loved or ever will love."

Another gust of wind rattled the trees outside Rachel's bedroom window. She glanced over at her sleeping husband, tried once again to go to sleep, then with an impatient sigh threw back the covers on her side of the bed and got up, careful not to waken Ted. Slipping a robe on, she tiptoed out of the room and crossed the hall into Jamie's bedroom. He, too, was sleeping.

Looking down at him, she thought back to the night when he was conceived. It was the most thrilling night of her life—the night she had discovered what the word passion really meant. And love. That, too.

And Steve had made the very same discovery. She was as sure of that as she was that she was standing in this room looking down at their son. Steve's and hers.

For all the good it was doing her now.

Rachel's eyes filled with tears. *It wasn't fair that Alice should marry Steve, when Steve belonged not to Alice, but to her.*

The wind had increased in volume, and now, with a splatter and shake, the rain began. Rachel went to the window and stood looking at the storm raging outside.

She wiped her eyes with the back of her hand. *Crying didn't help. It never had, and it never would.*

If you wanted something to happen, you had to make it happen. She had done it before. She could do it again. And not only could, but would.

So let Steve have his precious honeymoon with his precious Alice. He only wanted it—and her—because he'd had to work so hard to get it. Because he had to prove to himself he could do it. Miss Unattainable. Now Mrs. Steven Frame.

Rachel made a face.

Steve didn't love Alice. He loved the idea of her. And how long could a man stay in love with an idea?

Not very long.

And then, Rachel thought to herself, *it will be my turn. And I'm going to take it. Somehow, some way,*

I'll make you see, Steve, that I'm the one you really love, the one you really want, the one you really hunger for. Our son is living proof of it.

And when I make you see that—and I will—then Jamie will have you for a fulltime father. And I, not Alice, will be Mrs. Steven Frame.